# BREACH OF THE PEACE

## C R DEMPSEY

CRMPD MEDIA LIMITED

# CONTENTS

1.  Enhanced negotiations                       1

2.  New beginnings                              8

3.  The little lord                             15

4.  Getting familiar                            26

5.  With rank comes responsibility             35

6.  What would Desmond do?                      43

7.  What would Seamus do?                       51

8.  A rock in the spokes                        57

9.  The changing of the guard                   66

10.  Long live the King                         73

11.  Old folly                                  83

12.  The bargaining chip                        90

13.  A meeting by the river                     97

14.  The blossoming of love                    104

15.  The bargain                               115

16.  The return of the pretender              129

17.  Back on the acquisition trail            136

18.  The lust for revenge                      139

19.  Opportunities landed                      146

20.  The letter from across the seas          152

21. Man of the hour                                    157

22. The legacy of tapestries                           168

23. The second front                                   173

24. All this for a hill                                179

25. The ambush                                         184

26. A bargain in the shadows                           193

27. Night work                                         200

28. Impostor syndrome                                  209

29. Moments of happiness                               213

30. The cave                                           222

31. The kiss of summer                                 235

32. The Blackwater                                     242

33. Cartography                                        253

34. The bloody ford                                    260

35. The battle of the rain                             267

36. Robbed by mud                                      272

37. A winter's truce                                   276

38. Return to court                                    283

39. The lonely tower                                   291

40. Return of the land agent                           298

41. The pleadings of a prodigal son                    307

42. The mildew wall                                    312

43. The gathering storm                                322

44. Battle of Yellow Ford                              328

45. The final charge                                   336

Also By                                                350

Fullpage Image                     356

Fullpage Image                     357

Clans and military formations      358

About Author                       362

Acknowledgments                    363

CHAPTER I

# ENHANCED NEGOTIATIONS

"**I**s that it?"

Taaffe pointed to a small house on a hillock surrounded by bog-land, with clutches of trees dotted around the vicinity. At the bottom of the hillock were more shack-like dwellings resting in the crevices of the land, paying their meagre homage to the house on the hill. He had brought with him land surveyors, the local magistrate whom he had appointed to assist him in his duties as sheriff of Sligo and a selection of soldiers and thugs, but it was mostly interchangeable, which was which.

The magistrate consulted his records.

"Yes, lord. On the maps, these are supposedly the lands of Turlough O'Hara."

Taaffe stroked his beard.

"I'd say these could be worth maybe fifteen to twenty pounds. What do you think, Sean?"

The surveyor applied his skills to the hillock and its surroundings.

"That'd be about right. A little more if you didn't record that part of the lands are in a bog. The landlords in Dublin will never know."

"Right you are, then. Let's go acquire some land." Taaffe slapped his hands together to signal to his men to venture forth.

Turlough O'Hara looked out the door of his house and saw a band of armed men walking up the hill. He signalled to his sons to fetch the pitchforks and old swords. Taaffe and his men strode up the muddy path to the house, past a couple of domestic pigs, a handful of young cows, and scattered the skinny chickens in their wake. Turlough O'Hara, a thin, old man and a veteran of many a famine and war alike, stood outside his house waiting for them.

"That's far enough for now," he said. "My son has his bow aimed at you, and he can reload faster than you can run up the hill. State what you want from a safe distance for both of us."

Taaffe brought his men to a halt.

"I'm here on the Queen's business and it's an offence to interfere with that," said Taaffe. "I know the Queen may not feel like much to you isolated on your hilltop and all that, but she rules all these lands and all the surrounding oceans as far as the eye can see and she's appointed me to do her business. Therefore, I'd advise you to treat her servants kindly and not be pointing arrows at them and issuing threats."

"These hills are all I have. I've been beyond to visit far-off clans and the markets in Galway, but I've never seen this Queen of yours, so you could be here just to tell me tales. State your business, or else move on."

The grin gave away Taaffe's intentions.

"That's no way for you to treat a man that's here to make you an offer."

"And who is that man?" said Turlough.

"I'm William Taaffe, the sheriff of Sligo, right-hand man to Governor Bingham. I'd come up there, shake your hand and make your acquaintance, but I don't want an arrow in my head for my troubles."

"I've heard of you," said Turlough. "You and your master wrongfully took Drumahair Castle from the O'Rourke. They say the castle sits on the ridge of the two demons. I must be talking to one of those demons."

Taaffe gave a throaty laugh.

"Now there's no need to be a gossipmonger nor resort to name-calling. We can both sort this out like reasonable men."

Taaffe made a hand signal behind his back to his men. Some of them slipped off.

"What is this offer you've come to make me?" said Turlough. "I haven't got all day. I've got crops to attend to."

Taaffe stood a foot on a tree stump and rested on his knee.

"There doesn't look like much here to pay the chieftain when he comes looking for his coign and livery. That must be a real burden to you?"

"I do just fine, thank you. Why are you so concerned about my welfare?"

"Who better to protect you than the Queen? Have you ever seen a more impressive army than hers? All she wants is a reasonable steady rent and you get all the benefits of her protection, her laws, her army, all of it."

Turlough scowled.

"I've heard about all them Queen's laws. You note all these things down on your papers, things that you've apparently agreed and then you get dragged in front of the Queen's court and someone reads out the same piece of paper and everything is different. A den of cunning thieves is what that court of yours is. Now begone with you before my sons let loose."

Taaffe laughed.

"The Queen will be so disappointed to hear that's what you think."

With that, Taaffe's men, who had sneaked around the other side of the hill, came from behind two of Turlough's sons and slit their throats from ear to ear. Turlough and his other men turned to see what the commotion was, and Taaffe saw his opportunity and stormed up the hill. Turlough only had the time to dispatch one of his sons' murderers before Taaffe and his men felled Turlough and the remaining O'Haras in a rain of blows.

Taaffe wiped his mouth of blood from one of the few O'Hara retaliatory blows that landed.

"Bring him to me." Taaffe pointed to the beaten body of Turlough.

They dragged Turlough in front of Taaffe, kicked the back of his knees, and one of them grabbed him by the hair and held up his head. Taaffe thought it best to administer a few punches to the face before commencing negotiations. Turlough's head lolled from side to side.

"Wake him up," said Taaffe.

The two men dragged him over to a nearby puddle and shoved Turlough's face in it until he choked in the water. They picked him up and placed him in the previous position of on his knees and head held up by the hair. In the meantime, the land surveyor and magistrate gingerly walked up the hill, having turned away so as not to witness the violence.

"Now, let us get something straight. This is the Queen's land, not your land. Don't give me any of that Mac and Oe nonsense about the land belonging to your great grandfather's uncle. This is the Queen's land and always has been. Tell me you understand?"

Turlough's head remained bowed, but unmoved.

"Nod his head, will you?"

Taaffe's man grinned as he tugged Turlough's hair up and down.

"Now I'm the Queen's agent, so I act for her and follow her instructions on what she wants to do with her land. Have you got that?"

Turlough's head was nodded for him once more.

"Now I'm here to give you a chance. It's up to you to take it."

They nodded Turlough's head again.

"Now you either agree to pay the Queen's rent or I'll have to evict you from this land for being a squatter. What is it to be?"

Turlough's head remained limp and unmoving.

"Is he still alive?" said Taaffe.

A swift kick in the ribs and a yelp confirmed he was.

"Pick him up."

Turlough resumed the same position.

"Now this land is worth more with tenants on it. Since you're here, I'll give you the first option. Do you want to be the Queen's tenant?"

Turlough did not move. Taaffe slapped him across the face.

"I need an answer. Are you to be the Queen's tenant?"

Turlough roused and spat the blood out of his mouth.

"The O'Haras will not be slaves."

"What was that? I can't hear you. I need a yes or no."

"The O'Haras will not be—"

Taaffe whipped out his knife and slit his throat. The men let go and Turlough fell to the ground. Turlough's life drained into the bog he had done so much to defend.

"Secretary, mark this land down as untenanted, assign a value, and get the magistrate to write it up. Let's move on to the next farm. Nothing more to be done here."

Taaffe and his men rode back to Drumahair Castle several days later. The flags of the Governor of Connacht flew proudly from the towers. It was a green and pleasant land with a handsome rental income, and the ground was soft underfoot for Taaffe's column of men. The tents of the English army and the supporting companies supplied by the loyal gentry of Connacht surrounded the castle. The Governor always travelled with a large force, for rebellion was rife in his province. But Taaffe was his most trusted man, almost an extension of his cruel arm.

The Governor needed men like Taaffe, for the wilds of Ireland was a place for adventurers. These resourceful men could take advantage of opportunities as long as they were not limited by the lengths they would go to exploit them. It took a callous man to succeed, especially in the hinterlands of Connacht, which was at best filled with bandits and, at worst, having another armed succession or territorial dispute.

Taaffe was an excellent example of a man who prospered in such conditions. He had been born the second son of wealthy Catholic landowners in county Louth. He was a large handsome man with a chiselled jaw, hands like paws, and an appealing personality until you got to know him and his brutish ways better and realised how far he was prepared to go to get what he wanted.

Taaffe had left his family land to be inherited by his older brother and found employment with Sir Richard Bingham and risen to the rank of the sheriff of County Sligo. He assisted Bingham in his brutal subjugation of Connacht and became a wealthy landowner in his own right because of it. His master wished to auction off more of the land occupied by the native Irish to the gentry of Dublin and Munster, and Taaffe was instructed to requisition it.

The gates opened upon the confirmation of the sight of Taaffe, and he rode straight in. Taaffe was sent with his officials straight through to a secluded room in the tower of the castle, for Bingham did not want the lords of Connacht to intrude on his private business.

Taaffe invaded the room with a sack full of papers, a churlish grin, and the odour of the bogs of Ireland.

"I got you some prize pickings this trip, lord," said Taaffe as he placed the first of three satchels of deeds on the table in front of Bingham. The states of the pages reflected the efforts he had to put in to obtain them. He organised the papers into three piles. He shoved the neat pages pile across to Bingham first.

"They should be tenanted lands, where they signed the deeds with little coercion."

He pushed across a second pile, frayed around the edges with scrawls for signatures.

"We had to employ enhanced negotiations for some of these, as the locals proved stubborn in their stance. They're mostly untenanted, where we had to remove the farmers for being rebels and suchlike."

He pushed across the final pile of mud-stained, torn and sometimes blood-stained pieces of paper where the previous owners of the land had spent their last defiant energies hurling the pages back in the face of Taaffe.

"They'll be the disputed ownership lands that we had to revert to the Crown to prevent any festering disputes that could lead the locals astray to side with the rebels. The boys have marked down the prices accordingly to reflect the risk."

Bingham grinned from ear to ear as he inspected a sample of the land deeds from each pile.

"You've done splendidly again, my dear boy," said the Governor to Taaffe. "Have your men leave their valuations and other notes on the table. I assume you have marked out the tracts you want in lieu of your payment?"

"I have, lord. But I have something else to ask."

Bingham put the deed down.

"What is it? You're not going to raise your rates now the rebels are getting a bit feisty?"

"No, lord. I wish to play a bigger role in our venture. Are you going to introduce me to some of your buyers? I have served you well and feel I could serve you better by describing to your gentlemen friends first-hand what they are buying and get you a better price."

Bingham rose from his seat and walked around the table. He put his arm around Taaffe's shoulder and escorted him to the door.

"Dear boy, we have the perfect arrangement. Never have I met one as efficient as you in gathering up land we can package up to sell to English landlords and help the poor people of this island get a bit of civilisation. We are going to be very busy with the amount of rebel lands that is going to fall into our hands and I don't know how I could resell it all without your help. How about the next castle we get can be yours? Make yourself a nice home. Very soon your estate will far outstrip the estate your father gave to your brother instead of you, and all the Taaffes will look up to you. You are a man of distinctive talents, and we have the perfect arrangement. So why don't you have a wash and relax, for I have many other missions for you."

Before Taaffe could protest and argue the matter, he found himself outside the room with the door closing on his face. He walked off, cursed to himself and swore revenge against the man who made him what he was today, but denied him his right to further advancement, just like his father.

# CHAPTER 2

# NEW BEGINNINGS

"Ow! Be careful where you poke that needle! It hurts!"

"Don't be such a baby."

Eunan was in the uncomfortable position of being a clothes horse again with Dervella beneath him, trying to measure and pin his clothes so he could look his best for the ceremony. He wobbled on the stool, unsure of his balance. His strength and agility were returning slowly, but this balancing act was proving a severe test. Dervella lent him the occasional steadying hand and gripped the pins in her teeth. Pin and tooth made a formidable grin.

"Do you remember the last time you stood for me on a stool and I adjusted your clothes?"

Eunan frowned.

"How could I forget? You dressed me so respectably for my trial, only for Donnacha to strip me and put me in rags as soon as my foot touched the shore."

"Yet look at you now. A young man, all respectable and far better dressed. You have much to be grateful for."

Eunan was confused. To who did he owe this gratitude? Had God especially smiled on him to bless him with such good fortune? The last time he was in Enniskillen he had been put on trial for murder and had barely escaped with his life. Was it to himself when he made the brave choice to decapitate Donnacha? Or was the gratitude due to her husband Seamus and all of his conniving? All of this came at the expense of the death of Desmond, his mentor and the most father-like figure that had been in his life. Dervella, being the more blessed of the two in social skills, knew when to subtly press for a reconciliation between the two most important men in her life.

"OW!"

Another pinprick centred Eunan's wandering mind. But boredom and constriction of his soul in such fineries soon had it wandering again.

He looked around. The rays of spring beamed through the window frames of Enniskillen Castle and the crisp air wafted in and cooled his face and brought calm as he slowly breathed in and out on top of his stool. The sky that he could see was blue with scrapings of fluff as decoration. He was alive and could feel the strength return to his body. In his darkest moments in the prison cell in the same tower that he now stood in, he could not have imagined where he stood now, on a stool being measured up for his wedding clothes. Invited by the Maguire, no less, to get married in the chapel in the castle. It was an honour indeed, for if the nobility of the Maguire were not getting married on Devenish Island, they would be married in the chapel.

The Maguire had been more than generous to him and he had stayed in the castle to recuperate after the trial and the Maguire had dispatched some of his finest men to see to the upkeep of his house, farm, and cattle in his absence. Eunan thought it may have been guilt for letting one of his most faithful men be put on trial as a traitor, but Seamus told him to make the most of his newly found good fortune and try not to destroy it by over-thinking.

"How are you, boy?"

Seamus strode into the room, the chills of spring blowing through the open training ground having blushed his cheeks. He looked like a veteran, almost respectable lord, for he had helped himself to fresh armour and clothes since he was also basking in the fine favour of the Maguire. He placed a bag in the shadow of the door.

"You make a mighty fine husband in that outfit," said Seamus. "'Tis not often enough you bless our eyes by wearing full-length trousers."

Eunan was almost embarrassed by his red pants, yellow shirt, and green fur-trimmed coat. Seamus laughed.

"You might even get away with that garb on the streets of Dublin. But I wouldn't go creeping around any forests in that get-up. You'd fall to the first arrow."

Dervella tutted through her pin-gripping teeth.

"Don't come here just to poke fun at him. It's difficult enough to get him to stand still as it is."

Seamus went to a table on the far side of the room and poured himself a mug of wine. He pulled up a chair opposite Eunan and flopped himself down with his feet up on the table.

"Ah, this is the life! Many, many people said you wouldn't turn out well, but they were wrong and I was right. I always stood up for you. I did."

"Seamus," Dervella said. But her stern growl did not stop him.

"Now this one is a looker, apparently. I can't say for sure, but everyone else reassures me she is. Way better than your first wife, approaching that of your second. But at least she won't persuade your best friend to try to kill you!"

The fury overcame Eunan and Dervella tried to distract him with a prick from her pin.

"Ow!"

But Eunan had tumbled off the stool and landed in a heap on the ground. Eunan yelped again and Seamus roared laughing. Eunan picked himself up and snarled at Seamus. Dervella wagged her finger at a surprised Eunan.

"Don't you be going and undoing all my work and getting into a fight with him!"

Eunan took a breath and gritted his teeth. Seamus kicked a chair towards him.

"Sit and let us talk like men whilst you're still not betrothed."

Dervella picked up the stool and her measuring tape.

"The night before his big day is no time for laziness. Get up there on that stool for I'm not finished, nor will I let you get married in the only ceremony I will attend, looking like you got dragged through a bush."

Eunan hung his head in defeat and mounted the stool once more. Seamus laughed.

"Don't you go laughing at him, Seamus MacSheehy. I'll make your life not worth living if you spoil the day tomorrow for the boy."

Eunan looked down from the lofty heights of his stool.

"I'm not a boy."

"Well, soon with your new promotion, you'll be off to play war and we'll see what that makes you."

Seamus smiled and sipped his wine.

"See? You're an important man now. Independent too. You'll be glad to know that the O'Donnell would not release me, and the Maguire had to find himself a new adviser."

Eunan secretly smiled, but looked at the top of Dervella's industrious head beneath him to hide it.

"But I can still come and help you out. The fine marital match I got for you does not need to be the last of my assistance."

Love and anger swirled through Eunan's head. The mighty warrior being dressed up to become a caged bird.

"I don't want to marry this girl. I love Cara," said Eunan.

The words barely escaped his mouth, for it was his first public admittance of such feelings.

"Love is for the bushes and the brothels," said Seamus. "Important men such as ourselves have to sacrifice for position and the greater good of the clan."

"OW! Please be careful with your needle, sweet Dervella," said Eunan. "It is not your wayward husband perched upon this stool."

"Don't use the boy as your pin cushion, my wife. I'm just trying to teach him the ways of men of power. Now, where was I? Yes. Now, I'm not saying you can't love Cara, just that you have to marry someone else for power and prestige and the alliances of the Maguire. You can have a wife and love Cara, but you can't keep them in the same place."

"OW! Dervella! You drew blood!"

Dervella hunched over the pinned section of Eunan's trousers as if it were a stewing pot about to bubble out her fury.

"That wayward husband of mine will be sleeping in the bushes tonight and it'll be the snout of a wild pig he'll be cosied up to, not the lips of some filly."

"Dervella, Dervella, please!" said Seamus. "He is the nearest thing we'll ever have to a son, and I can't mollycoddle the boy. He has to know how the world works. Especially now he's so important."

Dervella growled and continued her measuring.

"Double, therefore, you should teach him to be a decent, respectable man. All those years on the run have hardened and embittered you. Pass on the wisdom you have gained and keep your bitterness to yourself."

She gave her husband a contemptuous look.

"You, get off that stool and out of them pants. I have to do a smart bit of sewing before you are called. Go talk to your uncle whilst I finish up."

The chair Seamus had previously kicked into the centre of the room received another invitational tap from Seamus's foot.

"Sit. Let us talk. We won't get a chance once everything starts."

Eunan pulled on a pair of old trousers and sat in a huff of petulant youth. Seamus laughed.

"As if by magic, I can still turn you into a boy."

He reached back into his bag and pulled out a bundle wrapped in leather. He placed it on the table in front of Eunan.

"Look. I found these in the castle."

Eunan took the package and unwrapped it. His childlike state continued, but the surly nature of the teenager regressed into the wild-eyed delight of a young boy.

"I thought they were gone forever! Thank you!"

There on the table lay before him the three throwing axes that Desmond had given him. He had carefully guarded them and only lost one of the four throwing it in the Battle of Belleek. There stirred within him a deep well of gratitude and joy never directed towards Seamus before. Seamus had retrieved what reminded him of Desmond the most in the world. He could not help himself. He smiled at Seamus in the manner of a young boy receiving his first weapon from his father. Seamus smiled in return, but such a positive display of emotions only brought up in him deflection.

"So I know next time to get you an axe instead of another bride."

Eunan's withering look showed that Seamus had spoilt the moment. But on reflection, such a moment with Seamus was finding a gold nugget in an icy stream. He would cherish it all the same.

A knock came on the door.

"Is the young lord ready?"

Eunan did not react. Dervella had a much greater recognition and sense of urgency.

"That's you, that is! Distract the man at the door momentarily whilst I finish sewing your pants."

The last pin was removed, and the last stitch was applied. Eunan stood sullen-faced, to be admonished or admired. Sarcasm landed Seamus somewhere between the two.

"You're a right little lord now, aren't you?"

Dervella adopted the veneer of a proud mother, as best she could, for she lacked both experience and spousal support.

"You look so handsome. Any bride would be glad to have you."

She ran over and began a systemic poking, preening, and pulling until Eunan's hands playfully beat her away.

"Get off me. I feel constricted enough in these fine clothes without you ensuring they always flow a certain way."

Indeed, his red pants followed the contours of his muscular legs, their outline chased by a line of stitching through their every curve and crevice. The yellow shirt gave a little more freedom and was prone to rippling, for to hem in Eunan's muscular frame would have been to risk a stress-relieving tear at an inopportune moment and Eunan's sophisticated facade to come tumbling down. The fur-trimmed coat added for status and warmth for the spring only brought promise and not warmth itself.

"You'd fit into any court in the north, Eunan. Wouldn't he, Seamus?"

Dervella's face said any unsupportive comment would not be tolerated. Not even to his wife could Seamus resist the urge not to be told what to do.

"Sure they wouldn't chuck him out in those clothes to get them pinched by all the beggars outside."

Dervella ignored him.

"She's a very lucky lady."

Dervella beamed a reassuring smile.

"And the Maguire got a fine alliance."

"If you're just going to be sarcastic, keep away from the boy. It's his big day. Don't spoil it for him!"

"I'm not a boy," said Eunan.

But his defence of his newly found maturity deferred to a knock on the door.

"Are you ready now? Everyone is waiting."

CHAPTER 3

# THE LITTLE LORD

E unan and his entourage strode across the castle courtyard. Darkness had descended by now and a torch-lit path lay before him, from the outhouse to the main tower. Well-wishers lined the way and showered him with cheers and spring flowers. Those onlookers who held bitter memories of the trial to their chest and expressed their support for Eunan's former prosecutors through curses and derision were chased from the crowd by the zealous MacCabe Galloglass. Such a cacophony haunted Eunan's memories, and he tried to hide his shaking hands but remembered to smile and wave at the well-wishers, even though the only smile he could muster was a pale shade of meek.

"You are a lord now, and these are your people," said Seamus. "Act with confidence and gravitas or we'll all be packed off home quicker than your arse can rest itself on its lordly seat."

Eunan stuck out his chest and raised his hand into a more discernible wave and was rewarded with an upping of the decibels of the cheering and a blossoming of smiling faces that lined his walk. They reached the tower, greeted the guards and began the slow climb up the stairs.

The stairs were lined with servants carrying food and the lords and gentry of Fermanagh, who elevated their importance to the guards on the door hoping they could gain entry into the spatially restricted main hall. Eunan was the guest of honour, but still had to queue in the claustrophobic stairwell.

"The memories we have here, hey?" said Seamus.

Eunan could remember well, his mind went to a brutal place. But even after fighting the English on the stairs for his life or pursuing Seamus up them to get some perceived revenge, his stomach never churned as it did now.

"Shouldn't it be the bride stuck here on the stairs, whilst I warm myself beside the fire?" said Eunan.

"Be grateful you are here and think of where you have come from," said Seamus. "You should be so lucky to be the subject of such an illustrious wedding today."

"Is that why you stuffed me into this shirt? Is it some kind of revenge?" said Eunan.

Seamus laughed.

"Think of it as a rite of passage. You have done the dirty work to rise up the ranks of the Maguire, and now is the pantomime to confirm it."

Eunan stood and shook his head, dreaming it was Cara he was about to marry, not some unknown girl. The door to the great hall swung open.

"The Maguire will see Eunan Maguire now," said an official.

He boomed his call down the stairs, kept his gaze upon the wall and let it be known he would not be searching.

"I am here," said Eunan.

The hand of a frightened young boy quivered in the air, but a hand that wished him to become a man pushed him in the back.

"Get up them stairs!" said Seamus.

Eunan arrived in the doorway to be met with torchlight and a sea of curious faces. The light was too bright compared to standing in the stairwell, and a single glance was not enough for a dazed Eunan to pick out individual faces. But this was no time to linger and pick out friends. The crowd parted, and a steward stood back and showed the way. Seamus gave him another gentle shove in the back. He walked forward through the smiling faces, polite clapping and occasional cheers. He waved and smiled with the same vigour as he did in the courtyard.

At the top of the corridor of faces sat Hugh Maguire, who appeared to Eunan as another young stuffed shirt. However, the splendour of the fine clothes imported from the port of Galway and the impression they left on those who just saw the image and did not know the man meant the efforts were not wasted. Beside Hugh was his new adviser, who he hired after Seamus declined his offer by hiding behind his obligations to Hugh O'Donnell. Fachtna Óg O'Gallagher Maguire was a wise man of numbers and ledgers and not a man of the axe or gun. Someone reliable that Hugh could leave behind whilst he went off and fought his war. Fachtna Óg was a nondescript, rounded man of a sombre temperament, but he knew how to make dignitaries and guests feel welcome. He had wisdom to share and not much experience in the machinations of the Maguire, but he was not a snake like Donnacha. His key attribute was his impeccable connections, being from the west Fermanagh branch of the O'Gallagher clan, solidifying Hugh's support to the west of Enniskillen. This branch of the O'Gallagher clan was closely related to the O'Gallaghers of Tirconnell, led by Eoghan McToole O'Gallagher, consolidating his support there. Given the fracturing of the Maguires over the past number of years and the growing strength of Connor Roe, bolstering his support was exactly what Hugh needed right now.

Beside Hugh Maguire, Eunan saw Cormac MacBaron, but there was no sign of his bride. Cormac was not in his usual military attire and appeared older than his forty-plus years, the sides of his sparsely covered head having greyed considerably. There was a glint in his eye, for even though his formal demeanour rarely gave much away, he seemed happy it was his daughter's wedding. Behind Cormac stood several other dignitaries, both known and unknown to Eunan. Eoghan McToole O'Gallagher represented the O'Donnell and Eunan nodded to him. Among those unknown to him were Eamon O'Reilly, Uaithne O'More, and Brian Óg O'Rourke, but Seamus walked behind Eunan and waved and acknowledged them all.

Seamus and Eunan stood before the Maguire and bowed their heads. The warmth of Hugh's smile encouraged all to applaud.

"Greetings, my friends," said Hugh. "I would like to acknowledge the years of faithful service you have given me."

He got up off his chair and embraced them, and the room reverberated with applause. Hugh sat down again.

"But I do not wish to make speeches, for we have much to discuss this evening and I'm sure that you, Eunan, would like to meet your new wife while the rest of us get on with the feasting."

Eunan tried to hide his head behind his hand, and the room laughed. Seamus joined in and slapped him on the back.

"First, I would like to right some wrongs. I would like to put behind us the trial that you were subjected to in my absence. Whatever charges may have been laid against you, the Maguire absolves you of any crimes, and you shall not be put on trial for these accusations again."

The room was silent, and Eunan nodded his appreciation.

"I would also like to recognise you as the O'Cassidy Maguire, and hereby, if anyone has a dispute about the legitimacy of your title, they should take it up with me."

A light ripple of applause spread across the room. Seamus once more slapped Eunan on the back as they erupted with smiles of delight.

"The third announcement I have before we begin Eunan's wedding ceremony concerns our dear departed friend, Desmond MacCabe. He was a long and loyal servant to my father and me. I cherished his advice and tried many times to convince him to come out of retirement so I could benefit from his wise counsel. Alas, he would only take up formal work one last time to protect his protégé, Eunan Maguire, when he was on trial. His reward for standing up for the law and what he believed in, was that he was heinously murdered. Now that Donnacha and the perpetrators of these injustices are dead or imprisoned, we no longer have a leader for the MacCabe Galloglass. I hereby offer the position of head of the MacCabe Galloglass to Eunan Maguire."

Eunan juddered. How could he replace Desmond? He was not worthy of such an honour. How could the Maguire have thrust such a yoke upon his shoulders? The room took an audible intake of breath. With the return of the

Maguire, it was expected that he might make amends with Eunan. But acknowl-
edging a dubiously obtained title was deemed to be the rumour's limit. The
two most delighted faces in the room, Seamus and Cúchonnacht Óg, clapped.
The dignitaries joined in and low-level applause broke out in the audience in a
limited show of solidarity and deference to the wisdom of the Maguire. Eunan
turned, stunned, and raised his hand to acknowledge the applause, but his eyes
knew not where to settle.

Hugh turned around and one of his men handed him an old axe with a highly
embellished handle and head. He smiled and held it below the head and at the
opposite end of the handle, and presented it to Eunan.

"May you, like Desmond MacCabe before him, serve the Maguire clan with
all your wisdom, energy, and endeavour."

Eunan thought of Desmond, his old mentor, and said what words seemed to
follow his memory after taking the knee.

"It is an honour to serve the Maguire and the greater clan and may I serve thee
well until the end of my days."

"Arise, I'm sure you will serve me well."

Eunan rose and took the axe from the Maguire. His head spun and he looked
for the reassurance of Seamus, and the pride on Seamus's face gave him some
courage. He held the handle in his right hand and turned to the crowd.

"May I serve all the people of the Maguire well and I promise to act fairly and
honestly in all my dealings with you."

The clapping was a little more enthusiastic now, as the idea had settled in a
little.

"Yet still we have more for you in our celebration of your loyal service to the
clan," said the Maguire.

He clapped his hands and then sat down.

The entrance doors to the room gently swung back, and the crowd parted. A
wave of emotion engulfed Eunan as he turned to get the first glimpse of his new
bride. She was dressed in a long, white, flowing dress with lace ornamentation
around the hem, neckline and sleeves. A white floral pattern danced along her
hips and midriff, its stems clinging to her shapely curves. She wore a veil upon

her face, but Eunan could see her long locks of brown hair protruding past the hem. Her slimness was the feature that stood out most for Eunan, and his interest was piqued. Eunan imagined it was Cara beneath the veil and this was to be the happiest day of his life. Seamus saw he was entranced and placed his hand on the ceremonial axe handle.

"Why don't you let me look after that for you? I think you're going to be busy now."

Eunan had barely noticed that his bride-to-be was followed in by her father, Cormac MacBaron, and an escort of MacDonnell Galloglass in ceremonial dress. Behind them came some MacCabe Galloglass, also in suitable attire for the wedding of their leader. The room had become a blur of faces except for the mysterious woman in white who slowly walked towards him. Seamus smiled and congratulated himself that his match-making skills were getting better.

Eunan received a tap on the shoulder and emerged from his trance. He turned to see the Archbishop of Armagh standing before him. The archbishop smiled and held his hands out to show that Eunan's bride now stood beside him. Eunan turned, looked to his left and then downwards. The veiled face looked up at him, and from the traces between the holes, she smiled.

"You may lift the veil."

The words sounded distant, like he was in a dream. He had been here before and thought of what had happened to his previous wives and wished that such a fate would not befall this one. Would it be Cara beneath the veil? He felt a finger between his ribs.

"Stop gawking and lift the veil," whispered Seamus.

Eunan came to and looked down at his bride. He bit his lip, for he knew when he lifted the veil it would not be Cara and he would be betrothed to another. But the emotion of the day had been too much for him, firstly replacing his mentor Desmond and then being married in the castle of the Maguire. He helplessly bobbed on the ocean of his emotions. His hands nervously floated in the air as he tried to see where the edges of the veil were. His aim was to be romantic and make the most of what he had been given. If he failed in that, at least not to be clumsy. He cursed his callused hands, hardened by years of axe work. A fear shook his body that he would accidentally hurt her and then she would reject him. He yearned for a return to his sensual youth. His fingertips felt for the edges of the veil. He rubbed the edges between his fingers to ensure he could still feel. From between the micro gaps, he could see his bride was also nervous. He took a firm grip on the edge of the veil and paused.

"Lift the veil," whispered Seamus.

His voice was injected with nervous urgency, exactly what Eunan did not want to hear at that moment. He took a sharp intake of breath, closed his eyes, and lifted.

"You can look now," came a sweet whisper.

Eunan opened his eyes to see two watery dark brown pools of eyes looking up at him. As he looked, he felt he could see down to her sensitive soul. She was a young girl, out on the most exciting adventure of probably her sixteen years. She smiled a nervous smile that engulfed her whole body down to her shaking hands. Eunan took her little hands in his, and they both shook together. It was not Cara, but she was beautiful all the same. The emotion of the night washed over him and cast him on the shore. It seemed as if there was no one else in the room except for these two quivering souls.

"If you two lovebirds have quite finished," whispered Seamus.

Eunan shook off his daze and looked at the archbishop.

"May we begin the wedding now?" asked the archbishop.

The ceremony was a blur to Eunan as he had been through variants of it twice before and the archbishop was very obliging as to nod wherever his bride and himself had to take part. Thoughts and emotions overran Eunan as he stood surrounded by a sea of smiling faces. She was so young and fragile. Who would give someone like that to a brute like him? Both his previous wives were dead, and he had a lover of vaster experience than himself, who he had no desire to be rid of. All he could think of was how he would accidentally crush this delicate flower.

"Now we shall bind the hands," said the archbishop.

Sorcha MacBaron put her hands forward and held them together as she prepared to commit herself to leave her family and her clan and live with this stranger. Eunan smiled sweetly, for he liked her and knew there was no way back now. He took her extended hands and wished for the best. A priest wound the ribbon around their intertwined hands and the archbishop blessed them and wished them luck. The ceremony ended and Eunan's lips flew down to Sorcha's before he realised what was happening. They smiled at each other and laughed. They turned and raised their intertwined arms to the crowd to rapturous applause. But those who looked the most pleased were Seamus and Hugh Maguire.

The room was temporarily cleared as the servants of the Maguire brought in tables and prepared the feast. Hugh invited Eunan and Seamus and some of his guests to converse with him in an adjoining room. Sorcha was escorted away to get changed and meet Dervella. Eunan felt some sobriety, for he knew that the temporary joy of being wed was now over for the price of his newly found status had to be paid. Seamus escorted Eunan into the back room where his new father-in-law, Hugh Maguire, Eoghan McToole O'Gallagher, and a young man he had never met stood waiting for him. Cormac went straight up to Eunan and shook him by the hand. The hand was warm but stiff and the handshake firm.

"Congratulations! Welcome to the O'Neill clan." He dropped Eunan's hand. "I hope you'll take good care of my daughter?"

"I told him you had nothing to do with the deaths of your previous two wives," said Seamus.

Seamus laughed as he avoided Eunan's protruding eyes.

"What? It's common knowledge. Of course he was going to ask."

Hugh walked over to play the diplomat.

"She will be well taken care of. Don't you worry about that. She has a large farm in south Fermanagh with an ever-growing herd of cattle and she always has a home here in Enniskillen."

"I will ensure your daughter will be safe," said Seamus. "You know me. I helped arrange everything so you have my personal guarantee."

Cormac's face tensed, but knew he had to dampen down his fatherly concerns to represent his brother to the best of his abilities.

"I trust you, Seamus MacSheehy, and would not have let go of my young daughter to anyone else. As long as you remain her guardian, I will be as happy as a father can be to have lost his daughter."

Eunan tried to reassure him with kind words and a smile.

"Think of it as having gained a son."

"A son with too much responsibility to visit his father. It is best we move on now, for I fear time is the only cure and not words, however well placed or well meaning."

"Let us sit and have some wine as a starter for the feast," said the Maguire. "I apologise for talking business now, but fear we'll not get the opportunity at the feast and time is of the essence."

The Maguire invited them to sit and instructed his servant to give them a mug of wine. Eunan sat to one side of the Maguire with Seamus and Cormac on the other.

"Now, Eunan, as I have learned over the last couple of years, along with great prestige, comes great responsibility," the Maguire said. "I have conferred upon you the honour of leading my Galloglass, because you are the most trusted and capable of my men. Don't believe the rumours you may hear that Seamus turned it down first."

Seamus grinned and raised his mug to the Maguire.

"War should return to us in the summer or autumn, as the Spanish have promised to land with a mighty army. Therefore, we must learn to co-ordinate with the O'Neills. Tomorrow you shall travel to Dungannon to train with your father-in-law."

Eunan gave a surprised smile.

"You can bring my daughter, and we can all get to know each other better," said Cormac.

"I would like that," said Eunan.

"Don't worry, your uncle will not get off easy," said Eoghan McToole O'Gallagher.

O'Gallagher smiled and rose from his seat. Seamus looked worried.

"It's like that, is it?"

"The O'Donnell has done you many a favour recently and as you were expecting, he wants something in return."

"Your master charges a high price to the recipients of his favours."

"You and your nephew appear to be doing very well from serving him."

O'Gallagher waved his arms around in a sign of the role he perceived the O'Donnell played in their upturn in fortune.

"What is my new mission?"

"Step forward please, young man."

O'Gallagher gestured to the man in his mid-twenties, who neither Seamus nor Eunan had met, to step forward.

"This is Captain Richard Tyrell."

He was a muscular young man with brown wavy hair, but with an air of experience that belied his age. He knew how to hold his own in a room that reeked of importance and ego.

"He used to serve in the English army, but has defected to us."

"So how do we know he is not a spy or will defect back again where the opportunity presents itself?"

"I have pledged my loyalty and that of my men to the O'Neill," said Captain Tyrell. "The English have devastated the lands of my family and some of my relatives were killed. I wish to fight for the freedom to live as I want to live and not end up as some tenant farmer for the Crown."

"Nice words, and you'll get plenty of opportunity to test their resolve."

"As will you, Seamus," said O'Gallagher.

"No! The last time was a disaster." It dawned on Seamus he was being sent back to Wicklow.

"The last time you brought Hugh Boye back, and he was invaluable in our negotiations with the Spanish. Anyway, Fiach requested you specifically."

"And here was I, thinking our friendship had just worn away."

"The O'Neill has promised to supply Fiach with the men and materials to wage war with the English on a suitable scale to distract a sizeable number of their forces."

Seamus pointed to Captain Tyrell. "Is he the new commander?"

"He is the first part of your mission. You must introduce him and his men to Uaithne O'More to prop up the rebellion in Leinster."

Seamus glared at Eunan.

"I think you got the far better end of this deal. You get to go on a jolly up with your new wife while I get to return to a dreary tent on a windswept mountain."

Eunan grinned, saluted him, and downed his mug of wine.

# CHAPTER 4

# GETTING FAMILIAR

E unan's head pounded. He felt trapped in his skin. He opened his eyes and saw the ceiling of his room in the castle. A little voice chirped in his ear.

"Good morning, my love."

Eunan's memories were returning very slowly. Yes, it was the morning after his wedding. No, he had not married Cara, no matter how much he tried to convince himself he had. He remembered smiling faces and seemed to have wanted this new girl yesterday. But the pain in his head evaporated the euphoria of the day before. He was now married and had to make the most of it. Seamus told him he had only one job to do, but the conversation was a blur. Slowly, he pieced together Seamus's advice. He grabbed the blankets and began searching for blood. He found some. Eunan fell back and heaved a sigh of relief. Sorcha saw him searching.

"Oh, don't worry about that, my love. I cleaned most of it up. You hit the doorway hard with your head when we stumbled in, and I had to get your uncle to come back and help you into bed."

Eunan scowled. Failure.

Sorcha fell on the bed as if a feather were floating and landing beside Eunan's drunken bulk.

"You need to get up, my love. We leave for Dungannon today."

Eunan bolted upright. He never agreed to this. Or at least he could never remember agreeing to this. He tried to piece together the night before, but had to tread carefully.

"How much should I pack?"

Sorcha laughed.

"If you owned anything, I have yet to see it. Your clothes can ride on your back, and your belt can hold your weapons. My father must have taken it on faith that you are a man of wealth."

Eunan was none the wiser for her response. He would have to seek his uncle to find out what was agreed.

"Is there any water? My mouth is as dry as a grain sack."

Sorcha smiled, and she ran over to a table to fetch a mug, her long brown hair bouncing behind her. The guilt gripped Eunan's chest. She was so delicate, and he could only hurt her. Why did Seamus have to set him up with a little flower? Cara could take the rough and tumble of the life of a Galloglass, and he could take her with him into battle, and she could look after herself. This little lady would soon have the disappointment of seeing her new husband go off to war and maybe never come back. No wonder he wanted Cara beside him, for he would live day to day.

She skipped back with the water and handed it to her new husband. He gulped it down greedily.

"Thank you. Has your father mentioned to you where you shall live?"

Sorcha smiled at him.

"There is plenty of room in my father's castle. We'll be safe there from anything. He has so many soldiers."

Eunan's brow knitted. So much more to this agreement than he remembered.

"Why are we going to Dungannon first?"

"I don't know. To visit my uncle? I know nothing of such things."

She skipped to a large chest on the floor and opened it.

"Oh, what shall I wear today? What do you think I should wear, husband, on the first day of our marriage?"

Eunan threw his legs over the side of the bed and sat holding his head.

"Something warm. The wind will rip through you. It is always cold travelling north."

Sorcha looked over at her husband, all bundled up in a ball of pain.

"I'll make sure a physician looks at you before we go. I can't have you die on me straight after we got married."

Eunan sighed. All he thought about was he must see Cara before he left.

Eunan received a summons to have breakfast with his esteemed hosts before they all once more parted ways. Arthur was given the honour of summoning him. Sorcha greeted him with all the air and charm of a fresh spring morning. She breezily invited him into the room and proudly pointed him to the hungover mess perched at the end of the bed that was now the leader of the Maguire's Galloglass. Arthur walked over and tapped him on the shoulder, as he had not emerged from his ball when he was invited into the room. Eunan raised his head.

"Oh, that's a nasty gash. Did you let your wife near your throwing axes last night?"

Eunan groaned.

"Please spare me. I'll get enough grief from Seamus, never mind what my new father-in-law will say. I started off with the best of intentions, but after our hands were tied, it was a blur."

"Let me fill you in as best I can, but I didn't see that much. Hugh and Cúchonnacht Óg were keen for you to ingratiate yourself with the MacCabes as soon as possible, and unfortunately, that involved your new men pouring as much wine down your throat as they could without your father-in-law noticing. Everyone noticed in the end, but most were as inebriated as you."

Eunan hid his face in the bowl of his hands.

"Oh God! What kind of fool am I?"

"One that has to face the music. Put on some clothes and hurry. You'll definitely draw attention if you show up last."

Eunan arrived once more in the great hall and had turned up last. He tried to hide his head behind Arthur's back but he was jeered when he poked his head around the doorway and jeered until he took his place beside the Maguire.

"I see your desire to turn your new bride into a fighting woman already got the better of you," said the Maguire.

Masculine jeers rang in Eunan's ears as his face turned red. Seamus came up behind him and ruffled his hair.

"So I make that three weddings and, at a guess, one successful wedding night?" he whispered in his ear. "Don't worry, you'll get another go in your father-in-law's house and he'll release you when you can evidence you have done the deed."

Eunan squirmed into a peculiar shade of purple.

"Not in front of the men," said Seamus.

Eunan looked down the table at the grinning MacCabe constables, who winked at him. The glints in their eyes made Eunan paranoid, for he could not recall meeting them or their names. His eyes turned to his father-in-law, and he saw the anger behind his sullen face.

"Maybe a child in her belly would make him happy," said Seamus. "You could do far worse than become an O'Neill."

Eunan felt trapped. The pulsating pain in his head. Seamus's taunts in his ear. Not being able to recollect the night before. What amused everyone so much at the table? Having so many important people to please. He felt his stomach churn, but the last thing he could do was excuse himself from the table and go and vomit. He sat, drank his ale and ate his bread, and hoped no one would pay attention to him. No such luck.

"Eunan," said the Maguire.

The formal tone chimed with Eunan's new standing and additional levels of responsibility.

"You will leave for Dungannon today and take with you our finest MacCabe constables. Your father-in-law has agreed to have them trained by the Spanish officers and his ex-English army officers so they can come back and train the Maguires. Our mission is to have the next finest army in the north after the O'Neills. It is up to you, Eunan, to fulfil that mission."

Seamus slapped Eunan on the back. It was supposed to be in congratulations, but the force reverberated up Eunan's back and circled inside his skull.

"Eat well, for we have a long journey ahead of us," said Cormac.

There was foreboding in his voice, no joy. Eunan wracked his brains to figure out what could have offended him so.

"I need to pack and tell my wife of your plans," said Eunan.

"No need. She is my youngest daughter and my most precious. I will show you how I expect her to be looked after."

Eunan looked to the Maguire who smiled back at him. His face seemed to say do your duty. Seamus smiled and looked out the window, trying to avoid getting involved.

Breakfast ended, and the Maguire had signalled to his men that they needed to attend to their duties as he said goodbye to the last of the wedding guests. Eunan stood by Hugh and nodded and shook hands when appropriate. The men and carts of the O'Neills and the other guests assembled in the courtyard of Enniskillen Castle and the surrounding areas, as the courtyard was too small to contain them all. Eunan realised he was running out of time. Through the crowd of men gathered in the room saying their goodbyes, he saw Arthur lingering at the entrance. He swam through the sea of bodies on the way to the door.

"Arthur, I need your help."

"What is it, lord?"

"Don't call me that. You've known me since I was a boy."

"Then no better than me to train your ears to hear it, for most people will address you as that now."

Eunan shook his head. He did not have time to deal with that now.

"I need you to find Cara. I need to speak with her before I leave."

"Are you sure that is wise, Lord, with you being a married man and all your relatives here?"

"Don't you worry about that. I'm a lord now. I just need to speak to her. She'll find a way."

There was only the O'Neills and churned-up mud left in the courtyard now. Sorcha had packed up Eunan's belongings and the quarter-filled sack paled into insignificance alongside Sorcha's three trunks. Eunan's bloodstained and ripped clothes should have been cast into the fire rather than packed for reuse, but Sorcha was too afraid to get rid of them lest her little-known husband be angry with her. Nevertheless, his rags would have a short lifespan as she had already planned his new clothes and the rags would make a nice kindling for a fire and warm them in their new home. She sat waiting patiently on their cart for him.

"Eunan, Eunan," she called when she saw him at the castle tower door. "Come and sit with me."

Seamus was right behind Eunan and laughed.

"You'd better get over there and keep her happy before her father and the Maguire arrive."

Eunan stood in the doorway and stroked his stubble, both in frustration and to restore some feeling into his body.

"Did you know it was going to be like this?"

"No!" Seamus protested.

But his inability to hold in his laughter stifled his sincerity.

"Really?"

"No. I only vet them for looks, so you aren't a laughing stock like with your first wife."

Eunan stormed off towards the gate. Seamus went after him.

"You're going the wrong way."

"No, I'm not. I'm going to find Cara."

Eunan hurled the words over his shoulder, not relenting in his pace. Seamus ran after him, placed his hand on his shoulder, and whirled him around.

"No, you're not. You have a responsibility now. Your priority is to make that young girl happy, keep her father happy, and keep the alliance between the Maguires and the O'Neills on track. I only sent her to the island to get you to stop moping about Caoimhe so you could win your trial."

"YOU WHAT!?!"

Eunan wanted to explode his fist into Seamus's face.

"Eunan?" called Sorcha from the cart. "Where are you going? We're going to set off soon. You need to say your goodbyes."

"Exactly," said Seamus. "Cara has returned to Munster, so be a good boy and do what your wife says. We can discuss this later if you haven't already worked out that it all worked out for the best."

Eunan battled with his better nature not to hit Seamus, but Seamus shoved him towards his wife.

"Go do your duty, little lord!"

Eunan sloped off towards the cart and Seamus returned to the door to the tower just as the Maguire and Cormac MacBaron emerged. They were deep in conversation. They lifted their heads when Seamus approached.

"Ah, Seamus, we were just discussing you and your important mission. The one hundred shot and Richard Tyrell are ready to leave. Once you have established a safe route south, Cormac here will send men south regularly."

"They'll be safe with me."

They looked over to Eunan and saw him lean up and give his new wife a peck on the cheek. She blushed and beamed with delight. Seamus and the Maguire saw a visible thaw on Cormac's face.

"He'll see her all right, don't you worry," said Seamus.

"He better have. A lot is riding on this," whispered the Maguire.

Cormac shifted his attention from his daughter to the task at hand.

"We are about to leave. What arrangements have you made for Eunan's lands, Seamus? I don't want him running off at the first excuse and breaking my daughter's heart."

"Let me reassure you, my wife will take charge. She spent many a year in her youth looking after large tracts of land for no less a man than the Earl of Desmond himself."

"I need not remind you about how that turned out. My daughter may go live there one day when she is old enough if I deem it safe. The house needs work, a lot of work before it would meet my daughter's requirements. May I visit if I am in the vicinity to see how the work progresses?"

"You are welcome anytime, but a little notice would not go astray so we can give you the welcome you deserve."

Cormac nodded. "I look forward to it."

He shook the hand of the Maguire and turned away.

"May I ask one favour, lord?" said Seamus.

"Of course, you may ask," Cormac said.

"May I send one of my most trusted men with Eunan to be his bodyguard? It would mean a lot to me to know he is safe, and I'm sure your daughter would appreciate him being protected as well."

Cormac laughed.

"Are several units of your best Galloglass not enough protection for him?"

Seamus tried his most persuasive smile.

"It's a lot of change for him. It would cheer him up to see a familiar face. And if the boy is happy—"

Cormac walked off.

"If he needs to be mollycoddled so, then so be it. Don't make me regret agreeing to this. You wouldn't want to be on the wrong side of finding out how much I treasure my daughter."

"My boy will be no trouble to you at all. He'll be a ray of sunshine in your daughter's life."

But Cormac was out of earshot and already preparing his men to leave. Seamus was left facing the Maguire.

"I didn't know he'd be so sensitive about his daughter."

"This had better work."

The Maguire glowered at him and turned and went back into the tower.

# CHAPTER 5

# WITH RANK COMES RESPONSIBILITY

E unan felt like a prisoner. A soaking wet prisoner as the roof of the cart failed to fully protect the newlyweds from the northern rains. His hulking, sullen, soaking mass sat wedged in a seat beside the frail young girl resting her head on his muscular shoulder. The cart was being dragged along the dirt tracks heading north. The screen of men in front of them was reassuring, but they also churned up the already muddy ground. His Galloglass marched behind them, their axes slung over their shoulders, maintaining good order, for they were well used to such conditions.

The cart was in the grips of the mud as if it were another Spanish Armada being cast around by the storms along the rocky coasts of Scotland and Ireland. The wheels stuck and jolted him forward. His hungover brain rattled in his skull. The wheels slid back, and he had to get out and push until they were free. He soon found out what a delicate flower he had married, for as his brain was thrown around, the same went for his betrothed's stomach and she was soon sick all over his lap and the seat. Eunan did his best to clean the immediate seating area. His bloody rags his wife saved for him in a sack came to some use after all. He put his arm around her to act as a comfort and to steady her. She sank into his armpit and not once complained about the smell.

Faolán rode alongside them and tried to hide his smirks at the predicament Eunan found himself in. Eunan was glad that Seamus had arranged for Faolán to come with him, but not at this very moment. The last thing his blazing headache needed was taunting. But he did not vocalise his frustrations as he did not want to disturb the little bird sleeping in the nest of his armpit.

Cormac would ride back periodically to check on the welfare of his daughter. He grew so uneasy that he sent back his physician to tend to her. The physician looked concerned as he examined her on the back of the moving cart. He called for Cormac to discuss the diagnosis, having refused to discuss it with Eunan, despite his protestations that he was her husband. When Cormac arrived, the physician got off the cart and went and whispered in Cormac's ear. Cormac waved to his men.

"Change of plan. We head home to Augher Castle."

He pointed northwards and rode to the top of the column.

"I suppose you're going to see your new home a little sooner than expected," said Faolán.

"Don't say that," said Eunan.

He cringed as he considered that, at the moment he achieved some status, he lost control of his destiny. He climbed to the back of the cart to attend to his wife like a dutiful husband.

Augher Castle loomed like a monolithic slab of granite had been thrown out of the skies and jutted out of the ground as a monument to man's obstinacy to live where he pleased, no matter the conditions. There was no courtyard, no outer walls, no ornamentation or excessive decoration that may lead one to be distracted from the function of the castle: a gigantic granite impregnable rock to dominate the landscape.

Grey skies swirled overhead and the granite and cloud became one. Sheets of spitting rain linked heaven and earth and made a grim stairway to heaven through the towers of the castle. The heavenly downpour softened the ground, which was trampled and churned into mud, and turned the last steps home into an almighty slog.

The column wound its way slowly up the road and climbed the hill upon which the castle stood. Eunan sat in the cart, tending to his wife. The rain and the state of his coughing and convulsing wife robbed him of any feelings or desire to admire the castle or be impressed. He became deeply suspicious of Seamus, Hugh Maguire, and his father-in-law and wondered what he had been set up for. Sorcha's cart was the first to climb the hill, and Cormac rode out in front to clear the path for his daughter.

When they arrived at the doors of the castle, a flurry of women came to greet Sorcha. Attendants, nuns, and cousins were all led by her mother. It was almost as if they had expected her to come back in such a state. The women flocked around the cart and took Sorcha from the hands of Eunan, brushing him aside as if he was a servant. Eunan was insulted that nobody had even bothered to ask if he was her new husband. But the anxiousness brought about by the urgency to get her indoors was infectious. Cormac rushed in behind the women, leaving Eunan in the back of the cart. Eventually, one of Cormac's men came to give instructions. The MacCabes were to camp in some fields near the castle, but Eunan and Faolán were invited in.

The inside of the castle was as functional as the outside, the drab, sheer walls nurtured cold and damp, not tapestries which told tales of the past, unifying bonds that spoke of the clan and kinship. The only nods towards ornamentation were the weapons on the walls, which hinted at a history of militarisation and doubled as weapons of last resort. The doorways were rectangular blocks that perfectly performed their function of holding doors, but little else. Whoever designed it seemed to have put little more effort in than if they were designing a prison. Eunan now stood in this drabness, his dripping clothes only adding to the prevailing air of dampness and cold. Cormac emerged from one room into the main corridor and saw him standing there. His worries became a fury, and he clapped his hands for the attention of his servants.

"How can you leave him standing there so? He is Sorcha's new husband, who looks as if he may catch his death in the cold. Bathe, dry and clothe him, and direct him to the main hall for dinner."

A quivering servant appeared from another doorway and came and grovelled before his angry master.

"Shall I bring him to your daughter's room, lord?"

Cormac became angrier.

"Of course not! I cannot have him making her more ill. You can move him when we are sure she is well."

Eunan stood and shivered and wondered what he had got himself into.

It was now night-time and Eunan felt the best he had all day, even though that wouldn't be hard. He was in a small room by the kitchens, large enough to hold a bed and a chest of clothes. Eunan explained to the servant that all he had were the clothes on his back and he would have to sit and wait while the servant washed them. The thought of Eunan standing naked waiting for him frightened the servant so much that he ran off to his master and then around the various residents to beg or borrow some clothes that he thought would fit Eunan. He was also careful enough to coordinate what he had got, and a green giant with a tuft of freshly cleaned red hair was deposited in his master's hall ready for dinner.

Cormac had waited for him alone and looked out to the sky and wished for better fortune. The room had more nods to homeliness than the other parts of the castle and it was the efforts of Cormac's wife choosing to spend her time wisely as her husband was out on endless campaigns on behalf of his brother.

The large fire had some small decorative pieces on the mantelpiece. The walls had different weapons and shields the clan had used through the ages, and there was even a tapestry depicting O'Neill tales from the past on one wall. A jug of wildflowers had even crept onto the table. The meal on the long table was a simple one of rabbit stew, for it is hard to catch a lot of game if the master gives so little notice he is returning and will bring many mouths to feed. Cormac always preferred simple food, like what he ate during his endless campaigns, so he was satisfied.

"Sit, and let us talk," said Cormac, without turning around. "Have a good meal and hopefully you won't wake up tomorrow with a chill."

"I would like that," said Eunan.

He walked over to the table and pulled over a stool.

"How is Sorcha? Is she feeling any better? When can I see her?"

Cormac turned and sat on his high-backed chair with enough Celtic design on the upper rim to make it stand out and signify that it was for the sole possession of the master of the house.

"She is resting. I don't want to talk about her now. Let us discuss more practical matters, for it won't do anyone any good for us to sit around worrying about her when there are things to be getting on with."

Eunan was a little taken aback by this, but was not in a position to argue.

"Please tell me what you'd like to discuss?"

"First, we should send your men forward to Dungannon so they can start their training as we have business to attend to here."

Eunan grimaced as he tried to feign interest in what Cormac wanted to discuss while attempting to dismiss the creeping worry about his wife's mysterious ailments.

"Of course. What business do we have?"

Cormac saw his new son-in-law's pained expression at the mystery of his new wife's ailments. Cormac's jaw clenched and his hand made a fist for he realised he could not brush off the subject of his daughter with her new husband. It needed to be confronted now. He cleared his throat.

"The preparations for the coming war and also the welfare of my daughter. I wish to make my daughter happy as she is so vulnerable and precious to me. I have other children, but they are all able to look after themselves and are not afflicted as she is. Therefore, she can never stray too far away from her father's love."

Eunan leaned in.

"What sort of affliction? Is it curable?"

"She takes to the fever far easier than any father would ever wish and is a constant mystery to any physician a father could ever employ. Therefore, any man that takes her on and makes her happy will be well rewarded."

"I am a loyal and honourable man," Eunan said and bowed

"Indeed. The Maguire eulogised about your honourable qualities and that you were one of the few who stood by him in his hour of greatest need and single-handedly led the defence of the island with mere boys when if it fell the Maguires would also have fallen."

Eunan felt truly humbled.

"I was only doing my duty."

"Seamus told me of how dutifully you attended your mother who also was afflicted by aliments and that you also tried to defend her before her murder by the English."

Eunan's soul burned at such lies. His fury would have rebounded off the four walls and found futile expression in violence in his youth. But he clenched his knuckles white for no matter how his anger would send him spinning, he felt this conversation might lead to a route by which he could escape his past. He nodded and looked at the ground.

"I'm sorry, lord. The circumstances around my mother and her death still bring out the vehemence in me."

Cormac reached out and placed his hand on Eunan's knee.

"So it should. But such energies should be used wisely. But please call me Cormac in the family home or in private. We'll save the lords and other such titles for the battlefield."

Eunan smiled, for this was the first time he truly felt a connection with his father-in-law.

"Back to our business. In the absence of the Maguire himself, I want you to be the leader of the Maguire forces that fight with the O'Neills. My fee is the happiness of my daughter and in return, I will teach you how to lead. I know the cost of being a leader and such a position engulfs the lives of one's whole family. I also have no objection to making marital alliances with my able children, indeed that is their duty, nor having my boys being hostages or learning to fight. But being forced to marry off your ill daughter?"

Eunan looked disturbed.

"No, it is not like that. She wanted to be married and to marry you," said Cormac. "It would have been much easier if she married a farmer and lived out her days in peace and isolation. But no. She insisted on doing her duty like her brothers and sisters. I hope I can rely on you to do your duty too."

Eunan got down on one knee.

"I can solemnly swear on whatever you wish, but I will always do my duty to the Maguire, yourself, and my new wife."

"I'm glad to hear it. Now get up and sit. Our first task is a difficult one. I have received news from my brother that the Spanish King has ordered a vast armada to be assembled. It is reported that he is sending over ten thousand men!"

Eunan leapt from his seat and went for the jug of wine on the table.

"That is wonderful news, Cormac! Let us drink and toast our victory!"

Cormac held out a calming hand.

"It is no time to celebrate yet. If they have promised to help us once, they promised us a thousand times and turned up with little. But we must act as if the landing will happen. We must make provisions for that vast army arriving in the north and therefore have enough food to feed them over the winter until we secure the fertile fields of the south and can take advantage of their yields. We must therefore impose more hardships on our people by taking from the harvests as much as they can set aside and wait for the winter."

Eunan frowned.

"But the people have just endured another harsh winter of famine. Can we take what little food they have out of their mouths and have them face another year of famine?"

Cormac wore the face of a pragmatic warrior.

"With rank comes responsibility. We must tell the people what needs to be done and why, so they both understand and support us. We only wish to impose force on our enemies."

"Then let us build our stores, expand our crannógs, and bring our message to the people."

"First, let us eat and drink and leave the work to the morning."

Eunan poured the wine, and they gave their first salute to the evening.

## CHAPTER 6

# WHAT WOULD DESMOND DO?

The next day, Eunan woke in his small room at the bottom of the castle tower. The draught from below the door tormented his feet and the smell of bread being baked roused his nostrils. But what really woke him and made him kick his blankets off in the frustration of his slumber was a nagging feeling in his chest that he did not deserve his position as the head of the MacCabe Galloglass, that the Maguire knew this and he was only using him to secure his alliance with the O'Neill.

"Why am I in the servants' quarters and not in the bed of my wife! If I say that I want to sleep with her, no one should stop me from doing so."

He pulled on his clothes that were neatly stacked for him on a chair beside his bed and stormed out into the castle. He had barely stepped into the corridor when he ran straight into his father-in-law.

"Ah, there you are. Saves us from calling you," said Cormac. "Down there is the kitchen where the cooks have prepared fresh bread. Follow the smell, you can't miss it. Then I suggest you change for training starts today. I will have suitable attire sent to your room while you eat. Then if Sorcha is feeling up to it you can visit her in the evening."

But before Eunan could respond, Cormac was gone to attend to some business or other and before him stood a quivering boy.

"Lord, this way for the bread. You eat and I will fetch your armour. The lord has assigned me to look after you."

Eunan gave a slight shake of the head but the wonderful smell had made him hungry.

"Lead the way then, boy."

Eunan sat and a young woman with a flirtatious smile and her hair in a knot placed a plate of bread in front of him. The crust of the bread crunched as he tore it into neat strips and it melted in his mouth as his back teeth broke down the crust. If he were to be a caged wolf then at least he was well-fed

Cormac came to collect Eunan as he pulled on his mail shirt in his room. He stood in the doorway and said nothing as Eunan struggled inside his shirt.

"I hope it fits," said Cormac before Eunan could slip the mail shirt over his head and see what was in front of him.

It only made Eunan wriggle more in his determination to impress his father-in-law.

"Take your time. Don't injure yourself on my account," said Cormac as he saw Eunan struggle. "Today we will meet your men and those who will train them. I will also begin your training as a leader of men for I picked up the distinct impression that you are unfamiliar with the men you are leading and your new role was rather sprung upon you."

Eunan finally pulled the chain mail over his head, for it was rather a tight fit. His red face gave away his embarrassment at being caught in a vulnerable position by his father-in-law, but he tried to put that aside.

"Sorry, sorry, lord."

"Cormac. We are in private."

Eunan blushed even more.

"Sorry, Cormac. You caught me unawares. My instructions from the Maguire are that his men should be able to slip beside the O'Neills seamlessly and fight like them."

Cormac smiled.

"Then that is what we shall do. Let us walk down to the fields and inspect the men."

They were halfway down the hill when Cormac turned back to speak to Eunan again. Cormac ushered his captains away so Eunan could walk alongside him.

"I hear you have Spanish trainers in Enniskillen?"

"We do, Cor... lord. Survivors from the Spanish Armada, kindly taken in and sheltered by the Maguire."

"Good," said Cormac. "At least we have somewhere to start. You'll be pleased to know I have borrowed one of my brother's best men, the Spaniard Pablo Blanco of the Battle of the Ford of the Biscuits fame to train the men."

A skip came to Eunan's step.

"I was there. My men charged down the hills to complete the ambush."

"Then you know that well-trained Irishmen can beat the English in battle and what a privilege it is to be trained by Pablo Blanco."

"Let me express gratitude on behalf of the Maguire."

"The Maguires being able to hold their part of the line in battle and being reliable allies is all the gratitude I need."

They arrived at the field in front of the camp of the MacCabes and to Eunan's embarrassment they were still in the throes of forming a line for inspection.

"Preparing to run away, are they?" came a voice from behind Eunan and Cormac. The air was peppered with sniggers until silence was restored when Cormac turned to find the culprit. Cormac turned once more to the MacCabe who now formed a neatish line with their chins thrust in the air.

A man in a morion and a shiny breastplate walked over to Cormac.

"I have had worse to work with, here on this Godforsaken island," said Pablo Blanco in his thick Spanish accent, the years of living in Ulster having dented its strength a little. "They still look in love with their axes, like they want to chop down some trees. From the looks of some of them they would be lucky to get within swinging distance having not been felled by a bullet along the way."

"They have received training with both guns and pikes," said Eunan to protect the pride of his men. Cormac put his hand on Eunan's shoulder.

"Why don't you get to know your constables and let Pablo assess your men properly? Then we can see what we need to do."

Eunan waved towards his men and the constables peeled off and followed him back to the castle.

Eunan had recognised some of the grinning constables from the breakfast of the morning after the wedding, but those he had met on the night of his wedding were just a haze. Most of the men were considerably older than Eunan, grizzled veterans of whatever war or raid the Maguire ordered them to go on. Why would they be impressed by him? He received a slap between the shoulders. He turned to see the bristled grin of Faolán.

"I've been getting to know them, the men, the rumours, the genuine dirt. I'll help you out," Faolán nodded reassuringly.

"What is he doing here?" said one of the constables, pointing at Faolán. "He is not a MacCabe, he is not one of us."

"He is my bodyguard," said Eunan. "He stays by my side."

"What!?" said the constable. "Is several units of MacCabe Galloglass not enough of a bodyguard for you?"

"He has been with me through thick and thin and shown loyalty to me and I to him. Let it be a lesson on how loyalty works and how it should work in the MacCabes."

The MacCabe constables glared at Eunan.

"Get to know us first before you make assumptions."

Eunan's mistake dawned upon him but he did not wish to compound it by looking weak.

"That is what I mean to do. Come, our generous hosts have laid us on a feast. Let us drink and be merry and prepare for the war ahead," said Eunan and ushered them back inside.

The house servants had laid them on a lavish feast in the main hall and Eunan invited his six constables to sit. Eunan took his seat at the top of the table and Faolán pulled up a chair beside him.

"Why is he sitting there beside you?" said Cearbhall Flanagan MacCabe, one of the elder of the constables. "Do you think you invite us to breakfast and make such a poor impression that we try to kill you afterwards?"

All the constables laughed and Eunan twitched as he glanced at Faolán.

"He is not a MacCabe, he is not a Galloglass," said Feargal Beggan MacCabe a Galloglass constable from Connor Roe Maguire's lands in the east of Fermanagh. "If he wished to become a Galloglass let him train and prove himself and then he may sit at our table. But until he is a Galloglass constable send him away and do not do us the dishonour of sitting there with a bodyguard and pretending to be our leader."

The men banged their mugs on the table. Eunan froze. He turned to Faolán.

"You had better leave," he whispered. "We'll discuss it later."

Faolán turned red-faced and walked out to the jeers of the men.

"Now we can sit and talk as Galloglass, as men," said Feargal.

The constables stopped eating and over a hundred years of combat and leadership experience bore down on Eunan. He winced inside and hoped it did not put a quiver on his face. He remembered his guidance.

What would Seamus...

He paused. He thought back to his days spent with Desmond beside the lake, in the Maguire's court in Enniskillen, on Desmond's island and the final occasion they spent time together on Devenish Island just before his trial. All of Desmond's advice led up to this decisive moment.

No. What would Desmond do?

He steadied his voice and took hold of his mug to mask his quivering hand.

"Men, we have a war to win and the Maguire's honour to uphold," said Eunan. "Let us clear the air so we can work together and make the MacCabes the best fighting men in the rebellion. I have dismissed my man as you requested, and as a sign of good faith I will send him back to my lands to lead the south Fermanagh shot. Some of you may be familiar with how I rose to my position at such a tender age compared to yourselves but I raised the south Fermanagh shot from a bunch of farm boys to be one of the better units at the disposal of the Maguire. My trial is fresh in my mind and who took what side should be put behind us. I know I do not match any of you for experience or fighting prowess, yet we still need to work together. So let us clear the air. Ask me what you wish and then let us prepare the men."

There was momentary silence until another of the constables spoke.

"Why did the Maguire appoint you, a mere boy, instead of one of us?"

Eunan looked up and saw the question was being asked by Irial McDowell MacCabe, the eldest and longest-serving MacCabe and the person who every-one thought would be the new leader of the MacCabe. While the MacCabe were mainly made up of men from the clans of Fermanagh, Irial could trace his lineage all the way back to the original MacCabe mercenaries from Scotland as well as to the McDowell Scottish clan. The original MacCabe mercenaries had integrated into the local populations so their blood lines had been blurred and at the same time, the Maguire leaders had treated the MacCabes as their personal bodyguard and placed the sons of prominent men in the clan they wished to win favour with into these elite troops. Irial considered that he was the natural leader of the MacCabes and to appoint this young upstart was an insult to him and the good name of the MacCabe Galloglass.

"You would have to address that question to the Maguire as it was his decision. However, I will say that I stood with him at Devenish Island when the English took to the river and came to destroy him. I have no wish to cast aspersions but I was one of the few that stood with him. I also bring connections to the O'Neills, of whom you are guests today, and the O'Donnell. These would be among the reasons I believe he would give."

The constables sat and stared at Eunan as wolves would stare at a lone deer, as they digested the comments and contemplated whether it was a statement of fact or an insult to their loyalty.

"We also served the Maguire at that time in other ways," said Feargal. "Some of us took to the forests of western Fermanagh to keep the bulk of his forces together for when he wished to rouse himself from the islands. Some of us thought it was better to stand and fight than to run and be cornered."

Eunan saw the conversation beginning to run away from him.

"I can neither answer for the Maguire nor pass judgement. If you ask me to answer such a question the answer will always be wrong."

The constables looked unhappy and whispered amongst themselves. Then Irial spoke up.

"How do we know you are worthy of leading us? Sure, we have heard the rumours of Eunan Maguire, both good and bad. We know your uncle is Seamus MacSheehy and you have his protection and also the protection of your father-in-law. But when we are in some bog in Connacht, miles away from your guardians, how do we know we can rely on you to lead us to victory?"

Eunan's hand shook beneath the table, but he thought once more of his mentor, Desmond.

"My battle skills have brought me this far and mutual trust and your battle skills and experience and my leadership will ensure that Desmond's legacy with the MacCabes will endure."

Irial smiled and sat back in his chair.

"Your mentor may have given you selective highlights of his time with the MacCabes," said Irial. "You still offer us nothing to reassure us you can lead us. You can give us guns and tell us where to point them and for us all to fire them simultaneously. This may pass for leadership in some circles but does not make you a Galloglass. My forefathers would turn in their graves if they saw what the Galloglass have become. We need someone who can face off any enemy with the nerve to present themselves before them and cut them in two with a stroke of their axe. You can hide in your bushes and fire all the lead bullets you wish into the sky and hide behind your smoke but all should quake in fear when the

MacCabe Galloglass take the field. Are you such a man? Like Brian Boru or Sigtrygg Silkbeard? What enemy would be too afraid to face you?"

It was now Eunan's turn to ascertain whether these were disguised insults being hurled at him. His heart hardened and his sense dulled.

"So what must I do to prove myself to you?" he said. "I am your leader appointed by the Maguire himself but apparently this is not good enough for you. What must I do to win your trust?"

Irial sat forward.

"Every Galloglass faces a trial to show he is worthy of being a Galloglass. So you must show you are worthy of being a MacCabe."

It was Eunan's turn to smile.

"I shall put down my ale and we can start my trial in the fields yonder. I would gladly do such a trial if it would earn your trust."

"I am pleased you have accepted my offer," said Irial. "However, you have been foolish in your haste to accept. The last thing the MacCabes need is a foolish headstrong youth to lead them."

"Why is that?" said Eunan doing little to hide his anger.

"It is because you accepted before finding out the terms," said Irial. "Since you aspire to be our leader the person you shall face in your trial will be me."

Irial sat back, half expecting Eunan to try and weasel out of the commitment he had made. All the constables waited to see if Eunan would subject himself to such a trial. Eunan placed his mug on the table.

"My ale is down and the field awaits us. Let us waste no more time here and begin the trial."

# CHAPTER 7

# WHAT WOULD SEAMUS DO?

F aolán sat on a rock halfway down the hill upon which the castle was perched and contemplated what he had got himself into and whether he should go back to Seamus and ask for another role. He saw his master storm out of the castle and down the hill alone in front of the MacCabe constables. Eunan signalled the rebuttal of Faolán's offer to join him. Faolán saw Irial walk ten paces behind Eunan, in sombre contemplation. The other constables followed, smiling and whispering in each other's ears. Faolán guessed the morning discussions had reached a detrimental conclusion for Eunan and slipped away to get Cormac and the O'Neills.

Eunan arrived at the training field and stood apart from the rest of the Galloglass and went through the Galloglass fighting drills that Desmond and Seamus had taught him, hoping the rules which had not yet been explained to him excluded lethal weapons.

Irial would not be so foolish as to kill Cormac MacBaron's son-in-law in the fields in front of his castle? Would he?

Eunan tried to put this out of his mind for he had to deal with whatever trial they devised for him and assumed he would do so alone. He went through the drills again and again. He had to assume that Irial had trained these drills hundreds of times so he would need a trick.

The MacCabes reached the bottom of the hill and the constables examined the flat patches of ground to find an area of suitable size free of rocks and divots.

"This will do," said Feargal as he drew a circle around himself with his finger and stomped on the turf to ensure its solidity.

"You stand over there," Irial said as he pointed to the edge of the invisible circle. Irial stood opposite and took off his cloak and handed it to Feargal. Eunan had no cloak bearer so he stripped down to his shirt and threw his outer garments on the ground.

Cearbhall stepped between the two combatants and handed each of them the traditional Galloglass six-foot combat training staff used as a substitute for an axe.

"The rules are the same as for a MacCabe Galloglass initiation test," said Cearbhall. "The one who strikes the other to the ground three times is declared the winner which can only be superseded by what the majority of constables would deem a death blow. If Eunan wins, he will be a MacCabe Galloglass and our rightfully appointed leader. If he is defeated he should decline the Maguire's invitation to lead his Galloglass. Are we agreed?"

"Agreed," said Eunan and Irial in unison, and they took the sticks and assumed a position of combat readiness.

"Then, FIGHT!"

Both men circled without committing themselves to the attack. Irial had taken off his chain mail and tied his long white hair into a ponytail.

"Come on then, boy," said Irial. "Show me what Seamus taught you. Surely he'd be ashamed to see you dance around me like this."

Irial thrust the butt of his staff forward in a feigned attack. Eunan skipped away.

"It will be all the worse for you if I have to come and get you. Accept the blows of your defeat and you can skip off to Enniskillen to resign and then return here to enjoy yourself with your wife."

"The only blood in the mud today will be yours!" cried Eunan and he aimed the top of his stick at Irial's head and thrust downwards. Irial stepped to the side and delivered a blow to the back of Eunan's head. Eunan fell to his knees.

"That is one blow," said Cearbhall.

Irial stood back and smirked. He did not want to deliver a perceived death blow. He wished to play with Eunan and ensure his humiliation was complete.

"Get up. I have no wish to strike down Seamus MacSheehy's plaything in such a manner. Assume the position and get your revenge."

Eunan spun around to where Irial had positioned himself and raised his staff into a defensive position.

"I have no reason to hurt you, old man, and we have far greater enemies than each other," said Eunan keeping a careful eye on Irial's every movement.

"Land a blow before letting out such hot air. You are here to impress us with your fighting, not your dancing skills."

Eunan charged and Irial committed himself to deflect Eunan's blow. Eunan then switched to a low blow which Irial blocked. Eunan then spun his momentum upwards, withdrew his staff and tried to force the other end down towards Irial's head. Irial raised his stick and blocked him.

"Well done for getting a sequence right," and Irial threw Eunan back. "But it takes more than blindly recalling your training to become a Galloglass." Irial suddenly jolted his staff downwards putting Eunan off balance. He forced his staff upwards and deflected Eunan to the side. Irial then delivered a blow to the ribs and did not pull it. Eunan went crashing to the ground holding his side.

"That is another blow. Are you going to move in for the death blow?" said Cearbhall.

Irial backed off.

"That would be unfair on the boy," he said. "The least I can do is test the faith the Maguire placed in him."

Eunan struggled to his feet using his staff as a prop.

"You can surrender now, boy, if you wish. Put down your staff and no one will think any the less of you."

Eunan steadied himself and held his staff in a defensive position.

"I am not done yet. Let's fight."

"So you are a fool," and Irial held his staff in an offensive position once more.

He charged towards Eunan to bring his futile resistance to a swift end. This time it was Eunan's turn to parry and with that parry, Eunan stabbed the butt of his staff downwards onto Irial's calf. Irial howled and fell to the ground.

"That is a blow to Eunan," said Cearbhall with the tune of amusement singing in his voice. Irial hit the ground and heard the faint noise of laughter. He was supposed to be the master of staff combat. Everyone had considered it unfair to challenge Eunan to a test of strength where Irial showed such prowess. Irial rarely participated in this section of the final trial of endurance for would-be Galloglass, he usually left it to the more junior Galloglass, the ones that were getting their first taste of real combat.

Irial hauled himself up to his feet. His calf ached but he could shake it off and stand sufficiently to finish Eunan. He held his staff in a defensive position. Over Eunan's shoulder he could see Cormac MacBaron and his guards striding towards them with the MacCabes trotting further behind, conscious not to get ahead of their hosts. Irial knew it was now or never. Now was his chance to rid himself of this upstart in the position that should be rightfully his, his birthright, his by virtue of length of service, his because he was the most powerful Galloglass. He roared and charged across the turf.

It was all a blur to Eunan. His ribs ached but he could hold his staff. Irial moved so fast and with such fury that he knocked Eunan's staff out of his hand and delivered Eunan a blow to the head. Eunan went down and hit the ground hard. He opened his eyes and saw Irial walk over to his shocked-looking fellow constables.

"He is no Galloglass. It is better to find this out now rather than on the battlefield. We may exchange harsh words with the boy's father-in-law, but the Maguire will understand. If we have insulted our hosts we can fight with the O'Donnell instead. We can hold an election for a new leader when we get back to Enniskillen."

Eunan's eyes welled up as all his dreams seemed to melt into the sodden Tyrone earth. The ground shook as he heard his father-in-law and the O'Neills approaching. This would be it. He would live forever in his father-in-law's cupboard at his wife's beck and call. It was all for nothing, it would all end here.

He thought of Desmond and all of the effort he had put in, all to be lost in this moment. He thought of his father and how this would be another chance to call him a failure and a monster like his birth father. He thought of Seamus and what he would think of his ultimate failure. He could have cried if his head did not ache so much. He felt around him for the ground seemed wet and he could not tell if this was him dying of a head wound. He felt his staff. He could wrap his hand around it. What would Seamus do?

Eunan gripped the staff in his hand. He looked over his shoulder and saw that Irial had turned and had his back to him. Eunan grasped the end of his staff, squeezed his eyes shut for a quick prayer and summoned all his strength. He spun over on the ground and raised his staff and struck down as hard as he could on Irial's exposed ankle. The crack and accompanying yelp of pain pierced the sky. Irial fell to his knees and keeled over onto the ground. Eunan hauled himself up with his staff and hobbled over to the fallen Irial. He held his staff above Irial's face.

"Death blow," said Eunan before he collapsed on the ground beside Irial.

Before Cearbhall and the other constables could protest they found themselves confronted with a prickle of O'Neill sword points.

"The boy, as you so disrespectfully address him, is correct," said Cormac, his face red more with anger than from the effort it had taken him to get there so quickly. "He may have been three points to one down, but your constable turned his back on his enemy without delivering the death blow or obtaining his surrender. Those that disagree with the rules will be held responsible for such disrespectable behaviour toward their hosts and as such will be hung from those trees over there. Are we all in agreement that Eunan won the contest within the rules and he is the rightful leader of the MacCabes?"

The constables looked at each other and grunted, "We are."

"Take that fool and send him back to the Maguire," said Cormac pointing at Irial. "If I hear anything about this trial not being fair or any type of revenge being planned against your rightful leader, then I will put a bounty on your constable's head and if you wish to protect him you will have the wrath of the O'Neills to contend with. Is that clear?"

"It is." The constables looked to the ground but nodded their heads.

"Now be off with you." Cormac now turned to his men and pointed to Eunan. "Pick him up and bring him to the castle. The rest of you continue your training."

Cormac turned and strode up to the castle with the men supporting Eunan following behind.

# CHAPTER 8

# A ROCK IN THE SPOKES

The men of MacBaron carried Eunan into the castle and Cormac directed them to bring him to a room on the second floor of the tower on the same floor as his wife. Eunan was still conscious and immediately noticed the better quality of the bed when his back was laid upon it. A physician was diverted from his wife's room to attend to him. After some prodding and poking, the physician went to address a shadow in the corridor. Eunan propped himself up on his elbows for he wished to hear how he was doing.

"He'll live, lord," said the physician to the flickering shadow on the wall. "Sure, there'll be tenderness and bruising for a couple of weeks, but there's nothing broken and no organs have been permanently damaged. A few days of bed rest, but no training for a couple of weeks. Now, please excuse me, for I must attend to your daughter once more."

The shadow grew and became an amorphous blob on the door frame until it manifested itself into Cormac MacBaron. He entered the room but did not lighten it with his demeanour.

"It was a foolish thing you did today," Cormac said. "You could have died, or we could have had a riot by the MacCabes and proper blood been spilt. You cannot solve all your problems with violence. You have a responsibility to me, your men, the Maguire, and your wife to name but a few. The age of the Galloglass is gone, no matter how much Irial tries to resist. It is now the age of the gun. Spend your time convalescing with your wife. I'll deal with your men and their training. I'll return to speak with you again, but be prepared to lead when you return to the field. May you heal with God's speed."

Cormac nodded and was gone. The quivering boy from the morning came and stood in his place.

"Is there anything I can get you, lord?"

Eunan rested his head on the pillow and turned to the window.

"No, let me sleep. Wake me when I can see my wife."

Eunan closed his eyes and smiled. The pain had been worth it.

He was out as soon as his head hit the pillow. Gone were the hardships of the last couple of months to be replaced by a comfortable bed and a head full of dreams. He dreamt of Cara and being trapped on Devenish Island, alone with her. They were married down by the pier and went to live in the house in the woods. They lived their lives happily there as war and strife raged on the mainland, but could never penetrate the lakes to pollute their shore. He drifted into semi-sleep and pondered had their love ever been real or was it all some plot by Seamus to keep him quiet and content while he waited to be put on trial. His love certainly felt real, and it looked real in the depths of Cara's eyes. A foot slipped from the comfort of his blanket and protruded out into the cold. He remembered where he was and the role he had to play. He was married now and had a responsibility to his clan to ensure his wife was happy. He had to banish Cara from his mind and play the dutiful husband. But he drew his foot back beneath the covers into the warmth and had one more island dream.

The room smelt of potions and medicine, of things Eunan did not understand but could only place faith in. The shutters had been partially closed, spreading darkness and shadows across the room, which draped themselves over Sorcha's contented sleeping body. Eunan sat beside the bed cursing the timid boy, for he was supposed to tell him when Sorcha was awake, not imprison his master in silence on a wobbly stool. The stool was no good for his injuries, sending sharp pain up his back and down his side. No matter how restful his wife looked, he had to get up and move about to relieve his own pain.

"Father, is that you?" said a meek voice from the middle of the voluptuous bed.

Eunan held out his coarse hands and searched the shadows of the bed until he could wrap them around Sorcha's dainty little ones.

"No, it is I, your husband."

Eunan gave a warming smile, but Sorcha saw lumps, bruises and shadows where there had been none before.

"Is that really you? Has the war restarted whilst I was asleep? Let the light in so I can see you properly."

Eunan obeyed and went and set the creaking shutters back into their resting position. He stood with his back to the light, hunched over, gripping his aching side, placing his weight on his uninjured left leg, his face a mess of bruises, stubble and crusty scabs.

"Oh my love, what has happened to you? Come and lie beside me so I may rest my head on your chest and make you better."

Eunan lifted himself into the bed, lay on his back, and stared at the ceiling. Sorcha lifted her head onto his chest and proved herself right. Eunan did feel better. They were soon asleep.

As Eunan convalesced in the castle, he was allowed to visit his wife every day, as Sorcha noticeably brightened up when he was around. Eunan would encourage her to get out of bed and he would help her walk around the room before she would be exhausted and return to her bed. After several days, she could walk with Eunan's support to the window and they would look out together. Sorcha would show Eunan the topography of the land and name the castles, villages, rivers, and forests visible from the tower. In response, Eunan would point to the formations of soldiers training in the surrounding fields and explain what their training comprised of and why they were doing it.

"Do you long to be out here training with your men," said Sorcha, trying not to betray the hint of jealousy at the amount of attention Eunan was paying to the goings-on outside, "rather than be in here with me?"

Eunan took her pale hand in his and the side of his face was bathed in sunlight as he turned to his wife.

"Of course I would prefer to be here with you, but as you say yourself, our lives are not our own. We may claim ownership of these cold castle walls for a period of our lives before we pass them along, but it claims our time and attention through obligations. Obligations to our family, to our clans, to our way of life."

Sorcha looked away and climbed down from the window. Eunan tilted his head.

"What's wrong?"

Sorcha grasped the outside of his hands and held them together.

"Do you love me, my sweet?" she asked, as if her own love was a pain she could not bear.

Eunan's head tilted again. The marriage of a lord was not meant for love, but for alliances, property, and status. But Sorcha was so delicate and innocent, she certainly seemed to take this marriage seriously and he, her heinous husband, spent his time thinking of Cara. But he should do his duty and make this girl and everyone else happy. He should make the sacrifice for all that he was given. After all, Cara was just a trick Seamus played upon him. He smiled at his wife.

"Of course I do. Why would you ask in such a manner? What's wrong?"

Sorcha smiled for such sweet words lingered in her ears. She pulled her hands to her chest and placed them on her small but well-formed breasts. She led Eunan onto the bed.

"Do you have an obligation to me, to your wife?"

"It would pain me to describe it as so," said Eunan, his facial expression mirroring his words.

"Will you give me what I most desire in the world?"

Eunan pulled his hands away.

"I feel my heart wrench whenever I think you are unwell or unhappy. Name your desire and I will see if it can be granted to you on God's earth."

Sorcha looked coyly at Eunan and meandered towards him.

"We may need God's help, but I mainly need you. My biggest desire is to give birth to a boy. Your child. A healthy baby boy that can be brave and strong, a mighty warrior. All that my ailments prevent me from being in this world. My father has looked after me all of this time and all I have been to him is a sickly disappointment. But I wish to reward him with a grandson. A grandson better than all of his sons and other grandsons. You can give that to me, for you are a handsome, brave warrior and my husband."

Eunan's face went blank. A child? Never had he thought anyone would ask him to be the father of their child. He was loath to think what he would spawn, with the bad blood swimming through his veins. Surely God had prevented his mother from having another child so she would not have another one like him? His head filled with memories of his mother. The play in his head distorted itself into contortions on his face. He saw in front of him his mother on her bed in the main room of his childhood house. The room carried a claustrophobic gloom barely relieved by the dots of candlelight dispersed as if they were little stars. Blood leaked from her groin onto the blankets beneath her, which subsequently dripped onto the floor. A well-to-do man stood with his back to Eunan and placed his hands between his mother's legs. He turned around and held up a little child in the air and blood dripped from the child down the man's arms and onto the floor. It was his sister. The child was translucent and did not make a sound. His mother made up for it.

"It is all your fault she is dead! GET OUT!"

Eunan went white, reeled back, and fell off the bed. He reached out his hand to his mother.

"You cannot be with child, for you are barren, I know it, for I made you so, and all your children will be born dead."

But he did not reach out to his mother, he reached out to his wife. A thousand faces of pity and hidden scorn merged with the look of horror on the face of her husband and she was once again the sickly little girl who guests would pity and be kind to gain favour with her father. No one would marry her, the sickly girl in the back room. But now it was her husband who declared her womb was dead.

"AM I THAT HIDEOUS TO YOU? GET OUT!"

Eunan snapped too. It was no longer his mother that was crying and telling him to get out. It was Sorcha. The O'Neill guards burst through the door and dragged the sprawling Eunan out. The door slammed behind him.

Eunan sat outside the kitchen under armed guard, nursing his wounds, his bruised ego, and his scrambled head. Eunan quivered like an autumn leaf as he tried to figure out what had just happened and what would happen to him now. The air vibrated with tension and violence. The castle was not large enough to escape the anguished howls of Sorcha as she cursed her marriage to him at the top of her fragile voice. A curse would come, be broken down by a croak and disintegrate into splutters and sobs. The servants ran around in a nervous panic, stopping only momentarily to glare at Eunan to remind him he was the source of their current strife. The call had gone out to get the lord and Eunan could see him striding up the hill, taking his fury out on the tops of the long grasses that bowed to his sword. Eunan was engulfed in visions of his sickly mother taking her fury out on him, and then the vision of his father striding back to the house to give him a thrashing.

"Where is he?" Cormac roared as he came through the kitchen door. Fearful directions were rendered in silence, and Cormac stomped in Eunan's direction.

Eunan shook, for it looked like a devil from the glen was before him, such was the redness and fury that burned from Cormac's face.

"Take him to my study and I'll speak to him there."

The men picked up Eunan by the arms and Eunan knew this was fury postponed rather than fury subsided.

Eunan sat in the study and waited. He had been given the liberty of the room, for the guards stood on the other side of the door. They had granted him a mug of ale, for they did not want his throat to go dry during the expected profuse apologies to their master. Eunan could only sit with his head in his hands and curse his mother for still haunting him. He could hear the hysterical cries of his wife and the pained shouts of his father-in-law from across the hall. There was one final shriek that drowned in her mouth, silence, then the sound of furious cursing. Eunan could only hope his father-in-law did not return armed.

Eunan heard Cormac outside the door tell the guards to come in if they heard violence, otherwise to stay put. Cormac opened the door and stood in the doorway. Eunan did not recognise this knot of anger. Such rage he only experienced charging towards him on a battlefield. But he had no weapon to defend himself except for his wits.

"How dare you come into my house and insult me so?" said Cormac as he prowled around the room, a sneer moulded to his face, a drop of spittle on his lips. Eunan leapt from his seat and tried to use his chair as a shield. It was as if he was in a flashback from his youth except, by the look on Cormac's face, it was not a thrashing that was at stake, but his execution.

"If you didn't want to marry my daughter, you should have said so and not come to my home and insult her for being sick and not living up to your sordid dreams."

"I have no such sordid dreams and you have this all wrong," said Eunan as he danced around the chair to avoid Cormac's lunges.

"I should just get my men in here and shoot you and tell the Maguire that it was a training accident. The MacCabes would support me considering you crippled one of their most esteemed leaders, probably for life."

Eunan clasped his hands together.

"Can we not sit and talk about this like reasonable men? I fear there has been a dreadful misunderstanding, all the fault of me and none because of your daughter," said Eunan hoping to somewhat appease his father-in-law so he could at least put forward his case.

"I can stand here and listen. But if you insult my daughter or her reputation, by God I'll shoot you myself."

"Here, take this chair." Eunan pushed the chair he hid behind towards Cormac as the beginning of a peace offering.

Cormac scowled and wrenched it out of his hand. "Make this quick or you'll also feel my wrath for wasting my time."

"Thank you for listening to me, and I meant no insult to you or your daughter," said Eunan as he grabbed another seat to sit in front of his father-in-law. He sat, hung his head, and composed himself. "I have never told anyone this before—"

"Stop mumbling and lift your head up," said Cormac. "Speak to me like a man, or don't speak at all."

That only made Eunan more nervous.

"When I was born in my village in Fermanagh, my mother experienced some complications."

"What complications?" The question sounded less harsh than Cormac's previous yelling.

"I don't know, nor do I think any man would. It is a dangerous endeavour our womenfolk take on, to give birth. Maybe it was the work of the devil, a curse by a bitter neighbour, or a trial sent by God. In any case, my mother was crippled and sickly from the day I was born until the day she was brutally murdered. She could not give birth to a living child after me and I had to sit and watch while the physician removed dead babies from her womb. When Sorcha said she wanted to have a child, with her being so sickly I thought of my mother and the pain and suffering she went through. I was cursed with memories of being a child after Sorcha proposed her idea. She knew nothing of my childhood and thought I was thinking about her. I am sorry I caused her such offence and disrupted your house, but before I could come out of my terrible memories, your daughter had taken offence and I had not the chance to explain."

Eunan watched the expression on his father-in-law's face cool.

"She is so upset by all the commotion she has taken to her bed once more. I fear her mistaking you for a brute that just wanted to advance his position at her expense has had a profound effect on her. It will take some doing by you to prove to us you are not this person."

Eunan was alarmed that he had to prove himself to both of them. Sorcha he thought he could win back, but Cormac would be forever looking over his shoulder. But his bed had been made. Now he had to get Sorcha in it.

"I just need the chance to repair all of this," said Eunan. "If I could see Sorcha and tell her what happened and how I feel, we would quickly return to the way we were this morning. Can you arrange that for me, for her?"

Cormac rose from his seat and made for the door, more his cold, aloof self.

"We shall have to see. As I said, she has now taken ill again and cannot be disturbed. I will mention to her your wish to make it up to her when she is suitably robust to take the emotional strain. However, I suggest you spend your time wisely making up with the constables of the MacCabe Galloglass you lead. Hopefully, it will ensure that one of them will refrain from shooting you in the back the next time you step out on a battlefield. I may even be impressed if you win them around. Your boy will attend to you and your quarters by the kitchen. Good day, and see you on the training ground tomorrow."

Cormac slammed the door behind him, leaving Eunan alone to contemplate what had happened.

# CHAPTER 9

# THE CHANGING OF THE GUARD

E unan was rudely awoken by a banging on his door.

"Get up! The lord says you must attend your men."

Eunan held his head to stop the reverberations and sat on the edge of the bed with his fire unlit and contemplated his new lowly status. This moment of reflection stopped when his feet touched the cold ground and did not meet the comfort of a well-placed rug or shoes for his feet.

"Boy! Why do you neglect me so!" Eunan hollered to the back of the door.

No boy came but the butt of a dagger, recognisable now as the noise that woke him returned.

"The boy has been reassigned to other duties. The lord expects that you also attend to your duties and do not abuse his hospitality. The Maguire's men will remain as long as the lord deems it necessary to train them to fulfil his agreement with their master. He does not want to see them lying about the fields and eating food that the lord could store for the winter."

Eunan slapped his knee in frustration. There was no point in arguing with the voice behind the door. He would have to ready himself and take to the field to win back the MacCabes, his father-in-law, and finally Sorcha. It was so much easier on the battlefield to drive your axe through someone's head than to navigate the sensibilities of politics, the clan, and the bedroom. But with rank comes responsibility.

Cearbhall and Feargal stood to the side of the field as one unit of Galloglass took to pike training, whilst another in the next field practised shot drills with Pablo Blanco and Arlo, the chief Spanish trainer for the MacCabes. Eunan has the indignity of walking down the hill alone, as if he were no one. He went and stood beside Cearbhall and Feargal, who both nodded their greetings but barely took their eyes off their men.

"How goes the training?" asked Eunan, trying to make small talk before he had to address the monumental issues he would have to overcome to gain the respect of his men.

"The Spanish trainers the O'Neills have are good," said Cearbhall. "Superior to our own."

Eunan laughed.

"Don't let Arlo hear you say that," said Eunan. "He is looking for any excuse to go home."

"Aye, he looks like a drowned rat in the rain, and an unhappy one at that," said Feargal. They all laughed and Eunan felt a pang of guilt from finding common ground with the constables at the expense of creating the unhappy drowned rat by not releasing him as promised when they previously encountered Spanish ships in Tirconnell. The guilt amplified in the following awkward silence.

"Are we to train with the O'Neills today?" said Cearbhall tentatively. The difficulties Eunan had with their host the previous day had spread like wildfire in the Maguire camp and most expected to be sent home.

"Today we must organise ourselves," said Eunan firmly. It was now time to grab the bit between his teeth. "Do we need to elect a new constable now that Irial has retired to Enniskillen?"

"Yes," said Cearbhall dubiously. "But such things are difficult as you would make a statement with whoever you chose."

"Of course I would make a statement," said Eunan. "He would be a man of my choosing."

"I beg your pardon, lord, I will explain myself," Cearbhall said. "Long gone are the days when the MacCabes all came from Scotland and the Maguire took them into his employment. Each subsequent Maguire would appoint to the MacCabes, sons of the men of Fermanagh whose support he wished to gain, who in turn would appoint their own men to what became his personal bodyguard. The MacCabes are essentially MacCabes in name only and are really the sons of the Fermanagh nobility or those of sufficient fighting prowess to earn their place. Those of rank reflect those of rank in Fermanagh, with Irial being the last with a line to the original MacCabe mercenaries that would be worthy enough to hold such a title. Therefore, whoever you choose would have to be agreed with the Maguire and would show which side you stand on with the factions."

Eunan wished for simplicity, but all he found were irritations.

"Enough. I grow tired of your political ramblings in my ear. Of course I'm on the side of the Maguire himself. Draw up a list of suitable candidates and bring it to me. Now let us train with what we have."

"Will you be participating today?"

"Alas, the injuries inflicted by Irial on me, the man the Maguire himself chose to lead his Galloglass, prevent me from participating for a while, but find me somewhere quiet to sit and I shall watch, assess, and get to know my men."

A chair was found for Eunan and he sat outside the constables' tent and watched the men progress through their drills. He had seen the MacCabes fight before in various raids and at a distance at the Battle of the Ford of the Biscuits and sometimes training in the fields around Enniskillen. He had never seen them up this close and they impressed him. They were not as good as the

MacSweeneys of the O'Donnell or the MacDonnells of the O'Neill, but they would be up there with the best of the other soldiers in their permanent retinue. They were far superior to his south Fermanagh shot, but he thought he needed to keep the loyalty of his old men and not abandon them and give the impression that he had moved onwards and upwards. He still held a large amount of land being administered by Dervella and Arthur, despite his being diverted north.

As the day wore on, he noticed Cormac had passed him by and gone to train his men in fields across the way separate from the MacCabes. He looked back to the castle and noticed that Sorcha was at the window looking out across the skyline as they both had done merely the day before. Eunan sighed in regret but hoped she was also looking out at him. He also noticed Faolán was lurking about, trying to keep out of general sight but making himself aware to Eunan. Eunan waved for him to remain hidden and then pointed back to the castle.

At the end of training, Eunan saluted his constables and trudged back up the hill to the castle. Faolán followed at a distance, sticking to the cover of trees and hedges, for he did not want the constables to see Eunan associate with him. Eunan entered the castle and made straight for his room. Faolán followed in behind him at a distance. When the coast was clear, Faolán followed him into his room. Eunan sat on his bed with a letter in his hand.

"Sorry, my friend," Eunan said. "I think your time here is done."

Faolán looked disappointed, but not surprised.

"If ever I am to win the hearts of the MacCabes, I must first win their trust. I cannot have a bodyguard with me, for they think it is to protect me from them and that I don't trust them."

"You don't," said Faolán.

"But I must if I am to lead them. Therefore, take this letter."

"Am I dismissed?" Faolán said, somewhat horrified.

"I could not dismiss you. We need good men like you. I need a man I can trust, like you. Therefore, this letter is my authority to run my lands in south Fermanagh with Dervella and Arthur. I also wish you to take command of the south Fermanagh shot and make sure it remains the best unit of shot besides the MacCabes the Maguire can call upon."

Faolán bowed as he took the letter from Eunan's hand.

"I am truly honoured that you would place so much faith in me. You won't regret it."

"I'd better not, or else you'll have me to answer to, never mind Seamus," said Eunan as he warmly smiled at him.

"If you need me, all you have to do is send for me," said Faolán, returning his smile.

Eunan got up and warmly embraced him. "Then let us fetch you a horse and you can be on your way."

Eunan put his arm around his friend's shoulder and walked him down to the stables, and gave him one of the best Maguire horses.

"Now be on your way, friend, and I hope we meet again soon."

Eunan walked back to the castle, having sent his only friend and ally away. As he walked back, he noticed that Cearbhall and Feargal were sitting on a wall, taking in the night air. Eunan had to pass right by them so he saluted on his way past.

"So you sent your bodyguard away. Does that mean you trust us now?" said Feargal with Cearbhall mirroring his grin.

Eunan smiled as he walked past.

"Don't be late for training tomorrow," he said and continued on back to the castle.

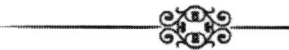

The weeks passed by and Eunan slowly healed. The MacCabe physician came and tended to his bruises every couple of days and they healed up nicely. He could then take part in the training, which did much to endear him to the men and to establish the foundations of respect with Cearbhall and Feargal. The

MacCabes also made steady progress in their pike, shot, and formation training, and even Pablo Blanco was mildly impressed by their progress.

Cearbhall and Feargal presented Eunan with several candidates to take Irial's place as constable. Eunan settled on an up-and-coming young man called Odhran McGoldrick from north Fermanagh, a Hugh Maguire loyalist who had spent some time in his youth as a hostage of Cúchonnacht Maguire around the same time as Eunan. He claimed to know Eunan and to have met him before, to which Eunan only nodded, for he had no recollection. Odhran excelled as a marksman and often recounted stories of when he went hunting with Hugh Maguire in his youth. He was boisterous and confident, but reliable and good in a fight. He was put forward to the MacCabes by none other than Hugh Maguire himself and Eunan could think of no better man to replace Irial.

However, getting back on the good side of his father-in-law proved much slower going, and he was no closer to reacquainting himself with Sorcha than gazing up longingly at her when she looked out the window of her room and he would try to catch her sneakily looking at him. He still had lingering thoughts about Cara but knew he had to banish her from his mind and take his marriage seriously. He had pressed his father-in-law to speak to Sorcha on his behalf and state his case so that he may be allowed into her room once more to explain himself. Cormac said he needed to rebuild the trust between them before he would intervene on his behalf. Eunan needed to wait for his opportunity to impress his father-in-law, and his efforts on the training grounds would not cut it. He did not have to wait long.

Raiding into Connacht had recommenced at a low level, and it was the perfect opportunity for a young man out to impress. Eunan had stayed put, but Cormac's son Rory had travelled west with some of his young companions to make a foray into Sligo. A messenger tore across Fermanagh and Tyrone with news of his exploits. He made straight for Augher Castle to pass the message to Cormac.

News quickly spread around the training fields surrounding the castle that Cormac had heard news of Rory. Eunan summoned his constables and climbed the hill to the castle. Cormac paced up and down the great hall, cursing and punching the backs of chairs set around the dining table. His constables dared not say a word.

"That stupid, foolish boy has gone and got himself captured by the sheriff of Sligo. He has admitted he is my son and now I face an extortionate ransom. I cannot be seen to pay, for the O'Neills will seem weak, yet cannot let my son perish."

Eunan pushed his way to the front.

"I can save your son. The Maguires know Sligo like the back of our hands. We are always raiding in and out of there. We are very familiar with the sheriff and his methods. Let the Maguires repay your kindness by rescuing your son."

Cormac sized up Eunan's offer.

"Let it be on your head if he dies. If you fail, leave him alive, so I may at least pay the ransom."

Eunan bowed.

"I will take my leave. You will not regret placing your faith in me."

"I'd better not," muttered Cormac. But Eunan and his men had already turned and left.

# CHAPTER 10

# LONG LIVE THE KING

T he demarcation point between the lands of the northern lords and those subject to the Crown or wavering in between was clear. Seamus and his men marched south through Fermanagh and although there was famine and the usual signs of lawlessness, the lands were intact and the peasants toiled. But when he crossed over into East Breifne, the contrast was stark. The scars of war had burned deep into the landscape of Leinster.

They knew they had crossed into East Breifne by the increase in the amount of smoke in the surrounding lands and on the horizons. The retributions between clan branches, families and fathers, brothers and sons had clearly not yet run their course. Bands of hard-faced men roamed the countryside, setting fires, stealing cattle and those who were desperate enough for the futile endeavour of trying to drive pigs without losing them or getting killed in the process. These rogue bands turned and ran when they saw this well organised column winding its way through the landscape. Seamus impressed on his men the need for speed as the attention they were attracting heightened the risk that they would run into formal opposition.

Seamus was put in command of one hundred shot, mainly drawn from the clans of Munster and south Leinster that had been part of the gangs of potential rebels that had flowed north as they had been evicted from their lands. They had sought sanctuary in Tyrone and had been trained by Spanish and ex-English army officers up to the same level of proficiency as the main O'Neill army. They were returning in disciplined lines, a musket and bags of bullets around their belts and a stern resolve in their hearts. They also had a screen of Kern to protect them, who scoured the lands ahead in search of both the enemy and supplies. They were under Seamus's strict orders to be discreet as they wished to pass through the lands unmolested.

Captain Richard Tyrell quickly impressed Seamus with both his abilities with the men and his knowledge of the terrain. Seamus was naturally suspicious and experience had both solidified and reinforced this. His best men had come from a history of service in the English army and it was a common background for swordsmen for hire. This always aroused the greatest of suspicion in Seamus for what would make a more able spy than an ex-army man? A prostitute, perhaps? But he trusted them even less. The easiest way to stab a man was when he had his trousers down. Richard had a perfect mixture of looks, ability, and gravitas that seemed almost too good to be true. Seamus warmed to him, but he knew the test of loyalty would come soon.

They worked their way down into central Leinster. There was a notable escalation of violence in the air. The sky was filled with smoke, bands of refugees roamed aimlessly across the lands searching for direction and the rivers were filled with the blood of the Irish and English settlers and the precious cattle they fought over. They came across a small abandoned village strewn with the bodies of their former residents as their houses burned around them. Richard got down from his horse, knelt, and examined the bodies to see what side they would have been on.

"All this senseless destruction," he said.

"I have seen much of it in my time in Munster," Seamus said. "But scars heal and the English would have deemed it worthwhile, for after the passing of a certain amount of time you would have a fertile land full of English settlers and the memories of the Irish there before would fade into the past. They put no price on Irish blood."

"Well, all the signs say that these were English settlers and recent ones. No wonder this village was burned out."

Seamus looked around at the fresh fires. He was nervous. Sure, his men could march in neat lines and load and fire proficiently in the field, but he had never seen them in a firefight. He was a long way from the relative safety of the north, and the tension in the air told him his men would be sorely tested soon.

"We'd better get going, for the English soldiers will be here soon. We don't want to get into a firefight in open country."

Richard raised himself from his knee.

"It's almost time for me to depart. We are near my family lands and I would like to take half the men to defend them, as we previously agreed."

"Aye, that we did. But I would much prefer to leave you in the hands of my good friend and ally, Uaithne and the O'Mores for there is a far greater chance of success than leaving you in a field with fifty men, waiting for you to run out of bullets."

Richard was determined to be his own man and at the beck and call of no one.

"The news of our rebellion spreads far and wide, and we draw recruits to our banner by the day. I mean to establish myself in my family's territory and draw men to me by news of my success."

"Your confidence is commendable, but your face betrays your youth," said Seamus firmly. "I was given command of this mission and I am happy to hand you over half my command once I deem it safe and not before. I will send men to find Uaithne. He had a short head start from Eunan's wedding and could not have travelled far. If you continue along our planned route, he will find us and then you can be released."

Richard looked displeased at not being given his leave, but held his tongue. Seamus gave the command to set off south once more.

They travelled for another day or so and the destruction became more and more widespread. The armed bands of men grew more numerous but none had the courage or strength to take on Seamus's men. Richard grew more agitated the further south they went.

"Be patient, my friend. Uaithne knows we are here and will come. Once he does, you'll see that patience was the right course," said Seamus.

The next morning, they came upon a burning village on the edge of the Earl of Ormond's lands. Seamus and Richard sat on their horses on top of a small hill and observed the raid as it occurred. The black dots of men on horseback rode through the flatlands and forests and left a trail of destruction behind them: the slime of a snail set on fire. Behind them were roving bands of Kern who mopped up any resistance and then removed any chattels they could get their hands on and directed them northwards.

"Besides the Pale itself, the Earl of Ormond is the main pillar of resistance to the rebellion that the English have," said Seamus. "If he could be turned then Ireland could free itself and would not have to swap vassalage to the English for vassalage to the Spanish. But he is not for turning. For even though he was born on this soil, he bleeds English blood."

Richard could hear the emotion in his voice.

"We'll return to Munster soon, don't you worry."

They saw below them at the bottom of the hill a group of riders approaching them.

"Hold your fire men until we establish if they are friends or foes," said Seamus.

They were quickly identified as being Uaithne and his men. Seamus grinned from ear to ear.

"I told you he'd find us."

Richard returned his smile and waited to be impressed.

They all sat by the fire and warmed themselves as Seamus ordered his men to hunt for rabbits so they could all enjoy a stew together before the next part of the mission. Uaithne was exhausted but excitable from his recent bout of death and destruction.

"What has you down here so far south so soon after the wedding?" said Seamus.

Uaithne took a swig from his water bottle.

"Fiach is on the offensive again. We have made our peace, reluctantly on my part, for the son he betrayed was my friend. He has called all the rebels of southern Leinster together in the Wicklow mountains so he can inaugurate Domhnall MacMurrough Kavanagh as the King of Leinster. A few of the sons and distant relatives of the old English lords of Leinster and Munster may be tempted to join us, so he asked me for a show of strength to persuade any waverers."

Seamus laughed.

"Well, we were impressed if it means anything to you." He clasped Uaithne on the shoulder.

Uaithne smiled.

"You must bring the men to the inauguration. It would encourage everyone there to show how much support the O'Neill will give them."

Richard scowled.

"But I need half the men to defend my lands."

Uaithne placed his hand on Richard's arm.

"Come with us. You will meet and make comrades of all the rebels of Leinster. You will no longer be isolated on your small patch of land. Once you come, we can all co-ordinate raids together and free ourselves of the English oppression."

Richard got caught up in Uaithne's boundless enthusiasm.

"I am with you, my friend. Let us set out at once."

Seamus was left out in the cold for he was unsure what reception he would get from his old friend, given how they had parted company the last time. He smiled and feigned enthusiasm nonetheless.

Their journey through the Wicklow mountains was one of relative ease, given Uaithne's knowledge of the secret pathways and where Fiach's men would be positioned to defend them.

"I was almost brought up in them," he would brag to Richard as he pointed to the south Wicklow mountains.

Seamus saw they would become firm friends with their similar ages, outlook, and military skills being the bedrock. It warmed Seamus's heart but it brought out a tinge of regret, for he could not see his nephew Eunan bonding with them in such a manner or sharing their aptitude for war.

They came upon Fiach's scouts, who seemed most pleased to see them and bore no outward animosity towards what had gone on in the past. They soon came upon Fiach's camp, which was spread over a sparse mountaintop in plain view. Fiach's men told Seamus that it was a show of strength not to hide the inauguration of the King of Leinster, but Seamus was not so sure of the wisdom or logic. They led them up the mountain to Fiach's tent.

The huge hulk of Fiach poured forth from his tent, a ball of energy and enthusiasm acting more like a youth than a man in his fifties. He looked more drawn than Seamus had remembered him, as if being the rebel of the mountains was finally taking its toll. One of his men pointed towards Seamus and his party and the arms dropped and the energy fizzled out. He coyly walked over like an apologetic dog, turning his head as he composed what he would say to his old friend. Seamus braced himself for the awkward reunion. Fiach approached Uaithne first.

"Welcome home. Forgive an old fool. You are like a son to me. A son that makes his father beam with pride. Soon the rest of Leinster will burn to add to what you have already achieved."

They embraced.

"Let bygones be bygones and the O'Byrnes and O'Mores be united once more," replied Uaithne. Fiach nodded, and Uaithne signalled to his men to make camp. Then Fiach was left standing in front of Seamus.

"Hello, old friend. We should talk before the inauguration takes place. We have much to catch up on."

Seamus gave a silent nod and Fiach invited him into his tent.

Conditions in the camp had further declined and Fiach definitely needed aid from the lords of the north. His tent was sparse, with a couple of trunks with clothes hanging out of the sides but with piles of old swords around the perimeter.

"We had to dig up poor old caches from around the mountains. Ammo is a precious commodity. Into the holes where the swords once lay go our guns when we have no more ammo for them. Such is the burden of the mountain bandit that absorbs the attentions of the English for his allies in the north."

Seamus tried to hide his disappointment for the sake of Fiach's fragile ego.

"If you write me a list of what you need and what types of guns you have, I'll do my best to bring what I can. The O'Neill is in constant discussions with whatever merchants he can hire to import as many guns and ammunition as possible."

"Thank you, my friend. Now sit and let us talk business and whatever else the past allows us."

Seamus perched on the side of a trunk. Fiach offered him some wine.

"How many men can you count on these days?" said Seamus.

Fiach became visibly irritated.

"Well, we still have most of the O'Byrnes and the O'Tooles, and an assortment of other rebels that seek sanctuary in the hills. With the crowning of the King of Leinster, I hope to get most of the remaining clans and some of the old English lords too."

Seamus did not want to extinguish his friend's nervous smile. He looked in need of hope and belief.

"So you could probably rally five hundred men at any one time?"

Fiach recoiled at such an estimate.

"We practise the art of the ambush down here. Our well-placed men can take down more than their fair share of English before disappearing back into the woods."

Seamus changed the subject and decided to count the men himself.

"I have brought you one hundred shot as promised by the O'Neill and I can bring down as many more as you need."

Fiach's eyes lit up.

"Are they trained? Do they know how to use their weapons?"

"They are good solid Leinster and Munster men who can fight as well as any O'Neill."

Fiach leaned forward and clasped his hand.

"Thank you, my friend. With five hundred shot we can keep the English tied down indefinitely. When do you have to leave? Can you stay for the inauguration?"

"I can stay for a week or so but then I must go, unfortunately, with half the shot."

Fiach dropped his hand.

"Why come and make promises you cannot keep? Why show me these men and then take them away?"

Fiach circled the room and gesticulated an angry speech he was giving in his head. Seamus gestured for him to sit again, but Fiach refused.

"I have a young man with me, a Captain Richard Tyrell," said Seamus, trying to change the subject to one more amenable to Fiach. "He used to serve in the English army, but family circumstances made him a rebel. Part of my mission is to set him up above Uaithne's territory so he can raid and harass from there. Another steaming pot of rebellion in Leinster will help draw the heat away from you."

Fiach's eyes lit up again.

"I must meet this young man."

Seamus smiled.

"That is why I brought him here."

"Let us celebrate then. Let us all hail the King of Leinster and throw the English into the sea!" Fiach roared.

They both got up to leave, but Seamus grabbed Fiach by the arm.

"Why didn't you become the King of Leinster? You are the most powerful Gaelic chieftain remaining."

"What? Is the price on my head already not high enough? Besides, the Kavanaghs cannot decide whether they are in or out. If they came in, we would double our men. Nothing better to help them decide than declaring their leader King!"

Seamus laughed, and Fiach invited him to leave the tent with him.

The next day the sun obliged and gave a cold and breezy day, the imitation of a blue-skied summer's day. All around the camp were celebrations inflated by the desperation of those seeking the smallest seed of hope. But Seamus was long past this and grew tired of weak men inflating their egos by granting themselves titles that genuine power had long deserted. Seamus sat on the sidelines, a little bored. He found all of this bravado to be empty and tedious. The words of Cormac MacBaron — that he would have to endure many such a ceremony to cobble together a rebellion — rang in his ears. Fiach was in his element making speeches, proposing toasts and herding everyone together to gain the sense of unity he hoped they would glean by his reach into the past. He was the puppet master, after all. Sure, the Kavanaghs brought men, but they were more bandits and boys than soldiers.

Their best skills were running away and hiding in forests and acting as bandits rather than causing an actual threat to the English. Domhnall MacMurrough Kavanagh sat on his throne as neither leader nor soldier but as a relic of the past. He had been a perpetual rebel and exuded an air of sophistication as some of his youth had been spent in Spain, but this was slowly evaporating as he could not live up to the Kavanagh myth. Over the years when he was a rebel, he was always subservient to Fiach. When he made peace, the English had slowly eroded his lands on the Leinster plain, giving it to English settlers, and Domhnall was powerless to do anything about it. He may have led small tantrum revolts, burning fields and stealing cattle, but the ensuing peace would always bring compromise in the form of the shrinking of his lands. Fiach was tired of the turncoat rebel and saw his crowning as the ultimate commitment to the cause. The King of Leinster would never surrender or run and hide like a common thief.

The younger generation lapped it all up. The romance of being rebels, of fighting for their heritage, the fight against the heretical Queen. Whatever it took to motivate them to join in the celebrations, Fiach included it in his speeches. Uaithne danced around with a mug of wine welded to his hand. He had reconciled with Fiach for they laughed, drank, sang and danced together. Fiach's remaining sons, except for Phelim, who saw himself as Fiach's heir apparent, his wife and the O'Tooles were more restrained and kept to themselves. The Leinster alliance was still rife with factions. Richard Tyrell joined in on the periphery but stood and observed most of the time and tried to work out who was who and who held the actual power. Seamus admired that, but Richard was still young. He did not know enough to work out that Fiach was doomed to die a rebel failure in the mountains unless someone such as the Spanish or the O'Neill came to rescue him. But Seamus was not sure he actually wanted to be saved since he seemed in his element here, the rebel puppet master of the Wicklow mountains.

"Come on Seamus, you ol' fool! Get some drink down ya!"

Fiach gestured to him to come and join in the celebrations. Seamus saluted him with his mug but declined to join in with the rebel songs. He sought Richard instead to give him the benefit of his Leinster political knowledge.

# CHAPTER 11

# OLD FOLLY

The Kavanaghs left several days later for the truce still held in Wicklow and Domhnall was keen for his men to plant their crops before the fighting season began. Uaithne and Richard were also keen to leave, for they had rebellions to foment. Seamus spent his time trying to devise several alternate routes that the lords of the north could use to supply arms and men to Fiach.

One bright summer's morning Fiach called them all into his tent and he hosted the meeting along with his son Phelim. He poured them all a drink, which led Seamus to ponder how Fiach always had such a good supply of wine, being that he was always up a mountain. The inauguration had given Fiach a new lease on life, and his enthusiasm still had not dimmed.

"The English snuck a message to me."

Fiach's face shone. Nothing inflated his ego more than thinking he was the most wanted man in Ireland. Which he usually was.

"What did it say?" said Seamus.

He was easily the most cynical in the room, which was otherwise full of the susceptible ears of youth.

"They want to arrange a meeting. They want to come to a more permanent peace."

"It's a trap," said Seamus. "All Russell wants to do is hang your head on a spike outside Dublin Castle."

"They say that if we can strike a permanent peace accord, they will consider giving me back Ballinacor."

"That is just red meat to bait the trap," said Seamus.

But it was Phelim's turn to adopt the sheen of enthusiasm.

"If we can win it back peacefully, then we must at least try. I can arrange an ambush for the enemy where they mean to meet to protect you, in case it goes wrong."

But Seamus was the mountain rain.

"Being stuck up a mountain must have dulled your senses. But if you must attend, it would be an opportunity for the O'Neill shot to familiarise themselves with the terrain."

"Then it is decided," said Fiach. "I will write back to them and suggest a suitably trustworthy O'Byrne to arrange the meeting."

"If there is such a thing," Seamus said. "I never knew there were any neutrals in this bitter war."

"I have a trick of my own," said Fiach. "If I hadn't, I would have been in the grave long ago."

"I'm sure the Lord Deputy is sharpening the spike on his castle walls for your head as we speak," said Seamus.

But Fiach was not listening anymore. He was caught up in the swirl of the excitement of planning to take back Ballinacor.

The meeting was on. The house nestled between lush forests in the picturesque foothills of the Wicklow mountains. With a stream to one side, it seemed a crime to blemish it with the constant war that raged in the mountains beyond and fill it with the blood of those who relied upon it to replenish their lands. It appeared the perfect place to nurture a truce.

"And the perfect place for an ambush," said Seamus.

He had gone ahead with Richard and Uaithne to scout the area for the proposed meeting.

"There is a huge amount of ground you need to cover to escape from the house if you need to quickly," he said.

"Yet Fiach seems to want this meeting more than he values his own life," said Richard.

"He is not my friend of old. He falls into folly too easily, very easy to persuade. I blame his foolish sons and the O'Tooles for he seems to lack sensible allies and surrounds himself with reckless youth."

"Who else are you going to persuade to live in these mountains?" said Uaithne.

He smiled, knowing he could easily be one of those reckless fools.

"But as usual he won't see sense," said Seamus, ignoring Uaithne's churlish grin. "Richard, organise the men so they can cover the house or at least provide a volley of cover if Fiach has to flee."

"They have chosen the house well. It is out of range for an effective volley," said Richard.

"We'll just have to settle for a noisy one, then. Let's go back to the camp. We only have a few hours to arrange everything."

Fiach had been in his customary jovial mood that had elated his spirit when he thought there was a chance to retake Ballinacor. He chose Phelim to come with him to the house. His mood had not been dented when Seamus had declined his invitation by saying, "The O'Donnell would be upset with my relatives if I threw my life away so foolishly and disregarded his mission."

Fiach did not respond, as he did not want to jeopardise his supply of men and materials, for he knew he could not continue the war without Seamus's help. He preferred to flatter the golden goose and offer him a command. It was an act to Seamus as transparent as water.

It was far from the first time that Seamus had to act on orders that he thought were foolish. He consoled himself by thinking of the randomness of battle and resolved to be on alert to take any opportunities that presented themselves. But his primary concern was to preserve his men and his second was to educate the youthful commanders in the art of war. He could only measure their potential in the heat and smoke of battle.

Seamus and Richard set up their men in the woods on their side of the house. They watched Fiach and Phelim cross the field to the house with their arms in the air to show they carried no weapons. The English officers on the other side of the field made the same gesture and walked from their side of the house. They both met at the front of the house and Fiach's cousin, who acted as mediator, searched them both and confirmed they were unarmed. They all went into the house.

"Keep the men ready," said Seamus.

Richard nodded, and all eyes were on the entrance to the house. All was quiet for about half an hour until the front door slammed open. Fiach and Phelim ran for their lives as the English captains chased them with swords.

"Hold your fire, men," ordered Seamus.

From out of the woods on the other side of the field charged the English cavalry. The neighing of charging horses, the shaking of the ground as they thundered sent a shiver down the spines of the Irish shot and lent a lightness of foot to Fiach and Phelim. The flashing of swords and lances as these Irish allies of the Crown thundered across the field put a curse and a prayer on Fiach's lips.

"HOLD!" said Seamus.

Fiach and Phelim ran for their lives.

"FIRE! FIRE!" cried Fiach.

"HOLD!" ordered Seamus.

The horses were gaining fast.

"DOWN!" shouted Seamus from in the trees.

Fiach looked confused and then tackled Phelim so they both fell to the ground.

"FIRE!" shouted Seamus.

With a billowing of smoke, one hundred guns let off an awful bang. The horses buckled and bucked. Riders fell to the ground and were trampled. The once neat line fled every which way.

"FIRE!"

The bullets were more of a threat to the tufts of grass in the field, but the tremendous bang worked its magic on the horses. The smoke settled in front of the forest and Fiach picked up Phelim and they both ran directly into it. Nobody followed them. Fiach collapsed in front of Seamus.

"They don't want to negotiate," said Fiach.

"I think I noticed," came the reply.

They fled through the mountains and forests and back to the camp with the English at their backs. The English pursued them like dogs chasing a rabbit into its burrow, with a gnashing of teeth and a howl for the approval of their masters. Richard and the shot from the north countered this threat by laying periodic ambushes for their pursuers to allow the main body of men to escape. A tired and dishevelled mob of rebels spilled back to their camp. Seamus did not bother to disguise his fury and immediately ordered his men to prepare to leave for north Leinster. When Fiach heard this, he called him into his tent. When Seamus arrived, Fiach seemed in a conciliatory mood.

"Come in, my friend. Sit and let us eat. We must plan your next return journey, and I need to give you the lists of men and provisions I need."

Whilst bread and ale were on the menu, Seamus dismissed the starter of idle chatter.

"Neither the O'Neill nor the O'Donnell would be keen to go to all the trouble of training up men, and equipping them with hard-to-get muskets, for you to recklessly throw their lives away at the first opportunity."

Fiach turned a shade of purple.

"So what have I been doing for all these years for them? Throwing away the lives of my family and friends to buy them time so they could grow stronger whilst I bled? They owe me!"

Fiach's shade of purple would have been intimidating for most people and have them worried for Fiach's health, but it only got Seamus's back up. He stood up, face to face with Fiach.

"What you did yesterday was reckless and stupid, and could've got us all killed. It was blatantly obvious that it was an ambush. Any fool could see that! If you get yourself killed, then this whole thing collapses. Why should I risk my own life and those of my men to traipse our way all across Ireland only for you to get us killed?"

"I never took you as a coward!"

A flash of anger left Seamus's eyes as quickly as it came. Seamus backed away and turned for the tent flap.

"It saddens me that our years of friendship have descended to this. You are not the man you once were. I will arrange with my masters for a more pliable escort for your reinforcements to come next time."

Fiach's anger dissipated as quickly as Seamus's and he chased after him.

"I didn't mean it. You have always been a good friend, and we have fallen out in the past but have always made up. I need you. The rebellion needs you. Yes, leave today, but come back with reinforcements as soon as you can. I will take care of Richard Tyrell."

Seamus turned to look at Fiach to respond but saw a pale shadow of his former friend. Where once had been the proud and powerful victor of the legendary battle of Glenmalure there now stood a greying old man clinging to his position and the glories of days long deceased. Seamus saw in him a bit of himself, but at least he had Eunan. All of Fiach's sons would kill each other in a bitter civil war induced by their O'Toole wives. He was so quick to sacrifice his most talented son for the lies of his wife. Seamus's temper told him to walk away, but what would he tell the O'Donnell?

"Richard and I'll leave before with half the men, as previously arranged. Give me your letters and I will press your case to the O'Donnell."

"Thank you, thank you. You are a loyal friend."

Seamus ignored him.

"Watch your back. Don't get usurped. There are several talented young, up-and-coming rebels vying to take your place."

Fiach's face dropped.

"And none of them are your sons."

# CHAPTER 12

# THE BARGAINING CHIP

Taaffe had now taken up residence in Drumahair Castle while the surrounding lands reverberated with the discontent of being under the heel of Governor Bingham, all stirred by the rebellious clans of the north. With great reluctance, Taaffe had to temporarily curtail his land acquisition activities to repel the many incursions from the lands of the O'Donnells and the Maguires. The clan structure of Sligo had fractured as some clans began to openly side with the rebels. Taaffe had assembled a force of English soldiers, men from the Earl of Clanricard and the Earl of Thomond, and men from the English settlers in the region. He was going to enforce the Queen's rule in the county in exchange for land that he would confiscate from the rebellious Sligo clans to pay the earls and the English settlers. However, such plans had to be postponed for the repulsion of a recent raid had yielded an unexpected bounty.

Taaffe stood at the top of the tower looking north, attempting to see past the low-hanging plump grey clouds to the borderlands and to plan his forthcoming campaign. One of his captains emerged from the stairs and approached him.

"How is our guest?" said Taaffe.

"Mouthy, since he realised his value to us," said the captain.

"Well, keep MacBaron's son away from the other low-value prisoners. We don't want his rebellious streak to spread. If any more of them claim to be worth a decent ransom, investigate it, and if any of them are found to be lying, hang them in the yard in front of the other prisoners."

The captain nodded and turned towards the stairs and the prison cells.

"Sheriff, sheriff," a shout came from the south facing section of the tower. "Governor Bingham approaches with a large body of men."

"Damn," Taaffe muttered to himself. He turned to his men. "Prepare to let the Governor in and I will meet him in the yard."

Bingham rode into the castle with his pikemen marching in behind him and they occupied the centre of the yard. Taaffe stood in the doorway to the castle tower. He put on a smile as he walked over to Bingham.

"Good afternoon, Governor. What brings you up here unannounced? Let me help you down from your horse."

Bingham scowled as he surveyed the packed courtyard.

"You've assembled a lot of men here, and from the banners, especially men from the earls of south Connacht. Why was I not informed of such a build-up? Is there trouble on the borders or are these men here for another reason?"

Taaffe ordered one of his men to place a stool beneath Bingham so he could dismount his horse easily. Bingham's mood was such that he deliberately dismounted on the other side and presented the man with the reins to his horse. Taaffe sensed the unease in the air.

"It is one of the biggest castles near the borderlands so it is natural that the men should seek shelter here," Taaffe said.

Bingham walked towards the castle door.

"I know you, Taaffe, and we need to have words, but not here. Come, and leave your men behind and mine will also stay in the courtyard."

Taaffe scuttled behind him.

"Whatever has you in such a mood is bound to be a lie. Our enterprises go well and the rebels dare not cross the Erne river. You can trust me," said Taaffe over Bingham's shoulder.

Bingham did not stop.

"As I said before, I know you and I know when a man is telling a lie. Let us not air our business out in the yard, but in private. Summon me some food and drink and we shall discuss our business in the castle's private quarters."

Taaffe stood across from Bingham and watched his master wipe the wine on his lips onto his sleeve.

"I've been in such a rush to get here I've barely had time to eat," said Bingham.

"I hope the meal was to your satisfaction?" said Taaffe.

"It was adequate, but I quibble. It is the best I can expect out in these backwaters," said Bingham, rushing to rid himself of the small talk and to get down to serious business. "Now I must press you for honest answers as to what you have been up to. You know my enemies bedevil me, and these Gaelic savages complain every time we squeeze their pips. Those soft fools in the Irish Council who wouldn't put a foot in the bogs of Ireland for fear of catching dysentery listen to every complaint without realising what you have to do to control the outer provinces. Now, in order to placate these savages and show that the Queen's law works, they want to put me on trial, and that means you going on trial too."

It was Taaffe's turn to be furious.

"No one has made any accusations against me! No one has come to arrest me or charged me with anything. I would ignore it. It is another negotiating tactic that the Lord Deputy is using to get a ceasefire with the natives before bringing men from England to crush them."

Bingham crossed his fingers and thrust them in Taaffe's face.

"We're like that, you and me, like that. What I do, you do and what you do falls on me. I know we are being blamed for driving them into rebellion for treating them so harshly. I'm being summoned to appear before the Council."

Taaffe gave Bingham a dismissive smile.

"The wind will change direction. Red Hugh will come pouring over the river Erne and they'll clamour for you to come back and send him packing once again. Hire a fancy English lawyer who can talk until there's no more air in the room and then they'll need you again. These threats have been hanging over your head for years and never came to anything and they won't this time."

"I wish I could believe that and I could if it were up to me alone," said Bingham. "But as I said, we are both in this together and I have heard many things about what you've been up to, so I've come to see for myself."

Taaffe's limited range of expressions did not extend to innocent.

"Nothing out of the ordinary, if ordinary existed in a place like this," Taaffe said.

Bingham smirked.

"I also hear the complaints. They don't only save them for the Council. What are all these men from the southern earls doing here? Rumour has it you're organising land sales behind my back."

Taaffe cringed but kept his composure.

"The Sligo clans are causing trouble again, so I thought it wise to raise a force, yet I still have to pay them. No better people to pay them than the troublemakers themselves. I thought it more efficient not to inform you so I wouldn't trouble you when you are so concerned with other things. Of course, you would still get the same cut of the profits."

"Oh, but of course," and Bingham's response came tinged with sarcasm. "That's why you didn't tell me about it and have sought the protection of the most powerful lords of Connacht. But we can deal with that later. We have more important business."

"Such as?" Taaffe raised a quizzical eyebrow.

"Such as the prisoner you hold in your dungeons. You'd better not have harmed him. I hear he is Cormac MacBaron's boy. If we could drive a wedge between MacBaron and O'Neill, and I get the credit, all my legal woes and also what you have dropped me in would fall by the wayside. My men are here to hold the castle until I can hand the prisoner over to the representative of the Queen and the Irish Council. I trust you have him here?"

Taaffe panicked. He had sent the ransom note to MacBaron, and he had received a reply that MacBaron agreed to pay. The proceeds of that and what he should make with his latest land grab would make him one of the wealthiest landowners in Connacht and get him finally out from under the shadow of Bingham. But he could not let his old master drag him down with him.

"He is not here. It's far too obvious. He is in Collooney Castle, safely hidden."

Taaffe felt Bingham's hot breath on his face, and an angry finger pointed in his chest.

"You'd better not be lying to me. I'll be back tomorrow and for your sake the prisoner should be waiting for me, for the English officer will arrive then. I'll leave some of my men here to ensure you don't leave the castle."

Bingham turned to the food lying on the table, picked up a leg of meat and stripped off as much as his mouth could hold and threw the bone back on the plate. He left without another word. Taaffe collapsed into a chair and held his head in his hands. The O'Neills were coming with the money and he had to do the deal right now before Bingham returned, furious and empty-handed.

Taaffe waited until he heard enough noise from the yard to convince him that Bingham had left. He went to the window to see the last of Bingham's entourage ride out of the castle gates. One hundred pikemen stood in the courtyard, their discipline leaving by the same gate as Bingham.

"Lazy Irish conscripts. This should be easy."

He furiously gestured out the window to one of his constables to come into the castle. They met on the stairs.

"As soon as Bingham and his men are out of earshot, get up on the tower and signal that a raid is coming," said Taaffe.

The constable looked confused.

"Then get the prisoner and throw a blanket over his head. We're going to smuggle him out the front gate."

"But... but..."

"Don't ask questions, just do it."

Taaffe paced the great hall, a bundle of nerves waiting for the signal. He had arranged to meet the O'Neills on the banks of the Erne the next morning. The sound of the horn signalling potential danger reverberated through every cavity in the castle.

"Raid, raid. The rebels are coming!" shouted Taaffe from the window of the castle over the heads of Bingham's raw conscripts. The conscripts looked nervously up at the bringer of bad news.

"We were given strict instructions to stay here and guard you," called up an English officer in charge of the conscripts.

"Well, someone has to stop the rebels from pillaging your master's lands. I am his sheriff, and the responsibility stops with me. You can always come on the sortie to guard me and see your first taste of action?"

The captain looked nervously at his men and decided it was not the time for their first taste of action. It was better they stay together as a unit rather than suffer the indignity of a potential defeat followed by obligatory desertions.

"Someone must guard the castle, and you know the lands far better than us. The Governor would understand, for it is no good for anyone if the rebels ravaged the land or the castle fell or was besieged."

Taaffe suppressed his smile.

"The Governor made a wise choice when he appointed such a canny captain as you. I'll rally my men and be back before the Governor returns with the lands secure and peace restored."

Taaffe left the window and called his captains. He left with a body of men and smuggled the prisoner out amongst them.

# CHAPTER 13

# A MEETING BY THE RIVER

R ory MacBaron was eager to impress any rebel that would pay him enough attention and considered his father's approach to be far too cautious. With all the verve of an eighteen-year-old who never had the blood of an enemy on his axe, had never had his stomach swell with famine nor had to win the hearts of other men to follow him because he was stuck in his father's shadow, he went to seek fame and fortune. He mistakenly thought that one or the other, or hopefully both, could be found in the bogs of Sligo or among the jagged rocks on the shoreline that impaled the Spanish Armada. He found out his dreams were all illusions on his first excursion across the river Erne with the youthful O'Neills he had persuaded to follow him after a drunken night in Enniskillen when he went there with some of his father's soldiers. His father's name did not inspire fear when English settler soldiers surrounded him; it just inspired their greed.

He now found himself tied to the reins of a horse with a hood over his head being led to either his death or, at best, exchange for a hefty ransom. The spirit had been kicked and punched out of him back at the castle, but Taaffe and his men had been careful not to damage the goods and left the face easily recognisable. Taaffe advanced towards the rendezvous with a gang of his best men drawn from the English settlers, all armed with swords and some shot from the Earl of Clanricard.

Eunan gathered together fifty of the men he felt he could trust the most and with his three constables set off for the arranged place of exchange for his brother-in-law. He had briefly met his brother-in-law at his wedding, but Rory had been far more interested in drinking than exchanging pleasantries with Eunan. But he was not doing it for him. He was doing it for Sorcha. Eunan had heard that she had taken ill again when she heard what had happened to her brother and feared that he was going to be taken away from her as well. The daydream front and centre of Eunan's mind was that he would ride up the hill with Rory in tow and Sorcha would run out of the castle and forgive him. That is, if she was well enough to run, if he could save her brother, and if he did not get himself killed in the process.

His father-in-law had given him the ransom under much duress. It was not because he was unwilling to pay it, but rather that if Eunan returned to Augher Castle without Rory and the ransom, that would be the end of his daughter's marriage. Eunan had to work hard to persuade his father-in-law to give him the responsibility. Cormac only agreed if Eunan would take along a unit of his MacDonnell Galloglass and have them stationed nearby but hidden, so if something did go wrong they could hopefully intervene and retrieve the situation. But Eunan had no plans to pay any ransom and was determined to return to Augher Castle with Rory and the ransom money. To that end he had brought the best bowmen the MacCabes had to offer. Eunan stopped behind a wood that led to a ford on a small river where the exchange was supposed to take place. He briefed his constables and his party split in three. He marched towards the ford with two chests and twenty men.

Eunan and his men made their way through the wood that invited them onto a plush carpet of moss and grass. Before them lay the ford, which was the place of exchange for Rory. Not being constrained by water or rock, the wood melted into the river to either side. The grey, bony branches of trees sprung out of the river, defying the gushing white water, clinging on to any clump of soil they could find that could bear their roots. The land radiated a green hue, of moss and grass, of plants festooned in the river, of the possessive clinging of the moss on the tree branches, be they of the wood or marooned in the flow. Reeds spiked out of the water, further blurring the division of river and bank.

Amidst the beauty of nature, on the other side of the green carpet, were a knurl of armed men waiting on the opposite bank. A seething boil was about to erupt amid the tranquillity. Eunan looked forth and could only assume it was the sheriff of Sligo. He dismounted and turned to nod to the men to reassure them that the time for action would soon be upon them. But all he saw were stony faces and twitchy hands on the grips of their swords and axes. He quickly faced forward to shield his nerves.

"What do we do now, lord?" said Odhran to Eunan as he walked up to him. Eunan much preferred the company of Odhran to the other constables, for he was the only one who seemed to respect his authority and Eunan had somewhat taken him under his wing, even though they were close in age.

"We go to the water's edge to hear his terms. Are you coming?"

Odhran beamed, a ball of enthusiasm. "I'd be honoured, lord."

They left behind the rest of the men still on horseback guarding the chests of money and walked down to the bank. The river was fordable here. The onrushing water would only climb up to your waist if you were on foot, and you could wade through if you were not too heavily weighed down. Eunan was familiar with the ford and the surrounding countryside, having used it many times when raiding Sligo. He hoped to use this knowledge to his advantage, but he could not guess who would have joined forces with his adversary, and their knowledge could be superior to his own. He noticed how some of Taaffe's men had broken away with their guns and taken up position in the tangle of tree branches that surrounded the clearing on the other side of the river. So far, it was all very predictable. It was now up to him to execute the plan. He stood on a rock by the river so all could see he was not afraid of their guns.

"ARE YOU THE SHERIFF OF SLIGO?" Eunan called out to his adversaries.

Taaffe stepped forward and thrust his chest out to make himself look intimidating. "WHO'S ASKING?"

"EUNAN MAGUIRE IS ASKING. I HAVE BEEN SENT HERE BY CORMAC MACBARON TO FETCH HIS SON."

Taaffe turned to his men on horseback at the rear of the clearing. "Let the boy down."

Rory MacBaron was ungraciously pushed off his horse and landed on his shoulder. Bravery could not suppress the corresponding yelp.

"I WAS TOLD HE WOULD BE UNHARMED," hollered Eunan.

Taaffe laughed.

"OF COURSE YOU'RE GOING TO GET HIM BACK WITH A COUPLE OF BRUISES. I'LL LEAVE SOME PARTS BRUISE-FREE SO HIS FATHER CAN GIVE HIM A SLAP FOR COSTING HIM SO MUCH MONEY!"

Taaffe dragged Rory up from the ground and yanked off the hood. An angry and shaken Rory glared at his captor, but he stood and held his head high so Eunan could identify him. Eunan gave him a firm nod.

"SEND RORY OVER THE FORD AND I WILL RIDE AWAY AND LEAVE YOU THE RANSOM," shouted Eunan across the ford and pointed to the two chests.

Taaffe laughed and grabbed Rory by the back of the neck. Rory could just throw daggers with his eyes in response, for his hands were bound, and a gag was in his mouth.

"YOU COME OVER HERE AND I WILL HAND HIM OVER. BRING THE MONEY WITH YOU. IF YOU TRY ANYTHING, I'LL CUT HIS THROAT FROM EAR TO EAR."

Eunan looked at Odhran to reassure him that everything was under control, as it was all very predictable to this point. Eunan signalled to four of his men standing behind and they took an end of each of the two chests and walked towards the river.

"ANYONE CROSSING THE RIVER MUST BE UNARMED," said Taaffe.

"WE ARE," said Eunan as he dipped his first foot into the river. The water was cold, the flow was strong and the bed a stony, slippery ankle trap.

Taaffe signalled to his men, and they raised their muskets.

"THROW DOWN YOUR WEAPONS OR YOUR NEXT STEP FORWARD WILL BE YOUR LAST," shouted Taaffe.

"WHATEVER I DO, YOU MUST RECIPROCATE," said Eunan. "PUT YOUR WEAPONS DOWN AT THE SAME TIME."

Taaffe nodded to his men and soon there was a pile of guns, swords and daggers in front of both of them.

"AND YOUR DAGGER," shouted Eunan.

Taaffe signalled to one of his men and he handed Rory and the dagger to him. The blade once more threatened Rory's neck.

"THE ONLY PLACES MY DAGGER IS GOING IS IN MY SHEATH AFTER I'VE BEEN PAID OR IN HIS NECK. NOW START CROSSING WITH THE MONEY."

Eunan followed his first foot with his second. He devised a route through the rocks, both on the riverbed and jutting out of the white water, and signalled his men to follow him. Four of his men joined him on the other side of the river, one on either side of the two chests full of the ransom for Rory.

"Place the chests in front of you and take a step back," said Taaffe, wary of having his enemies so close. "Open the boxes," he ordered some of his men. Two men crept forward and placed their hands on the latches of the boxes, and flipped them open. One of them turned to Taaffe with a twitch of nerves.

"Well?" said Taaffe.

"Cloth sacks, sheriff."

Taaffe's face boiled a sea of red.

"I can see that. Check for the money," said Taaffe. Anger and impatience reverberated in his voice. The man picked up a bag and felt it. He stared at Eunan. His eyes asked, even though they were enemies, how could he have betrayed him so, making him the bearer of such bad news to a master so intolerant of such a revelation. He held the bag upside down and onto the soft ground plopped four pebbles. Taaffe could barely control his shaking.

"KILL ALL OF THEM!"

On that signal, one of Eunan's men, who had remained on the other shore, threw a pebble into the reeds to Taaffe's right. The rest of the men either went for the pile of weapons on the ground or to weapons they had concealed. A Maguire man smashed through the skin of the water amongst the reeds and emerged with a bow strung. He let loose, and the arrow flew into the right ear of Taaffe's man, about to apply the blade of his knife to Rory's neck, and emerged through the left ear. The man fell like a dead deer. Rory freed himself from the fading grasp and ran towards Eunan. A clutch of bowmen emerged from the reeds and spat out their hollowed-out reed breathing tubes. They sprayed Taaffe's men with arrows and scattered those they did not fell. Taaffe grabbed a musket from the discarded weapons on the ground and fired, but he was more of a threat to the birds in the trees than the rebels as he ran and fired.

Eunan grabbed Rory by the elbow and pulled the gag from his face.

"You're all right, you're with me now," he said as he picked him up and placed him on his shoulder and ran back to the river.

Maguire men now ran from the woods on the opposite shore and waded past Eunan and Rory in eager anticipation of engaging with the enemy before they all ran away. Taaffe saw he had been tricked, all was lost, and took to his heels.

Eunan laid Rory gently on the opposite shore as the remains of the skirmish petered out behind him. Rory yelped, and Eunan rolled him over onto his front and cut the ropes that bound him.

"Sorry, I forgot about your shoulder," said Eunan. "Did they hurt you?"

Rory sat up and poked himself to see how injured he was. "They only dented my pride," he concluded.

"Your pride will heal. But that is good for I'll be able to return you to your father in one piece," said Eunan.

"That will dent my pride far more than any amount of kidnap and torture would."

Eunan laughed. "Well, may that be a lesson to you about getting caught, but I need to collect my reward from your sister."

"Could you not leave me off in some alehouse in Enniskillen and I'll write my father a pleasant letter instead?"

Eunan held out his hand to help Rory up.

"See, your pride recovered quicker than you ever thought. Get on your horse and come see your father. He'll be delighted to see you."

## CHAPTER 14
# THE BLOSSOMING OF LOVE

"You're a disgrace to the family! You almost broke us with the price we had to pay for your folly. What did you think you were doing, anyway?" Cormac paced the room and gesticulated furiously, his finger an angry wand.

Rory looked at Eunan, both confused and surprised. He had brought back the ransom, yet had not told his father. Eunan gave him a knowing look and took a step forward.

"Excuse me, lord," said Eunan. "I beg your pardon, but there may be some confusion here. The only monies that were spent were the ale and food for the men to celebrate the rescue of your son without a man lost, nor a coin in ransom surrendered and a humiliation for the sheriff of Sligo to boot. Your son stands before you with the bruises of a man and is blessed with the experience of what happens to prisoners without suffering himself."

Cormac barely believed his ears. "It cost me nothing?"

Odhran supported his master. "I hope this shows that you were right to place your faith in Eunan and that the Maguires are worthy allies."

An ebullient smile burst onto Cormac's face. "I always deemed him worthy, ever since he married my daughter. Speaking of her, come into the corridor and let us converse." Cormac walked over and put his arm around Eunan's shoulder and left Rory to come to terms with the fact that he was not the man of the hour, no matter what he had suffered, nor the ease of his rescue. Cormac was in the doorway to the corridor when he remembered and clapped his hands. "Men, my son has returned home to me. Prepare a feast and let us celebrate, for he will soon leave us once more for the war."

Rory smiled, a little diminished by the late acknowledgement from his father, but it vanished when he found Cormac had already gone.

Cormac and Eunan stood in the cramped stairwell of the castle, for even though he was the master of the castle, it was hard for Cormac to get some privacy. Eunan had the foresight to stand a couple of steps below his father-in-law for in life he had a couple of inches on him, but in the stairwell he would have towered over him. Eunan knew well that his opportunity was precarious. His words wished to jump from his mouth, but he decided upon caution and to let his father-in-law set the agenda. Eunan buried his nerves deep.

"You have done me a great service and are a worthy son-in-law," said Cormac, his warm, friendly smile an unusual sun to hover over Eunan's head. "Sorcha has been asking after you whilst you've been gone and every day she has devoured any morsel of story about you, whether true, false or rumour, and has eagerly awaited your return. I will speak to her on your behalf before we sit down with the men and hopefully lay the foundations for a reconciliation. Nothing would make her or me happier than to hear a young son of hers running through the halls of the castle. So take this opportunity now. Tell her it was all a misunderstanding. Tell her you love her and are truly sorry. You know what can befall you if you fall out with my daughter."

Eunan was coming to realise the downside of being married to Cormac's favourite child; with every opportunity there came a threat and there would always be three in this marriage as the possessive father-in-law acted as bodyguard to his child. But this was his opportunity, for war would soon part him from his wife, although he realised when he thought about it that he also harboured a seldom-mentioned desire to rear a son in his own image, as long as he was not cursed by the bad blood. But the first obstacle was his father-in-law.

"If you could but open the door, I'm sure my pleadings would fall on forgiving ears," said Eunan, bowing his head to gain his father-in-law's favour.

"As long as the truth springs from your lips and you bury no secrets deep in your heart, I'm sure all will be forgiven," Cormac said with a knowing but controlling smile. "If you attend my son's celebration feast, Sorcha will also attend, and you'll have her ear all to yourself."

"Then grant me your leave, for I must leave nothing to chance. I will bathe and change to be at my most presentable."

"Leave everything to me and soon you'll be in the sweet bliss of a loving bosom once again."

Eunan bowed and let his father-in-law leave their claustrophobic conversation first.

Cormac gathered as many men as he could into the cramped main hall and laid out a fine feast of venison from the forest to mark the return of his son. A table was laid across the back wall of the room with chairs behind, opposite the fire, with smaller tables around both ends of the table so as not to block the heat. Cormac made the centre of the table his, with the finest cut of venison in front of him, with Rory to one side and Eunan to the other. Beside Eunan sat Sorcha, who Eunan had not yet got to speak to alone. She smiled coyly at him after he had mouthed 'sorry' to her and she slid her arm under his, and sheltered her hand in the warmth of the nook of his elbow. Eunan smiled but tried not to show his elation or nerves. He subdued any itch or temptation to fidget, for he did not wish to give her an excuse to remove her hand. He would not feel secure until he had spoken to her in private.

Cormac seemed jovial but subdued. Duty was never far away from Cormac's thoughts and even though he had a new hero to celebrate and it was a joy to have his erring son returned, he was consumed with guilt. The people suffered and sacrificed as he imposed a harsh tithe upon them as he stored their goods in the anticipation of the arrival of a large Spanish army. Yet, here he was celebrating the redemption of his son's folly with a feast whilst the people suffered. But no matter, for now, duty pulled him in another direction. He stood and raised his mug and silence rippled outwards.

"I'm not really one for speeches," said Cormac, the nerves slightly tingeing his voice. "I leave them to my brother." His audience allowed him a ripple of laughter, for they were used to the brotherly rivalry joviality. "But I raise a mug to my returned son whom God looked favourably upon to return him to me." Rory gave a weary smile and raised his mug to salute his father.

"But I would also like to salute my son-in-law," said Cormac, "who saved Rory and gave the sheriff of Sligo a bloody nose whilst doing it!" Maguire and O'Neill alike roared and banged their mugs on their tables, united in appreciation of their new hero. Sorcha poked Eunan in the ribs. He turned for a kiss but received two eyes directing him upwards. Eunan leapt from his seat and saluted his father-in-law. Cormac grinned at him and returned to his audience.

"I am also grateful to the Maguire and his men and they have proved worthy allies." The three MacCabe constables rose on Cormac's invitation and accepted their salutes, and the rolling appreciation of mugs banged on the tables.

"But I would also like to show my gratitude to my son-in-law, who had to persuade me to trust him. He is a great chieftain, and I wish him to feel and appear more like one. Therefore, my gift to him and my daughter are two of my beloved Irish wolfhounds, Olcan and Sionn."

In front of the fire were the great hounds of the MacBarons, drying themselves as they lay sleeping. Two of them raised their heads at the sound of their names. A grey-haired beast and his white-haired companion. They had deep brown, expectant eyes sheltered in caves of fur. The tips of their fur were matted, and they smelt of the fields but they were fine healthy animals nonetheless. Eunan was ecstatic and Sorcha cried out her joy and clapped her hands until they stung with red. Eunan came out from behind the table and stood above the sleeping dogs, full of admiration for such generous gifts.

"Go take them, they are yours," said Cormac.

Eunan bent down near the fire and stroked the grey dog's head.

"His name is Olcan," said Cormac. "He's a sturdy dog of two years of age. He should last another six years with God's blessing. A fine hunter is he. You'll never go hungry in the woods with him by your side." Eunan beamed, for Olcan reminded him of Artair, his father's dog, and a shining memory of his youth.

"If only you could be half the dog Artair was to me, I'll die a happy man."

He stroked his hand once more over the dog's head and the dog lifted his shaggy eyebrows and his dark brown eyes looked deep into Eunan's soul. Eunan combed his wet fingers through the hair until it came to a gentle spike, just like he had used to do with Artair. He grinned, and the dog looked up at him again before laying his head to rest on his paws under the glow of the fire. Eunan knew they would be great friends. The white dog had barely raised her head and had quickly returned to sleep. Sorcha came up behind Eunan.

"The white one is Sionn, Olcan's sister. She is named after the fox, for she is wily despite her young age and slovenly behaviour," said Sorcha. Eunan turned and smiled warmly at her. "She is part of a litter from my father's favourite hunting dogs, so you should be honoured to receive such a gift."

"Oh I am, I am," said Eunan as he got up to stand opposite Sorcha.

"Enough of this," said Cormac. "Let the sleeping dogs lie and let us enjoy the evening and make new memories that we can look back upon." Cormac outstretched his arm and invited them both to return to their seats.

After several rounds of ale and wine, Cormac's official bard was invited to compose a poem about Eunan's bravery right there on the spot, much to Eunan's embarrassment. Eunan watched as Sorcha roared with laughter as the bard acted out Eunan, crossing the river and throwing rocks at the head of the sheriff of Sligo as his offer of payment for Rory. It was almost the perfect moment for Eunan as he watched his wife laugh and enjoy herself. He did not want to ruin the moment, so he took his father-in-law's advice and concentrated on enjoying himself instead of composing apologies for the past in his head to recite later. The night wore on and Eunan remembered how little of his wedding night he remembered and was very protective of partiers trying to refill his half-empty mug. Sorcha noticed and smiled bashfully. Rory somewhat melted into the background in this, second best to his brother-in-law rescuer. But he would not forget this.

"Oh, I thought tonight would never end," said Sorcha as she opened the door to her room.

"Neither did I," said Eunan, his tone missing that implied by his wife.

He got into the room, closed the door and wrapped his arms around her. Her slender body wriggled out of his grip. It would not be that easy.

"I'm sorry, my love," mumbled Eunan. He searched for the right words to unlock his wife's affections, but that was all he could find.

"What are you sorry for?" she said as she went and sat on the chair at the end of her bed. She moved quite freely now, will little sign of her previous ailments. Her face presented as if she sought a full explanation of her husband's failings.

"I'm sorry for my stupidity, everything that drove us apart in the past."

"And what drove us apart?" she said, going in for the emotional kill.

Eunan turned for he could not face her.

"When you asked to have a baby, and you are so ill, I thought of my mother. Giving birth to me did not kill her, as it does many brave maidens, but left her a cripple in body and spirit. She never let a moment pass where she would not remind me of what I did to her. She tried so hard to have another child but every one was stillborn and each death shattered her heart a little more. I saw her lying there when you asked for a baby. I grew afraid, for I thought I was cursed and with you so ill, I would curse you so you would be barren. Instead of holding my tongue, I insulted you and instead of facing up to what I had done, I was a coward and ran. For all of that, I am truly sorry and beg your forgiveness."

Sorcha went over to him and wrapped her frail body around his warm back to smother his past with her love.

"Every time you leave, you put yourself at risk for your master the Maguire, for my father, for the rebellion. I don't know if you will return ill, grossly injured or even dead. If you can put your life on the line for them, surely I can put my life on the line for my family? If I am to be kept in this room like a living doll, then there is no point in life at all. Let me live, let me at least try for my dream. Your life is at least as fragile as mine."

Eunan turned and embraced her. He felt fortunate that she could only nestle under his chin when he placed her there, so she could not see his battle with his tears. He tried to banish the images of his mother, his father, the birth of his dead sister and how he imagined his birth. Sorcha lifted her head, and he knew she needed an answer. Only one answer would save his marriage.

"Yes, my love. I wish to dream with you. Let's have a child."

Sorcha squeezed him hard. Her hands gripped his forearm with passion and joy. She extended her hand and invited Eunan to the bed. Eunan smiled and took her hand. The right answer.

Sorcha felt invigorated about being reconciled with her husband. Her previous ailments seemed to disappear and they could enjoy the remains of the summer together in relative peace. Cormac arranged for the MacCabes to train with his men, freeing Eunan from his responsibilities and allowing him to spend time with his daughter. They took to going for long walks in the lands surrounding the castle, walking through the woods and letting their dogs Olcan and Sionn roam free.

This was the first time he had spent quality time with his wife, away from her father, her physicians, her bed, and the claustrophobic confines of the castle. Running and laughing after their roaming dogs bound them together as they threw sticks for the dogs or chased after them every time they picked up a scent. The distance in ages of nearly eight years which mattered so much to Eunan in the beginning paled into insignificance. He noticed her sweet smile, her infectious laugh, her unbridled enthusiasm, and the way her cheeks would redden when she blushed. A joy for life possessed her when her ailments released her from their oppressive grip. She threw herself down on the grassy bank of the brook and cast up her hand in invitation for her husband to join her. Eunan reached down, and she grabbed his wrist and pulled him towards her. He fell over and she nestled beside him and rested her head on his chest.

"I cannot believe my husband is the hero of both the Maguires and the O'Neills."

Eunan hid his blushes behind her head.

"And you are my hero," he said. "I may battle against the enemies of our clans, but you battle against your illness every day but are out here with me and want to have my son."

Sorcha lifted herself up, took his hands, and rested her elbows on his chest.

"Our son will be beautiful, roam free like our dogs, and you will be master of all the land."

Eunan gently lifted her elbows and took her in his arms.

"I want to be master of nothing and live happily on my lands with you and my children."

He leant down and kissed her, and there was joy on his lips.

On the way home from a blissful afternoon as Sorcha skipped ahead after the dogs, Eunan wondered how he could cast such a beautiful young girl in the same light as his mother. She had far more joy in her heart than his first wife Róisín, but he had barely known her for a day. His mind wandered once more to Cara and whether what he felt about her was even real. Then Sorcha skipped back, tilted her head, smiled, and tucked her hand in his. He banished all the other women in his life out of his mind. He only had eyes for Sorcha.

He now realised that his wife was consistently poorly, be it with fainting, fever or vomiting, with only periods where she could leave her bed for joy and life to breathe a pale pink hue into her sallow complexion. Apparently, she had been like this since childhood, a fact both Seamus and the Maguire omitted when they were trying to sell the marriage to him. But he soon developed a fondness for her, a strange mix of admiration and atonement. He admired her resilience to her illness and how she remained in good spirits despite her constant affliction. The atonement part was because of the memory of his mother and how he used to wheel her around after she had been crippled in childbirth. Sorcha was his ill wife who had come into his life so he could look after her properly and make up for all that he put his mother through in his youth. He took on his task with the same diligence he applied to training on the field every day. He would attend to her every morning before he left for the fields, whether or not he stayed with her the night before. When training was over, he would dine with her if he was not obliged to dine with his father-in-law or his men. He would spend the evening in conversation with her or reading to her, dependent on how she was feeling.

As time passed and Cormac became more convinced that Eunan had more than a passing interest in his daughter, and did not view her merely as easy access to the upper echelons of the O'Neill clan, he increased the amount of time he would allow him to spend with his daughter, even when she was unwell. She would raise her head and smile sweetly when Eunan entered the room and sit and hold his hand as he read to her. Cormac was glad of the happiness that Eunan brought to her life, wanting nothing in return. If anything, Eunan seemed to him to be oddly content.

The autumn had been hard on the lords of Tyrone with the outlook for the winter bleak. It had also been difficult for the population as a whole. Whilst they were spared the famine of previous years, and the weather was not as harsh, the harvests had been meagre and the people wished to hoard food for themselves, both preparing for war and heeding the lessons of the difficult previous winters. But the lords raised their taxes, and the people had to hand over a greater share of the crop, bringing about near-famine conditions for most once again.

The people were unhappy, and some resisted. Eunan was sent out into the lands to gather food and supplies that could be stored for the impending arrival of the Spanish army. But he could not use the persuasion of the arrival of the Spanish force, no matter how rife the rumours nor how the O'Neill would try to subtly use the threat in his negotiations with the English. Eunan had to tear the foodstuffs out of the hands and mouths of the people, sometimes by force, much to his chagrin. Cormac would look with pride at the cart full of foodstuffs and columns of cows that his son-in-law had retrieved. He would become a great warrior yet.

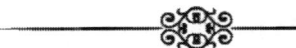

One morning after Eunan had left to train with his men, Cormac went to visit his daughter, who was still in her bed. One side of the blankets was still in turmoil whilst she sat propped up on some pillows on her neat side of the bed. Her father took a stool and pulled it bedside. He made himself comfortable and took her hand. Her cheeks were a pale pink with a flush of red and her eyes and mouth echoed faintly of happiness.

"It has happened, Father."

Cormac knitted his brow. It could be anything from she is finally dying to -.

"What has happened?"

"He did it."

Her eyes shone like little stars.

"He has left me with child."

Cormac wrapped both his hands around hers.

"That is wonderful, my dear. I am so happy for you."

The tinge of doubt in her father's voice disheartened her, but she knew it was true. She looked down at her stomach in a challenge to her father's disbelief.

"Is it true? I never thought it possible!?"

"Touch and see," said Sorcha.

She removed her blanket, and her father placed his trembling hand on her stomach.

"I never thought it possible, but it is true."

He caressed the gentle mound on his daughter's stomach.

"I will fetch the finest physician in the land to ensure both mother and child are well."

"Oh, please don't fuss. I feel like a delicate piece of pottery enough already than to be mollycoddled some more. Please, let me and Eunan live our lives as freely as we can within the confines of this castle."

Her father leaned in to her resting head.

"You may have your wish as long as your maids attend to you, but if you get ill, even in the most minor way, then the physician is coming."

Sorcha put her hand on his.

"That is the way it shall be, Father."

The next day, the physician arrived to help Sorcha deal with her morning sickness.

# CHAPTER 15

# THE BARGAIN

The winds of the Irish sea howled through the backstreets of Dublin. The fog caressed the tops of the houses, forming a blanket over the darkness of the streets and the twinkling of the stars. The skies almost told a lie to all of those who had to bear her tantrums beneath. Their calendars told them it was summer, the constant wind and rain made them question both their senses and their memories. Curfew cleared the streets. The rainfall was the only constant reminder the place was still alive. Compressed into this claustrophobic space, a civilisation stood on the edge of an abyss. But they could breathe a little easier. For now, the English navy had defeated the imminent threat from the empire of Spain.

To the north of the city lay the northern lords with their well-drilled armies, their honed skills of ambush and raid, and their constant threats to county Louth and the Boyne river. They seemed to gain more strength daily, as every man with a grudge to bear seemed to flock to them. To the west were the colonies in the fertile lands of central Leinster, which drew in colonists from Dublin, England and Scotland with offers of cheap land. Here chaos reigned. Bands of savage Irish burned and destroyed all they could, hoping to regain their old lands and push the settlers back into the sea. Why would they engage in such wanton destruction of lands and property they had no rights to, nor knew what to do with in the first place? To the south were the rebels of the mountains, a constant scourge to the city with their raids and banditry. Only the lands of Munster were peaceful. Civilised English men and Scots, from the old Anglo-Norman lords to the newer settlers who flowed in a small but constant stream from the mother country, had colonised those lands the most.

But the troubles of the hinterlands had come to Dublin. After years of complaints from the native Irish and rubbing the English elite in Ireland up the wrong way, the Governor of Connacht was put on trial for corruption and his conduct whilst exercising his duties. The trial was the sensation of Dublin, with various minions turning on their former master to give evidence.

The main minion Taaffe sat on the bench outside the courtroom. He looked at the floor as he went through his story one more time in his head. A battered pair of boots interrupted his view of the ground and the flow of his story.

"You know what to say?"

Taaffe looked up to see the granite face of Captain Williamson, the man who had facilitated his deal.

"I know who to incriminate and what to deny. What will the judge and jury do to me?"

"You don't worry about the grand and the good of Dublin. Once Bingham is gone, we'll have plenty of customers in Dublin for your lands in the wilderness. You just remember our bargain, what I told you to say, and you'll walk out of there a free man."

Taaffe shook his head, for he had not felt such a loss of esteem and control since he faced his father before he left home.

"William Taaffe, William Taaffe. Her majesty's court calls William Taaffe."

Taaffe's hand twitched, and he tried to purge himself of nerves and emotion. He nodded to Captain Williamson.

"I will see you later if you keep your side of the bargain?"

"That you shall."

William Taaffe had taken up residence in one of his family's homes in Dublin, near the port so they could supervise their export business. He poured himself a drink and was about to settle down and relax after an emotional day when there came a knock on the door. He took a candlelit lamp to the door, one sturdy enough to survive the inevitable gust of wind when the door opened and gave the lamp a thorough testing. A sodden Captain Williamson stood there, the gleam of his uniform dulled by the poor light and the worse weather conditions.

"Are you going to let me in or make me stay out here and drown?" the captain said, shaking his soaked sleeves on the doorstep.

Taaffe gritted his teeth.

"That depends on who you brought with you. There's a lot of soldiers here to guard him with the hood."

A man stood in the shadows with his hood pulled so far over his head that he had to be led along by his escort.

"We talked about this. You know who he is," said Captain Williamson. "He can't be seen on the streets of Dublin or he's a dead man. Now let us in or I'll renege on our agreement about today."

"On the cusp of your glorious victory? You wouldn't dare!"

But Taaffe stepped aside anyway, and the captain barged in.

The lawyer for Governor Bingham flicked through his notes before his descent on the key witness against his client.

"Are you not the sheriff of Sligo and did therefore comply with all plots and deeds connived by Bingham, the Governor of Connacht, and thereby were a willing participant and indeed a beneficiary of these plots and deeds that have been brought before the court today?"

Taaffe hooked his shirt with his index finger to claw himself enough room to breathe. He squinted towards the gallery but could not see Captain Williamson anywhere. Perhaps he had forgotten to bribe Bingham's lawyer, or had simply run out of money before he could attempt it? He realised he was alone on the stand, so he rallied his thoughts to defend his freedom.

"You lavish me with too much credit, lord," Taaffe said. "Yes, I occupied such a title, but the title is merely words in such a lawless land. We dealt with bandits and rebels daily, but mainly with the sword rather than the quill. Whilst we attempted to engage said rebels with the Queen's laws, in such an isolated place we did not have the benefit of such learned men as yourself to keep us apprised of the boundaries of the law. As such, the Governor in command of the Queen's forces was the law and I was his mere servant."

"But all the complaints from the lords of the region also mention your name. How can we accept your testimony here today and absolve you from any wrongdoing if your grubby hands are immersed in every accusation?"

"As I said before, I had the title of sheriff, but it is a title for the rebels to point their swords at, a symbol of our Queen. Therefore, every protest, every complaint is directed at the man the rebels see as representing the Queen. Does that mean that every accusation contains an element of truth or that the promoters of these accusations are against the Crown and her servants? Every land deed that bears my name also bears the Queen's seal and was prepared by a magistrate of the court and thereby, I assumed, followed the Queen's laws. Everything I did was under the Governor's instruction and thereby I thought derived from the wishes of Her Majesty. Once I realised the Governor was taking the law into his own hands and mistreating the native lords for his own benefit, I complained to the Dublin Council. I was instructed to gather evidence and the fruits of my labour were accepted today as part of the charges brought to bear on the former Governor today. Therefore, any criminal actions I may have unwittingly participated in were under the instructions of the Governor or the instruction of the Dublin Council, so I could bear witness to the misdeeds of my former master and have now been absolved."

Taaffe's mouth was dry, and he longed for release from the stand. A court clerk read out the list of deeds that Taaffe had complained the former Governor had done and what Taaffe had witnessed. He looked over to his former mentor and saw his head jerk with every allegation the court read out to him based on the evidence he had provided. He watched the confidence drain from his former master's face.

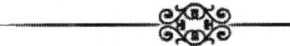

Taaffe found himself in the main room of his house with Captain Williamson handing over his sodden jacket to the manservant and being invited to warm himself by the fire. It was a room that told of the Taaffe family's wealth, decorated with fine furniture and paintings straight off the ships from England. It was orderly and reflected the place of business it was most commonly used for because the elder Taaffe and his other son spent most of their time on the estates of Louth and William in Connacht. They would use the house to conduct business deals, normally concerning land or the export of hides or cloth. As such, since the house was a place of trade, it would hold money and valuable documents in need of protection until the Taaffes could bring their items of value to a less obvious but nonetheless secure location. Therefore, they had to hire protection. This protection guarded both the external and internal doors to ensure that nobody could get in or out and that order was maintained in the household.

However, the house held a certain bitterness for Taaffe for despite all its fineries and the luxurious living it bestowed upon its occupants, it reminded Taaffe that he felt his father had overlooked him in favour of his brother and he felt like a tenant on the cusp of being thrown out by the landlord.

But no matter his feelings, his own follies had created a situation he needed to extract himself from and the foul weather of the day had thrust that problem right upon him. That problem was now the man in the hood who stood dripping in the centre of the room.

"Take his coat too," ordered Taaffe.

The man struggled to relieve himself of his wet clothes, which compounded Taaffe's contempt. But now was not the time for anger. He needed to bide his time and create some room where he could manoeuvre. Taaffe tried to ignore him and occupied himself by pouring drinks and handing one to Captain Williamson.

"That was some story you told in the courthouse today," said the captain as he took the drink with the air of smugness of a man whose plan had all come together.

"All of it was true. It was some adventure whilst it lasted," said Taaffe, determined to uphold his dignity.

"I'm surprised you turned on your former master. I noticed you left out the parts which would incriminate yourself?" said the captain.

"His time was done, and I told enough to fulfil that part of our bargain. He got arrogant and sloppy, and created too many enemies, or at least too many with the power to hurt him. He would have taken us all down with him to save himself. But do not underestimate Governor Bingham. It is one thing to get him to the courthouse and another to convict him and carry out the punishment. But I am safe, for I know he'll never trouble Connacht again."

"Well, it is for your moral flexibility that I am here. If you turn on your creator and mentor, you'll do just about anything."

Taaffe grimaced. Deal or no deal, he still had some pride.

"Be respectful in my house, please, Captain. I charge a hefty fee for my services. Crushing these Irish savages is a dirty business."

"And there it is again, that wonderful moral flexibility. Oh, how you can disassociate yourself from your fellow countrymen when the price is right."

"Don't jest with me about such things. You know we are not all born equal. Some of us are born into God-fearing respectable families and some born in a bush to become ragged savages hell-bent on killing themselves over some feud, whose cause is long forgotten."

The captain grinned at this response.

"I always wondered why you didn't go the whole hog and give up your Papist superstitions and take up the Queen's religion. I'm sure they'd make you a knight and give you a respectable position in the army and government."

All eyes were drawn to Taaffe's white-knuckled fist.

"It is not for me to question the religion my father gave me. The question of God is for other men and himself on high will guide them. It is up to me to sort things out here on this earth with God blessing my hands to do his work," Taaffe snarled.

The captain smiled to placate his host. He did not want to push too far with negotiations to be had next. He drew an audible breath.

"We need to be honest when striking the bargain, so each feels they have a fair deal and brings the bargain to fruition."

Taaffe's stomach churned with tension at being beholden to this captain. But he was eager to strike a deal and move on.

"I've concluded many a bargain in my time and won't be taken for a fool. Well!? Let's get on with it then."

The man in the cloak had gone into the corridor so the manservant could peel the wet clothes from his skin. He had now been dried and given some fresh clothes and came back into the room. Taaffe could see his adversary for the first time in years. They locked eyes. The hatred was visceral as if a black spirit had entered the room and possessed the air and turned the hearts of men who breathed it into black empty pits. It was as if two cocks, bred to fight with blades attached to their feet, had just been released into the ring and circled each other. The cruel smile that reeked of pleasure on Taaffe's face made him the favourite.

"I see you two remember each other?" said the captain. "You remember Sir Donough O'Connor Sligo, Taaffe?"

Taaffe laughed. He liked the captain's callous sense of humour.

"I remember him, but not with that outlandish title. But does he remember me?"

Donough twisted and contorted in body and soul. He stiffened as he remembered the eight years he spent both detained and incarcerated in London because of the accusations from Governor Bingham that he was conspiring against the government and the huge amount of debt he had taken on to get both his release and to launch this mission. But he gritted his teeth, as this was the next step.

"How could I forget you? I had little else to think about for eight years."

"Yet here you are now in my house, ready to make a bargain. Drink?"

Donough's face writhed once again.

"He'll have one and make it a large one. We don't want him dying of a chill before we get him back to Sligo," said the captain.

Taaffe turned and poured a drink for Donough and handed it to him. Donough stared at the outstretched hand as if accepting this mug would be a compromise of all he stood for and all he hoped to achieve. He was a thin man of sallow complexion, his hair having mostly left his head after years of worry and strife. Donough was in his mid-forties but looked much older. He had only recently become reacquainted with the fineries of life, most of which he received from agents of the Queen to encourage him to accept her terms. His stomach had still to get used to it. Each level he descended in the negotiations meant more and more compromise. He wondered when he would reach rock bottom.

"Take the drink," said the captain.

But the spirits of the past would not leave Donough's head.

"Take the drink."

Donough's hand shook as he forced it over the inches to the cup before finally grasping it and holding it unaided. Taaffe smiled. He had gained the upper hand.

"So what are we here to agree?" said Taaffe.

"Let us sit and discuss so we don't get too animated. These discussions may be more emotional for some than others," said the captain as he offered Donough a chair. Donough pondered and knew he would end up worse off than he had been when he entered the house, but he resigned himself and accepted the offer of a chair all the same and set his drink down on the table.

"Donough has already accepted an offer from the Queen and we have agreed to donate five hundred armed and trained men to his cause. In turn, we will recognise his Gaelic title of O'Connor Sligo. He will also be the constable of Sligo."

Taaffe carefully placed his drink back on the table.

"So, where does that leave me? I have a lot of land in Sligo, legitimately given to me by the Queen where I serve as her sheriff. I'm not responsible for anything underhand that Bingham may have done and you don't have to take my word for it, for the court in his trial will say it soon enough."

The captain paused to release some tension as it was building fast.

"Remember, we are all here to work together, as it is all in our collective best interests. We should let bygones be bygones, for the past will only prevent us from seizing the future."

"Well, if you want some agreement between Taaffe and me, we should get on with it and reach the crux of the matter," said Donough.

"Gentlemen, I have done this many times and believe me when I say it, you want to do this slowly. Both of you need to make compromises to make this work. Compromises you may not have contemplated and may take a while to get to."

"All the more reason to get to it. There you have your first area of agreement," said Taaffe. He theatrically threw his arms up in the air to show his frustration. Captain Williamson tried not to show his own frustration, but his facial expressions let him down.

"Then we shall proceed and hope you don't kill each other before you realise what is best for you."

The captain paused and took a drink.

"The Queen has regranted all the lands of Sligo to Donough."

Donough grinned at Taaffe, who turned bright red.

"My lands -" Taaffe choked.

"Except for the Barony of Carbury," said the captain.

Taaffe breathed again, and it was Donough's turn to feel hard done by.

"That is the pride of the O'Connor lands! It had the best castles and the most fertile fields. Why, after I have struggled so much, would you steal the home of my forefathers from me once more?" Donough slammed his fists on the table.

"The lands comprise the border with the O'Donnell and therefore must be fortified. Without a secure border to stop the raids, the whole province would suffer."

It sounded such a reasoned answer to Captain Williamson, but he did not realise what he had stepped into.

"Your lands, my arse," said Taaffe. "They never were your lands."

"You stole them from me!" Donough's seat flew back as his fury elevated him to his feet.

"Sit down," said the captain.

But it was too late. The fury had Taaffe too. He leapt from his seat and squared up to Donough. Taaffe was physically much larger, but Donough had lost his fear now that he finally got to confront one of those he blamed for his misfortunes.

"My uncle agreed with the Queen and her representatives that I should inherit his estate. You robbed me of that!"

"AND HOW DID I DO THAT!?"

"You had a bogus trial to say that my father was illegitimate so you could disinherit me and take the lands for yourself!"

Taaffe backed away, and the captain decided it was better for them to have it out now than hold in the resentment for later. He thought that both were unarmed and anyway had guards that could break it up if it got too heated.

"And how did I do that?"

"I won the first commission fair and square and then your master had to rig the jury with you on it so he could win the second. I went to appeal to the Queen directly for it was her the original agreement was made with. Those pleas were rejected, I'm sure, by rumours spread by your master, and then I was arrested for treason and you and he helped yourselves to my lands."

Donough was wheezing now, and the veins bulged in his neck. Still, the captain did not intervene.

Taaffe threw his hands in the air.

"And here we are now. What you Macs and Oes don't understand is all the land, the whole island belongs to the Queen. It is by her laws and her wishes that it is distributed. If you realised that, you wouldn't be a victim of these delusions. Accept where you are now. The past is the past."

The captain saw Donough was contemplating hitting Taaffe, no matter the consequences. Whilst it may have been amusing if Donough ended up dead on the floor of Taaffe's house, he would have to report that he had failed his mission. He could not have that.

"Taaffe is offering peace," he said, hoping Donough would see sense. "Accept his offer of a truce, for it may be the best offer you'll get."

"There'll never be peace until you honour the agreements your family made with me." Taaffe sat back in smug satisfaction that he had the O'Connor Sligo cornered. If violence resulted from his provocations, then all the better. He could dispose of the O'Connor Sligo with his own hands and then use his victim's lands to bribe the authorities to drop any charges. It had worked plenty of times in the past, so why not now?

His veins pulsating and purple in the face, Donough shook with anger before Taaffe, the ultimate tormentor of himself and his family. His family had been hunted out of their lands and banished, yet he was being brought back as some kind of puppet. When was he going to avenge his family's honour? If he took out his dagger to kill the monster who jailed him and stole his family's lands, who could blame him for it? He could die a martyr, a hero and the O'Connors of Sligo would rise up in his name. They would sing his praises and say he was the last great O'Connor.

The captain saw on Donough's face the cogs turning in his brain and decided nothing good would come of it. It was time to intervene. He took Taaffe by the arm and dragged him into the corridor, much to Taaffe's growl of protest.

"Do I have to remind you how our bargain was struck?" he said. "When I arrived at Augher Castle, Bingham was about to have you hung for lying to him and losing his prize prisoner as part of a botched enterprise to sell the said prisoner to the rebels."

Taaffe shook as he tried to control his anger.

"And I am eternally grateful for you saving my neck and pledged to make you a rich man from this wretched war, amongst other pledges."

"It is those 'other pledges' we are here to talk about. We are both here in service of the Queen and derive our power from Her Majesty. It is Her Majesty's request that you set aside your differences and co-operate with her appointed agent. If you wish to decline Her Majesty's kind offer, which could also lead to your considerable enrichment, I'm sure the judges can accommodate you in the dock in court tomorrow. I'm sure your former master will be more than willing to split the charges with you and tell us exactly which parts were your responsibility. And remember, he's a knight, so the hangman's noose will sit far easier on your shoulders than his."

Taaffe knew when he was cornered.

"I am ready to make this work," muttered Taaffe.

"Good. Now get back in there," said the captain, pointing back to the room.

Taaffe picked up his seat, threw it down and put his arm through the contents of the table, leaving all asunder.

"Speak then, O'Connor!" he roared at Donough. "If you want to be the master in Sligo, then name your terms."

Donough leaned on the table, a red-faced concoction of bad breath and uncontrolled temper.

"I wish for the Queen to keep her word."

Taaffe laughed and threw his hands in the air.

"How am I supposed to work with this? The fool knows nothing of the political world being locked up in his house in London for all these years."

Then for Taaffe, the penny dropped. Gone was the anger, and all that was left was an inquiry, for he wondered what cunning plots the captain weaved.

"Captain, you neither let him into the court today nor told him what happened?"

With a wave of his hand, the captain invited Taaffe to tell the story. Taaffe, in turn, invited the puzzled Donough to sit.

"I went to the commission today to turn on my former master. It was all written down, so you can check the records. Our woes were all his fault, as I told the court. He manipulated and intimidated all the other jurors and me into finding against you. I told the commission of his cruelty towards and mistreatment of you and the O'Connor Sligo. I did all of this with the captain so that we could set things right and restore you to your rightful position. I thought the captain had told you all of this?"

Donough grabbed for his heart and fell backwards. The hatred that had powered him for so long giving him energy and direction felt like it had suddenly been removed and it was as if he no longer had a spine to hold him together, a heart full of hate to thrust him forward and now, in a vacuum, his heart had stopped. The captain stood and gently supported his back and guided him to a chair.

"Do you want a drink?"

The captain offered Donough his mug.

"Is...is it over?"

"Something may be over for you, but for us, it has only just begun. Do you agree to our terms and do you also agree to work with Taaffe?"

Donaugh supported his head in his hands, for he could not believe what he interpreted to be his first piece of good fortune in years.

"Yes, yes," he whispered. "I can't believe it's all over."

"Well, we can't dilly dally here any longer. Now that you and Taaffe have made up your differences, you need to get ready for you are getting married tomorrow. Then we leave for Sligo before the end of the week."

Donough was dragged to his feet before he could reply and his cloak was thrown over him. Taaffe's visitors were gone as quickly as they arrived. Taaffe grinned, for he knew not what plot was afoot, but he realised its deviousness and considered himself to be on the right side of it. The O'Connor Sligo was a bigger fool than he ever thought him to be, but at least he was back in Ireland as the Queen's puppet and could be milked until dry for every last drop of profit. Taaffe laughed to himself as he poured another drink.

# CHAPTER 16

# THE RETURN OF THE PRETENDER

The wedding of Donough O'Connor Sligo and Eleanor Fitzgerald (Butler) was a quiet affair in Dublin cathedral, attended by government officials and distant relatives of the bride and groom either not afraid to show their loyalty to the Crown in such turbulent times or coerced to be there to make up the numbers. Captain Williamson kept to the shadows, only there to ensure the ceremony took place at all. He declined Taaffe's request for an invitation, considering it an attempt at gallows humour and also to prevent him from knowing too much about his plans.

Eleanor was almost the perfect wife the chief royal minister could have chosen for Donough. She was a plump woman of a dour complexion whose joy had been worn away by the many misfortunes that life had thrown at her and was driven by a seemingly bottomless pit of unfulfilled entitlement. But it was neither for her looks nor obstinate personality that the arrangement was made. She had an almost flawless combination of Irish gentry connections, to bolster Donough's credentials to a level sure to impress any Gaelic lord of Connacht who would be on the fence for declaring for O'Connor Sligo and pondering the lure of the O'Donnell's patriotic or religious call.

Her father was from the Butler family, and she was married to the 15th Earl of Desmond. She played a useful role for the Crown in her husband's various rebellions in the 1570s, such was her desire to retain her lofty social heights, which acted as a brake for any ambitions her husband may have had. She constantly urged him to stop his rebellions and reconcile with the Crown. At one stage when he joined rebels against the Crown she left him and declared her loyalty to the Crown only to reconcile with him once more and urge him to make peace again. When her husband was finally killed in 1583, she tried to secure his vast estates for her son, who had been taken to England in 1573 at the age of two as a hostage to ensure his father's good behaviour and remained a hostage ever since. However, royal officials refused to grant her a pardon until he renounced any claim to her husband's former lands. A pension was agreed upon, and she went to live in Dublin castle. The Lord Deputy soon reneged on the agreement, and Eleanor and her five daughters were cast into Dublin to live in great poverty. After several years, she escaped to London to plead her case to the Queen. The Queen agreed to increase her pension, and after much wrangling, Eleanor settled in London, where she could visit her son in the Tower of London.

The marriage was Eleanor's chance to renew her status and free her son. To sweeten the deal, the Queen granted Eleanor a small estate in Tipperary that once belonged to her dead husband. She took her new husband's arm at the altar with such zeal he momentarily mistook it for love. But Eleanor's radiating smile on the steps of the cathedral when the ceremony was over was not for him or for the pride of being his wife. It was for defiance of what she had been through. She had left Dublin a pauper and here she was married to the rising power in Connacht and at last making progress in freeing her son and regaining the lands she thought of as rightfully hers.

Captain Williamson smiled. Not only was the marriage the most efficient way to neuter the O'Connor's ambitions, but it was also the cheapest. He would hardly have to waste money on bribes or spies when the best agent for the Queen lay in O'Connor's bed. He just needed to release the O'Connor Sligo into Connacht and let him sow his seeds of chaos, and Taaffe would profit from the remains.

Donough rode across Ireland with five hundred men, avoiding engaging the raiders that criss-crossed Leinster. Uaithne soon got wind of such a large force travelling across the lands he laid claim to and passed that information back to the O'Donnell. Donough arrived in Sligo to find the county in disarray. The county had suffered the most in the conflicts of Connacht as it was the border of the province with the O'Donnells and the Maguires and also the northern part of the border with the O'Rourkes. Each of these three clans raided the county extensively, as it was the area beside them, with the greatest population of English settlers. Many of the castles were already in the hands of the rebels. He, therefore, went to his clan who readily accepted his leadership as there had been no other leader in years capable of holding the Crown's respect and they were slowly being subsumed into the English colonies. He then went to his homeland of the Barony of Carbury where William Taaffe was situated, having left Dublin before Donough's wedding. The reception was cordial as Taaffe now had greater respect for Donough, as he had rallied most in Sligo to his cause. Taaffe found it increasingly difficult to keep the O'Donnell at bay for he had only a small contingent of English soldiers and a mixed unit of English settlers and loyal Irish under his command. The combined force was poorly armed and suffered from low morale and constant desertion. Donough realised the O'Donnell would soon return, given his presence in Sligo. He had to rally enough support to resist the inevitable raids. With the support of the new governor of Connacht, Sir Conyers Clifford, he called a conference of all loyal or wavering clans to be held in Galway, hosted by the Earl of Clanricard.

As well as being a rallying call for all the Queen's supporters in Connacht, it was the first time that the loyal lords of the province and those on the fence would get to meet the new governor or Donough O'Connor Sligo. They all came out in force with the Earl of Clanricard, the owner of the largest estate in Connacht, laying on a splendid feast in his castle. The Earl of Thomond, one of the few Protestant leaders and the owner of the second largest estate, came, having been an avid supporter in men and materials in Bingham's campaigns. Several of the minor lords of central Connacht came but the most notable lord was Tibbot ne long Burke and his mother Grace O'Malley.

Tibbot arrived by boat, making the potentially dangerous trip through the Atlantic Ocean, but the skilled sailors of the O'Malleys stuck near the coast and avoided any potential dangers. Tibbot had to make such a journey for Mayo and the land route was being occupied by his great rival Kittagh Burke and Rory O'Donnell, who had a combined force of seven hundred men occupying the middle of the province.

Conyers warmly welcomed Tibbot, for he saw Tibbot and Donough as the two prizes he would need to break the rebellion. After the opening welcome speeches, Conyers singled out Tibbot as a man to speak to. He went over and sat at his table and threw out his hand.

"Sir Conyers Clifford, at the service of the Queen, all of her loyal subjects and hopefully yourself."

Tibbot stood and grasped his hand.

"Tibbot Burke, the leader of all the loyal Lower MacWilliam Burkes, is at your service, sir."

Conyers sat down, smiled, and raised his mug.

"I'll drink to that. I heard you arranged for your surrender and regrant and then the O'Donnell usurped you?"

Tibbot scraped the bottom of his mug on the table.

"He brought a large army, arranged a bogus inauguration and then rigged the vote. If he didn't, he'd never have got away with it."

Conyers' face was one of well-practised concern, for he had been given enough of a briefing to know that tanistry usually left a disgruntled opponent in its wake, one which was easy to recruit with promises of support for their 'just' cause.

"Well, the Queen has promised me as much support as I need to extinguish the rebellion in this province so we can all recover our rightful titles and get back to making money again."

"Amen to that. What do you need us to do?"

"After we've finished cementing our alliances and formulating our plans, go back to your castles and raise as many men as you can. We mean to go further than throwing them out of the province. We mean to chase them back to Tirconnell, overthrow the O'Donnell and finish this for good. You stand to gain a substantial tract of land and all the loot you can bring home. You'll be a rich man after this."

Tibbot grinned from ear to ear, but Grace, who sat quietly beside him, was unmoved, for she had heard these honeyed promises many times before and they usually only came to fruition for the benefit of the English governor.

"And I'll get my titles back?"

"That and more!"

Tibbot thrust out his hand.

"Tell me where and when?"

Conyers stood up to leave.

"I'll send word of where and when. Excuse me now, I've more flesh to press to build our alliance."

Conyers walked off to speak to the O'Flaherty, the clan from the mountains to the west of Galway. Grace O'Malley leaned in to her son.

"Remember, your brother was betrayed and killed by Bingham."

Tibbot was quick to anger.

"What choice do I have? If I join the rebellion, I become subservient to that thief Kittagh and potentially lose our lands if the English win. If I side with the English, our lands potentially get ravaged and they double-cross me. All I can do is side with whom I think will win and take my chances."

Grace looked unimpressed.

"Just like you did on all your visits to petition the Queen."

Conyers then turned his attention to the O'Connor Sligo. He found a thin-skinned, burning ball of resentment with the desire but not quite the ability to regain the lost prestige he believed his clan once held. He was quick-tempered and fond of the drink, so Conyers only needed to briefly inflate his ego before he was assured he was on his side. His men had given him a brief insight into Donough's background and Conyers realised that he would have to be watched. It was a fragile alliance based on fear, greed and resentment that he built that evening, but it was all for the glory of the Queen.

The time came for the highlight of the evening and Donough felt as if he had finally arrived. He sat in front of the top table under the supervision of Sir Conyers. The minor lords of Sligo and the surrounding districts queued up to pledge allegiance to him and to kneel and kiss his ring in a sign of submission. The O'Hara, the O'Maolcluiche, the MacDermott, the O'Devlin and the O'Gara all bent the knee and pledged their men to the O'Connor Sligo. A mixture of bribery, coercion and tales of the past when the O'Connors were high kings of Ireland were used in whatever measure would get the desired effect with the selected audience. Sir Conyers concentrated on the coercion and bribes, as he had the authority and the muscle to back it up, while Donough concentrated on clan ties and tales of long past greatness.

Taaffe laughed to himself at this pantomime of the past and sized up the amount of lands he could sell as each of these chieftains knelt in submission. He imagined them kneeling before the executioner, bowing to get their heads chopped off, the head then rolling and settling at his feet. The sooner his fellow countrymen could release themselves from the chains of the past and realise the opportunities of the redistribution of land—. Taaffe stopped himself mid-thought for on consideration, if they realised it, it may mean less money for him.

Leaving the natives to their games of who was the most powerful puppet chieftain, Taaffe immersed himself in the periphery of the conference where the leaders of the English settlers and the speculators met. They discussed their struggle with the locals and what opportunities lay ahead if the Governor was finally to complete the scheme of settlement in the province to a similar level to that in Munster and what it would mean for their pockets. Taaffe received a hero's welcome for his cruelty and underhandedness, and found a receptive audience here as they translated his actions into getting things done. They crowded around him, eager to hear how William had made such a success of himself and almost begged him to participate in their money-making schemes.

Ulick Burke, the Earl of Clanricard, hosted an enormous feast at the end of the conference and the loyal men of Connacht cemented their plans in song and spilt ale. They parted ways after making pledges to the Governor of how many men they could raise to fight on his behalf. Several weeks later, the loyal armies of Connacht invaded Mayo from different directions and Kittagh Burke and Rory O'Donnell were chased back to Tirconnell. It was more than Donough could have dreamt of on the voyage back to Ireland. He was now the master of Sligo, with the local clans all pledged to him and the might of the English army to support him.

## CHAPTER 17
# BACK ON THE ACQUISITION TRAIL

The conference of Galway had greatly inflated both the ego and greed of William Taaffe, a lethal combination for all who could fall victim to him. With a new gang of men, a pocket full of coin and as many promises to buy that his secretary could note, he set about slicing and dicing the lands of Sligo not in the hands of English settlers or promised to the O'Connor and his supporters, and began turfing the residents off their lands. The destitute clans of Sligo either fled north to the O'Donnell or the brave and naive ones took their complaints to the new O'Connor.

Taaffe rode back to Drumahair Castle, satisfied with his week's work, with plenty of paperwork to be completed by his growing band of secretaries and magistrates. He had moved the office of the sheriff and the Queen's magistrates' courts there, equipped with all the necessary seals and authority to approve the next part of his plan. Once through the castle walls, he quickly noticed the number of horses without saddles being led around by long-haired wild Irish.

"God damn him, O'Connor is here."

Sure enough, Donough O'Connor Sligo was waiting for him outside the main tower. Taaffe tried to ignore him, but Donough dismounted and walked straight up to him before he had the chance to dismount. Taaffe sighed. It had been a long week, and he did not need this at the end of it.

"Good afternoon, Donough. What has you here in such a tizzy?"

Donough's face was tangled like a cow chewing a cud and finding a stone ground on its sensitive teeth. It was an inopportune time for all that the O'Connor Sligo should finally muster some courage.

"We need to talk," said Donough.

His eyes protruded from his reddening face as he summoned up as much anger as possible, as he was unsure he could arouse enough gravitas to appear intimidating to Taaffe. He was not wrong.

"What is it? It is not wise to impede an agent of the Crown when they are trying to discharge their duties. Especially in front of a magistrate."

"We can talk inside," said Donough, for he was not for moving.

"If you must. Now step out of the way. A loyal servant of the Crown wishes to swing his leg so he can get off his horse. Thank you."

Donough took the smallest step to the side, enough to allow Taaffe to dismount. Taaffe grunted amongst his other thoughts about how he could violently avenge this slight. But then he remembered his deal with Captain Williamson and, despite what had happened in the past and in the courthouse of Dublin, he could still carry on his money-making ways.

They entered the building with Donough scurrying behind Taaffe. Taaffe pointed to the tables of the magistrate and the scribe so they knew to continue their work no matter what else was happening. Taaffe reached his office and threw his bags down on the ground and twisted and was in the face of Donough.

"What is it you want that you have to burst into the office of the sheriff like this?"

Donough recoiled. He looked for support, but his men had been prevented from following him. Everyone else in the building had their heads down at their desks, except for the two guards facing inwards at the door.

"We...we have an arrangement with Captain Williamson, and I believe you are in breach of it."

Taaffe bared his teeth.

"Oh, do you now? And how do you suppose I did that?"

Donough stumbled backwards, but Taaffe followed him.

"You are stealing the lands of the native Irish, those who, as the O'Connor Sligo, I am supposed to protect. Every time you do, you undermine me and drive them a little closer into the arms of the O'Donnell."

"I'll say to you what I say to them. This is not their land, this is the Queen's land. You forfeit your own and all of their titles through surrender and regrant. If you don't believe me, go read it for yourself. These people are in violation of the agreement you made on their behalf. If they get evicted, it is your fault. Now get out of my office before I put you behind bars."

Donough went white as his courage deserted him. Taaffe towered over him and grabbed him by the scruff of the neck. He marched him to the door and threw him out in a heap onto the courtyard.

"Never disrespect a Queen's official like that again!"

Taaffe slammed the door and marched down towards his desk.

"Magistrate, are the latest packages of land all finished and valued?"

"They are, sheriff."

Taaffe detoured to stand over the magistrate's desk.

"How much are they worth?"

"Depending on how they are packaged, three to five hundred pounds."

Taaffe's eyes shone.

"That's a pretty little total. Why such a difference?"

"It depends on where they're located, the chances of them getting damaged by raids, tenanted or untenanted, quality of the land, etc."

"Curse those rebels. They don't know what's good for them. Package them up into parcels that are the most sellable. I set off tomorrow for I have some very interested buyers in Dublin."

"At once, sheriff."

Taaffe smiled as he returned to his desk. Bingham or no Bingham, the Irish land trade was still as profitable as ever.

# CHAPTER 18

# THE LUST FOR REVENGE

T aaffe set out for Dublin the next day under heavily armed escort. It was a dangerous journey for an agent of the Crown, especially with such valuable goods as his satchel full of land deeds. He brought his magistrate and several secretaries, for at his journey's end was a heavy administrative burden that was not Taaffe's forte. He was more for boasting and selling and the secretaries would follow him around, making note of whatever transactions he left in his wake.

He had made this journey many times before, usually with or on behalf of this former employer and now the ward of Her Majesty, the ex-Governor of Connacht, George Bingham. Taaffe started by being the enhanced negotiator for Governor Bingham, the man he brought in when Bingham had failed in his persuasion. The negotiation enhancements would normally include fists and daggers but could require rope, axes or muskets. Taaffe did not resort to conventional torture, for usually a swift conclusion was required and the negotiations were impromptu in the person's home or surrounding area. The extent of the negotiations depended on whether the Governor wanted the land to be tenanted or untenanted, depending on what the market demand was and on how much potential trouble a prospective landlord would wish to put up with. Any style of negotiation suited Taaffe as long as he could choose the land for his cut.

Taaffe assembled a large estate in Sligo, most of which used to be Domhnall O'Connor Sligo's land, and an enormous fortune. He was now richer than his family in Louth, which somewhat went to ease the resentment he felt towards his family for passing the land to his elder brother who he considered feckless and lazy when they had a son with much greater abilities that were passed over. He also had his house in Dublin, which should be filled with distinguished guests the day after he arrived. How could these Macs and Oes be so stupid as to spend their energies fighting between themselves whilst someone like him could come and steal their land with all reward and almost no repercussions?

But he wished to settle down and stabilise his life somewhat, for his wife was sick of the constant turmoil in Sligo. It was a loveless marriage, in common with many of the other relationships Taaffe had with his family. After he left home, his first attempt at acquiring land was to marry a chieftain's daughter in the hope of a dowery of land. He quickly fell out with his new relatives and then with his wife and kept her around for appearances' sake, if she could bear to be around him that long. He had tried to persuade her to take the house in Dublin and he would use it as a base to carry out his various business activities. She was not particularly enamoured with that idea. He had suggested that he purchase some of the family lands from his brother and she could settle there. She did not like that idea either, as she found the idea of the constant raiding by the northern lords to be too unsettling. Taaffe said that he would acquire some lands in the far less volatile Munster and they could eventually settle there, but it would take time as he had to acquire more land and wait for suitable land to become available. In the meantime, she would remain in Sligo. But there was no better place to execute such a plan than the property market he had created in his own house.

He arrived in Dublin three days later after an uneventful journey, given the amount of raiding in previous months. He arrived at his house and immediately began preparations for the land auction the next day.

Taaffe cleared the rooms on the ground floor except for the desks of his magistrate and secretary and lined the walls with chairs so his guests could mingle and yet have access to all the land deeds he brought. He especially invited

Captain Williamson to lend some credibility to his land auction — as nobody from the Irish Council would attend in an official capacity — and to cement their burgeoning alliance. Taaffe invited previous purchasers, as their word of mouth would further enhance his credibility. They were also the easiest to sell to, as they were eager to add to their estates and some had deep pockets.

It had all been so much easier under Governor Bingham. Nothing said credibility more clearly than the governor of the province selling land within it. They only had to make the trip to Dublin occasionally, as before they could just go to Galway or one of the urban centres near large colonies of English settlers and sell the most risk-free land easily. The Dublin trips were only necessary for large tracts of land or uncleared areas that carried the risk of an uprising or properties where Irish natives of a certain social status or connections with the Gaelic lords of the north contested ownership. There was an abundance of wealthy merchants in Dublin who paid little attention to the volcanically charged politics of the hinterlands but wished to diversify their risk from just putting all their monies into risky trade voyages.

The autumnal winds blew the auburn leaves plucked from the sagging trees surrounding Dublin the streets and lanes that meandered out from the docks. Along these same lanes, avoiding the soggy leaves strewn along the edges of the puddles between the cobblestones, the well-heeled shoes of the merchants and gentry of the city were sucked down the lanes to the house of Taaffe. Well protected by their hired bodyguards, they came armed with bags full of money and were just as well stocked with ambition. There was confidence and hope in the air since such land auctions had resumed. The feeling was the rebellion was finally on its deathbed and they could get back to the serious business of making money.

Taaffe stood in the doorway and welcomed everyone in. The house soon brimmed with guests. Taaffe had a roomful of eager buyers but did not know what kind of reception he would get or how he would have to angle his sales pitch. He made sure that everyone who wanted a drink had one, and that his agents spoke to all of those who attended who he reckoned to be serious buyers. He was a little out of touch, having spent the last few months on the frontier, and had come to a couple of financial arrangements with Captain Williamson to ensure he had some eager buyers. Whilst his agents conducted their scouting, Taaffe took Captain Williamson aside.

"How goes the trial? I've heard nothing about it in Sligo. There are way too many other things going on than to dwell in the past."

"Then you'll not have heard that Bingham has fled the trial and gone to England to seek a pardon from the Queen. You'll hear no more about him, for lords that fall down the sinkhole of seeking a pardon spend years and their fortunes attempting to receive it and usually to no avail."

Taaffe scratched at his beard.

"Well, at least there'll be no revenge on me and my activities sought by him. But my primary concern is the credibility of the land deals we put together. The disputes I can handle, but is there anything I need to know that may put off my buyers?"

Captain Williamson smiled and patted him on the shoulder.

"When he fled, the case was put on hold until he could face the court and answer the charges. Anything outstanding reverted to the Crown. The risks are the same as always. I have every confidence in you that no plot will be unsold, and for handsome prices, too."

Taaffe slapped the captain on the shoulder, for that was what he wanted to hear. His chest swelled. He patted his pocket and walked into the middle of the room.

"Come forth, everyone. We have an auction of lands in the wilds of Ireland for you. All the plot sizes you could wish for, tenanted or untenanted, with current rents or we can estimate the rent. The Queen's agents verify all land transfers. All interested buyers come and talk to my secretary or me over there. The magistrate of Sligo town sitting at that desk there will immediately verify and approve all land transfers. Now hurry and let me know what you want, for it'll all be gone by the end of the day."

Potential buyers surrounded Taaffe, most if not all, with queries about the legitimacy and risks of purchasing the plot of land they were interested in. They would go to the secretary and give him details of what they were looking for, usually based on price or location. The secretary would hand them the relevant deed information and point them to Taaffe. The potential customers would then circle Taaffe, waving the pages for the land deeds they were interested in, and asking questions. Taaffe had an answer for everything.

"That one there," said Taaffe, regarding one set of plot details thrust in front of him, "I bought in good faith from one wild Irish who had no son and wanted to give his only daughter a dowery. He was sick and couldn't work the land. That stamp down there is the official approval of the local court for the land registry. The magistrate is sitting over there. You can go ask him."

Another came before him.

"Why is this cheap? Because I care about my customers, I do and want you to come back for more. It's untenanted, but could easily yield you five pounds a year in rent. It's also near the land of the Maguires, and they can be a bit wild, hence the discount."

Another piece of paper was thrust in front of him, followed by a heated inquiry.

"I got the deeds to that land fair and square. There is a succession dispute in the family, but as I tell everyone I have dealings with, the Queen owns the lands, and the Queen rules the seas. You can tell me all the stories in the world that your great uncle Mac something or other, owned all the land, but if you can't produce a piece of paper with the representative of the Queen's stamp on it, then he owned nothing. Now, if you have any trouble or need any help to resolve any such issues, then talk to my good friend, Captain Williamson. He is a genuine army captain on a specific mission for the Queen. He has men that can do any job for you, and I mean any job, and he can have that land cleared and sort you out with some good reliable English tenant farmers, as good as any you'd get down in Munster but for half the price. Yes, you heard right. Half."

Taaffe did a bustling trade and, if any explanation did not ensure a sale, the follow-up discount offer worked every time. A manic excitement possessed Taaffe, for he never envisaged he could be such a success without the benefit of his former master's gravitas to gain buyer confidence. He spun on his heels, answering questions to all comers until he received a tap on the shoulder.

"Have you got anything in Fermanagh?"

Taaffe barely gave the man a second look.

"No, dear boy, not at the moment. We hope to expand our operations to there over the next couple of years, but there's no opportunity there at the moment."

Taaffe went to move on, but Captain Williamson came and took his attention and brought it to the man who had tapped him on the shoulder.

"Taaffe, this is a good friend of mine, Cormac O'Cassidy, whom I would like you to meet. We have a good many business dealings in common and feel that if you both met, opportunities would open up for the both of you. He used to be a large landowner in Fermanagh until some rebels you may be familiar with dispossessed him, and he was wondering if you could help?"

Taaffe was irritated, for there was far easier money to be made in the room than anything he thought would come forth from this conversation. But he had the good sense always to be polite to the captain.

"Unfortunately, I'm only the sheriff of Sligo, so I don't have any jurisdiction there. When the English army subdues the Maguire there should be plenty of opportunities as they already have agreed to surrender their titles and regrant them English ones, but you'd have to ask the captain about that. I've got plenty of land in Connacht going if you're interested in that?"

"Anything on the Fermanagh borders, Cavan perhaps?"

"A bit risky for me these days. Again, ask the captain when the army will secure the area, then I'll have plenty."

Taaffe went to move away, for he had other potential customers with questions.

"Just one more thing. I have some rebels on my land. The captain says you could help clear them and give me good title to my lands so I could have them back. I would pay handsomely."

Captain Williamson butted in.

"I can vouch for him being a very successful merchant who can pay a handsome fee. I can't be seen to be involved, for I am in delicate negotiations with various parties in the county and can't be seen to be interfering in such a manner."

Politeness suppressed irritation, but Taaffe still wanted to move on.

"It's not something I can arrange in the here and now, but I can speak to my secretary who can deal with that for you. By chance, do you have the names of these rebels so I may pass it along and we can agree on a price?"

"Seamus MacSheehy and Eunan Maguire."

Taaffe juddered to a halt.

"I know that second man and owe him a bullet in the chest for robbing me and the predicament he left me in. As much as I wish my revenge upon him, I never let a vendetta impede business. However, once the auction is over, I am all ears. My man will be in touch. We will do some business in the future, I guarantee it. However, for now, I bid you good day, for I must not neglect my hosting duties."

Taaffe moved on to his next client as the party once more swirled in around him.

# CHAPTER 19

# OPPORTUNITIES LANDED

W hen Taaffe awoke the next day, elation sprung him from his bed, defying the gravitational pull of a late night, heavy meal and the drain of the persuasive energy spent to sell all of his plots of land. His head spun around the bed as he pulled himself free from the lure of his pillow and blankets. He went to fetch his clothes, which liberally decorated a chair and expanded onto the floor. He went to the window when he noticed some activity outside. He laughed as he leant on the window frame as the men who worked on the docks across the street made their way to work. Those 'good honest men' were fools. More little puppets dangling on a string to make another man rich. That life was not for him once he learned the trick to making money.

Never in his wildest dreams would he have imagined he could shop his old master without consequence, no matter how much he was entangled in his schemes, but even get rewarded for it! He had sold all the plots of land and even managed to profitably exit from some of his own more risky tracts of land in Sligo. Captain Williamson had proposed towards the end of the evening that they deepen their arrangement, that he would supply him with clients if he performed some tasks for the Queen that he could not assign to the army. Taaffe had, of course, agreed; he would not turn down the chance of some new deep-pocketed clients, and besides, the captain was drunk and would never remember, anyway. Taaffe was never drunk at any of the sales parties he attended. He was too busy and there was too much money to be made.

But he woke with some alacrity. Today was important. Today he was a target. With all the promissory notes and property deeds in his house, he needed to put them all in a safe place. He had brought some of his men from Sligo for protection, but it was cheap and easy to hire a gang of men, especially from those who hung around the docks looking for casual labour. A daring opportunist could easily assault the house and steal some of his papers, making it very difficult to prove good title even if his clerk and magistrate had made their way through the mountain of paperwork created by yesterday's party. The last thing he needed, besides being robbed, was a title dispute with one of his clients. The ensuing legal case, or unofficial violence it would take to resolve such an issue, would be unsavoury to his deep-pocketed merchant clients. They wanted him to deal with all the dirty work and give them clean title, and they would reward him handsomely for it.

But there he stood, one leg in his breeches and one leg ready to flee the cold when the heavy knock of metal on wood came upon his front door. He pulled his breeches up and tossed the room searching for a weapon. He stuffed the sheathed dagger he found under some discarded clothes in the back of his belt.

"Men," hollered Taaffe, deep into the bowels of the house. "Are you awake? Get your weapons and advance on the door."

The knock came with more ferocity than before.

"Someone look out the window!" shouted Taaffe.

The creak of floorboards was the prelude to a holler down the stairs.

"It's Captain Williamson. But he's brought some armed men."

"Well, I haven't violated the agreement enough to justify armed men. Let him in and let's see what he has to say. But be vigilant, men!"

Taaffe's men lined the hall, with swords, axes and daggers at the ready. One of Taaffe's men cautiously trod towards the door with Taaffe behind him.

"Open it," said Taaffe.

The man took the latch and released it. Taaffe stood behind him with a dagger hidden behind his thigh. The door opened. The captain stood nestled in a clutch of cloaked men with barely concealed weapons. Patience had long since deserted Captain Williamson's face.

"It's about time. It's freezing out here, this early in the morning." He noticed the nervous twitch on Taaffe's face and the hand hidden suspiciously behind his thigh. "If I wanted to, I could have robbed this place ten times over and owned half of Connacht for my troubles. That is, if your deeds are worth anything. You need to get more men. You can thank me after I've said what I've got to say."

Taaffe stood there dumbstruck, caught between the joy that he had not been robbed and killed and how Williamson had insulted him and his operation.

"Well, don't just stand there," said the captain. "I expect hospitality no matter how hungover you and your men are."

Taaffe went into the main room and organised a table and chairs so they at least appeared sociable. Williamson used his good arm to produce a handkerchief to wipe down his chair, and the top of the table provided for his usage. Taaffe was eager to erase the inhospitable welcome.

"Don't you go dirtying your good clothes like that. Let the men take care of that and let us discuss the urgent business that has you down here first thing in the morning."

The captain looked at him and smirked as Taaffe and his men cowered around him.

"I'll have some ale and bread whilst you're at it. Difficult to get some breakfast this time of the morning."

Captain Williamson made himself comfortable whilst Taaffe became decidedly more and more uncomfortable, for standing to the rear of the captain were the men he brought. Taaffe did not have to ask that these men were native Irishmen fresh into Dublin. He could tell that from the smell. The one with the horned helmet that covered most of his face had the most intrusive eyes. If anyone was going to revisit the house to help themselves, it was him. Taaffe needed to deflate the building tension.

"Would your men like to sit and eat? I'm sure breakfast is as scarce this hour of the morning for them, too?"

The captain turned and nodded to the men as if their job was done.

"Shea Óg and his men will take some food, and they can return later when you have considered my proposals."

Shea Óg grinned from beneath his helmet and followed the directions out of the room from Taaffe's men. A plate of bread and meat was placed before the captain and Taaffe had to watch the top of his head as he ate in silence. With the plate empty, the captain sat back and slowly savoured his ale.

"I've had worse, and I've served in all of Her Majesty's recent wars. I assume the good stuff was eaten last night to loosen the purse strings of your clients?"

Taaffe got up and took the plate away.

"I'm sorry the meal was a disappointment to you. I don't mean to be rude, but such a sale as yesterday's creates a lot of paperwork and jeopardy for those who need to process it before cash and title are exchanged. So what has you knocking on my door so early on a day like this?"

"I have another opportunity for you. The men I brought today will join your entourage if you are agreeable."

Taaffe got suspicious.

"Why would I not be agreeable? Are they spies? You are not such a fool you would lumber me with your dirty work and hinder me with spies?"

The captain laughed.

"If only I could exert such control over Irish vagabonds. No, they are men that can fight for you, but they also have another mission, the sort that you have taken on when you need to 'clear land'. They'll gladly do some of your dirty work, but are an expensive pain in the arse who seldom do what they're told."

"You're not exactly selling them to me. Desperate cut-throats live in every bog and forest in Ireland and are more than willing to emerge to do any job for a couple of coins. What's the upside for me?"

The captain leaned forward.

"You get paid to take them. Do you remember I introduced you to Cormac O'Cassidy yesterday? The merchant from Dublin?"

"Did he buy anything?"

"Not that I know of."

"Then no."

"How about the man with whom you have Eunan Maguire in common?"

Taaffe bared his teeth.

"I remember him now. I would not be in this predicament if it were not for Eunan Maguire. I said I would do business with him, but I did not think it would come so soon."

"This ex-chieftain is so hell-bent on revenge that he doesn't care when he gets it, how long it'll take or how much it will cost. All you need to know is he will sponsor you until his revenge is achieved."

Taaffe raised an eyebrow.

"Will this man be my master?"

"He will remain anonymous, and you will discuss all matters through me. We have higher objectives to achieve together and this is only some cash in our spare purse."

"I'll take them, but if they cause me any trouble, they're out. I can take care of Eunan Maguire on my own."

The captain nodded in appreciation.

"They'll answer to me for any trouble they cause, so don't let it worry you. Just take the money."

"What is their mission?"

"To avenge the death of Cormac's son, daughter and cousin and the dispossession of his lands by bringing him the head of Eunan Maguire."

"That is a serious amount of revenge. Where were his lands again?"

"South Fermanagh."

Taaffe shook his head.

"There are so many clan disputes over land in that area, I could never keep up. Does he know that barring defeating the clans of the north, it will be a long time before we get to dividing up Fermanagh?"

"Don't be so pessimistic about the fall of Fermanagh. They barely survived a couple of years back. Don't worry, your sponsor is patient and has an expansive purse. In fact, he gave me this to pass along to you as an introduction and an expression of his gratitude that you would take on his men."

The captain placed his hand in his pocket and pulled out a fat bag of coins and threw it on the table. The clattering of the coins centred everyone's attention on the bag. Taaffe's eyes lit up. He weighed the bag in his hand and quickly shoved it into his pocket.

"It's a wild and dangerous place out west. I bear no responsibility for the lives of his men."

"He knows the risks. He would also be willing to pay a generous price for the deeds of any lands adjacent to his old properties."

"Then he and I could become good friends. Tell him I will take his money and his men and set out west once more when I recruit a body of men. He should come to one of my land auctions the next time I come to Dublin, but bring money to buy something. I'm always far more receptive to requests when they have bought something first."

"Put on some warm clothes," said the captain. "Let's go to the port before they hand out the jobs for the day and recruit some men. The sooner you're out west, the sooner we'll all be rich and the sooner you'll have your revenge on Eunan Maguire."

"I'll drink to that!" Taaffe raised his mug and barked orders to his men to prepare to leave.

CHAPTER 20

# THE LETTER FROM ACROSS THE SEAS

I t started as a black speck on the Killybegs bay horizon. The speck grew larger and larger as the O'Donnell fishing boats congregated around it, first to confront it and then to escort the boat into the bay. The boat moored up in the harbour and the occupants came ashore. Once the occupants were recognised, they were greeted as heroes. Alonso Cobos had returned.

It took several days for news of Alonso's return to Ireland to penetrate the outer reaches of Ulster as Red Hugh sent messengers to all the major lords. Hugh Boye MacDavitt was also sent for as it was considered that he had built up a certain rapport with the various Spanish delegations and developed an understanding. The O'Neill was not available, so he sent MacBaron instead.

Alonso was brought to Donegal Castle for in the balance of the options available, the O'Donnell wished to impress rather than ensure the delegates' security. Cormac MacBaron arrived at the castle the day after he had received instructions from his brother. He had brought with him Eunan as his right-hand man and left his son Rory behind so he could train and get familiar with his father's soldiers. Cormac had by now realised that his son would fight no matter what he said to him, and it was now time to complete his training in the ways of war.

Eunan made his way behind his father-in-law, up the windy staircase to the great hall of the O'Donnell. Cormac skipped up the stairs with a giddiness

Eunan did not recognise in him. Cormac turned to see the vacant look on his son-in-law's face.

"Sorcha will be fine in your brief absence," Cormac said. "I have the best physicians in all the north at the end of her bed and a messenger at the ready to ride to fetch us should anything happen to her."

Eunan caught up with Cormac on the stairs.

"But she was well for such a short period of time. I hope I have not brought this upon her by getting her pregnant."

"You did what she wanted and I have long since given up trying to guess why she ails and for all of my money, the physicians do not seem to be able to give me a consistent answer. But we are men of responsibility and we must resolve the issues at hand. She'll be waiting for you when you get back."

Eunan nodded but could not shake the niggling worry about his wife from the back of his mind. They reached the door of the great hall and made their way through the throng of delegates from the northern lords, all eager for news of the Spanish invasion. Alonso would not disappoint his crowd with MacDavitt as his enthusiastic bellowing mouthpiece.

"The good King Phillip of Spain sends his warmest greetings to his fellow Catholics," MacDavitt translated. "Your years of oppression under the blasphemous Queen are nearly at an end. The King implores you to hold out for a little longer with hope in your heart and a prayer on your lips. For his armies will soon come to liberate you."

The Irishmen roared their appreciation. Red Hugh got off his seat as if he were a man on the cusp of greatness.

"Now we have heard from our guests," he said, "that all our sacrifices will soon be rewarded. But we must hang on a little longer for one last big push. Our guests must go now so that we may complete our plans and they can get some rest. But be assured soon the blasphemous Queen and her thugs will be thrown into the seas and the whole of Ireland will once more be ours!"

The men roared once more and banged their mugs on their tables. Alonso was guided in triumph through the crowd after the O'Donnell, a rain of congratulatory slaps falling upon his back.

Cormac grabbed Eunan by the sleeve.

"Come on. Now it's time for the business proper."

They followed the O'Donnell and his entourage up the narrow stairs to the top level of the castle tower. The men in the great hall sang their battle songs, veering from boisterous songs of victory to mournful songs of loss. The ale flowed and the revellers' spirits were high as the floor of the hall shook beneath their dancing feet. The Spanish contingent chattered excitedly on the stairs, to the delight of the O'Donnell. He grabbed the outstretched arm of Eoghan McToole O'Gallagher to assist him up the last steps.

"Victory will soon be ours," Red Hugh whispered in his friend's ear. "I can feel it in my very bones."

The guests came into the upper room by invitation only. Anyone not specifically named by the O'Donnell were requested to return to the great hall. The Spanish were given pride of place and presented with beef and ale. The O'Donnell held forth his arm, and invited Hugh Boye to begin. Alonso put down his utensils and took out a letter from his pocket and read. Hugh Boye translated for him.

"The greatest King on this earth by the grace of God will send ten thousand of his finest men to assist his God-fearing Irish allies to lift the yoke of blasphemy from their backs in a crusade against the English. May all those be blessed who stand behind the banners of the Pope and the one true God."

"To the Pope," said O'Gallagher. He raised his mug as he caught the mood almost perfectly. All stood rigid and saluted "the Pope."

"We are his humble servants and by his and God's grace we'll win this war," said Red Hugh, hoping to capitalise on this outbreak of piousness.

"The King wishes to know if you will summon all God-fearing Catholics the length and breadth of the country to rise and throw off your profane oppressors?" translated MacDavitt.

Red Hugh was pensive, for he considered the last comments to be leading in a direction contrary to the path he wished to tread. He lowered his cup to the table and the mood of the room lowered with it.

"We have a fine army here in the northern hills. Once it unites with the might of your King's army, the people will welcome us with open arms. With that in mind, what does the King suggest?"

Alonso cowered a little at the change in tone.

"Maybe we should talk in private to avoid any misunderstandings?"

"These men, before you, have persuaded their clans to make many a sacrifice this winter, in the middle of both a war and years of prolonged famine. They have made promises to them based on what you told us. The least I can do now is to be honest with them if I have to tell them all their sacrifices have been in vain. Do I have to turn and tell them that?"

All eyes turned to Alonso. Alonso looked to the stairs to see the O'Donnell men blocking it off. His hand shook a little as he raised it to address the O'Donnell.

"I need a map," said Alonso. "I need to show you the King's plan so you don't misunderstand."

"Eoghan, a map please," and as Red Hugh turned back to Alonso, expectation sat restlessly upon his face. Alonso stood and tried to mask his shivers as he waited for O'Gallagher to return. O'Gallagher rolled out the map on the table in the middle of the hall and all gathered around so they could see what was being discussed. Alonso whispered in MacDavitt's ear and they both muttered to each other in Spanish.

"You are here to translate Hugh Boye, and if you wish to retire, I will call in my old debts," said Red Hugh.

Hugh Boye frowned at Alonso and issued a sharp Spanish rebuke.

"Momentarily, lord. Once I have the fullness of the plan, I will tell you, lord."

"I hope they haven't cooked up something so complicated that it will fail before leaving the kitchen. Give me command of the Spanish forces and witness our foes flee in terror."

"They mean to land here." Hugh Boye's face stiffened as his index finger quivered over the map.

"Please move your finger, for it obscures the map," said Red Hugh. He studied where the finger had just been and calmly contemplated his answer. "Galway is not too bad a destination. Reachable from here, but still in the lands of one of our powerful enemies. Why didn't the King listen to us and send his armies to us up here in the North? I have no wish to sound ungrateful but I don't wish to put our joint endeavours in peril before they even get started."

Alonso was well rehearsed for such arguments and had been instructed by Hugh Boye that flattery was the quickest way to endear yourself to the O'Donnell. That was a straightforward assignment for a seasoned diplomat such as Alonso.

"The wind and the seas do the devil's work and devil's teeth surround these lands. My King has no wish to tempt the devil when he crosses the seas with such a large army. Galway bay was chosen to meet you halfway. Your raiding skills are legendary, even making it as far as the court of the King of Spain. To launch such a raid should be no bother to a man of your prowess. You should even get rich whilst doing so. To launch such a daring raid will go down in the annals of time, and from there, it should be a straight path to Dublin."

Red Hugh's chin lofted high.

"And when will this landing take place?" he said.

"Before the swells of the winter sea."

Red Hugh turned to face his men. His youthful exuberance took possession of the room.

"Lords of Ulster, gather your men. We will go to Connacht and strike two blows for the glory of the O'Donnells and their allies. One, we'll banish the usurper O'Connor Sligo back to his rat hole they call London, forever!"

The men roared and raised their mugs.

"And second, take Galway Bay for the freedom of Ireland and the glory of God!"

The men roared, stamped their feet, and embraced their fellow guests. Alonso placed his hand on Hugh Boye's shoulder and nodded. His work here was done. He could return to his master the King and report his mission a success.

# CHAPTER 21

# MAN OF THE HOUR

T he elation at the resumption of the war swept Eunan and Cormac back to Augher Castle. Eunan wished more than anything for the clash of steel where the MacCabes were put to battle after months of drills. He would finally prove himself and silence the numerous detractors he had accumulated in the Maguire nobility and the MacCabes. They rode up to the tower of Augher Castle to see the sunken white faces of the MacBaron women waiting for them. Cormac's wife approached his horse.

"It is our daughter..."

Cormac dismounted and tried to conceal his shaking hands. He paused but could not face his wife.

"Is she dead?"

"No, but the child..."

But Cormac had brushed past his wife, swiftly followed by Eunan. What wild emotions stirred in Eunan also begged to remain hidden. But fear of the worst consumed him. They climbed the curling stairs of the tower, each step being precarious, such was their haste until they were on the same level as Sorcha's room. They ran to the door until Cormac nodded to the two guards standing in front of it. Cormac ran in to see his daughter, but the guards stood in Eunan's way.

"That's my wife!" But his pleadings fell on deaf ears and silent lips. He fumed and fumbled for his throwing axes but thought better of it. He was shown to a seat and made to wait. He sat for what seemed an age but the shadow of the sun merely changed its position by inches. His ashen-faced father-in-law emerged, his jowls drawn to the floor. Eunan's anger dissipated with the look on Cormac's face.

"I have grave news," he said as he placed his hand on Eunan's shoulder. His hand was warm, but Eunan banished such sentimental gestures to a cold place in his heart. His father-in-law had shown him his place when he acted without thinking.

"Please, tell me of my wife," Eunan said.

Cormac looked at the floor.

"Your wife lives but is gravely ill. Your daughter was not so lucky."

Eunan tried to choke back the tears.

"Can I see her? Can I see my wife? Why did you stop me from seeing my wife?" The tremble in his voice gave his feelings away.

"She is almost ready to sleep, but she should be able to rouse herself to see you. Let me ask." But before Eunan could assert himself more, he faced Cormac's back, then the back of the door. As he stared at the door, he felt more and more like a stud horse who had been assigned to mate with a sick mare. No matter how often they brought in the stud, the mare would reject him or it would not work. Eunan wondered how many more times they would bring him in before they would give up and at that point would Sorcha's health give in, or would they get rid of him? He had to find another way, a way to make himself indispensable to his father-in-law and earn his trust. That would surely be on the battlefield.

Cormac eventually came out.

"She is ready to see you." Eunan nodded his appreciation and entered the shadows of her bedroom.

Sorcha lay propped up on pillows, her face as pale as her clean white sheets. Eunan studied her carefully to see if she was awake. He was cursed by memories of his mother and her tormented failure to have another child after he had ripped out the life-bearing magic of her womb. He saw the pain etched on

Sorcha's face, every twitch a maelstrom of the physical and mental pain that melted into his visions of those same pains he saw in his mother. Was this an opportunity to make things right, to put the pain of his childhood to rest? He would have to wake her and play the loving husband, not the traumatised child.

"Eunan, is that you?" mumbled Sorcha with half-closed eyes, sensing someone creeping around in the shadows.

It was too late. He would have to take his chances with whatever his face revealed of his state of mind.

"Yes, my love, it is I, your husband. How do you feel now that fate has taken away our child?" He squeezed her hand and gave a faint smile whilst fighting back the tears.

"I told them not to take the crib away when the ladies came for the child. My husband is a fighter, I said. Upon his return from his important quest, he will urge me to try again and this time I will bear him a son. God may have struck me down with a permanent affliction, but it is only to test me. It will not prevent me from being a good daughter, mother and wife."

Eunan sobbed and stretched out his other hand to sandwich her limp hand between his.

"Get better soon, for I only have a short time before I am called to the war. Then we can try for a son."

A faint energy possessed Sorcha's hand, and she gave him a gentle squeeze.

"I would like that," she whispered, barely lifting her head.

"That is enough excitement for today. Come now, Eunan, let my daughter rest."

Cormac stood impatiently in the doorway. Eunan kissed his wife's head and relented to Cormac's wishes. He could not help but glower at his father-in-law as he passed him in the doorway. He was beginning to resent the man.

Eunan only made it down as far as the great hall before events overtook the limited space he had elbowed out to grieve the loss of his child.

"Lord, the Maguire summons you to Enniskillen," said Odhran, bearing an official letter from their master. "We must leave at once."

Eunan glowered at him. He had not had the chance even to sit down. "Am I not master of the MacCabe? Do I not say when we leave?" he said.

Odhran stood back, for this was a side of Eunan he had never seen before. He let his lord pull up a seat and enter a state of contemplation, fuelled by the heat of the fire on his outstretched hands. Surely hell would omit such heat and crown his achievements with such torment. Odhran fidgeted in the background as he contemplated rephrasing his message to inspire a sense of urgency in his master. However, Eunan's father-in-law came in from the kitchens. The mask of duty covered any unwanted feelings from public view. He knew of Odhran's message and had no qualms about relaying it to Eunan.

"I have ordered the cooks to prepare a meal for the death of Sorcha's daughter," he said. He placed his hand on Eunan's shoulder. "It is a pity you cannot attend as duty calls. The Maguire is assembling his men to support the O'Donnell. I may follow you, but I await my brother's instruction." He then adopted a hushed tone, as if purely for Eunan's consumption, some consoling words perhaps if he could manage it, but it was within earshot of all who heard his previous message. "I feel for you, I do. Many a family event or crisis had to be resolved in my absence. I have spoken to Sorcha on your behalf. She understands, and wishes you good luck and a swift return home to her."

Cormac slapped him on the back and walked back towards the kitchen to continue his instructions for the dinner. A rage boiled in Eunan, for he felt reduced to a boy and searched for the prying eyes of his detractors, such was his paranoia. But no eyes were met for all were too embarrassed to look the mourning father in the face. Eunan glared at Odhran for he was the only one lowly enough to absorb his anger and fear responding and was the original bearer of the bad news. Eunan cursed and stomped off to his room to pack. He was gone within the hour without having spoken again to his wife.

It was a solemn march from Augher Castle to Enniskillen for Eunan. The men, knowing little of Eunan's troubles, were buoyant, eager to join battle and test out their newly acquired skills. They laughed, joked and played pranks to amuse themselves on the march home and their leader left them to their joviality. However, time and brooding had only multiplied and intensified Eunan's troubles and he pulled up his horse as the men marched on.

"What is wrong, lord?" asked Odhran as he pulled up beside Eunan. He could read his master's moods better now and realised that he could approach. "Enniskillen lies before us. We are almost home."

The word 'home' rang in Eunan's head. He had stayed in many places for periods of time that could have led him to associate them with 'home', but Enniskillen was not one of them. It had become for him a viper's pit of backstabbing and political intrigue, both of which he had not the stomach for now.

"I have urgent business to attend to on my lands. Lead the men to Enniskillen and I will be but a day behind you."

"Is there anything I should be concerned about, lord?" said Odhran.

"No, only that the men should be prepared to march on the order of the Maguire."

"The men know the way to Enniskillen, but you, lord, cannot ride alone in such hostile times."

"I have my dogs to protect me." Eunan pointed to Olcan and Sionn simultaneously sniffing and pissing on a tree.

"The men would never forgive me if I allowed you to lose the MacCabe mascots," said Odhran, trying a different tack. "Let me protect them whilst you go about your business."

Eunan laughed.

"They would object to being tied up and play havoc with the local rabbits, which may wear out my welcome. I'm sure the dogs would appreciate the company."

They both rode southeast with the dogs running behind them after Eunan had instructed his men to continue without him to Enniskillen.

It was half a day later when Eunan first caught sight of O'Cassidy house peering through the rolling hills of south Fermanagh. It was a glorious day with the sun high in the sky, the clouds pared back to a bare minimum and all above dominated by cobalt blue. If ever there was a time to view the house, it was now, for the summer framed it perfectly.

As they rode nearer, the birds sang from the trees of their undisturbed happiness in the place they had made their homes. Such songs soothed Eunan, for many was the time such warbling accompanied him in his youth as he sought his own undisturbed solace.

The hills disappeared underfoot one by one and the latest pretender for Eunan to call 'home' came into view. It presented a grand claim to be the home of a chieftain. The thatched roof had been repaired, and the facade had been given a new grey render. It was almost like it used to look when he first came to the house, even though that sheen had been severely dented by the treatment he received once he entered. It felt like the place in the world he could most call home until the spirit of Caoimhe, his dead wife, possessed his thoughts. But no such melancholy would be allowed to cloud his thoughts, and he quickly banished her back to the grave. No more did he think of treachery and corpses when he rode up towards the house. He was no longer the boy that bravely rode up to face his uncle whilst tormented by the dreams of his parents and his real father.

He closed his eyes and filled his nostrils. The gentle breeze smelt of flowers, for the wildflowers beside the path had grown back. Pleasantries remained until flowers were replaced with the smell of cow dung and his eyes jolted open. He saw further on that the fields had been tilled and the cows he had fought so hard to win were being tended to and the evidence that they were well looked after was easily discernible from their fattened bellies. Eunan pulled up his horse and called his dogs. A couple of farm hands were the only people there to greet him. One came forward to help Eunan off his horse, but he was not needed.

"We were not expecting you, lord," said the man with a quiver in his voice. "The master and mistress are in the fields in that direction and your soldiers are in the opposite direction. Shall I fetch them all for you?"

"You fetch the soldiers and I will meet you here," said Eunan. "In which direction is the mistress again?" The man pointed south. Eunan nodded his thanks. Odhran matched him stride for stride as he set off.

"Wait here for the men," Eunan said. "This is something I wish to do myself. Make sure the dogs don't attack my livestock. Cormac says they are superb hunters who will do us a fine job of fetching food deep in enemy territory on a raid, but I don't want to wear out our welcome."

Eunan walked down to the fields and observed all the hard work that Dervella and Arthur had put into the house and the surrounding fields. No more were the remains of the wedding raid that Oisin had been too negligent or lazy to fix. The stone walls around the house had been repaired and all that surrounded Eunan radiated the beauty of summer. They had done him proud looking after his lands.

Dervella saw him coming across the fields.

"Eunan? Is that you?" She dropped her spade and ran towards him. Eunan became awash with emotions and they ran and met mid-field and embraced. Eunan held Dervella by the waist.

"The land has been good to you and you to it. It is like you were born to manage estates," Eunan said, overcome with joy and gratitude.

"I still remember my time on the great estates of the Earl of Desmond when the soil was so good there was no requirement to nurture, you just had to plant a seed in the ground and it would grow. Once you relieve this land of its bad memories and bad spirits of times past, it accepts the seeds and just wants to flourish." Dervella stepped back to take all of Eunan in. "You seem to have come back to me as a man, even though barely four months have passed."

"If you have been this good to my lands in four months, imagine what you could do in a year?" said Eunan as he took Dervella by the hand and led her back to the house.

"Now don't you go changing the subject and making it all about me. It is you in the possession of youth that has the whole of his life ahead of him and is shooting up in the world." Dervella stepped in front of him, giving him no option but to stand still. "Now, stand here and tell me in the privacy of this field how your married life is going? Are you due to be a father yet? Seamus and I would be so proud of you if you were."

Eunan walked past her and towards the house again. The dam that kept his feelings in was about to burst forth.

"Marriage is... It is difficult to try to be an O'Neill when you are an outsider. There is so much more to it than just being with my wife. It would be so much easier if I could live here away from everyone, and it could just be the two of us. But that is not to be."

"Nobody told you it would be easy. Nobody would give such a gift to a boy from south Fermanagh with only a distant family of vague importance to speak of. It was always up to you to make the best of a bad hand."

Eunan looked to the ground in a last effort to remain in control. "No one told me it would be this hard to lead." He winced and looked mournfully at Dervella. "I wish Desmond was here. I miss him and didn't realise the value of his advice until he was gone."

Dervella cupped the back of his neck and brought his head to her shoulder. "Everyone is the poorer from Desmond being gone. But he'd be so proud of you for what you've become. If only I could take you back a year or two and show you how far you've come."

Eunan nestled into her neck. He felt a blissful contentment he was rarely familiar with. Dervella felt his emotions pour out.

"Now the O'Cassidy-Maguire can't be seen to be vulnerable. Get yourself together and come back to the house and meet the others. You'll be surprised how prosperous this little strip of land has become even without the Pale merchant coming to call." Dervella smiled and took his hand once more.

Eunan gave her a sheepish grin and composed himself and walked back to the house. He was greeted outside by the warm embrace of Arthur and the broad smile of Faolán.

"So they didn't kill you yet?" said Faolán as he slapped him on the back.

"Kill me? Some of them may now even respect me."

They both laughed and went into the house. Eunan's heart leapt as the interior somewhat resembled the house of old. Faolán noticed his look of delight.

"We got a lot of help from the local villages as they were as keen as us to consign the past to the past and to restore local fortunes, despite the proliferation of famine," he said.

"I...I just don't believe it," he choked as he saw the local people who he thought despised him so much had shown him such kindness.

Faolán slapped him on the back. "Well, you restored local pride with the South Fermanagh shot. Once the people saw how much you elevated the area in importance with the Maguire, they wanted to show their gratitude."

They led him to the main room where Dervella called for a feast to be prepared.

"Don't trouble yourself on my behalf," said Eunan modestly. "Unfortunately, I am only staying the night. The Maguire wants me for now I command his MacCabes."

That only encouraged the celebrations for Eunan's back stung with congratulatory slaps and good wishes rang in his ears. He was ushered to the seat at the top of the table and his mug immediately filled.

Darkness filled the window frames with only wisps of cloud, and the sky was beautifully decorated with stars. Eunan's men made a great fire, and they all gathered around it and ate, drank and sang the songs of old. Friendships were renewed and pledges of loyalty and friendship were reaffirmed. But all such nights, where wonderful memories were created to recall with old friends or to provide a lift when times were down, had to end.

Eunan stood by his horse the next day with Odhran, with a pounding head trying to ensure his recall of the night before was somewhat coherent. The two dogs sniffed around his feet, the local population of rabbits a little lighter than when they arrived.

Faolán approached him first and shook his hand. Eunan was almost insulted.

"Come here to me," said Eunan as he pulled him into an embrace. "You're not coming with us this time?"

Faolán let go and straightened himself up. "Not this time. We've been told to wait for instructions from the O'Neill. Apparently, it is us and Connor Roe's men that are covering the eastern flank, so you can have your fun."

"You'll be sorely missed but we'll meet again for battle soon."

Next came Arthur. The hug Eunan reserved for him was heartfelt and wholesome. Eunan released him somewhat but held him at arm's length.

"You've done a fine job here, you were wasted cooking fish on a little island."

"My cooking certainly wasn't wasted on you. You're a fine strapping lad now."

"Look after yourself and Dervella. I'll be home soon and I may even bring my wife."

"We'd look forward to that and would appreciate a bit of notice to make the place fit for such a fine young lady."

Arthur stepped back and left Eunan some space to say goodbye to Dervella.

"You've looked after me like you were my own mother. Now you have created a beautiful home for me. How can I ever repay you?"

"You owe me nothing, child. You are the boy I never had. You're a far better man than your father ever was and could ever have been. Instead, be the man your uncle Seamus could have been. You're more than capable. If circumstances had been different and the Earl of Desmond was still around he would have been a great man. But you can be better."

Eunan hugged her, for not only was he awash with emotion, he needed to hide the tears in his eyes for he thought it unbecoming of a man of his position. He let go of Dervella and turned, mounted his horse and set off for Enniskillen.

# CHAPTER 22

# THE LEGACY OF TAPESTRIES

As the hangover wore off, Eunan felt the energy seeping back into his veins. But along with his energy returned his doubts. The blackness and gloom that haunted his memories of his past life, in the little village with his parents, the intimidation he felt creeping up the path to the house of the O'Cassidy Maguire, and Seamus. Oh yes, Seamus. He could not banish the niggly doubts he still held about him, no matter how much he loved Dervella, the mother he never had.

A revelation occurred as his horse plodded along the track back towards Enniskillen. He realised he needed more exposure to kindness and to people he loved than to be forever masking his feelings in order to deceive, be it in the court of the Maguire, the O'Donnell, the O'Neill or wherever he may find himself. A life of the cloak and dagger of politics was not for him. He preferred the simplicity of the axe and what he could do with just its sharp, narrow blade. Every plod that shuddered through his body said to him he was on someone else's path and he should have stayed back in O'Cassidy house and beside the lakes he loved so much. He longed for the simple life, the one he sometimes deluded himself into imagining he once had, that of the peaceful farmer's son going from one abundant crop to another, at one with nature in a structured family life. But those daydreams were for idling away the endless hours spent on the back of horses being deluded by the beauty of the land and forgetting its call for blood for the honour of declaring oneself master of it.

They came to the familiar rolling hills and forests below Enniskillen, where they met the patrols of the Maguires who gave directions to the castle, whether or not wanted. The tower castle on the island came into view and Eunan wondered what had changed with the passing of Donnacha and the loss of power to the secret allies of Connor Roe, and Eunan wondered if Fachtna Óg would be friend or foe.

He soon found himself at the castle gate, recognised and greeted, his horse taken from him to be fed and rested and him on the circular staircase to the hall of the Maguire. He climbed slowly, each of the uneven steps a burden on foot, thigh and soul. Each step dragged out some of his elation and replaced it with a rock from the burden of duty. His melancholy was disturbed by a sound from below: the rhythmic sound of wood on stone echoed from the stairwell behind him. Eunan shook his head and thought no more of it. He continued his climb.

He found himself in the hall of the Maguire with Cúchonnacht Óg and Fachtna Óg O'Gallagher Maguire. Autumnal light shone through the windows, creating columns of gold. The giveaway for the time of year was that the heat these columns alluded to had to be supplemented by the heat of the fire. The mood was jovial, peppered with laughter, with the Maguire himself seemingly the most invigorated, walking around the room pointing at the tapestries and recounting the tales of Maguire glory in the distant past, skipping the reign of his father, a time of politics, peace and placation. His audience listened and smiled patiently. Eunan bundled through the door, breaching the mood, a ball of restless energy covered in the dust of the road.

"And here he is, at last, the leader of my MacCabes. I hope we did not disturb your idleness with the inconvenience of duty?" said the Maguire through a sly grin.

"I am never idle, master," said Eunan as he advanced into the room. "If I am not training your men by day, I am by night having political relations for you with MacBaron's daughter."

"You'll never sire a son with bed talk like that!" roared the Maguire.

They all laughed as Eunan went to the table and poured himself a drink.

"Well, I hope you have completed your mission and left a baby boy in his daughter's belly so you may return to do my work?"

"With God's grace," and Eunan bowed to the applause of laughter.

"Well, I'm glad you are back anyway and we'll see what God will grant us," said the Maguire. He pulled a letter from his pocket and stiffened his cheeks, signifying the beginning of business.

"The O'Donnell has summoned us to raise our men and follow him into Connacht. We will leave the day after tomorrow."

"We?" said Eunan.

"Oh yes, you may not have heard. I'm tired of playing politics in between the walls of this castle and long to get back onto the battlefield again. I will lead the Maguire horse."

"Is that wise, lord?" asked Eunan. "If you should be killed, we could be thrown into the hands of Connor Roe and all the turmoil that may bring."

"I have left Fachtna Óg in charge. He is more than capable. Anyway, I will not be gone for more than a month."

The clacking of wood on stone slowed now but still continued at a rhythmic pace, echoing up the stairwell. Eunan dismissed it as his brain playing tricks. His attention returned to the point at hand and trying to sink the Maguire's new plan.

"Are you going to lead the Maguire army from the rear? How will you resolve this with the O'Neill and O'Donnell?"

"I will lead and fight with the horse. If they wish to stand at the rear and point their fingers, so be it. I'm not there to usurp anyone. I want to return to something simpler, something I am more attuned to. Cúchonnacht Óg is coming too." The Maguire's brother came up and joined him. Hugh put his arm around Cúchonnacht Óg's shoulders and they beamed in delight at the prospect of testing their prowess on the battlefield.

"Why the sullen face? Are you not happy for us?" said the Maguire. "They will sing songs of the Spanish armies and the Maguire brothers throwing the English back into the sea. They will make a tapestry for us and I will hang it here in this very hall. It all starts tomorrow. Why aren't you happy? You are the famous Eunan Maguire, the scourge of Connor Roe, defier of the hangman's noose, a hero of the Ford of the Biscuits and many battles which I will ensure the bards reference and remember. Yes, I was there for some, bickering in this great hall for others, but I want to be in the heat of the battle, make our foes feel Fermanagh steel, to make the Maguires feared as they were of old. All of that starts tomorrow. Here, have a proper drink and help us celebrate and stop being so glum."

Eunan's cup soon overflowed onto his sleeve until he withdrew the cup from beneath the jug the Maguire was holding. He laughed and sipped off the excess until he could hold the cup without spilling it more.

"So, who is going to defend Fermanagh while you are gone?" said Eunan.

The sound of wood on stone got louder and then suddenly stopped.

"He is," and the Maguire pointed to the door.

Between the frames stood Irial, supported by a walking staff, his ankle in bandages, with two MacCabes standing behind him. Irial gave Eunan a certain steely stare that sent shivers down his back, which he dared not show or he knew he was done for. He steadied himself, determined to get the first word in.

"I take it you've retired from the MacCabes if you now perform this service for the Maguire?" said Eunan.

"I should have known that a relative of Seamus MacSheehy could stoop to such trickery and deception, but more fool me for being so naive. Since you have crippled me so I have to put my skills to other ways of being of service. One such way is my experience and my knowledge of the glory of the Maguires through the annals. Hugh is a worthy successor to the generations in the past who have stood and fought for the glory of the clan and will prove himself a skilled commander to add to his accolade as the leader of the Maguires. He should use his youth wisely to lead the Maguires to glory and leave the trivial matters of managing the lands until his return to Fachtna Óg and me. I expect you to do the same and lead the MacCabes from the front, just as my ancestors did."

Irial hobbled across the floor to where they were standing.

"Now is a time for war boy, and for every man to prove himself. Since you have robbed me of my opportunity you must make up for it and make the MacCabes the most feared Galloglass in the north."

Eunan remembered back to his days when he used to assist Desmond in the affairs of the court and how Desmond used to rail against any talk of fighting based on the glories of the past given the O'Donnells and the O'Neills loomed above them. He felt it was his duty to his mentor to continue his line of argument.

"The Maguire must stay alive to lead his people through these troubled times. He is no good to his people lying in a bog with a bullet in his chest," said Eunan.

"Don't poison your master's head with doubt. Such sentiments are unworthy of a leader of the MacCabes."

"The Maguire owes a duty to his people not to throw away his life on some folly," said Eunan.

Irial struggled to seat himself and laid his staff to rest beside him.

"If you didn't wish to fight, why did you cripple me to command the Maguire's best men? Or is it to follow in your mentor Desmond's footsteps when he took over the MacCabes and destroyed their fighting capabilities and reputation by never letting them fight?"

That pricked Eunan's pride.

"I am here to fight and give my life for the Maguire if needs be," he said. His hand twitched above his throwing axe. The Maguire had no desire to see another one of his advisors die at the hands of Eunan. He stood between the two men.

"Let us set aside our differences and have a drink to what tomorrow brings." Hugh lifted his mug. "To the greatest glory the Maguires have ever seen!"

"To the Maguire!" everyone saluted. Hugh hurriedly filled their mugs again.

Eunan emerged from the tower several hours later, his head in a spin wondering what folly he had gotten himself into.

# CHAPTER 23

# THE SECOND FRONT

S eamus returned to the O'Donnell to give him news of the mission to
Leinster and Wicklow and what he had done with O'Neill's men. He
returned with mixed feelings, as if his friend's decline in ability and reliability
was a reflection on himself. Seamus remembered back to the glory years of
Fiach, to his victory at Glenmalure. He was untouchable then. Other lords
had led their petty rebellions, which usually ended in dramatic failure, a result
mainly of their incompetence and ineptitude and their inability to construct
wide-ranging alliances in the disparate clans. But Fiach had remained in the
forest, ever the rebel, as his power and prestige waned. It was mainly the O'Neill's
ability to construct such alliances that encouraged Seamus to give rebellion one
last chance, though the O'Donnell's impatience, jealousy and lack of strategic
thinking threatened to undo it.

He arrived at the O'Donnell castle to find that the O'Donnell was not there.
He was directed to Eoghan McToole O'Gallagher who was left in charge. Seamus had his horse quartered, and he and his men were fed before O'Gallagher
was ready to see him. Seamus was directed up to a small room in the tower to
wait. Time passed and the walls of the room crept in to suffocate him. Seamus
grew impatient and went over to the window and looked out onto the lands.
The sky was an empty blue and the sun a strained yellow dot doing her best to
remind everyone it was the middle of summer, but being too stingy to exude

enough heat to prove it beyond doubt. The town was busy with the summer fair and market, and the fish trade bustled. The farmlands in the region were showing definitive signs of recovery from the decades of war and famine, and the faint ray of hope was reflected in the sun. Seamus could not help but think that with the war coming, this would be the last time Tirconnell would see such peace and tranquillity in many a year.

O'Gallagher entered, his face etched with concern. His beard and long hair, for years singed with grey, had suffered a decisive defeat to stress and middle age and was beginning to jump ship in parts, having fully succumbed to grey in others. Seamus pointed to the window.

"The town looks well, far better than you do."

"This is what responsibility does for you, just so you know and will recognise it when you see it," said O'Gallagher.

"I've got plenty of responsibility and I'm sure you're going to burden me with some more before I leave?"

"Well, if you ever washed all the mud off you, you may discover the scars of responsibility on yourself."

Seamus smiled and went to the table to pour them a drink from the jug on the tray that the servant who followed O'Gallagher had brought.

"The men were safely dispatched in Wicklow and your young rebel set up to fight in the midlands as you ordered," he said, handing O'Gallagher a mug of ale.

"We have high hopes for Richard Tyrell. You're a good man, Seamus, for a mercenary. If only you could truly serve the cause, you would be one of our greatest assets."

"I served, as my father and his forefathers before him, the Earl of Desmond. When the rebellion goes to Munster, you'll see me serve the new Earl of Desmond."

"When that happens, you'll be the first to know. But there is still much work to make that happen."

Seamus sat and smiled.

"That is why I'm here. To convince one little lord after another to turn to our cause until we have created ourselves a corridor to Munster and hope whilst we have our backs turned that these newly rebellious lords do not place a knife in it."

Seamus sarcastically saluted O'Gallagher with his swishing mug.

"And you're just the man for the job with your multiple powers of persuasion. But we have a more serious mission for you this time."

"Oh, what is that?"

"We wish you to return to Wicklow with a large body of men to reinforce Fiach. We need him to open up a second front to tie down as many English soldiers as possible."

Seamus was confused.

"How does that differ from our normal plan?"

"Our sources tell us that a Spanish invasion is imminent. They are expected to land here in the north. Still, if Lord Deputy Russell continues his obsession with Fiach, they will be suitably distracted so the Spanish army can land successfully."

Seamus was unmoved.

"I say again, how is this different from our normal plan? They all end the same way, 'and then the Spanish will come and rescue us'. Fiach bleats out that line to me regularly as if it would be a miracle from God."

"You saw out the window how Tirconnell crackles? The O'Donnell has given the order that a great food store is created. The people endure, not for themselves but for hope. The O'Donnell has not told them about the potential arrival of the Spanish army, but still, they toil, even after years of famine, in the hope of being free. Would you deny them their hope? The freedom of Munster depends on it."

The outburst made O'Gallagher a little red-faced, but he was a man under pressure and would not tolerate any insubordination, even if in jest. But Seamus was again unmoved.

"The only thing guaranteed with waiting for the Spanish is that it will make you old. If you saw Fiach's camps and the fragility of his alliances, you would not stress yourself out. You would be on your knees with your hands clasped together!"

Seamus tumbled out of his seat and onto his knees and held his prayer hands to the heavens.

"It is the wrong place for blasphemous jokes, Seamus. The O'Donnells take such matters very seriously."

But Seamus could see the tremble of a smile on the edge of his friend's lips. Seamus lifted himself up and slapped his friend on the shoulders.

"Don't worry. I'll take your mission and more besides. In any foray south, we should always supply Uaithne and Richard."

"We have plenty of rebels from Leinster and Munster that make their way here. Three hundred more men are waiting for you in Enniskillen. Two hundred for Fiach and one hundred for Richard. If you get them through, I will do my best to twist the O'Donnell's arm to ensure you are one of the first into Munster."

Seamus thrust out his hand.

"We'll shake on that, for I know all you can give me is your word and you're good for that. Leinster will burn so Munster can too!"

Fiach's face lit up when he saw Seamus march up the hill and into his camp at the head of two hundred shot. He ran down the hill, passed his guards, and embraced his friend. He released him and held out his hands in astonishment as the men marched past him.

"How? How did you get — how many?"

"Two hundred," said Seamus, his smile almost as large as the valley beneath them.

"Two hundred fully armed men across Ireland and to here?"

"Well, I can't take all the credit. Uaithne is an invaluable ally for us all. His men are the scourge of the English all over Leinster."

Fiach could not contain his delight.

"Thank you again, my friend. Did you bring anything else for me?"

"The men brought enough ammo for one campaign if you use it sparingly and only when you have to. I will try to get you a regular supply, but you'd be better off if you could arrange your own or continuously steal enough from the enemy. Anything else is a private conversation away from prying ears."

"Of course, of course. Come to my tent and give me all your news."

Fiach ushered him in that direction.

They arrived in the tent and Fiach unfurled the maps that Hugh Boye had made for him during his stay. Seamus stood over the maps beside him.

"How goes your alliance-making?" said Seamus.

Fiach sighed.

"With such twists and turns, it makes me dizzy just trying to keep up. The O'Tooles are still with me but half still ponder on which side to pick. The northern O'Byrnes have sided with the Crown. The crowning of Domhnall Mac-Murrough Kavanagh brought over the Kavanaghs, some Kinsellas, O'Kennedys and O'Nolans, and we always have the dissident factions of the families of the great earls."

"How many men can you count on in a fight?"

Fiach had to think hard.

"Maybe five hundred in the mountains and the same again in Wexford under Domhnall?"

Seamus did a calculation in his head.

"So really, that's about five hundred, including my two hundred men and the men I brought you before?"

Fiach scrunched up his face.

"Now that's a little unfair."

"I don't want them to run away from me when I expect them to have my back."

Fiach shrugged his shoulders.

"So what is the best way to get the attention of Russell?" said Seamus.

Fiach's eyes lit up.

"Assault Ballinacor!"

Seamus was more sceptical.

"Do you have enough men to take and hold it?"

"Nothing would be a better rallying call to the O'Byrnes and all of south Leinster than to take Ballinacor!"

"I'll take that as a no."

Fiach did not take the dousing of his enthusiasm well.

"We will take and hold it and my sons will prove themselves worthy of the O'Byrne name."

"Well, I hope so for my sake, for I cannot leave until the war is in full swing here."

# CHAPTER 24
# ALL THIS FOR A HILL

F iach was true to his word, for if he loved anything, it was Ballinacor Castle. Word had gone out across Leinster of Fiach's planned assault on Balli-nacor. Most of the O'Byrnes had rallied to his cause, hoping if the castle was retrieved, Fiach's lust for war would finally be satisfied. The King of Leinster came with his assorted force of Kavanaghs, O'Nolans, O'Kennedys and Kin-sellas. Although they were the largest body of men, they were the worst armed and trained. Seamus considered them an ill-disciplined rabble, only good for absorbing bullets and acting as a distraction from the main attack. The O'Tooles had also turned out in force and lined up under Barnaby O'Toole, Fiach's wife's brother. Fiach's son Phelim took command of the O'Byrnes. However, the pride of the assault was Seamus's contingent, a force of O'Neill's men and recruits trained by Richard Tyrell, and Uaithne O'More. It was an all-or-nothing gamble by Fiach, for if they were defeated and defeated decisively, then the rebellion in Leinster would be dead.

Their objective was Ballinacor Castle, Fiach's home, base and centre of power for the O'Byrnes in Wicklow. It was positioned on a hill at the head of a valley, nestled in between the forests of Wicklow. It commanded the surrounding lands, allowing nothing to pass through the valley north or south undetected. The valley was the primary route into central Wicklow or south towards Wex-ford, besides the coastal road. Lord Deputy Russell realised its strategic value and cut away some of the forests around the castle to make it harder to assault. He had installed a garrison of mainly raw native Irish recruits, but most of the English army in Ireland was in Connacht and they were not expecting an attack in Wicklow.

The Queen had raised men in England and sent them over to Ireland to quell the rebellion. However, they were poorly trained and prone to illness and most that arrived through Dublin port were unfit for duty. They remained in Dublin and convalesced and waited to be retrained. As such, they were unavailable to the Lord Deputy. Fiach knew most of this through his network of spies. If ever there was a moment to strike, it was now.

Fiach devised a plan for the assault in consultation with Phelim as he wished to avoid having a general conference about it, for he knew Seamus would disagree and it would just end in an argument and spies would leak all his plans. Once the plan was agreed upon, he called the leaders together and assigned each of them a role. The Kavanaghs and allies under Domhnall would block the valley, Richard, Uaithne and the O'Neills under Seamus would provide supporting fire on the castle and act as a reserve, and the O'Byrnes and O'Tooles under Fiach would assault the castle. Fiach waved away any protests or accusations that the O'Byrnes were trying to hog all the glory by taking the castle and leaving the other clans to do the dirty work. They were, but it was his home and he was in charge.

On the chosen morning of September 9th 1596, Fiach ordered his Kern to spread out over the valleys and surround Ballinacor. The Kavanaghs followed swiftly behind. Fiach and Seamus made their way slowly up the valleys, waiting for news of the size of the enemy force.

Ballinacor was lightly defended by a garrison of around forty men. Politics had interrupted Lord Deputy Russell's vendetta against Fiach and he had sent most of his men to Connacht or to guard Dublin, both as the result of the ongoing trial of ex-Governor Bingham. Wicklow had been quiet for about six months with only low-level skirmishing, and the Lord Deputy was concentrating his efforts on shoring up the border against the northern lords.

Seamus and Richard marched with their men through the forests on the other side of Ballinacor. They had several hours before they were due to arrive and surround the castle with their shot. Seamus surveyed the landscape as he passed through it, looking for any advantage it would afford him. He noticed how tall the trees were on this side of the valley.

"Taller than any castle," he said.

He ordered the men to halt and take out their axes and follow him into the forest. Richard ran after him.

"Seamus, you're going the wrong way! We'll be late if you do not return to the road."

Seamus ignored him and pointed out the tallest trees he could find.

"That one, that one, and that one. I want twenty trees, all of that size. Tie ropes to them so we can control them."

"What are you doing?"

"It's an old forest battle trick. I'm surprised that Fiach doesn't use it but it can backfire. Go fetch Uaithne for me."

Uaithne came and was dispatched to get some specified supplies. Seamus set back upon the road and the men carried his tall trees onto the top of the valley and hid them in the forests where they were to take up their positions. Seamus laid out his shot as Fiach asked him to and waited for the assault to start.

The element of surprise was quickly squandered. The garrison of the fort soon discovered a large force coming their way and locked themselves in the castle and lit their distress pyre at the top of a nearby mountain. The smoke could easily be seen in Dublin before Fiach's men put it out. Fiach was determined that the assault should take place, for if he failed he feared Ballinacor would be lost forever. He ignored the pleas for caution by his allies and ordered the first assault. Seamus obliged with a couple of volleys before Fiach's men charged out of the woods. The defenders picked off a few of Fiach's men as they charged across no-man's-land. But most of Fiach's men congregated below the walls. The castle was a large fortified house, and the English had added a set of walls to create a walled courtyard, which space the garrison could use as it pleased in order to withstand a lengthy siege. Fiach's men had no siege ladders or cannon, so they could neither scale nor knock down the walls. Fiach's men knew they had to get out of there before the defenders used them for target practice.

In the meantime, Seamus ordered his men to build large protective shields out of wood. They ran out into no-man's-land to a certain distance from the castle, set the mobile walls down and laid down covering fire to protect the men at the bottom of the walls. They also dug small holes behind the protective shields.

Seamus went to find Fiach to discuss his Plan B and discovered him in a panic at the side of the woods facing the castle.

"It didn't work, it didn't work," said Fiach.

He looked as if he was losing his nerve.

"We always needed something more than just surprise. I can keep them pinned down, but fear we are in a stalemate until a relief force comes for them from Dublin."

"Well, if we don't take Ballinacor now, my alliance is dead. Have you anything in mind?"

Seamus's eyes lit up.

"As a matter of fact, I do. An old forest fighting trick you taught me all those years ago, back when we used to fight in these woods."

"Well, if it's one of my tricks, it'll be good."

Uaithne returned with several barrels of oil, as Seamus had requested. They lined the trees up out of sight of the castle and greased them with oil. They were then distributed throughout the forest, as Seamus instructed. His shot readied themselves for several rounds. Fiach then appeared from the side of the forest and signalled to the constables of the men trapped under the walls to ready themselves to retreat to the woods. Everything was in place.

Seamus gave the signal. The shot on the edge of the woods and from behind the wooden shields in no-man's-land let out several volleys to pin down the defenders. Fiach came out from the woods and signalled to his constables. The men trapped under the walls of the castle ran out across no-man's-land. Seamus gave his second signal. His men ran out from the woods carrying the cut-down trees. The men carrying each tree ran for a different wooden shield in no-man's-land. The men at the front had the tree stump and ran for the hole behind each shield. Once in the hole, the shot who had previously hidden behind the shield retreated. The stump hit the hole and the men at the back grabbed the ropes and pulled the tree forward as hard as they could. Men with flaming arrows stepped out of the forest and took careful aim. The trees burst into flames. Some trees flew as planned. A sheet of flaming tree collided with the walls of the castle and spat flames inside, setting fire to the house and courtyard. Some of the tops of the trees broke off on the walls and fell flaming into the courtyard. Some of the trees bounced off the walls and fell harmlessly in no-man's-land and spent their force scorching the grass. Some trees caught fire too early and flames shot down the greasy ropes and set fire to those brave souls that had carried the tree and been rewarded with a layer of grease for their troubles. The archers put the lucky ones out of their misery.

Fiach and Seamus stood on the side of the woods and let the flaming trees do what they were going to do and tried not to choke on the bellowing smoke. Soon the gates of Ballinacor opened, and the defenders came running out. Fiach accepted their surrender and once the last defender had evacuated, he ordered his men to douse the flames. Ballinacor was Fiach's once more.

# CHAPTER 25

# THE AMBUSH

Eunan assembled his men in the forests of western Fermanagh and waited for instructions from the O'Donnell. The buoyant mood in Enniskillen Castle proved infectious to the men in the forest and under the leadership of Hugh Maguire, they were eager to charge into Connacht. Eunan was one of the few commanders to express any caution. There had been an influx of young men to join this raid and the Maguire had appointed many young commanders as the ranks had swelled, most with good connections rather than combat experience. Eunan had come to an accommodation with the MacCabes and their leaders, and he hoped the raid would at least bind them together as a more cohesive unit. But at least he now had his war dogs. They would not let him down.

The Maguire called his commanders together and distributed a list of clans and persons the O'Donnell knew collaborated with the English or who recently swore loyalty to Donough O'Connor Sligo. It was to be open season on these people. Everyone else was to be spared unless they offered resistance to the rebels.

The O'Donnell gave the order to attack, and the rebels swept everything before them. While the Governor was expecting the attack to come, his forces melted away, for most of his Irish recruits deserted and his new raw recruits from England did not need an excuse to run. Donough O'Connor Sligo tried to rally his men, but once those minor clans who had rallied to his cause realised that the O'Donnell was singling them out, they quickly pledged to the O'Donnell. The O'Connor Sligo soon took to his heels.

Taaffe considered he would be safe in Drumahair Castle, but such was the velocity of the rebel assault he realised if he stayed he would find himself far behind enemy lines. Most of his men from Sligo either took to their heels to defend their land or fled, expecting the rebels to sweep through only to be chased out by the Governor swiftly afterwards. Taaffe climbed to the top of the castle tower to see the streams of rebels coming over the low hills. He saw that his men on the ramparts of the castle could see the same thing, so he ran down the stairs and assembled his captains.

"We need to leave, and now. However, our strength is keeping the men in good order, so assemble them in the courtyard and tell them we are to join up with the army of the Governor and the rebels will be no match for our combined forces."

"The men will run at the first sign of the rebels," said one captain.

"Draw them up in their formations of pike and shot and wait in the yard. I need to collect my valuables," said Taaffe.

He walked calmly into the tower and ran to his office when he was out of sight of the men. He ordered his magistrate and secretaries to load all the papers into trunks and went to retrieve his chests of coins. He had so many chests of coins and other valuables that he would need to keep the garrison intact to transport it safely to Galway with an adequate escort.

The men brought the chests into the courtyard and loaded them onto carts. The watchmen on the ramparts shouted the rebels were clearly visible now. The men looked jittery. Taaffe ran back into the tower and retrieved a bag of coins. He gave a coin to each man that had kept their formation.

"That's one coin for every man that does not desert or run now and one coin for every man that makes it to Galway," shouted Taaffe around the courtyard. More men picked up their weapons and fell into line.

"Good," roared Taaffe as he mounted the cart with the most loot. "The carts are to be protected by pike front and back, shot along the flanks, and horse screening in front and defending the rear."

The column left the castle and wound its way towards Galway.

The Maguire horse rode ahead with Hugh leading from the front. Hugh's horse lapped up the miles, and he felt invigorated about being out on a raid free of the constraints of having to be the Maguire. Eunan tried to shadow him, but with most of his men on foot, they were always miles behind, trailing the horse. Hugh's scouts soon spotted Taaffe's column winding its way south.

"Lord," said the chief scout as he reported to the Maguire. " I think the Governor's baggage train is in the valley ahead. It looks lightly defended."

"Can we take them alone without having to wait for support?"

"It would be a risk, but we could lure them into a trap if the MacCabes would hurry along."

The Maguire turned to his brother. "Get your friend to hurry along. We'll drive him eastward towards the river and spring our trap there. We'll be the hammer and them the anvil."

Cúchonnacht Óg saluted and took some men and dashed southward.

After being hurried along by the Maguire's brother, Eunan spread his men out along the forest, seeking contact with either the enemy or the Maguire horse. His men soon found the scouts of the Maguire and brought them to Eunan. Eunan greeted them warmly and sat them down to eat some rabbit stew, a fresh contribution from his war dogs. Eunan let them eat first, for they were famished.

"The governor's column will wind its way through the gap between the forest and the river, probably this afternoon. The horse have funnelled them this way."

Eunan called his men together and assigned each of his three constables a section of the column to attack and sent Cúchonnacht Óg back to his brother, with the suggestion that the horse should pick up the stragglers as they fled. Eunan did not know whether the Maguire would listen to him and co-ordinate or would do as he pleased. With this worry in the back of his mind, he took command of the group that would attack the enemy's centre and set his plan in motion.

The Kern had been sent to follow the column at a distance and to report back to Eunan that they were still on the route he thought they would travel and what time they could ambush them. Eunan and his men hid behind a low hill where Eunan would peek over the brow to ensure the plan was still in place. Cearbhall MacCabe hid his men at a spot where the forest came down almost to the river, creating a narrow path to cross so he could block the column's advance. Feargal MacCabe and his men shadowed the column at a distance, ready to cross over any escape route and trap the column.

Taaffe and his men continued on, unaware they were being followed, as Taaffe was more concerned with keeping his men together as a cohesive unit. So where bullying did not work, he resorted to more bribery and when that reached its limit, he thought of more threats. Shea Óg O'Rourke and his men marched in the front, ignoring the moaning of the Irish conscripts. They had chosen their side, were well paid for it, and knew their time would come. They marched with the river on their left-hand side and the forest closed in on their right. Shea Óg ordered his men to march on while he waited for Taaffe and the main part of the column.

Taaffe ordered his shot to pan out and cover the flank beside the forest. Shea Óg walked alongside the cart.

"This makes me nervous. If I were to spring a trap, this looks like one place I would do it," he said.

"What would you have me do?" Taaffe said. "I can barely keep the men together. If I look jittery, then they'll run for the hills."

"More jittery than you look now?"

A messenger rode up from behind them, eager to get Taaffe's attention.

"What is it, boy? Let your tongue do its work."

"Rebel horse are behind us and coming up fast. We don't have enough men to hold them off."

Shea Óg looked up at Taaffe. "It's begun."

"What would you have me do?" said Taaffe, shrugging his shoulders. "Galway is a day away at most. Take your men and surge forward and find the Queen's soldiers to help guide us to the city."

Shea Óg sighed, but nodded his head. He also knew that there was nothing to be done.

Eunan and his men hid in the forest. They had recruited the help of some of the local clansmen who were sympathetic to the rebels to help them choose the best place to lay their ambush and now Eunan lay behind some cover with one hundred of his finest Galloglass. He watched first the screen of horse pass by, then the shot and then a formation of pike. He knew from experience that the next section should be the middle of the column and he would have to contend with shot on the flanks before he could penetrate the main column. He had armed his men with bows for in the dense forest the only thing the shot would hit were the trees. His men were used to hunting deer in the forest with the bow, so the Queen's men should make easy targets. He just needed to see the prize of the baggage train.

He sat and waited until on his right he heard a branch crack and looked over to see some of his own Galloglass waving in apology. The soldiers in the column shouted and shot aimlessly into the surrounding forest. This was as good as the element of surprise would get.

Eunan leapt from his hiding place.

"THE CRY OF THE MAGUIRE!"

A hail of arrows came upon the column from the surrounding trees felling cart horse, driver and protective soldiers alike. The shot turned their attention to the trees, but all their firing did was create a haze of smoke and frighten away the crows. This gave Eunan and the MacCabes the chance to rush out and make up the ground between where they hid and the enemy column without the inconvenience of having to dodge random flying balls of lead.

Eunan broke out from the cover of the forest but most of the enemy had taken to their heels. He charged with his six-foot axe, flailed it around his head and brought it down in a semicircle, striking the shins and knees of several of his foes and bringing them screaming to the ground. A captain tried to rally his men, but Eunan impaled him on a cartwheel, driving the point of his axe into the spoke. It became stuck and foes charged at him left and right. He reached for his throwing axes. One man went down, an axe firmly lodged in his forehead. Another came from behind, but Eunan swung another axe from his belt and the man fell. The battlefield became engulfed in smoke and screams. A man leapt off the back of a cart and knocked Eunan to the ground. The man raised his dagger to thrust it into Eunan's chest. Time moved in slow motion and the sky blurred. A deep-throated growl came from a distance away. The sound became blurred with rapid motion. A hairy body flew over him and the growl intensified. Eunan got up and threw the man's legs off him as his war hound mauled the man's neck. Eunan grabbed another axe from his belt and flung it at the back of the head of an enemy soldier of rank. With the disintegration of the man's skull so collapsed the resistance of the enemy. They ran for the river only to see the Maguire horse on the other side waiting for them. They ran for the forest but Eunan did not have enough men to pursue them. Eunan lent on a wheel of a cart, for he was exhausted.

Taaffe heard the volley go off at the edge of the woods. He leapt off his cart and ducked for cover with the river behind him.

"FORM THE CARTS INTO A DEFENSIVE CIRCLE!" he roared. Some men had followed his lead and hid behind the carts. He glared at them from behind the cart wheel and pointed them towards the forest, gesturing to them to attack. What men followed his instructions never returned. Taaffe looked over the top of the cart towards the smoke of battle and saw the charge of the Maguire. He spread his hands over his precious chests and shed a tear for all the efforts he had made to accumulate such wealth, and now it would be so easily stolen from him. Several arrows thudded into the body of the cart and Taaffe knew it was time to go. He patted the chests once more.

"Farewell!" he cried, and he ditched everything of weight on his body and jumped into the river he knew met the sea somewhere near Galway.

Shea Óg reached the first line of shot at the front of the column. The forest receded and opened up into a clearing. The land was flat and the port and towers of Galway were clearly visible. A boy emerged from the forest, waving his hands.

"Bring him to me," ordered Shea Óg

The boy came and held out a letter for Shea Óg. He took it and read it.

"'Go to Galway and don't look back. Someone will contact you about handing over Eunan Maguire.'"

Shea Óg could hear gunfire from behind him.

"Is this a trick, boy?" growled Shea Óg.

The boy shrugged his shoulders and wriggled free of the grip of Shea Óg's men. He ran back into the woods. Men started running towards Shea Óg.

"The rebels are coming!" they cried.

Shea Óg grunted and pointed ahead.

"To Galway, men. There is nothing for us here."

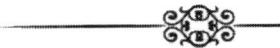

The Maguires made camp in view of Galway town alongside the O'Donnells and the other clan allies of Connacht. They hitched the carts as they were to the horses, for they did not want to get caught out in the open looting the baggage train. They set up their tents around the carts and Hugh and Cúchonnacht Óg picked up their axes and smashed through the locks and flipped open the boxes with their axe blades.

"There must be half the coin in Sligo in these boxes!" exclaimed Hugh, who looked like he had never seen so much money in all his life. The Maguire ordered Eunan and his Maguire constables to open up the other chests. Some were full of coin, some full of jewels and some full of paper. The Maguire stood back and stroked his chin. He called Eunan and his brother to him and ordered the MacCabes to disperse the onlookers.

"What are we going to do with all this?" the Maguire said. "No wonder they travelled so slow."

"Money is only good if you are alive to spend it," said Eunan.

"Are you to be my sober adviser now Desmond is gone?" said Hugh.

"I will be what you need me to be whether you realise it or not, as long as I am of service," replied Eunan.

The Maguire slapped him on the back.

"Well, what do you think I should do with these chests then, oh sober one?"

"Dig a shallow hole, bury the chests and cover them over so no one will know where they are until we know what our next move is. Put a large tent over it and have a feast for the men in the tent. Therefore, the chests are always guarded but no one will know their location. Then we bring them back to Enniskillen at the first opportunity we get."

"Ha! That sounds like a great plan. Get your MacCabes to do it, for I have been summoned by the O'Donnell. When I return, I expect it to be as if those chests were never here at all."

"Your wish is my command," said Eunan as he bowed in a half joking manner.

"Like they were never here," said the Maguire over his shoulder as he walked away.

# CHAPTER 26

# A BARGAIN IN THE SHADOWS

T he Maguire spent a week at the camp of the O'Donnell while his brother took charge of the Maguire camp. The provisions of Drumahair Castle had also been hastily loaded onto the back of some carts by Taaffe only to be captured and the ravenous Maguires quickly consumed them. The ale lasted a little longer as the Maguires partied for several days on top of the buried treasure. The men were strewn around the tent and the alcohol proved too much for the discipline of some young men and fights broke out. Into this chaos the Maguire returned.

Galway town heaved at the seams with all the loyal Queen's subjects that sought the protection of its wall. It was a large town for western Ireland and was well defended but not set up to take such a large influx of men. Sir Conyers Clifford, the Governor of the province, had taken refuge in the residence of the Earl of Clanricard and he fumed at the reversal he had suffered.

"Why do they send me the dregs of England to defend this godforsaken place? There is way too little to steal here to compensate for the constant war, illness, and famine. These bogs will be the graveyard of my career, as it has been for so many others. How can you stay in such a place as this?"

Ulick Burke, the Earl of Clanricard, the largest landowner in the region and the most loyal servant of the Crown, poured him a drink.

"You have to carve out your place in the flesh of both the people and the land. Strength is the only currency here. Most of your men ran at the first sign of the rebels and those Englishmen of yours are halfway across the country to catch the next boat home. Let us seek solace in our maps and plan on how to send the O'Donnell home."

They unfurled the maps and read out loud the correspondence from their scouts and spies and placed upon the map where they considered the dispositions of both forces to be. Clifford placed his finger where the O'Donnell camp was situated.

"Why would they stop there? It has a commanding view of the city, but why did they not attack when we were in disarray? Why wait?"

Burke shrugged his shoulders.

"They needed to rest?"

"No, there is something else."

Clifford ran to the door and shouted at his secretary to bring the latest correspondence from England. The man ran in with a satchel full of letters.

"What is the most important news that I missed when I was in the field?" he asked of his secretary.

"A Spanish fleet sank off Cape Finisterre?" he said, hoping it was the answer his master was looking for.

"That's it!" cried Clifford as he ran back into the room. "They are waiting for the Spanish!"

He ran over to the map and surveyed its contents. "They must not know about the fleet's demise yet, but soon will. We must strike when they are at their lowest. Secretary, send word to the Earl of Thomond and Tibbot to raise all the men they can and attack from the west and the south. We'll sortie out of the city. We can counter attack and smash the rebellion in one pincer movement."

He picked up his mug and smashed it into Burke's.

"To the final victory and the end to this wretched war!" cried Clifford.

"And the Queen's ongoing good health," said Burke.

Clifford drained his mug for he could taste victory in the dregs.

Taaffe staggered through the gates of Galway town draped over the shoulders of two men along with hordes of other stragglers who had no clan to return to, did not know the way to Dublin port, or had got swept up in the general retreat and feared getting executed as a deserter. Taaffe was covered head to toe in mud for when he entered the river, he saw the Maguire horse on the other side, which prevented him from wading across. He ducked beneath the water, held his breath, and swam. Once under the water, he was in the power of the current, which drove him thrashing through the rocks and rapids until he lost consciousness. He awoke on the bank of the river to hands riffling through his pockets and leaving him for dead. His head bled into the mud banks until two passing men recognised him and saw that he was not dead. They had tidied and bandaged his wound and taken him to Galway town.

"To the house of Ulick Burke," mumbled Taaffe. "He will look after me and see that you are rewarded. That man owes me, he does."

"And which way would that be?" said the man under Taaffe's right shoulder.

"The big house overlooking the port," said Taaffe. "Any fool knows that."

"It wouldn't be any fool that would pick you up out of the mud half dead with your reputation. We expect to be well rewarded since we saved your life."

"You will be, and you also knew that with my reputation, you'd have to put up with my temper. Now I can hardly see, but I think it is straight ahead. If you see any of Burke's men, ask them the way and tell them it is me that is asking."

The streets of Galway were heaving with men who had run to escape the rebel onslaught. Bodies lay everywhere, taking advantage of this slim opportunity for some sleep, in various states of drunkenness or various states of injury, from a stomach wound to a severed arm, to bleeding to death on the streets. The men of Clanricard tried to instil some kind of order and to sort the men out into those that were fit and well and those who were wounded or dying. They sent what able men they could find back to their original units. But they were quickly overwhelmed by the sheer weight of numbers.

They staggered along the street seeking directions to the Earl's house but getting rebutted by his men, for everyone was claiming special status and the protection of the Earl. A man stood before them, his face mostly obscured by his helmet's huge nose guard.

"I'll take this man from you now," he said, pointing to Taaffe.

"Not unless you're a man from the Earl and are here to give us our just reward."

Shea Óg raised his axe.

"This will be your only reward if you don't release him to me."

Taaffe raised his head. He was feeling a little drowsy, but he recognised Shea Óg.

"These men saved me. Pay them well and send them on their way."

Shea Óg laughed.

"Pay them with what? We're as poor as they are now. Let my axe do its work. Don't tell me you've gone all soft because you are hurt?"

"We don't want no trouble. We were just being good Samaritans and helping an injured fellow soldier. Tell us where to put him and we'll be on our way."

"Over there, and be quick about it." Shea Óg pointed to the side of a house where his men were resting. The two men laid Taaffe down gently and scurried away before Shea Óg changed his mind.

"You're lucky you hired me, hey? You got a guardian angel thrown in for free," said Shea Óg to the squirming Taaffe as he tried to find a comfortable position to rest.

"Let me sleep awhile and when I can stand, we can seek the Earl and get some accommodation."

"You may as well, for that is the only place you'll find your fancy bed." Shea looked down at Taaffe, but he was already asleep.

Shea Óg and his men made their little camp on the corner of the house and made themselves a fire by stealing straw from the thatched roofs of the nearby houses, which the locals were powerless to defend. They got a little of the bread and ale being distributed by the Earl from the rations of the local English garrison. Night fell, and they occupied themselves telling tall stories about the stars in the clear sky above them. Taaffe slept on and Shea Óg occasionally checked on him to see if he was still alive. Nothing of note happened until Shea Óg received a tap on the arm.

"Do you wish to gain revenge on Eunan Maguire?" said a small boy who looked at him and wondered what the man's face looked like under the helmet.

"And where did a young boy like you learn about bad men like him?"

"From the man in the house over there who said he would give me a coin if I repeated his message and got you to go over and speak to him." The boy pointed to a house across the street.

"It must have been a pretty coin for you to approach me."

"It was, and the man said all the soldiers would be gone if you listened to him."

"Well, if you put it like that, lead the way, boy."

The house across the way was bathed in shadows and the owner led Shea Óg into the main room, where a man in a hood stood in the shadow of the fireplace.

"I give you and your master a message, Shea Óg," he said.

"Why should I not come over there and drag you into the open and beat the message out of you?"

"Because I come as a friend and we both want the same thing. Eunan Maguire dead. You can enrich yourself with the same information if you wish."

"Why get me to do your dirty work?

"Do you ask so many questions when your English masters assign you a task? I can give you the location of Eunan Maguire, and where the monies you stole from the people of Sligo are hidden, but we are prepared to overlook that for the death of Eunan Maguire."

"And who is prepared to overlook it? I like to know who I am working for."

"We offer you the chance for revenge and to enrich yourself and all you can do is ask questions?"

"So why come to me and not offer the information to the English? You'd get a lot more money."

"It is not money I am after. You have your reasons to see Eunan Maguire dead, and so do I."

"I get very suspicious of anyone who says they don't like money." Shea Óg raised his axe.

The man drew out a blade and Shea Óg saw the flash of a familiar design on it. Shea Óg lowered his axe.

"So you are Galloglass?"

"I am that and if you and your men assault me, even though I may die, I will take you with me."

"It is a strange honour you're showing to be such a traitor to your master."

"The Maguire dishonoured us by imposing Eunan Maguire, who is not even Galloglass, upon us. We must remove this stain and replace him with a true Galloglass and our honour will be redeemed. We cannot kill him ourselves, but it would benefit the both of us to see him dead."

Shea Óg's greed overcame his suspicion.

"Well, it's not worth a dagger in the belly to defend the honour of a traitor."

"Don't insult me, for I will remember you. Our truce ends at Eunan's death or your failure to kill him this night. After that, we shall meet on the battlefield and let the axe decide."

"That is the kind of bargain I like. Tell me where and when and I will release you into the night."

"Then the bargain is struck."

The hooded Galloglass whispered his secrets and disappeared into the shadows.

# CHAPTER 27

# NIGHT WORK

T he Maguire returned to camp at barely a trot in the early evening. He made his way through the camp and gave the briefest nod to his men, and he retired straight to his tent. He sent his bodyguards to summon the leaders of the Maguire to him. Eunan entered the tent to see his leader slumped in his chair staring out into space.

"What is the matter, lord?" he said as he silently contemplated whether he wished to hear the answer.

"We must wait until all the leaders are here," the Maguire mumbled.

The members of the Maguire aristocracy arrived in the tent in various states of sobriety for the men had found another source of ale.

"What is it, lord?" said one of the more inebriated clan leaders. "Have you summoned us here for one last bout of drink and song before we descend on Galway and burn it to the ground?"

The Maguire lifted his eyes in contempt and jealousy that one could remain in such high spirits given the news he was about to hear.

"The Spanish fleet is no more. It sank to the bottom of the sea with all its soldiers. We are alone once more."

The news was met with a deathly silence.

"Do we attack Galway now and take it while it is at its weakest?" said Feargal Beggan MacCabe.

"The O'Donnell has given the order to retreat. We leave for Fermanagh in the morning."

An audible groan rang around the tent.

"Contain your disappointment, men. We won a brilliant victory driving the enemy back so far. But we should take back the proceeds of the raid and regroup. The clans of the north will strike again but tonight we must rest before we set off home."

The men groaned and muttered amongst themselves as the Maguire dismissed them.

"Eunan, please stay," said the Maguire. "I have another mission for you."

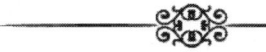

Eunan cleared the large tent in the middle of the camp of revellers who wished for one last night of alcohol before the sobering march home. The men may have grumbled at being evicted from their fires and comfortable seats, but Eunan ignored them, remembering his promise to the Maguire. He covered the sides of the tent and dug.

Shea Óg and his men saw the lumps in the shadows on Eunan's tent. They thanked God for their perceived good luck.

"Open the door and drag him out," said Shea Óg.

"Why don't we attack the tent?" the man whispered.

"In the middle of the camp?" said Shea Óg. "We're lucky they're so distracted by drink to get this far. Grab him by the feet and I'll bash him over the head as you pull him out."

An axe quietly sliced through the strings that tied the door to Eunan's tent. The man felt for Eunan's feet but could not find them. He stuck his head in the tent so he could see inside. An excruciating scream of pain quickly became muffled. Shea Óg looked around in panic. The surrounding tents were beginning to move. Shea Óg knew he had just one chance. He reached inside and grabbed his man by the shoulders and tugged as hard as he could. The man's lifeless body fell out with the jaws of an Irish wolfhound wrapped around his face. Sionn let go and growled. Olcan bit his way out of the other side of the tent to support his sister. He emitted a blood-curdling low growl and slowly paced forward, drool falling from between his teeth. The intruders huddled together and swung their axes to keep the dogs at a distance. Maguires emerged from their tents, armed themselves, and called for their comrades. Shea Óg pushed his men towards the dogs to buy himself some time. With the dogs' attention suitably distracted, Shea Óg saw his chance.

"Run!"

Taaffe had recovered enough, mainly motivated by the thought of getting his treasure back, to come on the mission. He had found enough of his men still sufficiently reliable to be trusted in a night assault to crawl up the hill upon which the Maguires were camped.

"We must get to the large tent in the middle of the camp. Pretend to be O'Haras if anyone asks. They turn coat so often nobody ever knows whose side they're on."

The Maguire guards were lax that night and Taaffe and his small party pene-trated far inside the camp and waited hidden in the shadows of the night while they watched Eunan dig.

Eunan and his men dug out the various treasure trunks and loaded them onto covered carts. He heard the commotion coming from his section of tents and dispatched some of his men to investigate. The moon ducked behind a cloud and Taaffe signalled to his men to attack. His men crept around the tents. They set upon Eunan's men and gained temporary control of the carts.

"WE ARE BEING ASSAULTED! WE ARE BEING ASSAULTED!" cried Eunan towards the Maguire's tent.

Taaffe and his men had little stomach for the fight and fled into the night. The Maguire and his bodyguards rushed out only to find Eunan tending to the wounded remains of his men. They searched the area as best they could, but found no one.

"Look, lord!" One of the Maguire's men pointed south.

The fire torches of a large body of men crawled across the landscape in their direction. Another man shouted from the west of the camp. A similar body of men was visible, aimed at the camp of the O'Donnell.

"What shall we do, lord?" asked the Maguire constables of him. "Shall we stand and fight? Shall we charge out with the horse? Shall we send messengers to the O'Donnell to co-ordinate with him?"

But the Maguire knew that the news of the sinking of the Spanish fleet had hit the O'Donnell hard and sapped him of his will to fight.

"Summon the men and tell them we leave now to retire to Fermanagh in good order. The O'Donnell and our allies will make the same preparations. The MacCabes and the horse will cover our retreat. Eunan, get that baggage train moving."

Eunan nodded to his master. He had not been asked for much, only to lug heavy treasure across Connacht and hold off all the Queen's forces while doing so. He went to rally his men.

Taaffe and Shea Óg rallied in a prearranged spot in a nearby forest through bird calls to show who they were.

"Were we set up?" said Taaffe.

"I think we were sent in good faith," said Shea Óg. "I didn't kill Eunan Maguire."

"I know. I met him."

"What shall we do? We won't kill him this night."

"But I can still get my treasure back. Clifford sallies forth from Galway and soon the rebels will run. You can't run with all that loot, so we can steal it back."

"So all we have to do is wait?" said Shea Óg.

"A little more than that. They'll never be able to tell us apart in the dark. We will disguise ourselves as O'Haras once more and wait for our opportunity to strike."

Eunan loaded the carts as rebel fires were stamped out all along the ridge. The night sky decorated by patches of thick cloud were of no use to either side so it had to be watched carefully to move at the most opportune time while both sides tried to creep around to disguise to the other side what they were up to. Discipline was on an axe's edge on the side of the rebels. The Maguire rode around the camp encouraging the men to take their tents and their pikes, the first items a running man would usually abandon. The discipline of the allies the rebels picked up on the march south proved to be much more volatile and they soon took to their heels, abandoning anything that could slow them down. However, the Maguires had begun their retreat in good order.

It had drizzled constantly for the past couple of days, but whilst the night was dry, the ground underfoot was waterlogged and, as the carts were loaded up, they sank in the mud. Eunan and his men tried to dig out the wheels, but some carts were stuck fast. Eunan got a poke in the back as he and his men tried to free one cart.

"We've got to go," said Feargal. "The enemy horse is climbing the hill and will soon engage us. We'll all be dead if we're caught out in the open. No matter what is in these chests the Maguire won't thank you for losing his best men."

"The Maguire told me to bring the carts and I'll do just that. Hold the line in front of us to allow the rest to leave. I'll send the carts that can move to catch up with the main column and free the rest. Have courage, my friend. The darkness of the night will protect us."

"There are many creatures of the night I have no wish to meet and fear they are all coming towards me. I can give you some time, but not much blood of my men."

"Let me push, and I'll let you fight. One last heave, men, and this beast will be on its way to Fermanagh."

Odhran returned from the camp with some men and the dogs of his master. The dogs jumped up and licked Eunan's face. Eunan pawed them away. He wiped his mouth.

"That is blood I taste and not my own," said Eunan to Odhran.

"Some fools tried to attack your tent, and we found your hounds mauling their dead bodies."

"If only all men could be as loyal as my dogs. Odhran, wrap your men around that wheel and we'll give this cart one more push before we contemplate abandoning it."

They gave one last almighty heave and dislodged the rear wheels from their pit. Some men filled the pit with hard wood so the wheels would not roll back again.

"Get this cart on the road and only two more to go."

Eunan struggled as the night wore on until morning, such was his determination that the Maguire should return home with his booty. By the time he freed the final two carts and set them on the road, the Maguire horse had engaged the enemy and the Crown shot was almost within range and patiently waiting for twilight. Feargal MacCabe was already fending off scouting parties making their way up the hill. Eunan gathered his men to screen the carts and sent Odhran ahead to catch up with the other carts so they could all travel together.

Daylight broke and the forces of the Crown stormed the ridge and any men covering the rebels' retreat were dislodged and a full-blown pursuit began. Feargal MacCabe soon caught up with Eunan as he was on foot, trailing behind the last of the carts.

"You'll have to abandon them or you will sacrifice all your men for nothing," said Feargal with a tut in his mouth.

"Why are you so insolent towards me, the head of the MacCabes and your master? Why are you so insistent that I leave the carts?"

"Being a Galloglass and the leader of the MacCabes is not about throwing the lives of your men away all in the search of glory. You must preserve your men, for they are the most precious resource you have. There'll be other raids and more loot to be had."

"Until the Maguire tells me different, then I am staying with the carts," said Eunan obstinately.

"If you insist on such a course of action, I will go ahead with my men and find the Maguire and send him back to you."

"I order you to stay and defend the carts!" said Eunan.

"If I lived to tell the tale, I could not look the families of the men we would lose in the eye and explain why their brothers and sons had to die. Goodbye, Eunan Maguire, I hope you find the glory you are looking for."

Despite Eunan's protests, Feargal and his men marched past him to catch up with the rest of the clan.

Taaffe and Shea Óg welcomed the morning light, for the night had not looked favourably upon them and left them in a forest to lick their wounds. It had not taken long for them to spot Eunan and the carts, but there were too many rebels around for them to steal their loot back. They shadowed Eunan and the carts at a distance until they saw Feargal MacCabe march away from him.

"Now is our opportunity." Taaffe grinned at Shea Óg.

"There are plenty of vultures around now it is light," said Shea Óg. "It won't be long until the Queen's forces catch up with them. There is no time for us to whisk the carts away."

"Exactly. That is why we must take possession of them now and lay our claim. You must lead the attack, for I am still hurt. Do you have enough men to take them?"

"If we make enough noise, hopefully, fear will do most of the work for us."

The land in front of Eunan was flat and he could see the rears of the different rebel armies grow ever distant whilst the horse of his pursuers grew ever nearer.

"Should we abandon the carts and run back and join the Maguire?" said one of Eunan's men in his ear.

"He promised he will come and he will come. Have faith."

The path meandered through a gap between two large rocks protruding from the ground. Eunan walked up towards the gap in front of the carts. In the distance, he could see a body of men advancing towards them.

"Come men, hurry along. The Maguire is here to protect us."

The men whipped the horses to go faster, and the carts passed through the rocky gorge. As they did, a volley of darts struck them and Shea Óg and his men jumped from behind the rocks. They fell upon Eunan's men and their surprise was complete due to exhaustion and the replacement of vigilance with hope.

Whilst his men fell around him, Eunan was lucky, for he was out of range for anyone to leap upon him from an elevated position. Taaffe's men leapt down and struck who they landed near. Eunan advanced upon them and swung his six-foot axe. A stomach was sliced open. A blow came from the side, but Eunan parried and took out the knee with a swing of the axe. He had no time to finish the opponent off for a blow came towards his head. This one connected and sent him reeling. It was a dull thud, and he felt no blood on the side of his face. Shea Óg had spotted Eunan, and his men circled him like wild dogs. Eunan saw his men fall one by one and Taaffe's men swarm all over the carts he had sacrificed so much to defend. Shea Óg and his men closed in on him.

"I've been waiting a long time for this," said Shea Óg.

Eunan felt a pain in his head and then nothing.

## CHAPTER 28

# IMPOSTOR SYNDROME

Eunan awoke surrounded by friendly faces. Through the blur, he made out Odhran, Cúchonnacht Óg, and some men he served with.

"Am I dead?" he said.

"Well, let's see, shall we?"

Cúchonnacht Óg took out a flask and poured a little down Eunan's throat. He coughed and spluttered as feeling followed the water down his oesophagus.

"Well, I never heard they had water in heaven," he said.

"Nor in hell," came the reply.

Feeling gradually returned to Eunan's body, and he heard the trotting of the horses and the rolling of the wheels over uneven terrain. Cúchonnacht Óg tried to pour more water down his throat, but Eunan reached out, took the flask from him, and helped himself. Everyone left Eunan alone until he had sufficiently recovered his senses to ask the obvious question.

"Where are we?" and the next obvious question: "What happened?"

"You're all right and that's the main thing," said Odhran.

"What happened to the carts?" said Eunan, as his memory flooded back. "And the men?"

Odhran and Cúchonnacht Óg looked at each other, inviting the other to speak first. Cúchonnacht Óg knew Eunan the longest, so he took the responsibility.

"Odhran made it back to the main body of our men and told us of your obstinate defence of the carts because the Maguire had told you to do it. We knew it was foolhardy, so Odhran, my brother and I rallied some men to go back and rescue you. By the time we got there, the carts were lost, and you were surrounded. They were about to descend upon you, so the men fired a volley of missiles, one of which accidentally connected with your head. Luckily, your head is so thick it just bounced off and knocked you out. It did the trick, however, and we could retrieve you and some men. Thanks to your efforts, however, we kept half the carts that you sent ahead, and the Maguire is giving back to those clans that support the O'Donnell what they can identify. We are almost back in Enniskillen where you will remain until you are well enough to return to Augher Castle."

Eunan lay back, his head a mixture of guilt and pain.

"Am I one of the few survivors? Did I throw those men's lives away for nothing?"

"Rest your head and get some sleep," said Cúchonnacht Óg. "The sacrifice of you and your men gave the rest of the Maguire army the chance to escape. You are a hero in Enniskillen. The duty of a Galloglass is to cover the escape of the rest and you did just that. Sacrifice is part of war. Rest for you will soon be in Enniskillen and everyone will want to shake your hand."

But he was up on his elbows once again.

"Odhran, my hounds? Where are my hounds?"

"Rest, lord. They have been sent back to live with your wife while you recuperate. Now rest, lord."

Eunan lay his head down and before he could contemplate what had happened, he was asleep.

The next time Eunan awoke he was on a bed in Enniskillen Castle being tended by the maids of the Maguire.

"You need to get better for tonight the Maguire holds a feast in your honour, lord," one cooed as she fluttered her eyelashes at him. Eunan neither recognised the girl nor the bed where he lay. His pain returned with such a speed his memory could only trail in its wake. He tried to move his legs. They ached both in pain and in the longing for a stretch. He lifted his head only to trigger more aches and pains in his back.

"I have to walk first and God only knows I can't tell you the last time I took a step," Eunan said.

"Sling your legs out of the bed and let me help you up. If you can walk to the door with me as a crutch, you should at least be able to make it to the great hall."

The young woman stretched her arms out and, with some gasps and wheezes, helped him first place his feet on the floor and then support his body weight. They stumbled across the floor until Eunan could support his own weight. He could soon walk the length of the room unaided.

"Has someone sent word to my wife that I am all right?"

The young woman looked at the ground.

"You would have to ask the Maguire. You'll meet him soon enough."

A servant came to give notice that Eunan was soon to be called to the great hall for the celebration in his honour. Eunan arrived with only the torn shirt on his back, so Cúchonnacht Óg had arranged for some clothes to be sent to him. They were laid out on the bed and when Eunan showed little interest in them, the maid took it upon herself to make a selection.

"My, you look quite the lord," she said, admiring her taste as it covered Eunan's body.

"I hate getting stuffed into these clothes," Eunan said. "It just makes me feel more of a fraud."

"No one will see beyond the handsome, heroic warrior that stands before me," the maid said as she brushed down the creases in the folds around Eunan's shoulders.

Eunan scowled in the mirror as the maid placed a hat on his head to hide his bandages. There was a knock on the door and when it was opened, it revealed two scowls worse than Eunan's.

"The Maguire has instructed us to escort you to the celebration," said Feargal, who tried to speak in a monotone to hide his discomfort at being given such a task.

"If you must, then we'll go," said Eunan. He brushed off the attempts by his two constables to take his arms to help him walk.

"As you like, lord," said Cearbhall.

But it was as he liked until he reached the foot of the stairs. Eunan held his arms out.

"There is a time for every Galloglass to do his duty."

The MacCabe guards on the door of the great hall patted Eunan on the back before they flung open the doors to the cheers of those inside. Feargal gritted his teeth as he helped Eunan hobble past the cheering Maguires and he and Cearbhall supported Eunan to the hero's seat beside the Maguire. Feargal and Cearbhall sat at the edge of the top table. Feargal shuffled in his seat as he watched the Maguire salute and celebrate Eunan's exploits.

Eunan's head ached a lot worse as he had to drink some ale every time some-one proposed a toast to him. He wished the floor would open up and swallow him, for he felt like a complete fraud in receiving the accolades of the Maguire when he felt they were using him to cover up a defeat and the disappointment of the Spanish fleet sinking. He longed to get back to his wife. But it would be many a toast before the Maguire would release him. But his heart warmed when the men of the MacCabes came and saluted him.

He went down amongst the men to receive their accolades. Feargal MacCabe came up from behind him.

"Congratulations, you convinced everyone you understand the ethos of the Galloglass when what you did was out of lust for glory. The Maguire may trust you but he is young and foolish with no regard for the lives of his men if they impede him from being immortalised on one of his precious tapestries. The MacCabes had to come and rescue you and all they got was you back and the false praise to cover up a defeat. Let that be a lesson to you."

Feargal stepped away. Eunan's head spun. Such was the state of his jumbled memory that he could not remember if Feargal saved or abandoned him. He would have to tread carefully to find out which.

## CHAPTER 29

# MOMENTS OF HAPPINESS

Eunan had to endure a week of celebrations before the Maguire released him. He was seen off to the gates of Enniskillen Castle by the Maguire himself and given two hundred MacCabes to go north with him to Augher Castle so they could train while Eunan convalesced. Eunan sat in a cart for he had not recovered enough to ride a horse and his men made their way north on a blue-skied day in October.

Eunan was granted even more time to mull over the dreams that skulked in the back of his brain, only to emerge when he was most vulnerable. He was at the birth of his sister and his mother rose from her bed holding his newly born sister by the leg upside-down and invited Eunan to come nearer. As he did so, he could see the blue of his sister's skin flow down towards her head. Out of the shadows came Sorcha, and his mother passed the blue baby to Sorcha, who took it by the other leg. Sorcha walked towards him with the dead baby held aloft. He always woke up at that part. He pulled his blanket over himself, but it was little comfort. If he was not dozing off, slipping into his dream, he was overcome with guilt for abandoning his wife just as her dream had been ripped out of her.

A MacCabe rode ahead to the castle, so when Eunan emerged from the woods and the castle came into view, a little party was waiting outside to cheer the Maguire hero up the hill. The cart rolled to a halt and Eunan dropped his blanket, stood up, and waved to acknowledge the well-wishers. There below him stood his wife, her head poking through a thick blanket.

"Welcome back, my hero." Her smile was as radiant as any summer sun.

Eunan climbed off the cart and took her in his arms. His face held a pinkish hue, not just from the wind on the exposed hill.

"I'm no hero. You're far braver than me to lose a child and then have your husband run off."

"I always knew I had to share you. We both have duties to do."

Eunan wrapped his arms around her shoulder and they walked through a line of cheering well-wishers and into the castle.

Eunan, the new hero, had to endure a celebratory dinner as the guest of honour with his relatives. He had to raise his glass and smile to every salute as Sorcha played footsie with him and tried to sneak her bare foot up his breeches. She smiled up at him, but it was bittersweet for Eunan as she looked unwell, as if she should have been in bed. When the toasts were over and the feast had broken down into drunkenness, Eunan leaned over and borrowed his father-in-law's ear.

"It is time for this hero to retire and get reacquainted with his wife."

Cormac grimaced and stroked his chin.

"Be careful with her in body and in heart. She is my delicate flower."

"And mine," Eunan said. "I will join you with the men tomorrow, but for now, I bid you farewell." He smiled at his father-in-law to be once more met by his grimace.

Eunan flung open the door to his wife's room and carried her across the threshold. Sorcha laughed as she draped her arms around his neck. Eunan's romantic gesture did not last long for his two hounds bounded over to greet him, almost bowling over their master and mistress. Eunan placed Sorcha down on the bed and went to cuddle his dogs.

"I have missed you both so much," Eunan said as he ruffled the fur on the crowns of their heads. "No home is complete without a hound."

Sorcha smiled sweetly from the bed. Eunan smiled back but realised how she had interpreted what he said.

"No, I mean every home should have a hound, not that this is my home because my hounds are -"

"Why don't you shut up whilst you're ahead," Sorcha said.

Eunan sat on the bed and tried to hide his blushes. Sorcha watched his mind work as he finally decided what he thought was the correct thing to say.

"I am so glad to be back here with you -"

"In your home."

"Well, I have my estates in south Fermanagh that I thought we would always go to live at?"

Sorcha tilted her head.

"Do you think my father would let me live there?"

"Yes, yes, I do actually. It would be far better for your health than living in this windswept tower."

Eunan got off the bed and paced.

"He would never let me leave," Sorcha said.

"I can persuade him. I am the hero of the north. He cannot refuse me."

"I know how we can persuade him."

"How?"

"If I prove I am well."

"And how do you do that?"

Sorcha drew herself to the end of the bed and stared at Eunan.

"By having a baby."

Eunan clenched his fist.

"You are barely over the death of our first child. Are you well enough to try for another? How can I fight knowing I have made you ill and potentially that you may lose another child?"

Sorcha's smile evaporated and her face hardened.

"So you can do your duty, but I cannot do mine?"

"It is not about duty."

"Then what is it about? My health? I can do it, I know I can."

Eunan turned his back on her.

"I don't know if I can do it again so soon."

Sorcha reached her hand out to him.

"You are here for the winter. You can leave me with child in the spring when you return to fight."

Eunan turned around.

"Let me have one night in peace with my wife and I will consider it."

Sorcha leapt out of bed and threw the blankets to the side.

"Your bed awaits, my lord."

Eunan spent most of the winter suffering the castle's cold and exposed location and not appreciating its strategic positioning, which was far more apparent in the months of spring and summer. Every arrow hole was an orifice to be penetrated and violated by the gusts of freezing wind. Each hole would whistle its distress as the wind blew through. On his restless nights, Eunan dreamt of English saboteurs sneaking into the tent of an ancient O'Neill and making a mischief of their drawings for a new castle. If only besiegers knew they would only have to wait until winter before the defenders would go mad with the cold and howling of banshees.

But the winter conditions did not seem to affect Cormac. To him, it was like a solid army camp on a hill. A constant hardship to ensure one did not go soft. But the womenfolk of the family insisted that he hone those sharp edges so their rooms were on the less exposed eastern side of the castle, with fireplaces and tapestries to provide warmth and home comfort. Eunan flittered between both worlds, between his duties as a soldier or a husband, but not to his convenience.

After witnessing the effect the winter had on Sorcha's health, Eunan wondered why such a sickly woman as his wife would be confined to a windy tower on a hill and why her father, a man of obvious wealth and influence, would not build her a house in a valley. Perhaps beside a wood to act as a windbreaker for the northern winter winds and leave her to convalesce and see if she could fully recover from whatever ailed her. It would be far better than the string of priests praying for her soul, the constant bloodletting and the occasional unconventional physician that Cormac would get from all the ends of Ireland, who would promise the world and leave her paler and sicker than ever.

But through these cold winter months, a husband would visit his sickly wife and his warming embrace would get more serious and in the morning, the wife would be happy and hopeful. When the illness would return, she would embrace it and spend her mornings as her husband trained in the fields debating with her physicians whether this symptom or that was outside her normal pattern of illness so that she could conclude she was pregnant. Most mornings she was disappointed, but some mornings left her with hope. When her husband returned from the fields, she would persuade him to return to bed, no matter if he was tired or if he did not want to bear the responsibility of making her feel unwell again.

Then one afternoon as her husband trudged up the hill home for what he thought was the thousandth time she called out to him from the tower.

"Eunan, Eunan, come to me."

A panic overcame Eunan for he thought his wife was sick again. He ran up the hill, up the stairs, and to her room. His wife stood side on, her dress pulled up so her belly was exposed.

"Look," Sorcha said. "Can you see it? If you look at it side on, you can see I am with child."

Eunan was now worried about his wife's sanity and her health. She was obsessed with becoming pregnant and Eunan felt once more like a stud horse. He tilted his head, if more to humour his wife than with any belief that her skinny white waist had expanded any.

"Have you eaten recently or is a deceptive shadow cast upon your belly?" Eunan said.

"No, it definitely looks bigger."

Cormac stood in the doorway and pondered his daughter's stomach. Sorcha's calling for Eunan had attracted Cormac's guards at the same time who had gone to fetch him.

"No, I definitely think it has grown bigger. I'll fetch the physician, but you should get into bed and keep warm just in case."

Sorcha became the centre of attention once more as the physician declared she was pregnant and her father was determined to mollycoddle her up to the point of her delivering the child. Eunan became an observer.

Spring came, and the skies cleared of their grey swirling porridge of rain and sleet and sometimes would even be a clear blue. The winds barely relented, but at least it was consistently a little warmer. All during this time, Sorcha endured her pregnancy. From the day she told her father, she was ill. Eunan fought with her father for access as Cormac did not want her to be overwhelmed with visitors and suffer from tiredness and stress. Eunan went to visit her every day and held her hand and read to her to keep her calm.

Cormac saw how good Eunan was for his daughter's wellbeing and had a more favourable disposition to him now it appeared his daughter's pregnancy had taken, so he recalled the Maguire Galloglass from Dungannon and borrowed some trainers from his brother and allowed the MacCabes to camp beneath the hill and train there. Eunan seemed much happier to descend the hill each day and train with his men, and his wife would wrap herself in a blanket and go to the window in the tower and watch her husband train all day. He would return in the evening and if she was feeling well enough, they would sit at a table in her room and eat their evening meal. Eunan would regale her with his adventures of the past, suitably tailored for his audience, and Cormac would hear his daughter's faint laughter echo through the corridors.

The MacCabe trained in the fields of the MacBaron over the spring of that year. Red Hugh raided Connacht but did not invite his Ulster ally to join him. The MacCabe were becoming formidable units of shot and pike, as good as any the O'Neills could field. Unfortunately, they only numbered one hundred men as that was all the Maguire could spare as he was supporting the O'Reillys in reclaiming their land and he also needed a force for a deterrent against Connor Roe on one side and Sir Conyers Clifford on the other.

One day Eunan was out on exercises with the men when Cormac sent for him. Eunan ran up the stairs and down the corridor to Sorcha's room. There was a wall of wailing women outside her room, blocking the door.

"What's happened?" said Eunan to anyone. "Is she...? It can't be."

He forced his way past the women and the two hapless guards and into the room.

The room was dimly lit with candles on the table and the windowsills surrounding the bed. Melancholy hung in the air like the black smoke of a burning carcass. Cormac sat on the edge of the bed, a pale hand in his. Eunan forced his way past the physicians and maids. Panic possessed him as a madness of the mind.

"No, it can't be!"

He looked down at the bed, and Sorcha's chest moved up and down with a gentle wheeze. But beneath her chest was a bed and blanket covered in lashings of blood. Her belly was empty.

"He could do nothing about it."

Cormac pointed to the physician. The emotion trembled in his voice. The rock of the O'Neill generals shed a tear from his eye but quickly hid it in his sleeve.

Sorcha's face was a pale shade of white, in a certain light translucent. Eunan sat on the bed on the other side from her father and took her other hand in his. Her hand sat cold, pale and limp in his palm, with the occasional twitch to show she still lived.

"Excuse me, master."

The words were faint, as if at the bottom of a well. Cormac looked up at the ceiling and prayed, hoping the angle would force his tears back into his eyes.

"Excuse me, master."

"What is it!?" Cormac hissed.

"If we wish to save your daughter too, then we need to clean her up and get her warm again. May you take your leave and let the maids and I do our work?"

Cormac lay his child's hand gently on the bed and rose to his full height.

"The baby was -"

"A boy, lord."

Cormac shuddered, but years of command on the battlefield allowed him to regain his composure quickly.

"Wrap the boy in swaddling clothes, and we will bring him to the family graveyard. He will be buried as an O'Neill."

Cormac signalled to Eunan to follow him, for they would bury the baby together.

# CHAPTER 30

# THE CAVE

The taking of Ballinacor in September 1596 was a pure provocation to Lord Deputy Russell, and he immediately launched an offensive into Wicklow with all the forces he could muster. He quickly recaptured Ballinacor and an attritional war to the death began. The towns and villages of Wicklow burned as they changed sides multiple times. The failure of the Second Spanish Armada in October of that year was an immense blow to Fiach, his men deserted and his alliances collapsed. This was compounded with the death of Barnaby O'Toole in January 1597, Fiach's wife Rose's brother. Fiach tried to shore this up by marrying more O'Toole women to his sons, but to no avail. He was soon left with his core O'Byrne/O'Toole supporters and the men Seamus had supplied him with. They were low on hope and ammunition, and the winter bit them cold and hard. Fiach sent his wife Rose to the local English commanders to see if a secret truce could be negotiated.

Seamus had left soon after Fiach took Ballinacor, for he had to report back to the O'Donnell regarding his mission. He had attempted several times to reinforce Fiach with men and ammunition over the winter. Still, Russell had cut off Wicklow, so Fiach made do and Seamus resupplied Uaithne and Richard instead. Uaithne also attempted to penetrate into Wicklow but was foiled every time. Fiach was on his own.

The death and destruction of the ongoing war erased any sympathy for Fiach or pretence of neutrality for most of the north Wicklow O'Byrnes and they actively joined the hunt for Fiach. Phelim O'Byrne took it upon himself to escape the mountains and seek help. He dodged the English hunting parties in the mountains and reached the plains below. He rode for where he thought Uaithne may have set his camp but discovered only the ashes of long burned-out fires. At a point of high despair, he set out north. He remembered the way to O'Cassidy house and when he arrived, Dervella and Arthur redirected him north to Tirconnell, where Seamus was busy training the O'Donnell's men. They gave Phelim a guide and a good meal and several days later, Phelim arrived in Donegal town. Once the guards at Donegal Castle established who he was, an audience with the O'Donnell was arranged and Seamus was summoned to the castle.

Phelim sat in a small cold room in a tower in the castle, a picture of nervous exhaustion. He was young, but the stresses of the past six months would wear down even the most resilient mind. He sat and ate the best meal since he left Wicklow except for the one at O'Cassidy house. Seamus was the first to arrive, and he greeted Phelim warmly. Phelim was glad of the embrace, for he was unsure of what kind of reception he would get given their differences in the past. Seamus held him by the elbows with sincere concern.

"How is your father? Have they finally trapped him? What can I do to help my old friend?"

Phelim pulled away, physically and mentally exhausted.

"I fear this is it. He is hunted like a dog. The only way I think we can save him is to smuggle him up north. It is no longer safe for him in the mountains because his family seeks to give him up. But I fear he will never leave."

The O'Donnell entered the room preceded by O'Gallagher. He also embraced Phelim warmly.

"Sit. Tell me, what news of the rebellion down south?"

"I have only grim news to tell you, lord. I have come alone and put myself in danger by coming here, but if I remained and we were not rescued surely we would all die."

The O'Donnell, O'Gallagher and Seamus stood around Phelim. The O'Donnell slapped Seamus on the back.

"No better man than this one here to save you. I had many a task lined up for this man, but none more important than saving my lifelong allies. I remember when I escaped from Dublin and I lay by the roadside wondering if death would take me in the prime of my youth, the O'Byrnes and O'Tooles came and saved me, for which I am eternally grateful. Therefore, consider one of my best men and whatever he needs to fulfil his task at your disposal. I'm sorry if it appears rude that I must leave now, but you'll understand if my actions in the next few weeks draw the heat away from Wicklow and allow you to retreat or resupply, whatever you think is best. You have my best wishes and my resources at your disposal."

With that, the O'Donnell bowed and left with O'Gallagher not far behind him.

"You'd better tell me what you need then?" said Seamus to Phelim's obvious delight.

They waited for several weeks, for as promised, the O'Donnell drew many English soldiers from Leinster into Connacht and allowed Seamus and Phelim to proceed south virtually unmolested. Phelim wanted to take a considerable body of men with them to fight and also to carry supplies of ammunition. Still, Seamus cautioned against and they brought some hand-picked men with them to ensure they got through rather than bring supplies. They met up with Uaithne once more, who escorted them through Leinster. The resistance was more considerable in the Wicklow foothills, so they had to go around and through the lands of Domhnall MacMurrough Kavanagh and approach from the south. English patrols criss-crossed the mountains and Phelim did not know where his father was hiding. They had to lie low for a week whilst Phelim located his father and worked out how they could safely go to him.

He hid in a farmhouse down by the south coast. He had been caught out by the English patrols led by loyalist O'Byrnes who knew the mountain passes as well as Fiach but had lesser knowledge of his many hideouts. Fiach's scouts immediately recognised Phelim and sent him to the house with Seamus. A much paler and thinner Fiach hobbled out of the house to greet them.

"My boy, why did you leave me? I thought your head was turned, and you joined those hunting me down? And you, Seamus. Are you my saviour? Have you swept down from the north with guns and men to free me?"

Seamus looked around at the men Fiach surrounded himself with. Three veterans, a handful of men he had brought from up north, and farm boys surely timing their defection. Seamus spat on the ground and walked towards the house.

"If this is all you've got, I've come all this way to be sent to my grave. If you can't muster any more men than this, we're leaving, and if you're smart, you'll come with us."

Fiach ran after him, a panic in his voice as if Seamus was the last log to be thrown on the fire and a freezing night was ahead.

"No, no. There are bands of my men all over these mountains. We just don't want to gather right now because the English were too strong. We hid some weapons and evacuated some men when your master up north went on the attack again, but Russell came back with renewed vigour. But I've survived up here for all these years and Rose has gone to negotiate a peace settlement and there'll be another truce. There always is. All I've got to do is hide out for long enough."

As Seamus turned to face him, his lips trembled.

"I have indulged you on my master's behalf for long enough. I have not come here to die. Pack your things and let us leave."

Fiach waggled his finger and walked backwards into the house.

"I'm not leaving. If you want to go, then go now. Don't offer me hope if you don't mean to follow through with it."

Seamus turned and signalled to his men.

"Leave the guns and the spare ammo. We are going home."

Uaithne obeyed, but Phelim pursued to argue.

"You can't abandon my father like that!?"

Seamus kept walking.

"I can and I will. This place is not safe. I won't sit here and argue with him whilst one of those boys sells him for a silver coin. He has taken leave of his senses."

Phelim looked back at his father walking into the house. His heart was a mixture of frustration and anger. But he knew his efforts would surely be better spent scouting for English patrols than waiting in the house with his father. He followed Seamus but left his father with a couple of guards.

They found a campsite in a couple of caves higher in the mountains. The trees were tall and climbable and would make good lookout posts. But that would be for the morning. A thick blanket of clouds cut them off from the night sky so it was a time for rest, not spying. Seamus set his watches up on the top of the mountain and they all settled down to get some well-earned rest.

"Seamus! Seamus!"

Seamus woke up in a daze. Was it his body waking him up because he needed to piss, or did someone really want his attention?

"Seamus! Seamus!"

He had his answer and the urgency in the voice said he needed to respond before he could relieve himself. He left the cave and looked around to see where the voice was coming from.

"Seamus!"

It was from the trees he noticed would make good lookouts.

"There's a plume of smoke coming from Fiach's house. It's a signal there could be something wrong."

Seamus ran back into the cave.

"Everybody up and arm yourselves!"

They grabbed their weapons and spread out across the forest to spot and evade English patrols. They soon came across several and had to retreat and regroup. Seamus stood in the centre of his men after they reassembled in a forest clearing.

"Uaithne, can you draw away the patrols into the mountains and Phelim and I will check out the house? We'll meet back at the campsite at nightfall."

An agreement was reached and Seamus and Phelim made their way cautiously to the house while Uaithne provided the distraction. They hid on the other side of the clearing opposite the house. An English patrol was examining the scene and digging some graves for their dead. Fiach's bodyguards were left lying on the ground. The smell of smoke was almost overwhelming.

"There's nothing for us here," said Seamus. "If they have your father, dead or alive, they'll be dragging him back to Dublin. Let us go back into the mountains and lie low. We can send out our spies to find out what happened."

Phelim nodded his agreement, and they set off back into the woods.

They spent several weeks roaming the mountains under the guidance of Phelim, using the many hideouts that Fiach had spread across the range. They got suspicious when the number of English patrols fell and rebels did not come to occupy the gaps they left. They went to the top of the mountain range to observe what was occurring in the county. Uaithne observed from the foothills of Dublin, all the way to the mountain peaks and back down to the Irish sea.

"They are definitely withdrawing," he said.

Seamus was not blessed with such good eyesight.

"If they're withdrawing, they have either completed their mission and Fiach is dead or a major offensive has been launched up north by either side and they need the men."

Phelim looked nervous.

"My father will hide in a cave somewhere and will emerge, eventually."

Seamus was more realistic.

"Something's not right. He would have emerged by now."

"Then we should head south and seek my brother. He may know what happened."

They spent the next couple of days picking their way through the forests and mountain paths, being sure to avoid the English patrols until they were in the foothills. Redmond O'Byrne had found himself a farmhouse in Kavanagh country, where he could hide out. His spies quickly spotted a gang of renegades clambering down the mountains, the mud on their clothes giving them away if the smell did not. Phelim was quickly recognised and his brother warmly welcomed him into the house.

It was a modest building with all the rudiments a farmer would need, a large kitchen and table, a porch to clean himself off, a roaring fire to warm him after his day's labours, a pantry for the storage of food and two bedrooms so the parents would have the luxury of not having to sleep in the same room as their children. This house had been adapted, however, at the planning and instigation of rebels, with hiding places both as coverable pits outside and the entrances to tunnels inside so the occupants could hide themselves and weapons should the soldiers come.

Redmond's wife was inside the house alongside her husband and offered warm replacement clothing as she asked for the clothes of the mountain rebels to see if she could clean them and make them fit for reuse. Redmond put a pig on the spit, gave refreshments to his guests and sat to exchange news with his brother and Seamus.

"Where have you been, Phelim? How come Seamus is here? I fear you have come too late."

Phelim eyed his brother nervously.

"Why do you say that? Where is our father?"

Redmond's face dropped.

"I am sorry to bring you such sad news, but his head is on a spike in Dublin Castle. There was an enormous explosion on the Dublin docks. Our spies tell us it was an accident and someone set off barrels of gunpowder as they were being unloaded from the ships. All of Dublin was in mourning for hundreds were killed and tremendous damage was done. Russell blamed our father and said it was sabotage. He tripled the price on his head and all the loyal or wavering O'Byrnes came running. One of our brethren gave away his hiding place and led them to him. Our father defended bravely and fought his way out of his hiding place, but was wounded in the battle. He fled into the forest and hid in a cave. One of his few remaining bodyguards went to get a physician he thought he could trust. He brought him back, and the man examined my father. Under the pretence of going into the woods to get herbal medicine, he fetched a patrol instead and his escort were killed. They then went to the cave and dragged my father out and beheaded him."

Redmond's final few words were pregnant with emotion, and the room fell silent. Seamus almost fainted. His stomach went into contortions and blackness descended upon his soul. He cast his arms out as if a blind man.

"I've got to get out of here."

Redmond's wife opened the door, tears streaming down her cheeks. Seamus guided himself along the walls as his eyes welled up and he almost fell out of the door frame when he came upon it. He stumbled through the farmyard past the distressed chickens and wallowing pigs. Their smells did not even register on his nostrils. He fell by a fence and threw up.

Phelim followed him out, the guilt a torturous black cloud upon his face.

"We could have helped him."

"I know, I know."

Seamus sobbed bitter tears into the sleeves of his fresh shirt.

They stayed in the house and its vicinity for several days mourning, for nobody could do much else such was the shock of the severing of the patriarchal head. Seamus was cast into a black pit. He had not been in a pit so deep since the death of his father. He could barely raise the energy to leave the house. Guilt had him in a vice, and he took to the drink and Fiach's sons watched as another heroic warrior seeped in the myths of the Galloglass of the past diminished before them.

Seamus wandered in the woods, wondering what beast had swallowed his friend, the bear of the Wicklow mountains, the colossus of Glenmalure, the most feared rebel in all of Ireland. That he of all people should end a sad husk of a man, betrayed by his own family and slain in a cave. Seamus went back to his youth, to his first days as a rebel in the mountains as part of a band of MacSheehy Galloglass who fled the defeat of their master, the Earl of Desmond, to take to the highest hills they could see before Seamus's eyes dimmed and betrayed him. Fiach was a few years older than him and took a shine to him. He had taught him how to fight in the mountains and woods, how to spring the perfect ambush, and how to live off the land. Fiach was his rock when he wallowed in the pity of the defeat of the MacSheehy, and how did he repay him? When Fiach was at his lowest, he walked away thinking he was teaching him a lesson but really leaving him to his death. But was this Fiach's ultimate revenge, to steal away his yearning for revenge, to re-establish the MacSheehy to their former glories, to leave him an empty aimless soul? The forest swallowed Seamus, and the night swallowed the forest.

"Seamus! Seamus!"

Seamus awoke damp and cold beside a felled tree. How could responsibility have been so cruel as to burden him with the hopes and dreams of his friend's sons when they should have died alongside their father? They called for him again but he did not respond even though he clearly heard. Why could an obese wild boar not charge him down and skewer him with its tusks? That would be a worthy death for a once proud man from a once proud family that was now reduced to a bandit in the woods. Why should he take the hopes of these young men just to lead them to their deaths?

"Seamus! Seamus!"

He should run the other way and leave them to fend for themselves. Maybe, without his encouragement, they would give up the bandit's life and become farmers and concentrate on impregnating their wives and feeding their children. Who cared if it was to a Queen or an O'Byrne or a Maguire to whom they paid their rent? They would more than likely be happy to live their lives on their farms and let the world pass them by instead of getting their heads split open by an axe in some bog or forest for someone else's benefit.

"Seamus! There you are!"

Seamus saw the only person who could motivate him, the son he never had, the son he would have been most proud of.

"Uaithne. You know better than to scream down the forest. What's so urgent that you must tell everyone where I am?"

"The English are coming. They're sweeping down the mountains, arresting anyone they vaguely suspect could be a rebel."

Seamus jumped to his feet.

"Then we must leave."

He had found motivation again.

They ran back to the house and Seamus ordered everyone to pack their things.

"We are setting off to Tyrone. You may return when it is safe. If we all die here today, the rebellion will die with you and Fiach will have sacrificed himself for nothing."

The sullen young men were silent and went and collected what few belongings they had and what morsels of food they could find to take with them on their journey. Redmond went to get enough horses for everyone. Phelim came to Seamus. The life of the rebellion and his father's legacy weighed heavily upon his shoulders.

"We must save Domhnall, the King of Leinster. The people will rally around him if anyone comes when we return. He will be hard to persuade, but we must do it."

Seamus had experienced a revelation on the way back to the house. Even in his old creaking, cynical bones kindled a sense of duty, as he had before when he fled from Munster to the Wicklow mountains. Just as Fiach had sheltered and protected him, just as Fiach had fought against what he perceived as injustice, and fought for what was right, he should do the same. He had to give meaning to Fiach's death. This was it. This was Fiach's legacy. Seamus put his hands on Phelim's shoulders.

"You are the O'Byrne now. We will do what you think is right. Let us rally the men, fetch Domhnall, and head north."

They rode south to the castle of the Kavanaghs. For all their youthful folly, lack of talent and questionable marital choices, Seamus admired each individual member of his motley crew. Uaithne was the most talented, his attributes encompassed bravery, tactical acumen and the ability to motivate men and keep them loyal. He was the natural leader, but his clan had been smashed by the colonies of the King's and Queen's counties and were now reduced to roaming bands of rebels with no permanent base. Since Fiach had got his oldest and most talented son executed, Phelim was his natural, if only worthy successor. Diligent and enthusiastic, his prime motivation was not to let down his father, which was a high bar. Redmond was a follower, handy in a fight, but if Phelim died, Fiach's legacy would rapidly diminish.

They arrived at Domhnall's castle with the Queen's colours flying from the mast. Seamus leaned over from on top of his horse to borrow Phelim's ear.

"This flag could mean many things from Domhnall's death to his changing sides or some kind of subterfuge. I don't know the man, so only you can interpret this. Do we approach or turn north?"

Phelim stared ahead, not knowing which way to jump. Seamus wished to remove him from the spot.

"What kind of man is he?"

Seamus could only manage a gruff patience for old habits die hard but he was used to hand-holding a hereditary leader who thought they could decide but really could not.

"He is as slippery as an eel," said Phelim. "My father always said you could not trust him as he would slip out of your hands and turn around and bite you. That is why he tried to trap him in the ceremonial trappings of Kingship, for he could not slip away if all eyes were on him."

"Then we head north?"

"Then we head north."

Seamus nodded when he thought it looked convincing that the decision had been Phelim's. Seamus pointed in the direction of the road to the midlands.

# CHAPTER 31

# THE KISS OF SUMMER

E unan held his wife's head to his chest, and she cried. She cried until she ran out of tears. Dry-eyed, she fell back to her bed. The maids came in to set her bed for her and Eunan was banished from the room. He retreated to his room to hide away to deal with the anguish of losing his son.

The castle became a mournful place, and only sadness echoed in its hallways. Cormac declared a week of mourning where everyone would attend mass daily and afterwards sit with Sorcha until she got so ill she had to dismiss everyone from her room. Eunan could barely get a word out of her, such was the deepness of the pit she was in. Eunan would sit in her room while she was asleep or pretended to be as his heart wrenched out of pity for his wife's dreams being destroyed.

On the seventh day, Cormac had a feast, a wake of sorts for the child, with music and merriment to which the residents of the castle and the principal officers of the MacCabes and MacDonnells were invited. Despite the efforts of Cormac, the atmosphere was despondent and Cormac decided it was time to have a word with Eunan. He slapped him on the shoulders as Eunan sat and drank and Cormac signalled to the men sitting around that they should give him some space.

"How are you feeling now after the death of your son?" Cormac said as he sat in front of Eunan.

"If I can be honest with you, as much as I hate to leave my wife in her time of need, I would like to get back to the war to forget my troubles."

"A soldier's answer," Cormac said, "and one I can sympathise with. But we must speak frankly, even now, because the pain is still so raw. You must give up this folly of trying to have a son with my daughter. I could never tell her this as it would destroy her, but I suspect she could never have a child. You should stop making her try."

Eunan dug his fingers into the sides of his knees and paused for breath.

"However much I want to — for I fear that with every pregnancy she is a little closer to death — but I cannot steer her away from her plan. She sees it as being her duty to have a son. I also fear my marriage would not survive if I didn't join her scheme, for it is her ultimate dream to have a child and as soon as she recovers from the trauma of this, she will try again. You have many respected physicians in your employment. Use them to persuade her, not me. That is, if you still want me as your son-in-law?"

Cormac moved back in his seat.

"There is no persuading her, no matter how I try. But the war may be a blessing for both of you. For you to forget your troubles and for her, your being away will mean she cannot get pregnant. Long may it continue."

"Let us not fall out about it, father-in-law. Let me be a proper husband and you'll have a happy daughter."

Cormac looked down at the floor.

"I try my best, but I'll leave it to you. Let us hope the melancholy leaves her soon."

"I'll drink to that," said Eunan.

They chinked mugs, and Cormac got up to speak to the other guests at the wake.

Time passed slowly for Eunan. His wife had taken ill and had lost the will to make herself better. He was consumed with worry, for he could not bear to lose her, especially so soon after they lost their son. Losing children was common in the north, especially in times of famine, but Eunan felt especially hard done by for he knew of no one that had to go through so much to have a child. He went to his wife to console her.

He knocked on the door in a manner to be kind to the sick on the other side. When Sorcha saw it was him, she dismissed her maids and physician and invited him in. No smile greeted Eunan and when she looked at him, only dull eyes met his. He sat on a stool beside her and took her hand.

"How are you, my love?"

Sorcha turned away from him.

"Barren and bereft, if you must know. When do you leave for war to compound my feelings with loneliness?"

"I shall stay as long as duty allows. Nothing is more important to me than your welfare."

"Do you see how lucky you are? You can leave and escape and I am trapped here in this bed, between these four draughty walls."

"How can I help you, my love? I may not be trapped in a bed, but my heart aches to see you distraught."

Sorcha turned around to Eunan and gripped his hand, her eyes burning.

"Say you will not abandon our plan, or abandon me. I know my father will have been trying to get you to give up, but say you will continue our quest to have a son and you can leave the room knowing you have made me happy."

Eunan shook and fought back the tears.

"Every time you get pregnant destroys a piece of the both of us. I don't know if I have the strength to go through it again."

"If you have the strength to leave me to go to war, you have the strength to leave your wife pregnant. Be a good husband and leave my father to me."

Eunan squeezed her hand and sobbed.

"If you want me to get out of this bed, give me a reason to get out of it. Keep your word."

Eunan bowed his head.

"I will try one last time, if only to make you happy. May God damn me to hell if I kill you in the process."

Sorcha leaned over him and kissed him on the forehead.

"Thank you, my love. Come back to me tomorrow and you can walk me around the corridors."

Hope was rekindled a short time later for Eunan and Sorcha when the morning sickness started once again. She was bedridden and isolated once more from the main residents of the castle, and the guards were extra vigilant early in the morning so no one could hear Sorcha throwing up. However, the sickness attacked her with such violence that even with a muffled sound, her retching could be heard in the courtyard. It was not long before the pattern of morning sickness nurtured rumours she was pregnant once more.

Cormac became anxious and, because of that, quick-tempered and irritable. No one dared approach him unless they had to. Eunan had no such luxury to remain a loving husband and potential doting father. He had to go through the gatekeeper.

"Is she all right?" he said, peering over Cormac's shoulder at Sorcha lying in the bed.

"She'll live, but we must keep a close eye out for the child," Cormac replied. "I told you I was against this, but foolish youth paid no attention to me. Still, duty calls you once again. Sent for your constables, for we must once more speak of war."

"Who will look after my wife?" asked Eunan.

Cormac rose from his stool and gestured to Eunan to leave.

"You have a duty to your clan and your chieftain. Let the maids look after your wife, for the best thing you can do is ensure your wife remains safe."

Cormac led Eunan away and there was nothing Eunan could do about it.

The constables and leading men of MacBaron's lands gathered in the great hall. Cormac was grim, having submerged his anxiousness in his sense of duty.

"Men, once more we are called to war. A new Lord Deputy is in place and is eager to impress his Queen. Therefore, he has ordered a two-pronged assault on our free lands. We will subsequently divide our forces to deal with these dual threats. The Maguires under Eunan will once more depart back to Enniskillen to counter the threat coming from Connacht. The O'Neills will go to the Blackwater, where the new Lord Deputy awaits us on the other side of the river. Both parties will depart today, for our enemies have struck swiftly and we must make all haste.

"But before you depart, let it be known to those who do not know me well enough that I am not one to encourage or participate in gossip. However, I have it on good authority that the O'Donnell has received emissaries from the King of Spain. He berated them for their failure to appear last October. But he has once more received assurances that the King supports our cause and means to send an army to support us. I realise that many of you may feel such bitter disappointment from being let down in the past, but I feel it my duty before sending you off to battle to dispel any falsehoods or rumours you may hear. The King of Spain may help us or he may not. But let it be known that the O'Neills have the bravest, most skilful, and best trained army on this island. Under my brother's skilled leadership, we have defeated every army the Queen has put in front of us and my brother will deal with this new threat without delay. To the glory of the O'Neills!"

"The O'Neill!" came the roar in response.

MacBaron made straight for the exit whilst the men excitedly chattered about the prospect of a new campaign. Eunan moved to intercept his father-in-law.

"Lord, may I see my wife before I depart this time?"

Cormac pondered in the doorway.

"Yes, but do not get her overexcited. I shall see that news is sent to you if she keeps the baby past the month's end."

"It would certainly inspire me if I could be kept abreast of such news."

Eunan found himself above his wife's bed, his hand shaking as he leaned over to remove the hair from her face as she slept. Such fair and sensitive skin could no longer remain sleeping when a hand roughened by wielding an axe in such a harsh environment brushed across it.

"I was sleeping, restful for the first time today," she said. "Why must you wake me?"

"I must leave for war once more with your lust for children a burden on my heart, for with every stillborn child you grow weaker in body and more disconsolate."

"My heart cheers for you can go out to battle, do your duty and hold your head up amongst the sacrifice of family and friends. But no, I shall wither away in my darkened room so you can feel better."

"Your duty will be the death of you," said Eunan.

"You should be so lucky to die for something worthwhile and not just rot away. If you can provide me with neither love nor comfort, then wield your axe and become a legend that people without knowledge of you will sing and admire. For if I may not do my duty nor will you leave me with child, then you are useless to me as a husband and may as well become the anonymous dead warrior, the hero of the bards."

"Let me place my hand on your stomach and whisper in your ear of my love so I may use it to comfort me as I lie down to sleep in the damp, cold bogs of Connacht."

Sorcha leant over and kissed him on the cheek.

"Think of a suitable name for our boy on your adventures. One that tells of the Ireland of old, the glory of the O'Neills and the greatness of God."

"If there is such a name out there, I will find it for you," Eunan smiled. "Now farewell my wife and write to me and tell me how your duty goes."

Sorcha kissed him again, but a knock came on the door and it was time for him to leave.

# CHAPTER 32

# THE BLACKWATER

S eamus returned to his wife at O'Cassidy house deep in grief from the death of his friend. The southern rebels had been put on the road to Tirconnell. He rode up to the house well in advance of the northern rebels he had rescued from Wicklow. His mind was firmly in the past. His friendship with Fiach had realistically died the year before when Fiach's willingness to sacrifice his better judgement to cling to his position had severed their ties. But he should have stuck by his friend throughout his woes, if not for him, but for the rebellion. The Seamus of old would have found a way. But once he caught sight of the house, he consigned the past to the past.

Dervella stood in the yard waiting for him. There were others there too, but Seamus only had eyes for his wife. Seamus rode up to the door of the house, dismounted, strode up to her and took her in his arms and tried to squeeze the love and warmth into himself to submerge the feelings of guilt, loss and frustration as the emotional dam collapsed at the sight of his wife.

"It is rarely you come home in this state without a gash, wound or broken bone to show for it," Dervella said as she caressed his cheek with the back of her fingers and saw the hurt in her husband's dulled eyes.

"The wounds I have run far deeper and take much longer to heal," Seamus said. "Let us retire into the house and be alone to catch up. We can talk of emotions another day."

"I have nothing prepared, for I was not expecting you."

"You were here to greet me and I am satisfied. Lead me to your room and let us rest."

Dervella took her husband by the hand and led him into the house.

Seamus spent the early summer quietly convalescing in the company of his wife, not letting the outside world know where he was and forbidding any of the residents or visitors to the house from revealing his location. He left the training and recruitment of men to Faolán and the management of the farm to Arthur, and he spent most of the time alone with his wife. It was a blissful time for Seamus, where, after a couple of weeks, he was free of guilt, grief and stress and felt a joy of life he thought had long deserted him. They spent much of their time in the garden or making trips to the lake, and such was his restless energy, he barely knew what to do with himself. But his wife would bring him to the fields and he would spend his vigour breaking the ground and they would plant vegetables together. Seamus dreamed of another life as if he was a farmer alone with his wife. He looked across to see Dervella smiling at him as she sprinkled seeds into the freshly hoed ground. But he soon banished these fantasies for what they were, for he knew what followed productive soil was bandits, or worse, a landlord, and he would be forced to retrieve his axe.

But eventually, the dream had to die as the Maguire found out where he was, and he sent word to the O'Donnell. Once it was known about the planned attacks of the new Lord Deputy, a messenger found his way to Seamus. Seamus snatched the letter from the messenger and stuffed it in his pocket. But the etiquette of a Galloglass would not leave him and he directed the messenger to the kitchens so he could get a meal.

Seamus stormed around to the back of the house, where he was sure he would be alone. He left the unopened letter from the O'Donnell on the ground as he sat, closed his eyes and took in the sun. The outside world could wait. But it would not. He heard the faint whistle of a tune recently composed by the local bard. Seamus opened his eyes and slapped the ground.

"Please. Spare me your attempt at humour. Eunan Maguire has done nothing worthy of being put to song and I should know as I was there at both his greatest moments but more frequently to save his arse."

Faolán laughed.

"At least it's better than them wanting to lynch him every time he shows his face?"

"True. For one so naive he sure knows how to make enemies."

"Can I change your mind and get you to help train the men today?" said Faolán.

"I am busy calculating who told the O'Donnell I was here by working out who would benefit. By making your request, you have shot to the top of the list."

"You're the one being naive thinking you could hide forever with a reputation like yours. I saw the messenger arrive. When are you leaving?"

Seamus knew the outside world would wait no more. He broke the seal and read the letter.

"It is when are we leaving. Next time you share a drink with that bard of yours, get him to pen a song for the south Fermanagh shot. They and we are going to fight for the O'Neill."

"It will be an honour to fight with you, Seamus MacSheehy." Faolán bowed.

"That's enough of you taking the piss for if you do that in front of the men you'll see what a harsh disciplinarian I can be."

"This way, lord," and Faolán bowed once more as he directed Seamus to the training field.

Seamus laughed, stuffed the letter in his pocket, and followed Faolán to the field.

Several weeks later, Seamus found himself in unfamiliar territory. He was behind the O'Neill ramparts on the other side of the river Blackwater beneath Lough Neagh. The previous month the O'Neill had been besieging Armagh and Newry and the new Lord Deputy Burgh raised a large army of five hundred horse and three thousand foot, mainly of Irish conscripts, to relieve them. Once he had done that, the Lord Deputy was determined to relieve the Blackwater fort. But the state of his conscripted force was reflected in his own health. He came north with a retinue of physicians, as he needed them to apply leeches to a troublesome old wound. So the Lord Deputy frequently had to retire and have his physicians attend to him. Despite having more administrative than military experience, he was in high spirits and eager to bring the war to the Irish rebels.

Seamus had been sent a request by the O'Donnell to come and join him and lead one of his units of continental veterans. However, as the O'Donnell was unsure of Seamus's location, he sent his request to Enniskillen to be redirected. The Maguire was not there, and the letter was answered on his behalf by Irial. The invitation was declined and instructions were sent to O'Cassidy house that Seamus was to lead the south Fermanagh shot and join the O'Neills. So Seamus stood on the bank of the Blackwater river watching his men take potshots at the royal army as it entered the water.

Faolán came and stood beside him as he took cover behind a tree.

"They seem very reluctant to get in the water. It must be a bit cold for them southerners, even though it is the height of summer."

"We should think ourselves lucky they can only send the reluctant Irish against us. We should only assume they sent these to absorb the bullets and test our strength. The real assault is yet to come."

Seamus observed how his men performed and was pleased with their rate of fire and accuracy. As far as he could tell, they were prosecuting their tasks as well as any of the O'Neill shot. The attack faltered in the water, offering the prospect of a night of celebrations around the campfire, secure on their side of the river. Then that illusion was drowned with a concerted push from the other side of the river.

"There! Look!" cried Faolán, and he pointed to a group of men attempting to wade across the river in full plate armour, obviously better equipped and protected than the men who had previously attempted to cross.

"I'll give him this much," said Seamus. "If that is the new Lord Deputy he is more foolish than brave. Concentrate the men's fire on that group and try to end this battle before it starts."

Faolán returned to the line of shot and directed them to target the elite soldiers crossing the ford. The rebel shot zipped across the water and sometimes drowned with a splash and sometimes lodged with a thud in some flesh and polluted the water with loyalist blood. But the leader of the Queen's army did not sway nor veer off his target of the rebel bank. His charge proved an inspiration to his men and more and more piled into the river behind him until they became an unstoppable force.

"Fire on the men before they reach the bank," shouted Seamus, hoping they would hear his call and fire a sweeping volley into those invaders about to set foot in O'Neill land. But alas, they could only continue taking pot shots at them, and as it was only single individuals being felled as they crossed, this was not enough to put off the mass of the English army once they got their blood up.

"The O'Neill needs to send this lot back into the river with his pike. Pull the men back so we can force the English together to make them a more compact target."

Faolán followed his order, and the shot kept up a good rate of fire, but the English were now consolidating their position on the O'Neill bank.

Seamus slammed his fist on the trunk of a tree.

"If the O'Neill has refused to put his men in jeopardy, then why should I expose mine? Sound the retreat."

Seamus had distinctly less leverage with the O'Neill than the O'Donnell and he was reduced to the lowly position of allied commander and was not invited to dine with the O'Neill and his military advisors. They would talk and then send him orders. If he did not obey, they would probably cut off his head. Seamus liked to tell everyone that he did not care, but he did. That night he ate rabbit and stoked the fire and cursed the O'Neill for not taking advantage of the enemy when they were at their weakest, when they had a small beachhead with most of the men crossing the ford.

The next day, a messenger asked for the constable and handed Seamus his instructions and rode off. Seamus read the letter and then tore it up.

"What's wrong, lord? They didn't like your plan?"

"Give me an axe and send me back to Munster. I have so much wisdom in this thick skull of mine I could carve out a land for the MacSheehy myself."

"That bad?"

Seamus grunted and Faolán ran after him.

Seamus and his men positioned themselves as close to the crossing as they could physically get. What had once been a small ford across the river with woods on either side to provide cover for any defenders was now a cavernous space where all the trees had been removed to be replaced with a huge trench and earth ramparts.

"See! That's why we should have pushed them back into the river yesterday," said Seamus. He hated not having the O'Neill's ear and wished he had gone to Connacht instead.

"Maybe he has a plan?" said Faolán.

Seamus gave him a withering look.

"It's me you're talking to. You'll be trying to drag me off to mass next."

Seamus went and stood on the bank of the river and saw the steady flow of pack animals being led across the ford with the trunks of freshly cut trees downriver being guided across but with teams of men pulling long ropes tied to either end of the logs to get them across.

"If we don't root them out now, we never will," Seamus muttered as he walked back to his men.

If anything infuriated him more than not being listened to nor being seen as a person of importance, it was the fact that the O'Neill had insisted that all the Maguire forces were placed under the command of Connor Roe so he could 'show his loyalty'. Seamus feared that his loyalty would be cut down in a hail of enemy lead, nevertheless, he heeded the summons of Connor Roe of all the leaders of the Maguires to his tent before the engagement with the enemy began. From the smirks of Connor Roe's men that greeted him as he made his way to the tent, he knew nothing had been forgiven or forgotten. This was one pre-battle planning meeting where he did not want to have the leader's ear.

He arrived at Connor Roe's tent and joined the line of nervous men that waited for their surprise leader.

"Why aren't you leading us?" whispered one of the constables in Seamus's ear.

"They never asked," Seamus said.

Connor Roe emerged from his tent, resplendent in his freshly polished breastplate. He inspected his commanders and burst out in a grin when he noticed who some of them were, but the biggest grin was reserved for Seamus.

"Now we all know why we are here," Connor Roe said, "even though some of us didn't expect to be here. The O'Neill has given us a job and on this afternoon it is our duty and honour to the Maguires of old that we uphold the fine reputation the Maguire clan has as a fighting force in the north. I have assessed our strengths and weaknesses as much as I could have in the time allowed and have decided the mercenary Seamus MacSheehy will lead the assault with his shot and other men I will assign to him."

While others may have gasped as the O'Neill had given the Maguires a particularly exposed route to attack the fort, Seamus did not flinch. He knew from the moment they appointed Connor Roe that he would either try to kill him or place him in the moment of greatest danger, or both.

"It would be my honour to lead the attack, lord," said Seamus.

Faolán was about to protest, but Seamus signalled to him to be quiet.

"Please assign me my men and instruct me as to when the assault will begin," Seamus said.

"Take your men from South Fermanagh and I'll send you some men from Enniskillen and the west. You will attack the fort from the south after the O'Neills lead the assault from the north and west. Before that, you are to lay down a cover of fire, so the defenders dare not stick their heads over the walls."

"As you command." Seamus slapped Faolán across the chest as the signal to leave. They had got halfway back to where the men were positioned before Faolán worked up the courage to question his master.

"You know we are going to lose most of our men?"

"Which is exactly what Connor Roe wants. He can climb over the bodies of Hugh Maguire supporters and claim whatever glory he can muster as his own."

"And you accept that?"

"You sound like Eunan as a boy. From the position I'm in, I can merely stay alive and bide my time. There is a possibility that we could take the fort in just one assault, but it is a remote one. I will do enough to keep my masters happy but concentrate on keeping my men alive."

They got back to the camp and Seamus shared some reassuring words with the men and went to check the supplies. Nothing told you more about where you were in the clan hierarchy than your access to supplies, especially those of gunpowder and bullets. Faolán opened the tent flap, and they both looked in and then at each other.

"I knew we were low but not that low," said Faolán.

They had a large box of bullets, maybe enough for twenty shots for each man, but plenty of gunpowder.

"Search the camp and wherever else you can, and lay your hands on as many weapons as possible. On what we have now, we won't be musket men making this charge."

Faolán nodded and did not argue. He took a few men with him to collect what he could find.

He returned several hours later, mainly with weapons that had been retrieved from the battlefield of the day before.

"You get a better yield from a bigger battle, especially one where one side ran away," Faolán said.

"I wasn't expecting much, but even I am slightly disappointed," Seamus said. "But the other men to support our attack have arrived, and I'm sad to say that these are the type of weapons they deserve. Let's wait for the signal and keep as many of these boys alive as possible."

The O'Neills attempted to sneak up to the walls of the new fort and were only rumbled when they came within a hundred yards. The defenders let loose a volley on the attackers and the battle for the fort sprang to life.

Seamus waved his men forward.

"Lay down some covering fire upon the fort. Take out as many of them as you can."

The shot hugged the remains of the forest until they could release a couple of volleys which flew over the earthworks or hit it with a disarming thud.

"Get closer," shouted Seamus as he ran to catch up with them. "Those bullets you have are precious and shouldn't be wasted because you are too cowardly to stand out in front of the enemy and get in proper range."

The men shuffled out and came under sporadic fire. Seamus ran up behind them and turned back towards the rest of the men who hid in the forest.

"For the Maguire! For Fermanagh!" He raised his axe to signal the beginning of the charge. Men trickled out from the forest.

"Faolán! Get them moving!"

Faolán used whatever he could to get the men moving, which usually involved dragging or kicking them, but when that got too slow, he took a man's musket from him and fired just over the heads of a group of boys crouched behind a bush.

"The war is that way!" he cried before grabbing more of them and pushing them from their shelter.

The shot were running low on bullets and the din from the sections the O'Neills were assaulting grew ever louder. Seamus knew it was now or never and did not want to give Connor Roe the excuse to charge him with being a coward. Seamus raised his axe high in the air for all to see.

"FOR THE MAGUIRE!"

His voice carried over no-man's-land and even caught the attention of those defenders not diverted to stave off the O'Neill assault.

The men and boys cowering in the forest looked at Seamus, thinking him rather odd and wondered, within the pause of his shout and everyone else's inaction, what he would do next.

Seamus turned and charged towards the fort. He did not look back to see who was behind him. He ran forward as fast as he could. His eyes constantly moved from obstacles on the ground to defenders on the wall loading and having him in their sights. Tree stump. Move around it. Tree root. Jump over it. Something whizzed past his head. He looked up and saw musket barrels protruding over the top of the earthworks. He would have to be more alert. He took a few more steps and found himself in the air, coming down with a thud. His ribs were in agony, but his head seemed to have hit soft turf. He could move his arms and slid his right arm down his body. No blood. That was something. His fingers found the cause of the pain in his ribs. He removed a rock from below his right ribs and pressed gently. The pain told him they were probably broken. He looked behind him. The men had charged and were gaining in nerve as they ran, for few fell. He knew he had to get up and lead the men, at least until they engaged the enemy for boys that raw and nervous were brittle and easily broke. He lifted himself slowly to his feet, his body a ball of aches and pains, and his energy seemed to drain into the ground. The bullets whizzed past his head and his men were not far behind. He took his axe in his left hand and raised it above his head.

"FOR THE MAGUIRE!" This time, the response came back. "THE MAGUIRE!"

Seamus ran, but his energy seemed spent. It became more of a stumble across no-man's-land but the shot had nearly caught up with him and sent volleys of bullets towards the defenders. Some young boys in their foolishness caught up with Seamus, but their inexperience and vulnerability made them easy targets for the enemy shot.

"COME ON, MEN!" Seamus shouted. He was parched and almost hoarse. But he was twenty yards from the enemy ramparts. He would never have advised anyone else to do this for it would mean certain death, but as long as he was in no-man's-land and failed to engage with the enemy he would be in Connor Roe's grasp, which probably meant the same thing. He looked behind as bullets came ever nearer his head. A body of men were charging towards him with enough bulk to force themselves up the rampart and engage the enemy in hand-to-hand combat. It was now or never, or die where he stood. He mustered up the last of his energy reserves and charged up the ramparts.

The bullets whizzed past him. Some defenders resorted to throwing rocks, and they were better shots than those with guns. One such projectile hit Seamus on the side of his head, his morion helmet only offering partial protection. He stumbled and tore his helmet off and let it drop to the ground. He was stunned, but heard the men charge past him. One man fell from a bullet and rolled down the earthworks, knocking Seamus from his feet. He struggled to get up but saw the hand-to-hand combat breaking out in front of him. He got to his feet and once more raised his axe to rally the men.

The next wave hit the ramparts. He charged to the top and thrust his axe downwards. He looked down to be greeted with the splattering blood of a young man whose head his axe had penetrated. After throwing the body off the rampart, he told his men to charge up the earthwork. He turned to face another young man who trembled before him, but in his hands he held a gun. He pulled the trigger, and the bullet leapt out and seared through Seamus's right upper chest and shoulder. Seamus felt a rush of heat and pain and then nothing.

# CHAPTER 33

# CARTOGRAPHY

S ir Conyers Clifford could talk. He had persuasion down to an art. He could bring together the loyal lords and those on the periphery or in need of persuasion far better than Governor Bingham ever could. Bingham made fear his principal ally, but relied on having a professional army from England to back him up. But when his forces became reliant on Irish conscripts, it all collapsed. Conyers made everyone feel good about themselves and made them feel important, and this especially worked on the ego of Taaffe and the fragile confidence of the O'Connor Sligo.

Taaffe had been impressed with the new Lord Deputy Burgh's energy and thought he had a sensible plan to defeat the rebellion, even if the loyal Irish lords had to supply the means to execute it. He rallied what he could of the English settlers in Sligo and combined them with the few cut-throat Irish with whom he commanded respect. His right-hand man now was Shea Óg with whom he shared a ruthless affinity. He could do any job, no matter how unsavoury. They were a band of horse and traditional Irish-style Galloglass fighters, for men came and went before he had adequate time to train them and he needed men out in the field fast. He prepared his men in Drumahair Castle to join the march north when the main army supplied by the Earls of Thomond and Clanricard passed by the castle to progress northwards. He was so confident they would take Ballyshannon Castle and open up the north that he hired a new map maker and magistrate to accompany him on the trip so he would get the choicest set of lands to sell when they were confiscated from the rebels. Drumahair Castle emptied when Sir Conyers' army marched past.

The fortunes of the O'Connor Sligo rose and fell with the pull of the moon and the tides of the sea. His sun was Sir Conyers who would liberate Sligo, invigorate support for the Queen and camp in the middle of the county until all wavering clans pledged support for the O'Connor Sligo. But the O'Connor was strong and waged war on those clans who would not give up their loyalty to the O'Donnell. The O'Donnell was the moon and would strike in the shadows, a hungry wolf with an insatiable appetite for sheep. He would sweep in through Sligo and provide restitution for the clans that had remained loyal to him by confiscating the cattle and other chattels of the O'Connor Sligo and giving them to his supporters. The O'Connor Sligo would then become a vagabond, a vagrant with no lands over which to exercise title, and would have to flee to Galway to beg Sir Conyers to ride to his rescue once more. Taaffe saw the tides slowly but systemically eroding anything the O'Connor Sligo built, be that trust, an alliance, or a season's crop. Taaffe could supply the persuasion of fear, but his greed would destroy everything in his path.

When the O'Connor Sligo was back in possession of Sligo once more and built trust and prestige worthy of his title, he took the lands of those who supported the O'Donnell and the possessions stolen from him and his supporters. He then offered lands back to any that would recant their allegiance to his enemy. He was determined to end this loop of continuous invasion and reconquest and gathered all the men he could trust outside Sligo town to join with the Governor's army. He gathered three hundred men, mainly shot and pike and one hundred horse, the largest single force that any of the factions in Sligo could raise. His hopes were high for the loyal forces of Ireland had yet to arrange a two-pronged assault into Ulster and the loyal Irish lords considered the rebels to be vulnerable if their forces could be divided. The O'Donnell got wind of the planned offensive and sent an appeal to the Maguires and the O'Rourkes to come and assist him.

Eunan waited in the hall of Enniskillen Castle for the Maguire to arrive. He had the troubles of the world on his shoulders and could barely remove his head from the tribulations of Sorcha's bedroom and the dark mysteries of her womb. He had heard the tale many a time, especially recently, that his MacCabes would go home to their loved ones and before they knew it, like it or not, their wives and girlfriends would be with child. But it seemingly would not be for him. He was not destined for a simple life, his was to be a life of burden and duty. He longed to hear the heavy footsteps of Desmond through the halls, to revel in his joviality, to note down his advice, but death had separated them. He would have even settled for the battle-weary cynicism of Seamus, but all he had were a sprinkling of inexperienced young men eager to impress, or the cloak and dagger of the world-weary, personified by most of his Galloglass constables. His heart sank when he heard wood rhythmically striking stone. He poured himself another drink. He would need it.

The Maguire entered the room followed by his chief advisors, Fachtna Óg and Irial McDowell MacCabe. Hugh appeared with the excitement of a little boy and immediately called for food and wine. He sat down on his seat and leaned forward as if he was telling a secret.

"Men, we are going to war."

Eunan looked out the window. That was no secret. The Maguire seemed to lust after war, urged on by his advisors. Eunan could only hope that whatever happened this summer would be decisive and that he could return home to live out his life as a peaceful farmer in O'Cassidy house with his wife and, hopefully, some children.

"Eunan, how is the preparation of the MacCabes coming along?" said the Maguire.

Eunan was startled having been caught not properly paying attention.

"The MacCabes are ready and await your orders, lord."

"I hope you have been training your men in more manoeuvres than just the retreat?" said Irial with a smirk.

"I am expanding their repertoire beyond what you taught them," said Eunan. "I think you may find a much different force than the last time you graced the field. Our esteemed leader invested the proceeds of our last raid wisely by investing in many new armaments that our merchants purchased in Scotland. Equipment that serves well to both attack and defend."

"May I second that and raise my mug to Eunan without whom the Maguires would not be the primary ally of both the O'Donnell and the O'Neill," said the Maguire.

"To Eunan!" and they all raised their mugs.

With that, the Maguire rolled out the maps of Connacht and identified where the enemy was located and various points of strategic interest.

"The enemy now threatens Ballyshannon Castle and if they take that, then Tirconnell is open. They have landed cannons and are about to set them upon the castle walls. We are to sweep in behind them, take the fords on the river Erne, and trap them. We need to be quick and decisive and the main army is not ready yet. Therefore, Eunan and I will sweep forward and the O'Rourkes will support us while the main body of our men follow up and hit the enemy in the rear when they turn to escape. Are you all with me?" the Maguire asked.

"We are!" The room raised their mugs in support.

"Then we must prepare, for we leave as soon as we are ready."

The men hailed the Maguire once more and disassembled to prepare for the march. Eunan was bent over when he heard a whisper in his ear.

"You'd better pray you have the favour of God on the battlefield, for the Maguire and MacBaron won't be there to protect you."

Eunan stood up and turned to see who it was, but the culprit had been swallowed up in the throng of the room. The sound of wood on stone grew slowly distant.

Eunan took the veiled threat seriously. He took his dogs with him and appointed Odhran as his bodyguard. He met his men and the Maguire and his horsemen in the fields surrounding the castle.

"I'll lead the way," said Hugh. "We have no time to waste in securing the fords. Follow along the Erne and my men will contact you as I determine where the enemy are and where I want you to go."

"Be careful, lord," said Eunan. "Your clan needs you."

"They also need you," said the Maguire. "They need you to make haste to the fords. I will try to leave some of the enemy for you."

"Don't spare them on my behalf," said Eunan.

The Maguire raised his hand, and the horsemen took off east.

"You worry about him, don't you?" Odhran said.

"I wish he would lead from the castle and leave the field to me," Eunan said. "The politics of the castle are fragile enough without him needlessly risking his life."

Clifford swiftly advanced to the Erne to find most of the fords had been blocked by the rebels. However, O'Connor Sligo volunteered some of his men with local knowledge to be led by an English captain to capture a lightly defended ford when darkness could be an ally. The ford was quickly captured, and the army forced its way across. The ships of the O'Malleys were there to meet them on the shores on the other side of the river. They carried two guns from Galway that would be powerful enough to blow a hole in the walls of Ballyshannon Castle and cause it to surrender. They went and set up camp and laid siege to the castle. The siege did not last long for the next day, after he had witnessed his cannon balls bounce off the walls of the well defended castle, Sir Conyers received a message that rebel forces were attempting to cut him off from Connacht and Cormac MacBaron would soon be there with one thousand O'Neills. He immediately ordered the retreat.

Taaffe and Donough O'Connor Sligo, who had once been at the rear of the army, which was composed of the less well organised of the units, now became the vanguard. The few English units in the army and those units of the Earls of Thomond and Clanricard kept their shape and discipline whilst those of the lords of upper Connacht disintegrated. Taaffe gathered what he could of his freshly created maps and cartography equipment and joined in the dash to get over the fords of the river Erne and into the relative safety of Sligo. He was limited for he had a cart with all his equipment and therefore had to keep his men together to protect it. They stuck to the same road as they had crossed the Erne and the men stuck narrowly to the path for to spread out would be to have to queue to cross the narrow ford. But it was a fool's errand, for no sooner did they head southwards than the missiles of the ever-mobile Maguire horse pelted them. The Maguire would charge and swoop down in a semi-circle before the English shot set up and loaded and the horsemen would release their barrage of missiles. But Taaffe struck his horses hard and continued down the road no matter what obstacles were in front of him. The column continued for several miles, suffering attack after attack until some riders approached them.

Donough rode up to Taaffe in his cart.

"The rebels block off the way we came. The only escape route is through the Ballyshannon ford."

"Curse the O'Donnell, and his wretches. I thought this time would be different. But back we go again to Sligo."

"My men will clear the ford. By the grace of God, may we make it back."

"More by the power of the axe and the musket. If you get us out of this alive, I will save you a prime cut of land and may even give you a discount," Taaffe said.

"I only hope you check the legal title of the land first and not sell me what I already own."

"Stick with me, boy, and we'll both be rich. Who knows, I may even sell you back your estate one day."

Taaffe laughed. Donough spat on the ground and rode off.

Donough rode ahead with his horse and was driven back by the sporadic fire of the Maguire shot guarding the approaches to the ford. He retired to the main body of the English column, hurrying towards the ford. He rallied his footmen and got them into basic shot and pike formations. After a couple of exchanges with the Maguire shot, the enemy retreated and the way to the ford was open. Donough rode to the nearest hill to survey the approaches to the ford. All that was in the way was a small unit of Galloglass pike. The bulk of the army was right behind him and he needed to secure the ford as quickly as possible. He did not have the luxury of his shot picking off the enemy one by one. Desperate to restore honour and glory to the O'Connor Sligo name, he ordered his men to attack. Discipline had almost broken down and an armed mob descended on the ford.

# CHAPTER 34

# THE BLOODY FORD

With the other fords on the Erne secure Eunan and his men made a dash for the ford at Ballyshannon, which to his knowledge was behind the English army. The Maguire had gone ahead with the cavalry and the main army was still a distance away. Eunan selected a hill to survey the landscape with his constables.

"Look, lord," said Odhran as he pointed south. "The O'Rourkes make haste to cut off the ford from the south."

"And our forces are a couple of hours behind us to the east," said Cearbhall.

"Yet our leader makes a dash to the west," said Eunan.

"And the enemy lies to the north," said Feargal.

"Well, our master has left us with little choice," said Eunan, "for if our enemy were suddenly to turn, it would be him that would be trapped between the river and our foes. I cannot risk that he would be crushed on the very river that made and nurtured the Maguires. For it to cause our downfall would be a tragedy indeed."

"It is a time for bravery and fortitude," said Feargal. "Let us sharpen our axes, call out to our ancestors and put our faith in victory in the hands of God."

"It is all right for a crippled old man to yearn after a glorious death," said Eunan, "one which he will never achieve other than to look at those brave stalwarts of the Maguire Galloglass and ask them to throw their lives away."

"You mistake both Irial and me," Feargal said. "We may have urged caution in the past, but you need to recognise when there is an opportunity and also be willing to take it. Excessive caution leads to a war of attrition and those with the greatest resources and the know-how to utilise them will prevail. If you listened to any of the lessons of your former master Desmond, you would realise in a war of attrition only the Queen will win."

"I have no desire to fall into a trap, irrespective of if the Maguire himself has already fallen into it. I am the appointed leader of the MacCabes and what I say goes. Let us go to the ford at Ballyshannon but with the O'Rourkes to the south, always in our sight. That way, if we fall into an ambush, the O'Rourkes or our men coming behind us will hopefully mean that at least some of us come out alive. You will take the lead with your men, Feargal since you are the most eager to get there."

Feargal cursed to himself but nodded and set off to relay the instructions to his men.

Eunan succumbed to the nagging of his underlings and had so outpaced the O'Rourkes that they arrived alone and exposed. Eunan braced himself and became the leader he was appointed to be.

"Set up the shot in two lines on the north side and cover the approaches to the ford. The pike will guard the ford and the Kern will seek the enemy or the horse of the Maguire. Whichever comes first."

His constables acknowledged their instructions and set about their tasks. It was not long before scouts from the Kern returned.

"The enemy is almost upon us!" said the messenger.

"Then we must dig in," said Eunan.

"All the enemy, I mean all the enemy," the messenger said. "They arrive upon us with their full army."

"Where are the Maguire and the horsemen?"

"Nowhere to be seen, lord. If you asked me to make a guess, I would say that they are shadowing behind them. But it would only be a guess."

"Where are the armies of our allies?"

"The O'Rourkes are but half a day away at most," said Feargal. "If we were to make a stand here, then they would surely come and support us. If the enemy is in retreat and we hold all the fords, the O'Donnell cannot be far behind."

"Then we stand and fight. Feargal, get the shot to drive the enemy into our pike on the ford. We'll skewer the enemy on our pikes."

Feargal spat and without another word waved to his men to follow him.

Eunan positioned himself behind the pike as he considered this the best position to lead and inspire his men. He admired the ranks of the pike drawn up in front of the ford. They were one hundred men of vast fighting experience and each life lost would be a blow to the Maguires. Although he prayed for such an opportunity to test his skills of command, his hand shook at the thought of losing valuable, experienced men. But no more would he sacrifice so many men for carts of treasure that he would lose anyway.

The enemy horse burst into view, scattering the Kern and shaking off any missiles they threw at them. Behind them came the main army. It was mainly Irish in composition, from the lords of Connacht, and in its haste to escape the O'Donnell's trap had become an ill-disciplined mass of still dangerous armed men. They rolled forward like a runaway boulder towards the ford.

Feargal ordered the shot to fire into their flanks, but those that fell were quickly replaced.

They kept up a covering fire until the English horse charged and forced them back into the woods. The pikemen hunkered down to brace for the impact of the charge. Feargal made his way from the woods and came up behind Eunan to offer his opinion.

"The line won't withstand this charge. The enemy are too many and will sweep right through us."

"What would you have me do?" Eunan said. "If I let them through, they will escape back to Connacht, but if I stay, I can slow them down until our forces catch up with them and crush them. We have been going back and forth from Connacht for several years now. We may not get as good an opportunity as this."

"I don't believe the Maguire would have appointed you if he knew how reckless you were."

"There is no pleasing you, Feargal. But let us resolve our differences at a more opportune time for the men."

"If we see this day out I'll see you and your uncle sent back to your farm."

"Save your loathing for your foe who bears down upon us. Go to your men and position yourself there and wait for fate to show her hand. I will see you at nightfall, when hopefully our fates will have been decided."

Feargal turned without another word and returned to the shot and Eunan was glad of the silence.

He felt for his throwing axes and the shaft of the battle axe strapped to his back. He called Odhran over to him.

"Take my dogs over the ford and wait for me there. Don't come to assist. If you should lay eyes on the O'Rourkes, send them over to fight my battle for me."

"I want to stay and fight," said Odhran. "Can you send the dogs away under the charge of one of the boys?"

"I want you to obey orders. You can be my eyes on top of the hill on the south side, should you wish to make yourself useful. Now go. For if the combat starts, the dogs will run into battle and I will go through hell to retrieve them."

"They will pine after their master if they see him having all the fun."

"They can join in after him when the other armies arrive."

Eunan saluted him farewell and went to slap the backs of the rear pikemen to raise their spirits.

The English army rolled forward, but they did not so much resemble the disciplined ranks of the army that crossed the Erne days earlier but that of a mixed Irish rabble with only one means of escape. They sprayed the wall of pikes with musket fire, but the lead balls were more of a threat to lone birds in the sky than the massed ranks of Galloglass pike. The front ranks of the advancing rabble still had their weapons, but had completely lost their shape. They lost their will to advance further when they saw the tips of the pikes but suffered the funnelling action of the woods and the force of the weight of the men behind them propelled them forward. They spilt onto the pikes and dead men became wedged upon them as the men behind them pushed forward. These dead weights forced the pikes downwards and each pike felled meant the wall of spikes became a little less effective.

"FORWARD MEN, PUSH FORWARD!" shouted Eunan from the rear. His years of training with Desmond told him he needed to push the enemy backwards to free the pikes and prevent them from being pushed into the river.

But the weight of the oncoming men was too much and the ground under-foot by the river bank soon turned to mud with so many men trampling on it. They were soon pushed back.

"WHERE ARE THE SHOT?" Eunan directed his call to the woods on either side, but they were by now full of retreating men from the English army and his men had dispersed into the countryside. It would not be long before they were pushed into the river. The English sent marksmen into the reeds by the ford and they peppered the sides of the pike with lead. Eunan was losing men, and fast. He looked to the rear for some relief. On a nearby small hill, Odhran leapt and waved his arms about.

"ONE LAST HEAVE, MEN," he cried. "THE O'ROURKES ARE NEAR-LY UPON US."

The men gave their all-in-one final push and forced the mass of Irish loyalists back so that their momentum was temporarily broken. Then the English soldiers dispersed and Eunan called on his men to disengage and regroup near the ford. He admonished those who dropped their pikes and made them pick them back up. Eunan tried to count how many men he had left, but with the adrenaline pumping in his veins and the men moving about so much, he became confused and settled at around fifty.

"Way too few to hold this ford," he said, not wanting this crossing surrounded by a rocky outcrop to become his graveyard. But he still had no sight of his allies.

"Let us regroup once more and make our stand. Relief will come soon," he told his men as he pointed to where he wished them to draw up.

"But we'll die here," said one blood-soaked man who was losing his nerve.

"We are Galloglass and we make our stand for the good of the rest. We have three armies converging on this spot, and all we are doing is delaying the enemy until they arrive. Soon enough, we will retire."

"Why do they not deploy their shot and blast us off the road? Surely they have some discipline remaining to think of that?" said another of the Galloglass.

Could it be true? Eunan turned to address the man.

"You have inadvertently given us another reason to stay. We must remain here to see if they deploy their shot and in what strength. For if they don't deploy them, they must be out of bullets. If they are, they will be rabbits to be chased down by us, the dogs. Do not despair, we have hope, men!"

He ordered his remaining men to form a schiltron in front of the ford with pikes in every direction but the rear blocking the way of the enemy once again. They stood or knelt behind their pikes and waited. The English soldiers, for the main part, disappeared behind the woods and the nearby hills and regrouped. All the while Eunan bought valuable time. He looked to the rear and studied the ford and the surrounding topography so they would have an escape route if they needed it. Eunan had no intention of dying on this ford this day.

After around an hour, the English made themselves known again. They had, as Eunan suspected, regrouped and now marched in formation towards the river. At the front was a thin line of shot and behind them were several units of pike. Eunan now knew that they meant to drive him into the river and the best time to escape was before the pike engaged, for if they engaged, they would be locked together with the enemy until they died or were relieved. The English raked them with bullets and the Galloglass fell.

"Come on, men. We've done our duty today. Anything beyond this is folly. Bring your pikes if you can. Let's go. RETREAT!"

The bullets rained down upon them, striking the backs or calves of the unlucky, and as they fell their comrades tried to help but the English horse came at them. The brave wounded few tried to lift the pikes whose ends had been dug into the ground to stop the charge of horses so they could give their able comrades a chance of escape. Eunan was soon wading across the water, his axes held above his head as missiles fell around him. He dared not look behind him, for fear of his life more than fear of turning to salt. He could hear the rushing of water in amongst the screams of men in agony or anger and the neighing of horses who did not want to be there. His legs were released from the water and he ran for the cover of the woods, all without looking backwards. Once in the woods, he sought the sanctuary of a rock and looked back across the ford. He saw the last of his men follow him into the woods. A cruel cocktail of bitterness and guilt caught in the back of his throat for so few of his good men had survived. It all seemed so pointless as he saw the enemy horse take their revenge on the wounded he left behind and the enemy march to the ford in battle formation. He felt a hand on his shoulder and saw it was Odhran.

"We must go."

Eunan left behind a graveyard with his plot empty and that was that.

# CHAPTER 35

# THE BATTLE OF THE RAIN

O dhran led Eunan and the battered remains of his men to the other side of the woods, where Feargal and the shot were waiting for them. Feargal and his men had barely a scratch on them and had only lost one man. Eunan slammed his axe on the ground in front of Feargal.

"Most of my men died defending that ford while you lay idly by in a forest?"

Cearbhall, who had also survived the ford, remembered the strategic position and stepped between them.

"The time for recriminations is not now. We must act and tell our brothers where the enemy is, so our fellow Galloglass will not have died in vain."

"Tell me you have done something useful with your time?" Eunan asked Feargal.

Feargal's answer, whatever that was, was rudely interrupted by the sound of sustained musket fire.

"We must go, for the fight is not over," Eunan said. He raised his finger towards Feargal. "Neither is my discussion with you. If we both live to leave this battlefield today, we shall have it out in Enniskillen."

"I look forward to it," muttered Feargal beneath his smelly breath.

They tore through the forest with Eunan leading the shot. Stragglers from the English army had entered the perimeters of the forest to escape the heat of the battle or to desert. Under normal circumstances, Eunan would have let these men melt away but his blood was up and he wished for revenge for the ford and his axe made quick work of those he could catch. He reached the perimeter and below him, winding its way beneath the hills, was the English army. But it was far from unmolested. As it made its way over the ford, the O'Donnell was engaged with the rear of the English army. The O'Rourkes had finally arrived and were harassing them from the other side of the valley. The main Maguire army had also arrived south of the river and harassed the retreating English. Eunan was elated. The deaths of his men may not be in vain after all.

"Men, line up and fire at the enemy," he ordered the shot.

They did as he said and smashed volley after volley into the retreating English. The men from the ford had by now caught up with them and amused themselves by watching the English army writhe between the Maguire and O'Rourke shot as it tried to escape.

"Do we attack now with what we have?" said Cearbhall.

"We have done enough sacrificing today," Eunan said. "We'll wait until the Maguire reinforces us before we strike."

But Feargal was incensed.

"The only reason we can do anything now is because I preserved the lives of my men and now we can strike at the enemy."

Odhran ran over to Feargal to confront him.

"Eunan is a hero and the only reason we have the English army at our mercy is his delaying action."

"Well said, Odhran, but now is not the time to fight," said Eunan as he put his arms between them to break them up. "We can sort out our differences in Enniskillen, but now we have a battle to win. We shall wait for the Maguires, for we are heavily outnumbered on this flank, but our moment will come when we can attack."

They watched the English army go by below them and Eunan drummed his fingers on his axe shaft as he cursed his lack of men. But news soon came from the ford in the form of one of Eunan's few remaining Kern.

"The English army has finally finished crossing the ford, lord," said the Kern as he gasped for air. "The O'Donnell follows in behind with the Maguire and our horse at his side."

Eunan leapt from his seat. "Prepare yourselves, men, and look lively for your leader, the Maguire. Upon his arrival, we'll support his pursuit of the enemy."

"When our opportunity is gone," said Feargal.

"If you talk to your master like that once more, I'll put my axe through your head!" said Eunan as he went for his throwing axes.

"The battle is below, lord," Cearbhall said. "We need to replenish our ammunition. Shall we steal it from the dead below?"

Eunan's eyes lit up.

"Kern, go back to the Maguire, the O'Donnell or anyone of rank who can pass a message to them. The enemy is out of powder and bullets — you have that from a good authority — and they should be an easy target for your own shot. Go. Run and tell them and stop for no one."

The man nodded and took to his heels. Eunan sat and watched the English army scramble past as his men fired the last of their bullets into the army's flank.

"Now we have no ammunition left. Do we charge them?" said Cearbhall.

Eunan looked around and saw the exhausted hulks that occupied the bodies of his men and saw they were spent.

"They have done their duty for today."

A call came through the woods and Eunan's men signalled back and the Kern came back proudly walking in front of another one hundred Maguire shot complete with powder and ammunition.

Eunan embraced him when he came before him.

"Thank you, lord. I met the Maguire himself as he chased and harried the enemy's rear. I told him your message, and he sent these men to reinforce you. He said the O'Rourkes would wheel around the enemy and block their route south. The shot will soften them up before we move in for the kill."

Eunan was alive with energy.

"Men, replenish your pouches and prepare for battle once more. A glorious victory this day lies within our grasp."

They followed the enemy at a distance, but well within musket range. They released volley after volley. Each one would reveal their bounty straight after with the falling of the dead and injured from the edges of the limping column. The English could not retaliate for Eunan had guessed correctly, they were out of ammunition. They occasionally attempted to charge Eunan and his men, but every time they did, the shot would melt away and they would have to run back to the cover of the column again. But despite all the constant attacks, the column kept its order and momentum forward.

Cearbhall came to Eunan's side.

"It is late afternoon, and we must strike before nightfall comes to our enemy's aid. Have you heard from our forces attacking the rear or the O'Rourkes at the front?"

"I have heard nothing and only have the view from this hill. The clouds also gather above our heads, which darkens the skies. We need to strike to win the day but we are too few in number. Send a messenger to the rear to get instructions."

Cearbhall nodded and Eunan returned to leading the shot.

They had time to unleash several more volleys before Eunan felt a drop of rain upon his face. He did not flinch, for rain was not unusual in and of itself. But the skies went dark, and the men looked to the heavens. Then the rain came in sheets and buckets. The men were soaked through and those with any armour became weighted down with the additional burden of their soggy clothes.

"To the woods, men," Eunan cried, and they all ran for shelter in the trees. The trees on the edge provided little cover, such was the power of the falling rain, so they had to go deeper to regroup. Once inside, Eunan counted the men.

"Only a couple missing. Not a bad day's work for so many of the enemy felled."

"Lord, the powder is ruined," said Cearbhall.

"What do you mean?" asked Eunan.

Cearbhall held out a bag of gunpowder, placed his hand inside, and pulled out its soaked contents.

"The guns are now useless."

Eunan cursed.

"Then we attack with our axes," he said in desperation for a solution.

"You said we have too few men," said Feargal.

"Damn it!" said Eunan once more. "It must be the work of the devil himself that has denied us victory this day."

"Or God himself is unhappy with some of our actions this day," Feargal said. "If we had not reverted to only attacking with shot, this day would have been won already."

The torrent of rain ceased, and the sun returned and sent its beams of light through the forest.

"Let us cease arguing here in the mud and see if we are to be granted any more opportunities this day," said Cearbhall.

"To our previous positions, men," said Eunan. "Let's see if we can salvage anything from this day."

They returned to their former position to see the last unit of enemy pike march past them below. They were pursued by the Maguire horse who were kept at a distance by the pike. The main body of the army had passed.

"Shall we charge down and attack the enemy?" said Feargal.

"No, the men are spent and our powder being soaked is a sign that our day is done. Let us sit and watch the end of the battle and celebrate our victory."

But it did not feel like a victory for some, with so many of their comrades left on the field.

# CHAPTER 36

# ROBBED BY MUD

T he grasslands in between the bogs, protruding rock formations and woods that made up the approaches to the Ballyshannon ford were cluttered with the baggage train, carts and units of the rapidly disintegrating English army. Taaffe had already resorted to the whip to beat off any unwanted man he did not recognise as being under his command from mounting his cart or trying to commandeer it for transporting the wounded back to Sligo. The horse and Kern of the rebels bombarded the flanks of the retreating army with missiles and bullets. Taaffe was lucky enough to be out of range but unlucky to be caught up in the chaos in the centre of the column.

"Get this damn column moving before we all perish!" he hollered at where the column pointed towards the ford.

"We cannot move until the O'Connor Sligo takes the ford," came the angry response of one of the cart drivers.

"Then God help us all," said Taaffe as he turned and his whip connected with the face of a boy eager to mount his cart to assist his escape.

He remained there for what seemed like an age. Taaffe watched as the English sergeants worked their way down the column and forced the shot to deploy on the flanks to drive off the attacking rebels. This created space in the column and the sergeants restored some order as everyone waited for the ford to be cleared. A shout came from the front and the column moved forward.

Taaffe rolled down the well-trodden path to the ford as the men on foot ran past him in their eagerness to cross over to the other side of the river and what they perceived as safety. Taaffe watched as the sergeants supervised men throwing the bodies of Irish rebel and O'Connor Sligo supporter alike to the side of the road so the army could pass. The Erne ran red with the blood of friend and foe alike. All Irish blood flowing down into the sea. The muffled screams of those wounded rebels being finished off by vengeful O'Connor Sligo supporters intermingled with the sounds of the constant rebel attacks on both the sides and rear. The corresponding bank on the other side looked blissfully peaceful in comparison. But Taaffe could do nothing but wait in line until it was his turn to cross.

Donough O'Connor Sligo could see the open country before him. His tunic was splashed with blood, not his own nor that of a foe, but the residue of the impact of a lead shot with the head of one of his bodyguards. The fight for the ford was bloody and did not endear the O'Connor Sligo to his men as, in an act of recklessness, he sent wave after wave against the enemy until one of the English commanders made it to the front line and ordered in the shot. But he led his men across the ford first and at least half emerged on the other side relatively unscathed. There came a colossal bang as his head collided with the ground. He saw his horse's neck quiver in front of him as he lay there. His senses were deafened except for the searing pain in his leg. He pulled upon it, but it was trapped beneath his horse. He felt himself moving and feeling coming back into his leg. He saw the blue sky above him become surrounded by dark clouds.

"Lord, the enemy had lain in wait for us and we must wait here for help."

Taaffe felt the splash of water on his face as the wheels of his cart met the waters of the Erne. Never had he been so glad to have made it to a river. The bang of musket fire from behind him rang in his ears. He had not realised he had fallen to the rear of the column in everyone's eagerness to escape.

His whip became his means of escape, thrashing horse and cart intruders alike. The bullets lodged themselves in the rear of the cart. Taaffe allowed himself the luxury of looking back to where he had come from and saw English pike and shot fend off an ever-increasing force of rebels. The front wheels climbed the bank on the other side and horse hooves thrashed in mud as they tried to grip the bank and pull the weight simultaneously. Suddenly the cart became lighter and Taaffe turned to see the men behind him push the cart so they could clear the way to mount the other bank. The heave worked for the horses could now mount the other side and pull Taaffe clear.

He whipped the reins, and the horses broke into a trot. The trot soon stopped as the cart ran into bodies as Taaffe found out what awaited him on the other side. A unit of pike marched in front of him as rebel shot fired at them from both sides. The loyalist shot were reduced to searching the dead for powder so they could sporadically return fire to provide some sort of cover for their comrades.

Taaffe battled onwards, attempting to cut a clear path for his horses between the bodies and debris from the battle. But the rebels now had sight of him and liked the large target he presented. Another volley was discharged and amongst screams and frantic neighing, his front left horse fell injured, dragging the others down as he collapsed under the harness. Taaffe jumped from his seat and cut the horse free. She was still alive, but he had no time to put her out of her misery, for he was still under fire and had the chance to escape as he still had another three horses. He took the lead horse by the harness and dragged him so the wheels of the cart were free of the horse's former partner. He jumped back on his seat and whipped the reins.

He was reduced to the speed of the unit of pike in front of him, as the English army could only carve out a narrow path between the rebels.

Taaffe cursed the rebels as they used the cart and horses for target practice. The non-combatant men had now joined him on the cart and used whatever boxes and trunks they could as cover. Wave after wave of rebels attacked the flanks of the column and the cart was peppered with bullets and missiles.

All looked above them as the skies went dark. The heavens opened. Taaffe had his head, shoulders, and feet battered by the rain. The horses suffered the same fate, for neither man nor animal could seek refuge from heaven's wrath. The downpour stopped as suddenly as it started. All and sundry were soaked to the skin. The cart came to a juddering halt in the churned-up ground left behind by a fleeing army. Taaffe felt ill after his soaking but summoned up the energy from the depths of his soul and jumped off the cart and pushed on the wheel.

"Jump down and help push whilst the enemy is distracted," he called to those hitching a ride on his cart.

They reluctantly obeyed but his passengers were more useful for their brains than their brawn and soon exhausted themselves in their futile efforts to free the cart.

"It's no good," said Taaffe's magistrate as he rested himself on the wheel. "The rebels are not done and will be back soon and we'll die for the contents of this cart. Better to flee now whilst we still have our lives."

"The crust you earn is in this cart. Push as hard as you can, or none of you'll get paid."

They spent the last of their energies on a wheel that would not budge. They collapsed by the cart, exhausted. The magistrate had reached his limit.

"If it frees me from these bonds of obligation, I relinquish my fee. Slash the reins of the horses and set them -."

There was a swish and a thud and he looked down towards his stomach. The end of a javelin protruded out of it. His blood gushed down his leg. He staggered back and fell against the cart. He turned white and fell to his side. The shock of his companions was palpable. Taaffe leaned over the man to check if he was dead.

"I free you from your bonds," he whispered in his ear as his magistrate took his last breath. He turned to his men who had gathered around. "I free you from all of your bonds."

The men nodded and took to their heels.

Taaffe slammed his fists on the wheels of his cart and cursed his luck. A bullet whizzed past his head to signal it was time to leave. But his horses who were still strapped to the cart neighed and bucked for they also wanted to escape.

"You have also served me well and though I may deserve my fate you need not share it with me."

He cut the reins of his horses and set them off in the direction of the forest. He ran after his men.

## CHAPTER 37

# A WINTER'S TRUCE

The Maguires limped back to Enniskillen in dribs and drabs, for what should have been a glorious victory became tinged with failure. The Crown army had escaped and was still intact and the O'Donnell had chased them back to Galway and retreated once more when they heard of the failure of a third Spanish Armada and the death of the Lord Deputy. Hugh O'Neill had once more begun negotiations for a truce. Then there was the all-important point that the end of the fighting season led straight into the reaping of the harvest and the fighting men were required to bring in the crops.

Eunan limped back to Enniskillen with half of his pike dead, but with most of his shot. Cúchonnacht Óg was at the gate to greet him when he arrived. They warmly embraced and Cúchonnacht Óg took him aside as his men entered the castle gate.

"I have orders from my brother that you must stay until he returns."

"I have a sickly pregnant wife in my father-in-law's castle that I must see to. What is more important to the Maguire than my domestic bondage and his diplomacy with the O'Neills?"

"His Galloglass," said Cúchonnacht Óg.

"And what of them? They enabled what should have been our victory and if there was any fault in the campaign, it was certainly not down to them."

"There are stirrings of trouble in the court about it. I advise you to release the men for the harvest and see if you can replace those who you have lost."

"Lend me a scribe and a messenger and I will face my critics, but let it be soon, for I must return to my wife."

"I will see what I can do."

Eunan stayed for several days and heard the rumours of the stirrings against him. His recruitment efforts had been in vain, for such was the eagerness of the Maguires to reap what turned out to be a reasonable harvest and fill their crannógs for the expected year of war ahead. Eunan was granted a leave of absence by Cúchonnacht Óg to replace some of the men he lost before his conduct in the previous fighting season was discussed in the court of the Maguire. The next day he left for O'Cassidy house with Odhran by his side.

Seamus woke up. His body felt as if it had been marinated in treacle. His head throbbed.

"Water...please!" he croaked.

A blurred face peered over him and lifted his head. The sound was muffled. He felt his head being raised and life returning to his mouth. He coughed and spluttered, and his head raised more. His senses gradually returned to him.

"Are you all right?"

The noise sounded like it came from the bottom of a well.

"He's awake now."

That stung in his ear as the volume varied. Then a face he recognised.

"Are you all right, love?"

It was the creased face of Dervella.

"Prop me up a little so I can see," whispered Seamus.

He heard someone rushing around but could not see them. They placed pillows behind him and he still felt pain. He could still see Dervella but there was another person there which he could not quite recognise.

"It's me, Faolán," said the person and Seamus nodded in recognition for he felt vulnerable at the sight of the apparent stranger and wished to appease him in case he was a threat.

"Where am I?" whispered Seamus. "It can't be heaven, for they'd never let me in."

Dervella laughed and smiled at Faolán in relief.

"Well, we thought the devil might have you for a while but you mustn't have liked it and came back," said Dervella. "He left you with your sense of humour, anyway."

"My whole body aches and I can barely move my arm. What happened to me?"

Faolán's face came into view.

"Can you remember standing on the top of the Blackwater fort wall and calling back to the men?" he said.

"I can vaguely remember charging the wall."

"Well, that was only the start of it. You were shot and fell back down the wall and the men rushed it to save you. We were beaten back off the wall because Connor Roe failed to come and support us. We carried your body back to the camp where Connor Roe offered to take you so his physicians could attend to you. We refused, and that evening had to fight off assassins sent, no doubt by Connor Roe, to murder you. We could not let another sun rise without making sure you were safe. We smuggled you out of the camp before daybreak and you have lain here drifting in and out of consciousness for several weeks. Now is the longest you have been awake. A bullet went clean through your shoulder and it is healing. Your fever has finally cleared. Maybe now we can finally feed you properly and look to getting you out of bed?"

"He's going nowhere until I say it is safe," said Dervella, spreading her arms above Seamus's body and fending Faolán off with her eyes.

"I can decide for myself," said Seamus.

"Oh, can you now?" said Dervella. "Get out of bed then, if it is all up to you."

"All right, I will." Seamus felt his spirit return to him, but it was not his old body. His muscles ached, his bones hurt, and his limbs wouldn't listen. He could not even clear his legs from beneath his blanket.

"There. Can you admit I am right?" said Dervella.

"I haven't even the strength to argue with you, so I am at your mercy. Do with me what you will, woman."

Dervella tutted and turned to Faolán. "Would you mind leaving? I'm sure you have a thousand things to do better than listening to our bickering."

"I'm sure I do. Goodbye, Seamus, and I'll come back and visit soon."

"Go back to the war and don't let my men disgrace me!"

"Sure, that is all over for the winter. The Lord Deputy was a man with a strong head but a weak constitution and quickly succumbed to the Irish lurgy as they call it. The O'Neill is busy negotiating this winter's truce."

"So if Eunan stays out of trouble, then I have six months to recover?"

"That is a big if."

A month barely passed before Eunan and Odhran had O'Cassidy house once more in their sights. The crops were being taken in as they rode past, and the leaves of the trees had achieved a beautiful ochre colour and fell daintily around their heads. Men and boys trained in the lands surrounding the house and the whole estate seemed a hive of activity in stark contrast to his visits when he left Óisín in charge. Eunan was greeted by name as he rode up to the door of the house by men whom he recognised.

"Is the mistress of the house in?" said Eunan.

"And so is the master," came the reply.

"Well then, do not let me linger on the door and bring me to them."

The man led Eunan to beneath the oak tree where Seamus, Faolán, Arthur and Dervella sat around a fire with a rabbit upon a spit.

"What has you out here on a wintry day like this when my uncle generously donated a house to keep you warm?"

"EUNAN!" Dervella shrieked, and she almost bowled him over as she ran to hug him.

"Don't fuss over him, woman," said Seamus. "You'll embarrass him now that he's really important."

Eunan untangled himself from Dervella's limbs and greeted first Arthur, then Faolán and finally turned to Seamus.

"Don't get up for me or anything," said Eunan as he shook Seamus's upwardly extended hand.

"Look at him," said Faolán. "He's an old man now that he's got his war wounds."

Eunan looked downwards and indeed there had been a mass expansion of grey along the strands of Seamus's long hair and upon his beard. He had also yielded a lot of his bulk and was, in comparison, almost skin and bones.

"What happened?" said Eunan.

"Ah, just a stray bullet. I'll tell you another time," said Seamus.

"He single-handedly assaulted the Blackwater fort was what he did," said Faolán.

"And more the fool for it," said Dervella.

"I'll be fine for the next fighting season," said Seamus. "So what has you here besides seeking our delightful company?"

"I need some fighting men," Eunan said.

"That leaves it wide open to my imagination. What you have got yourself into this time?"

"Heavy losses in Connacht. I need to show some replacements before I face the Fermanagh court."

"How about him?" said Seamus, pointing to Faolán. "He's a sturdy lad."

"No, they've already met him."

"That'd be a good reason to reject him," and they all laughed. "The shot are pretty good," Seamus said. "I can give you twenty of them without leaving me short. Precious little pike and I'm sure you're not in the market for Kern now you've moved up in the world."

"The shot would be a substantial contribution. That would help me out a lot."

"Well, make yourself a seat and have some of this rabbit with us and tell us some tales of the escapades of Eunan Maguire," said Seamus. "If we're lucky, Faolán will put them to a tune."

The fire burned long into the night, fuelled by logs and stories until Seamus grew tired and they all went to bed.

A joyful week came and went before a messenger arrived to inform Eunan that the Maguire had returned to Enniskillen and had summoned Eunan to meet with him before the Maguire council of leaders. Eunan prepared to leave, but so did Seamus.

Eunan stood outside the house with his bags packed and his horse ready. Odhran was busy organising the twenty shot who were to go with him. Seamus emerged from the house with a bag squirming under his arm and his belt a snake that refused to be tamed. A tearful Dervella followed him out the door.

"You can't leave now. You're not well enough. Your wound will open if you ride on a horse," she said.

"Stop fussing, woman," Seamus said as he finally tamed his belt. "Eunan needs me. I'll size up those vipers in that castle and come straight back. Eunan's got to see his wife, so neither of us will loiter in Enniskillen for long."

Dervella ran up to Faolán. "Talk some sense into him. Make him stay."

"What makes you think I have any more sense than he?"

"At least go with him. Make it harder for his numerous enemies to kill him now he is in a weakened state."

"I'll go if he'll have me?" Faolán looked inquisitively at Seamus.

"Go get your things. But remember, you're a bodyguard, not a nursemaid," said Seamus as he nodded towards the door of the house.

Seamus put his bag on the ground and went to whisper in his wife's ear. "I'll be back in a few days. Now go say goodbye to the boy, for it could be a long time before you see him."

Dervella went to Eunan and wrapped her arms around him.

"Good luck and may I shower a thousand blessings on you."

"They would still be less than all the blessings you have given me and my lands. I will return your husband to you in one piece before the week is out. It is his fault he is so useful."

Dervella smiled and wiped a tear from her cheek.

# CHAPTER 38

# RETURN TO COURT

E unan found himself in the crowded hall of the Maguire, with the lords and military leaders of the clan to celebrate the end of another fighting season. Even Connor Roe was invited on the instruction of the O'Neill for his contribution to the assaults on the Blackwater fort. The room was tense, but ringed with Galloglass to prevent any trouble.

Eunan was summoned the next day to see the Maguire in the great hall. Eunan and Seamus climbed the stairs with Cúchonnacht Óg with whom they had been staying in a farmhouse he owned near the castle. They entered the room to find the Maguire seated in his chair with Fachtna Óg at his side. Along the wall sat Irial, Feargal and Cearbhall and some of the more powerful chieftains of the Maguire, who supplied most of the men for the army. The Maguire extended his hand.

"Please Eunan, come in," said the Maguire. "We have some matters to discuss concerning the conduct of the raid in Connacht and other items."

"Have we not just had the feast and now should take in the harvest to prepare for the next fighting season?" said Eunan.

"Normally we would. But the commanders of the MacCabes have brought up some issues with me we should discuss."

"There's none so bad that there's a noose waiting for him in the yard?" said Seamus.

He looked for a smirk in reply to his jest but only saw grim faces.

"I will be honest with you, Eunan, for you have always been an excellent servant to me. The issues they have brought up concern your fitness to lead the MacCabe and whether I was too hasty in appointing you to lead my best men. But as you have always served me well, I have done you the service to allow you to face your critics and for them to make their cases in front of you before I decide."

"Let us hear these allegations so we can dismiss them and get on with more important matters such as bringing in the harvest," said Seamus as he glared at who he perceived to be Eunan's detractors.

"I don't know why you are here, Seamus MacSheehy," said Irial. "You do not bear the clan name nor are you an agent of the Maguire. I believe the O'Donnell is your master. Then why do you speak of issues that concern the Maguire alone?"

"Eunan has a right to council and I am that for him." Seamus looked behind him and Eunan nodded in agreement to Seamus's self-appointed position.

"Then you should also listen," said Irial. "Eunan Maguire is accused of reckless negligence of his duties to the Maguire and his Galloglass, which has resulted in the decimation of the ranks of the MacCabes."

Seamus turned to Eunan and whispered in his ear. "You'll have to help me out here. I only have those tall tales you told us by the fireside to go on."

"They were the truth," said Eunan.

"Then I'll go with that."

Seamus turned to address the Maguire. "Since we are all here today, you must consider these allegations sufficiently serious that they need to be aired. Let us waste no more time and hear these allegations. I, for one, am needed elsewhere."

"Don't let us stop you," said Fachtna Óg. "The Maguires can sort out their own business."

"I'm sure the Maguire has no wish to compromise the important connections he has with the O'Neills or the O'Donnells by interfering with their agents," Seamus said. "Please, begin this inquiry and let us hear your hot air."

"Please present the first allegation," said the Maguire.

"The first," said Fachtna Óg, "is that Eunan Maguire did recklessly endanger both his own men and the rearguard of the entire Maguire army by ordering the MacCabes to guard some very slow carts that allegedly contained treasure."

"I was carrying out the orders of the Maguire himself," said Eunan.

"I very much doubt the Maguire would give such an order that would endanger his men if he was in full possession of the facts of the tactical situation?"

Wise old heads looked to the Maguire to see which side of the fence he would fall. The Maguire's cheeks tinged, and he stared into the blankness in front of him and no answer was forthcoming. But Fachtna Óg had read him well.

"So since we are all on the same side and have no wish for the roots of animosity to cast shoots into the semantics of words, whatever you were told or instructed to do was within the bounds of tactical adjustment. Would that be fair, Eunan?"

Seamus glared at Eunan for he feared any misplaced word would open him up to the wrath of the Maguire. They had to admit they were beaten in this line of argument.

"I went through the chests, not all of them mind, but enough to know that it would be the making of the clan to get them back to Enniskillen."

"Did you know the source of all these treasures?"

"Only that they were from the retreating English army."

"So they may have been stolen from our allies in Connacht?"

"That is a question for the Maguire," said Seamus. "For the distribution of booty and diplomacy is the bastion of the Maguire not the commander of the MacCabes."

"Thank you for your comments," said Fachtna Óg, trying to regain control of the conversation.

"And before you try to rewrite history, remember the Maguire held a feast in Eunan's name and declared him a hero for saving half the treasure and holding off the English from attacking our rear."

"Do not get me wrong," said Fachtna Óg, "we are grateful for Eunan's efforts. But now we find that most of Eunan's men are dead and they were the best men the Maguire has. We need to account for their deaths to their families and those chieftains who supply the Maguire with most of his men and see if they died in vain. We have a duty that is greater than Eunan's ego."

"Well, if you condemn Eunan for that last event, then you call into question the judgement of the Maguire for declaring Eunan a hero."

Fachtna Óg did not reply, but paced the room slowly, as if deep in thought.

"I did not want to say, for I wished to avoid sowing division, but some of Eunan's own commanders warned him of the folly of defending treasure carts that he inevitably lost. That commander's actions preserved most of the men."

"Who is on trial here?" said Seamus. "Eunan or this mysterious commander? As a commander in the field with decades of experience, I'd say on the facts you presented, the commander disobeyed the orders of his superior and jeopardised the mission by dividing the men and making Eunan weaker."

Fachtna Óg ignored the last comments.

"What we are trying to do is see what kind of man Eunan is, establish a pattern and then see if he is fit to lead our best men. The next point to consider is the defence of the ford in the battle of the rain and the near wipe-out of the Maguire's pike."

Seamus laughed.

"State your case. We can look at who is to blame afterwards."

"Eunan was instructed to seize and defend the ford and wait for support from the main Maguire army. Is that a fair summation of your orders, Eunan?"

"Within tactical interpretation, yes."

Seamus glared at him again for he knew that Fachtna Óg was just setting the trap.

"And what did you do?" said Fachtna Óg.

"I went and occupied the ford as instructed," said Eunan.

"What was the tactical situation?"

"I was ahead of the main army, looking for the Maguire horse and the O'Rourkes were not far behind."

"So you were alone?"

"At that moment in time, yes. But I knew that the ford must be held until reinforcements arrived."

"What men did you have at your disposal?"

"One hundred pike and one hundred shot."

"These were all Galloglass?"

"Yes, they were all MacCabes."

"And how many more Galloglass does the Maguire have?"

"Another hundred of each."

"Is that correct?"

"That was the number at the start of the campaign. As I'm sure you can imagine, the number fluctuates during the campaign."

"I'm sure it does. But I prefer definitive numbers. The estimate was the Maguire had another one hundred Galloglass at his disposal, doing various duties for him. Therefore, you had the active Galloglass under your command."

"If you say so."

"How long does it take to train up a Galloglass?"

"It depends."

"On what?"

"The circumstances."

"Humour me with a guess."

"Three years is good if they come to us as a lad."

"So, let me see if I have this correct. You have got ahead of the main Maguire force and hold a ford with most of the Maguire's Galloglass."

"On his explicit instruction."

"So where was the English army?"

"Bearing down on this ford for it was the nearest one to them."

"And what was the estimated strength of the English army?"

"Around two thousand men."

"So you are outnumbered ten to one?"

"Are you trying to write a ballad to him?" said Seamus. "Can you not do it in your own time?"

Fachtna Óg again ignored him.

"What did your constables advise you to do?"

"Is this all about Feargal and how he does not want me to lead the Galloglass?" said Eunan. "This seems a neatly crafted narrative that would match Feargal's version of events with the benefit of hindsight thrown in to make him appear wise."

"Just answer the question."

"The Galloglass constable's duty is to the Maguire and to obey his orders. We did just that."

"Were you not advised to retreat?"

"If one of the constables would like to come in front of the Maguire gentry and admit that he wished to retreat in the face of the enemy, I will not stop him," said Eunan.

"Please remain co-operative so we can resolve this issue fairly. Now the English army pinned you against the ford. At what stage did you retreat?"

"When I thought we had delayed the English enough so they would become trapped between the O'Donnells, Maguires and the O'Rourkes."

"Was it before you thought you would be wiped out?"

"We would have insufficiently delayed the enemy to justify holding the ford any longer."

"Then what happened?"

"We went to the woods and watched our sacrifice bear fruit as the English army was caught between our three forces."

"Were you able to attack?"

"The men were spent. Only the shot who quickly abandoned the pike on the ford to their fate were capable of fighting."

"And were the English crushed between the three rebel forces?"

"They certainly got a good hiding."

Fachtna Óg turned to the Maguire nobles.

"So there we have it. Two missions, with what could be described as both avoiding defeat and most of our irreplaceable Galloglass dead. What is to be done with this irresponsible youth who deceived the Maguire into trusting him and placing him in charge of his Galloglass?"

Seamus stepped forward in front of Fachtna Óg's audience. He was not going to take this.

"This eloquent pawn knows nothing of war, the code of the Galloglass, nor what it is to obey orders in the face of a vastly superior enemy. It takes guts to control all your constables and follow your master's orders, especially when you are risking the lives of your men. It is easy to criticise when you dissect every decision made with the benefit of hindsight to fit a particular narrative. We have heard Fachtna Óg's whining but still do not know why we are really here. We have heard the set-up, now execute your plot so we can see it all out in the open."

A silence descended upon the room which was pierced when the Maguire rose to speak.

"I have listened intently to both sides, considered my instructions and the lee-way I gave for their interpretation. But no matter what interpretation I explore, I cannot escape the fact that we have lost too many good men that I cannot easily replace. With the clan having faced several years of famine and no signs of the war coming to a definitive conclusion, I cannot risk hiring mercenaries to replace those we lost, especially when, if we could not pay them, they may turn on us. Therefore, I put the command of the MacCabes in the hands of Feargal Beggan MacCabe. Eunan will now serve as his constable and command the MacCabe shot. I am grateful for the service you have both given me."

The nobles of the Maguire, Fachtna Óg and Irial crowded around the elated Feargal who received their congratulations. Eunan's head fell to his chest and Seamus hooked his hand around the back of Eunan's neck and pulled him towards him.

"I know what's going on here," Seamus whispered in his ear. "I'll take care of it. Leave it to me. Go see your wife."

Eunan released himself from Seamus's grip and stood before the Maguire.

"What about my wife? May I have leave to see my wife?"

"You will be granted any leave that may be necessary and I will instruct Feargal accordingly."

The Maguire beckoned Eunan forward.

"I'm sorry," he whispered in Eunan's ear. "The nobles refused to give me more men to fill the ranks of the MacCabes if I left you in charge."

"I understand, lord. Give me time and I will strengthen your position. May I recruit my own men for the MacCabe shot?"

The Maguire nodded. Eunan bowed and left with Seamus. They got as far as the door when a Galloglass approached them.

"I was asked to give you this, Lord. I don't know what it is."

Eunan took the crumpled-up letter and stuffed it in his pocket. He had had enough of Enniskillen that day.

# CHAPTER 39

# THE LONELY TOWER

E unan sat in a chair by the lake on Cúchonnacht Óg's farm whilst he wrestled with the indignity of being stripped of his position as leader of the Galloglass. He also contemplated going to see his wife; the tattered old letter with the date torn off he had been given on leaving Enniskillen was from her. He reread it, held it down and resisted ripping it up. Eunan shuddered.

"How long has my wife been like this?"

He needed to bide his time before he could make his excuses and leave. He snapped to and paid attention to the here and now.

Seamus threw logs onto the fire and addressed him.

"All this is a plot between Irial and Feargal to remove you. The Maguire was foolish, no offence to our host."

"None taken," said Cúchonnacht Óg.

"But it was throwing a piglet into a snake pit. I told you they were all vipers, but your uncle Seamus will look after you as always."

"Be quiet," said Eunan. Seamus was about to take offence until he saw the white face of the offender.

"I received a letter from my wife and she has not taken well to being with child. I must go and be with her now."

"It's a pity you didn't receive the letter earlier. We could have got that trial postponed."

"Shut up, Seamus," hissed Cúchonnacht Óg.

Seamus made a fist. "Don't mistake my politeness to the boy as an excuse to be rude."

"I'm sorry. It has been an emotional day for all of us, especially Eunan. Forgive my shallow temper, for it meant you no malice."

"It better not have," said Seamus. "Eunan, if it is so urgent, leave now. Take Faolán with you, for you may need protection. I'll stay here and arrange things for when you get back."

"Thank you, but I'll ride alone."

"You have the choice of Faolán or me. You have responsibilities now and many enemies. What is it to be?"

"Faolán, pack your things."

"Cúchonnacht Óg is far better at insulting me than you are, even though you've had so much practice."

Eunan ignored him and packed his things for his trip.

The tower of Augher Castle looked lonely on the hill even though it was the centre of attention for the winter wind and the crevices between its bricks gathered the most rain. It had taken Eunan a day and a half to get there as he did not want to draw attention to himself and the roads had become dangerous because of the increase in the number of people made homeless by the war and driven to banditry. Eunan did not know what he dreaded the most: confronting the reality of his wife's illness and probable failed pregnancy, or having to face her father and explain why he had not written or visited and his subsequent loss of status in the Maguire clan. As he rode up the hill to the castle, he wondered if this would be the last time.

As he approached the gate, one of Cormac MacBaron's constables came out to take his horse.

"I barely recognise you. It has been so long."

"I suppose I'm in for more of that when I go inside?"

"I'll not speak for my master's temper lest to do so provokes it. My master and your wife wait for you inside. I hope for your sake you have some pleasant tales to tell."

"And I hope to tell them to receptive ears."

Eunan was shown to the great hall where Cormac and his constables sat eating. Where his mood had been volatile before, it now settled on black.

"My son-in-law returns to me. I should be honoured were it not for the extensive O'Neill spy network in Enniskillen. Whispers and rumours ride faster than a horse. Did you know that?"

"Hello, father-in-law," Eunan said. "I apologise for my tardiness."

"Your extended absence is way beyond tardiness."

"We have much to discuss, and I am weary. Perhaps it is better that I see my wife first, before we try to resolve the world and her woes."

"First, I suggest you attend to your son."

Eunan froze. Cormac continued to eat, not looking up at Eunan.

"Where is he?" said Eunan, his ears pricked to detect the crying of a child.

"In the graveyard at the bottom of the hill. One of the men will show you."

Cormac's anger at his son-in-law's prolonged absence simmered as he sliced off a strip of meat from a leg of roasting hot venison. A wave of shock shuddered through Eunan's body. His mind froze, and he looked at the floor.

"I had a son and nobody told me?"

Faolán caught his falling body and helped him to a chair.

"Someone get him a mug of wine," said Cormac. "May its medicinal qualities work on him far better than all the good the expensive physicians have done my daughter."

Eunan sat with his senses shattered. Faolán whispered "there, there," in his year, for nothing else would come to mind, such was his unease with this nursemaid's role. Eunan jerked upright.

"I must see my son."

"This way," said one of Cormac's men and he tapped Eunan on the arm.

Darkness enveloped the castle, the wind caressing the stone walls and the faces of anyone who stepped outside it. The rain pelted down, but it was good cover for anyone with uncontrollable tears. Eunan staggered downwards and cried out for his boy. Faolán grabbed hold of him and wrapped a blanket around his shoulders.

"This way," and their guide pointed down towards a group of trees.

They entered the graveyard with clumps of grass and commemorative stone all equally slippy underfoot. They went past all the patrons of Augher Castle from the past, their wives, then their children and finally their dogs. After all of that came a series of small graves at the back of children who never survived infancy.

"It is that one there," said the guide.

"What does it say?" said Eunan, for tears blinded him.

"Here lies Art Maguire O'Neill."

Eunan sobbed.

"I wouldn't have called him that."

Eunan had to be escorted back to the castle, for he was inconsolable. He was brought to his room and laid to rest. It was a week before he emerged again, for he was taken with a fever and assigned to one of Sorcha's physicians. It was a blessing he was ill, for some tempers cooled and some ears were more willing to listen when he emerged from his room, pale-faced and slightly skinnier. His father-in-law had a meal prepared for him and ensured that they would eat alone. Faolán was sent to fetch him and sat him down by his father-in-law in front of a meal of meat, bread, and ale.

"Eat," Cormac said. "I have never seen you so pale."

Eunan stretched out his shaking hand and took some bread. He noticed Cormac had somewhat mellowed towards him and at least was being civil. He put some bread in his mouth and chewed slowly.

"How is my wife?"

"You should ask her yourself. She'll be glad to see you. We have heard many rumours about you. They say you are like an eagle shot down in soaring mid-flight."

"I certainly feel like that. Enniskillen is a cesspit of intrigue and backstabbing. Every time I leave, there comes someone from behind me that wants to plunge a dagger in my back."

Eunan picked up pace as he ate as he felt the energy come back into his body.

"You're lucky your wife loves you so much. She wrote to you many times to tell of her woes. But she can talk down an over-protective, judgemental father."

"If I had known what she was going through, I would have come immediately. I only received one of her letters once my trial was over. I can only think that they were intercepted by my enemies in the MacCabes and tossed in the nearest campfire to hurt me and break my link to you. Given where I sit now and under the circumstances, you can definitely say I failed, but I could only do what I could do. I ask for your forgiveness for neglecting your daughter, but I have a duty to the Maguire, which I'm sure you understand."

"If I did not understand, I would not have reminded him of who you are married to and that I can be easily offended in matters concerning my family."

Eunan's fork paused in the side of the venison. Did he only keep a position in the MacCabes because Cormac threatened them? What would have been his fate had he not spoken up for him? Eunan remembered where he was and finished carving his meat as calmly as possible.

"Thank you for your kind words on my behalf. I wonder if it raised or lowered what the Maguire really thinks of me?"

"Definitely raised it," said Cormac as he stabbed the chunk of meat in the middle of the table so he could break off a large piece. "View this as no more than a temporary setback. There are people on your side working in the background for you. But the key to it all is keeping my daughter happy. Speaking of her, it is high time you went to see her, don't you think?"

Eunan nodded and threw down his napkin and waited for his father-in-law to finish eating.

He knocked quietly on her door until he was invited in. She would have leapt out of bed and threw herself at him and almost knocked him off his feet had she not been so sick in bed that the most she could do was raise a smile and extend her arm out to him to welcome him in. He gladly took it and fell onto the bed. He buried his head between her neck and shoulder and sobbed.

"I'm sorry, I'm so sorry. I would have come if I'd have known. Please forgive me!"

Sorcha wrapped her hands around the back of his head.

"I forgive you, for I know you would have come if you were not duty bound. I could just as easily ask for your forgiveness as I failed when I tried to do my duty, just like you failed when you tried to do yours."

Eunan withdrew his head from the bed since it spun from the last sentence and it seemed to play back to him in a loop.

"I failed...you failed...I tried to do my duty...just like you failed...you failed."

His tears dissipated into anger, but his brain hurt too much to process anything. He stopped, paused, and looked at his wife's smiling face.

"We may both have failed, but we still have each other."

Sorcha extended her arms, and he fell into them, and they exchanged forgiveness.

Eunan emerged, smiling, from his wife's room the next day, and met his father-in-law in the hall for breakfast.

"So are you staying, then?"

"For as long as yourself and Sorcha will have me."

# CHAPTER 40

# RETURN OF THE LAND AGENT

Having left his worldly goods and possessions behind to soak and the ink of the land deeds he had stolen to flow into the bogs on the battlefield of the rain, Taaffe fled to Munster. He came to call on his friend Richard Boyle to whom he had sold good deeds for the lands he stood on and was confident of a warm reception, for he had sold more land to him in the safer parts of Ireland on multiple occasions afterwards. His assumption was correct, and he stayed and convalesced for a week before his friend presented him with a bill for his lodgings. Taaffe took the bill with as much grace as he could muster and walked down to the seclusion of a tree-lined bank of the local brook. The sun glistened on the water, the birds sang in the trees and the bees busily collected their nectar. But the joy of nature could not penetrate the dark heart of Taaffe, for he could not lift his mind from plunging his hands in his pockets and finding only holes. He had to return to his former good fortune, but Sligo was ablaze while all his former allies were exiled or had turned coat. His hands left the emptiness of his pockets and plunged them into the earth. There was only one way he knew how to restore his luck and that was through the land.

He returned to Boyle's house with his bill for lodging protruding out of his back pocket. He got his friend to retrieve his collection of various maps for his friend aspired to be a large landlord but did not have the skills or determination of Taaffe to do whatever was necessary to possess that land and therefore was reliant upon him and men like him to package up the land for him. Taaffe did not want to alienate his friend, no matter how offended he was to receive a bill for lodgings, as his friend would vouch for him to potential buyers wary of the turbulence in Connacht.

Boyle laid out the maps on the table. Taaffe bent over the arbiter of his new fortune and studied hard. For what the maps lacked in detail Taaffe made up for with imagination. He divided up the land of Sligo into what he could remember he previously sold, what he owned, what Donough O'Connor lay claim to and the rest, which was what he thought he could sell. He drafted some promissory notes based on his past discussions with his magistrate. He knew he was selling risk. Instead of selling the land, he promised the bearer of the notes an option to buy the land cheaply once the English army had repossessed it. The notes were to be valid for five years and the monies raised would go towards raising mercenaries to free the land. He allowed himself a congratulatory smile on the genius of his plan. He persuaded Boyle to accompany him to Dublin to vouch for the legitimacy of his scheme. His friend agreed for it was the only way he would receive his rent and his additional fee.

Taaffe spread around Dublin to the good, the great, and Captain Williamson, the date and venue of his house. He discreetly sold whatever of his father's possessions in the house would generate quick money. He hired some bodyguards but could not stretch to a magistrate or cheaper legal advice for he had to keep the appearance of the house as respectable as possible for his esteemed guests.

The evening finally arrived, and he invited his guests into the house and gave them some alcohol in the vain hope of making them more pliant. The guests were far less numerous than his first event and the mood sombre compared to the ebullience of the previous party. Taaffe worked the room but was bombarded with questions.

"I heard Sligo fell to the rebels?"

"Why aren't you fighting with the Queen's army?"

"The lands you sold me last time are overrun with rebels."

The gentry of Dublin, disgruntled or curious, formed a circle around Taaffe, waiting for his answers.

"What you gentlemen need to know is that you are all buying risk. That is why you get these lands at such knockdown prices. What you gentlemen have to say to yourselves is, do I believe the Queen or the northern rebels will win? If you believe in the Queen, then form an orderly queue and buy your discounted land and present your certificate to the local magistrate when the lands are cleared and claim them. If you don't, then pack your bags and set off for England or Dungannon. I have my good friend Richard Boyle who will vouch for the validity of the land deeds and my other friend, Captain Williamson, who can vouch for the Queen's forces that they can clear the land and support claims to good title. So, who wants to buy some land?"

An awkward silence ensued. A brave soul embedded in a small round man and puffed cheeks raised his voice.

"Well, the last time you were here and filled us full of wine and venison I bought a large tract of land from you in Sligo where you are supposed to be in control. The men I sent disappeared, never to be seen again."

"Well, it's hard to get good reliable men these days. Some of those clans turn coat so often I swear they must be colour blind. Tell my men the details of your land and I'll make sure it is secure."

"I sent my brother there, a man of sound morality and who has my complete trust. He went to my land only to be chased off."

"Again, I'll sort it for you," said Taaffe. "Just give me the details. Now, who wants to buy some land at a generous discount?" Taaffe turned his back on the man.

But he underestimated the man's fury and received a tap on the back.

"He got chased off because they called him a rebel and said the land was being requisitioned for the Queen."

Taaffe turned around in a shade of scarlet.

"Well, there you go then. My men were protecting your land for you and you sent a stranger without documents to claim it."

"He had both the title deeds and my seal. Your men, for all intents and purposes, could only interpret him as being my representative."

"As I said, I wasn't there. I can only reply to what you tell me. Now, I am happy to resolve all your issues but am not in the position to do so now. Why don't you peruse what's on offer and we'll see if we can add a bit more to your lands with an extra discount? Now, who wants to buy some land?"

Everyone drifted away to pick up another drink, talk in huddled groups or edge towards the door. Taaffe decided there was nothing else for it. He hooked the man by the elbow and took him to the badly-dressed man sitting behind a desk who was the cheapest magistrate-looking man Taaffe could hire.

"Right then, court magistrate of Sligo, what do we have for sale in—" He turned to the man to prompt him.

"Oh, the north," he said, a little surprised.

"Yes, the north of Sligo. A fine part of the country, very arable land."

The stand-in magistrate shuffled through his papers and shuffled through some more. Taaffe's mistake dawned on him. His first question should not have been how much, but can you read? Taaffe reached out and grabbed the nearest deed.

"That's a brilliant suggestion. Let's have a look at the map."

He bypassed his hired hand and grabbed the map himself.

"Now look, it is there. How about that for twenty per cent under the asking price?"

The man took the deeds in his hand and studied the description of the lands for sale. He fumbled in his pocket for another piece of paper and laid them both side by side on the table. After carefully comparing both, he put a finger on both descriptions.

"These descriptions sound like the lands you are trying to sell me and have already sold me are the same!"

Taaffe grabbed both pieces of paper and looked from one to the other. He pointed to the man and stood apart from him.

"This man is an agitator sent by the O'Neill to spread lies about my land sales. Men, seize him and bring him to the Lord Deputy!"

The room turned to chaos as the guests made for the front door to exit. Some grabbing hands emerged from the melee to snatch property deeds by buyers who thought Taaffe could have swindled them. Taaffe's hired hands filled their pockets with anything of value and fled. The slighted man slipped away into the crowd. Taaffe tried to protect his land deeds and swung punches at those grabbing hands, hitting the innocent and the guilty alike. Captain Williamson went to protect Taaffe from harm because, for all his faults, he was still of use in Sligo. The captain grabbed him and dragged him out into the alley behind the house.

"You must leave Dublin now," he said.

"Why should I run? Have that man arrested for being a spy or an agitator!"

"It's easy to get a mob in Dublin and you aren't the most popular around here. Leave now whilst you have a chance."

"You get your men and I'll go gather my things."

"I mean it, leave tonight."

Taaffe nodded and ran back into his house.

The house had been ransacked and abandoned by all. Some of Taaffe's papers floated around in the debris. There was not much of the former grandeur of his father's house left: holes in the wall, all the furniture smashed and the front door knocked off its hinges. Taaffe scrambled around, trying to gather his papers, when a slow thud came from the remains of the door.

"Taaffe, I want my money back!"

Taaffe could hear footsteps by the front door. He grabbed what he could and went for the back door, feeling for his dagger in his belt. It was still there. He looked into the alleyway to see three looming shadows in the fading light. He ran for the front door only to be confronted by his disgruntled client and some hard men he had run off and hired.

"Whatever he is paying you, I'll double it," he said to the men.

"Let him show you his money first," said the client.

The men grinned at Taaffe and advanced towards him, preparing their fists to meet his face. Taaffe took out his dagger and cut a semicircle in the air and dared them to pass it. The men paused and spread out across the room. They approached Taaffe from different directions and Taaffe's semicircle began to diminish rapidly. They prodded with whatever weapons they had, a knife, a spade, and a big stick. Most of these had longer reach than Taaffe and they took advantage by whacking down upon his wrist to disarm him. The stick connected with Taaffe's knuckles, and he dropped the knife with a yelp.

"Surrender now, or I'll throw your corpse into the river Liffey," said Taaffe's client.

"You don't have the guts to kill me," said Taaffe.

From outside came the sound of musket fire and the thud of bullets lodging in the beams of the house.

"Leave this house or suffer the wrath of Her Majesty's men!" came the shout from outside. The thugs looked to the windows, dropped their weapons, and ran past Taaffe out the back door. Taaffe's client turned from a growling dog to a timid mouse.

"I can buy any land you wish to sell me and you can forget about the discount," he said as he tried to edge towards the door.

"I can sell to no one else after what you said. You'll pay for sullying the reputation of William Taaffe!"

Taaffe picked up his dagger and charged at the client. The dagger went through his arm and stomach and he fell to the floor to die in a pool of his own blood.

Captain Williamson burst into the room and saw Taaffe, knife in hand with a blood-soaked tunic hanging from his body.

"You definitely have to leave. This way."

Captain Williamson smuggled Taaffe back to his house, where he allowed him to wash and gave him a new set of clothes. Taaffe was huddled by the roaring fire, a blanket wrapped around his shoulders and a bowl of soup in his coarse hands. The captain sat opposite him and grinned.

"You really didn't have to kill him."

Taaffe looked up from his soup.

"He would have turned on me the moment he felt safe and ruined my business and got me hung. It was him or me."

"What are you going to do now? You can't stay in Dublin. You're lucky you made that deal and are still useful to me."

"I may not look it, but I am grateful."

The captain smirked.

"Everything comes at a price. You know that the Earl of Ormond is in charge now?"

Taaffe smirked back.

"We get news in Sligo. It's not that remote."

"You've got a charmed life. I sometimes wonder how you've got away with all you have."

"So you gave up wondering and got a cut for yourself?"

The captain shook his head.

"Don't interpret my rescuing you as anything less than friendly. I have much knowledge and many connections that can benefit us both, even with your sullied reputation."

Taaffe reverted to seeking to get on the captain's good side.

"Sorry, the excitement of the last couple of days has got me jittery. You were saying?"

"Well, he may not have told you that the Queen gave the Earl the mission of subduing the rebellion in the north, but few new men and little money to do it."

Taaffe shrugged his shoulders.

"What's the point of that? She seems determined to bury the reputations of her best generals in the bogs of Ireland. I put it down to all the political wrangling in her court and all the different factions battling it out as to who shall succeed her when she eventually dies without an heir."

The captain shook his head again.

"You don't get it, do you? Since he has no soldiers, all loyal noblemen of Ireland can raise their own men and pledge them to the Queen's army. You get to raise a force, get them trained and armed for free, and get a share of the spoils when the Crown eventually wins. The land sale you'll be able to have after that will make your previous ones look like a chicken market."

Taaffe slapped the table with delight.

"That is good news! I already have a small command from the English and Irish settlers in Sligo, but they now seem to be in the wind. Where am I supposed to get these men from?"

The captain pointed towards the window.

"Where are we now? Dublin port. The place of men's dreams of wealth and fame. You need to divert their attention away from being merchants, joining the navy or emigrating overseas. You need to sell them the idea that they can have lands out in the wilds that can be productive farms and they can become wealthy like that. You'll soon have an army of men behind you and as much land as you could ever wish to sell."

Taaffe jumped out of his seat and thrust his hand towards the captain, his smile as radiant as any sun.

"Put it there! I need a couple of hours to sort out my affairs and then we can recruit some men down the docks."

The captain shook his hand but remained seated.

"Sit yourself down before you get all excited and clear the docks of their porters. You need money to pay them and from the looks of you, there's not a penny in those pockets of yours to rub together."

Taaffe looked hopefully at the captain.

"You'll get nothing from me," said the captain. "There's nothing in the Queen's coffers for you. I hear there are a great many of your punters seeking their money back, to say nothing of the money you borrowed from the Dublin moneylenders. You need to raise your own money and your own men. If you can get back on your feet, you'll have the Queen's blessing once again."

Taaffe rose, and the blanket fell to the ground.

"Where are you off to in such a hurry?" asked the captain.

"My father's. If you and the Queen apparently don't owe me, then he definitely does."

# CHAPTER 41

# THE PLEADINGS OF A PRODIGAL SON

Taaffe pulled up his horse. It was a straight road across the flat plain to his family's house, and he could see it clearly in the distance. However, memories of past failure soured his body from his stomach to his mouth. It was now early summer, and the fields should have been filled with crops for the autumn harvest. But the sky was wounded as it choked on billowing plumes of smoke and the lands ached with the scars of the fires left by the raiders of the north. Would he bear the failure of all of this when he turned up, the prodigal son, at his father's door? The pain unleashed by his leaving the house would surely rebound upon him. He threw the bitterness of his father's rejection of him back into his father's face. Now he was back at his father's door to plead for sanctuary, hounded out of Connacht by rebels and of Dublin by creditors. All he had left was the family home.

He rode up to the boundaries of the house and then dismounted. He was alone for his men had departed as quickly as his fortune disintegrated. He could not find solace in the English army for those Irish who could join the rebels or make it home had all deserted such had been the scale of the defeat. He might have survived with the gentry of Connacht or the merchants of Dublin, but the promise on his promissory notes and land deeds had become illusionary and bounty hunters had been hired by those who sought the return of sizeable sums of money. Sure, if his father could not see it in his heart to forgive and protect him, the bounty hunters that followed him could send them both to hell. A man stood in front of the farmhouse with a posture to protect his lands rather than welcome strangers.

"Heaven help us, 'tis the devil himself who stands in my yard. Not content with all our worldly goods, he wants our souls as well!"

Taaffe hung his head.

"Hello, Father. The least I could have expected from you was a sermon. If I didn't even get that, then I must be truly dead."

"Well, you look like a ghost to me, son. A pale-faced body whose soul has long since departed."

Taaffe looked expectantly at his father but received not a flinch.

"Aren't you going to invite your son in? Is there a Bible verse you would like me to quote to remind you of your Christian duty if you abandon those duties of a father?"

"The good word would sizzle on your tongue before you could utter it and then steal its meaning. Come in if you must. The rebels are like a plague upon us. Your brother, who dutifully stayed home to look after his family, has gone to Dundalk to sell some grain. You can come in and feed and bathe, but it would be good if you were gone before he returned."

"I'll accept your hospitality, Father, but I am not here to relight old arguments. The world has changed and the lands will burn before men like me willing to graft and shape the country will have done our jobs and made it safe for farmers like you. In what I took from my brother in abilities, he repaid me by beating me out of the womb. Let us break bread before you scornfully throw me out to protect you."

"Go sit at the table. Your gift of the gab didn't work on your creditors and won't work on me."

Taaffe grunted and went to sit at his father's table for even pride needs feeding.

His father sat down beside him to share the meal. They shovelled food into their faces in silence until an absence grew in the mind of Taaffe.

"Where is mother?" he asked. "Has she also gone to Dundalk?"

"She's gone to the other side of the hill," replied father. "A savage's axe put her in her grave. You tell me you do all these evil deeds because you are supposed to protect me. Yet, here I sit, all alone and hungry. 'Tis as if God has passed judgement on your family already, yet not all of us are in the grave."

Taaffe held the bridge of his nose in his thumb and index finger but even that did not stop the flow of tears.

"I will seek revenge on those who have wronged you. All I have ever wanted to do is to prove you were wrong to give everything to my brother."

"Yet all you have done is prove me right."

They sat in silence as Taaffe contemplated the death of his mother.

"Lord Bagenal and the Earl of Ormond are busy raising an army to invade the north and end the war," said his father.

"Good luck to them," said Taaffe as he wiped his nose.

"They are paying a good bounty to those who can raise men to fight."

"And look where that got me."

"It can get you there again. Whatever you are, you don't quit, unless it is on your family."

Taaffe got up and threw the remains of his plate on the floor.

"You tell me of my mother's death and still you torment me. How am I supposed to have saved her when your other precious son did no better than I ever could?"

"Because you're a brute. You're an animal! You could have easily killed all of them and protected your mother. Now redeem yourself and raise some men to crush the rebels. Get revenge for your murdered mother!"

Father collapsed in a coughing fit, his face as red as if his lust for revenge came straight from the pits of hell and vomited forth from him.

"Father!" Taaffe cried, and he bent down to help the old man.

The front door slammed against the back of the wall. Taaffe's brother stood in the frame with a bag of coins in his hand.

"Have you come to finish the job?" said his brother as he threw the bag of coins onto the nearest table and went for his knife.

"I was trying to help him, but that would make no difference to you, for you never missed an opportunity to put poison in his ear."

Taaffe stood up to confront his brother.

"If you take out a knife, you have to be willing to use it," and Taaffe looked down upon the knife in his brother's trembling hand.

"Stop...." their father wheezed before he keeled over, gripping his chest. The brother paused.

"What have you done to him?" he cried.

But before Taaffe could answer, his brother had set upon him. Thirty years of resentment gouged an eye, bit a thumb, spat blood on the floor. Twenty-eight years of jealousy flailed fists, bruised a cheek, and kicked out repeatedly yet sometimes aimlessly. The knife entered the fray, slicing the skin of arms used as a makeshift shield. Four hands wrestled for its grip, the point being thrust in the face of whichever brother's energy wavered, only to surge when coming face to face with the tip of the knife. Taaffe realised he was in a stalemate. But as their arms intertwined in their deadly grip, he saw opportunity where only a person such as he could out of the corner of his eye. He shifted his body slightly until he won over both their senses of balance. He kicked his brother in the shin to knock him off balance and hurled them both towards the corner of the table. They were both quite hefty men, so they struck the corner of the table with such force it knocked it over whilst breaking several of his brother's ribs. The coins were liberated from the bag and flew all over the room. The brothers' brawl ceased to be a contest. Taaffe knelt over his brother, the knife having gone to the victor.

"You stole everything that was mine. My parents, my land, my dignity."

His brother could only hold his ribs and fight for breath.

"Now you start a fight that almost killed our father. But now it must end."

Eaten up with resentment and hatred, Taaffe held the knife in both his hands and thrust it into his brother's chest. There was one final wheeze, but it was from the other corner of the room. Taaffe crawled over the debris of the fight to his father's contorted face. He shed a tear, not because he saw his father's face but a flashing moment of happiness from his youth. It was all over now. He was alone. His sense of torment was dead. He had no one's ideals to live up to but his own. He picked up the coin bag and searched the room so he could refill it.

# CHAPTER 42

# THE MILDEW WALL

The winter was hard for all residents of Augher Castle. The residents of the castle shivered in the cold as the wind and rain took advantage of its lofty and exposed height and bombarded them relentlessly with rain, even though it was more sparing with the howling wind. The tents of the MacCabe, who Eunan had recruited and had been sent to train with the O'Neills, were decimated first by wind, then by illness which either incapacitated or killed many residents of the camp. All the while the rain poured down, the skies were grey, and the soldiers prayed in the gloom to God to forgive them whatever sins they had committed for him to punish them so and to reassure him that they were on the right side; the Queen was the heretic, and they were all doing this for him. Eventually, Cormac relented in trying to harden up the MacCabes as he found exposing them to the elements in non-fighting season was counterproductive and a waste of the efforts to train them if they were all going to die in a puddle of mud. The local population took in what soldiers they could under coign and livery and the remains camped in a nearby forest. The soldiers clamoured to go home, and the local population echoed their pleas. But Eunan could not leave, and he was their leader.

The winter was especially bad for Sorcha's health, for she caught a fever or a chill every time the wind howled under the door. Cormac was determined to scupper her plans to try for another child and since he could not say no to his daughter, the easiest way was to restrict Eunan's access. He made excuses and blocked Eunan at every turn, but soon the pressure from both Eunan and his daughter paid off and he finally relented. But not before having another word in Eunan's ear.

Once Eunan received permission, he went and sat with his wife. Cormac sat in the chair opposite. Sorcha lay in the bed, her pale skin morphing into one with her white sheets, her long brown hair shaped around her face and shoulders showing where the sheets ended and she began. Eunan choked a little, for she reminded him of a living corpse, a thought he immediately wished to banish from his mind but which refused to leave. Memories of his mother returned, and he clenched his fist as if it would flush out his mind. Sorcha opened her eyes, looked at the wall opposite and heard breathing to her side. She turned her head.

"Eunan!"

Her eyes lit up with delight. Eunan looked at her with both fear and delight: delight she was still alive, fear that she looked tired and dreary, as if looking at him was using up most of the energy in her body.

"Eunan, take my hand."

Eunan obeyed and slid his hand under hers. Her hand could only lie there limply, not able to grip his.

"That is enough. Don't overexert yourself."

Her concerned father had made himself known. Sorcha turned her head towards him.

"Oh Father, you have kept my husband away from me long enough. May we have some time together alone to speak? If I need you, I will call for you."

Cormac rose, a little put out in his own home.

"The physician is on his way here with the latest herbal medicine straight from the continent through the port of Galway. Please make your conversation succinct, for we have little time to waste if you wish to be better. Then you can spend all the time you wish with your husband."

Sorcha smiled but did not reply. Eunan nodded, but also kept quiet. It was not his home, nor ever would be. Cormac picked up his things and left. Eunan made sure Cormac closed the door behind him before he spoke.

"Are you all right my love? I sit outside day after day waiting to be invited in to see how you are. This is no way for a husband to be treated!"

"Please be patient, dear husband. My father may be possessive of me but he means well. I speak to him on your behalf to ensure you are well rewarded for all your patience."

Concern, insult, and emotional confusion broke out all over Eunan's face.

"I don't want to be well rewarded. I want my wife!"

Sorcha could only raise a faint smile of reassurance.

"I am sick, but I will get better. Then we can spend time together if the war does not take you away from me."

"I would wish you to be better before I leave. I don't want to be off in the bogs of Connacht, parrying the swings of an axe and worrying about you in the back of my mind."

"When you leave, you will have me in your heart, warming, loving, and protecting you. But only think of me in the night-time when you look up at the stars. During the day, you must do your duty and be a magnificent warrior."

Eunan grasped her limp hand in both of his rough, calloused ones.

"I shall think of you always and do whatever it takes to make you better."

"If you wish to make me better, give me what I want most in the world."

"Anything. I will do anything to give you hope and make you better. Tell me what you wish for and it shall be yours."

"What I want most in the world may be the least attainable and may cost me my own life."

"What is it?" said Eunan, his heart plummeting in his chest for he knew the answer before he asked.

"I want a son."

Eunan clutched his chest and reeled back in his chair. Tears streamed down his face as he pulled himself upright and clasped his wife's hand.

"I thought the doctor said you could never conceive again?"

"I believe in all my heart that I can conceive, and that is what I want the most in the world. Nothing would make husband or father happier than if I gave birth to a healthy son."

Eunan's hand shook as he hid his face from his wife. Would he have to sacrifice the life of his wife so she could have a son? Was she even capable? Could he bear the pain of another lost child? Noises came from beyond the door.

"That is the physician. My father will come soon. What is your answer? Do you want a son?"

Eunan looked at his wife and the diminishing energy in her eyes. Would she ever be well enough to procreate ever again? He could see her writhe in her bed the longer he delayed his response. He could see her disappointment gather in the corners of her dark brown eyes. Was he cruel enough to extinguish her last hope? He grasped her hand with renewed vigour.

"Remember, you left me alone in this lonely tower to bear the loss of our son," Sorcha said, driving her point home.

Eunan bowed his head to hide his shame.

"Of course, my love," he said. "We will try for another son as soon as you are able. But if we are unsuccessful, it must be the last time."

Sorcha smiled and tried to raise herself in the bed to hug her husband. The door burst open and through it came Cormac.

"Don't overexert yourself, my dear. Lie back in bed. The physician is here. Please leave, Eunan, you are overexciting her."

Eunan never got his celebratory hug.

Eunan was confined again to the bench outside Sorcha's room to wait to be summoned. The winds howled even in the insides of the castle, so much so that there was a ready supply of blankets beside the bench so those that stood and waited could keep warm. The wailing women became too much for him and his prayers dried up. But obligation and compulsion glued him to the bench. He took to observing the light on the wall and how it changed with the passing of time during the day. It was susceptible to the northern gloom, where the cloud cover was so dark and thick one would think it was night when really it was day. But the inconsistent light did not give Eunan the steadiness he required to keep himself orientated and on track. If his emotions shackled themselves to the northern gloom, he knew not where despair would lead him.

He fixated on a patch of mildew on top of the wall opposite the bench. The walls were brick and mortar with a huge wooden frame spine. Eunan would follow the beams up the wall until they formed a junction with another beam that jutted out onto the roof. Physicians from different disciplines would scurry through the corridor to offer their expertise. The northern gloom would dance on the wafts of warm air and deposit moisture into the junctions of the beams. A constant flow of bowls of soup would pass by Eunan, as that was all Sorcha could eat. The moisture would feed the white mildew lodged between the fleshy valley and ridges of the huge beams, and the wood would contain life once more. Sorcha's mother would take to the bench beside Eunan and pull on his clothes and wail, and when the tears and energy had died, use his muscular shoulder as a pillow and reminisce about her daughter's lost youth to illness. But the mildew would eat away at the dead flesh of the beam and weaken it to such an extent that, if not dealt with, it would render the beam dangerous and useless.

"Eunan, you should really attend to your men. You have other duties besides warming this bench."

Eunan awoke from his stupor.

"Yes, father-in-law, you are probably right. My poor wife has enough people attending to her while my men are neglected. Will you inform me should her situation change?"

The stern face in front of him had little concern for his feelings.

"You'll be the first to know. Now your men await you."

"You should really get the top of that wall seen to. Things will only go one way if that mildew sets in."

Cormac's eyes gruffly climbed the wall.

"Oh, thank you. Now take your leave."

Sorcha's recovery seemed to take an age, and Cormac's mood improved at a glacial pace. Eunan would seldom approach him unless it were for an update about how his wife was doing. Cormac seemed disinterested in any conversations longer than a sentence. But one day he summoned Eunan to see him in the great hall.

The fire blazed, and Cormac stood before it and stared at the mantelpiece. He had a letter in his hand, down by his thigh. Eunan's chest tightened. What bad news did Cormac have to build himself up to that he needed to tell him?

Cormac turned around when he heard Eunan come in and placed the letter on the long dinner table. He extended his arm and invited Eunan to "sit". Eunan duly obliged and looked expectantly at his father-in-law.

"Are you enjoying your stay here with us?"

Cormac's tone was formal but polite.

"I could not say that with the circumstance being as they are that there is an element of enjoyment in my stay, but you all have been excellent hosts and made me feel welcome."

Eunan paused for he knew he had to brace the subject some time, and it may as well be now.

"I would like to know when I can properly take Sorcha to be my wife, and I can see her at my leisure on my own lands. We have excellent physicians in Fermanagh and I'm sure the Maguire would make available every resource he has in Fermanagh should needs be."

Cormac's jaw dropped.

"No, she is far too unwell to travel. I do not know what sort of environment you have down by the lakes and whether it would be agreeable to Sorcha at all. Maybe one day, but she cannot stray too far from her own dedicated physicians. But this is not why I brought you here. This is a conversation for far into the future. It is my understanding from the discussions with the Maguire and Seamus and, indeed, from your own actions you are amenable to spending your time here in Augher Castle and by doing this, cementing the alliance between the Maguires and the O'Neills."

Eunan nodded, for he felt that was what he should do as Cormac intertwined his fingers to emphasise his point.

"If this marriage should yield any children, I would gladly let them adopt the O'Neill name should they or their parents wish them to do so."

Eunan nodded again, for that was what he thought he should do. To pass on the O'Neill name would be a gift to his children beyond his wildest dreams. But he feared this was not the actual subject of the conversation.

"But this is not why I have brought you here."

At last. A shiver went down Eunan's spine.

"I have received a letter from your master requesting that you return. Apparently, after the turn of the year, the war will begin. The O'Donnell is anxious about setbacks in Connacht and has called on his allies for their support. I shall soon take to the field myself but in service to my brother. That means we will both leave Sorcha. Therefore, the safest place for her to be is in this secure castle in Tyrone with physicians that know and are familiar with her. I'm sure you agree?"

Eunan nodded, for he knew that to be a rhetorical question.

"I will write to the Maguire concerning your stay here and give some very good feedback about the leadership skills, battle tactics and war strategies you have picked up during your stay. The rescue of my son is something I will mention. I will also say that you have a fine body of well-trained men who show good skills with both muskets and pike. I will also recommend to my brother that the Maguires are the highest standard of allies that can be relied upon to withstand the most brutal of battles and most steadfastly hold the line. It may even contribute to you getting back your former position. What do you say to that?"

"I would be most grateful if you wrote such a favourable report. It is a pity that I could not have had it before my trial. But I fear my men could be caught out if such high praise was taken as the benchmark for their martial performance."

Cormac laughed.

"Nonsense. You must push your men to achieve the highest results. You can achieve that standard and more if you apply yourself properly and have confidence in your own abilities."

"Thank you, lord. I am flattered that you deem me worthy of such high praise."

"You are a credit to both myself and your wife."

Cormac gave Eunan a pleasant but formal smile. Eunan braced himself for he felt the arrival of the main topic of conversation. Cormac pulled up a chair and sat opposite Eunan.

"Unfortunately, I need to return to the subject of my daughter. If the circumstances were different, a father-in-law would not need to brace these topics, but we are where we are."

Eunan nodded and tried to look Cormac in the eye, but Cormac looked away.

"My daughter is slowly getting better, and I have had a few conversations with her and her physicians about the state of her health and what she really wants out of her life."

Eunan nodded, but more slowly than before.

"She says that she has discussed what she really wants with you. Is that correct?"

Eunan had to think about that for a minute.

"We all want what she really wants for her so that she can be well and lead a relatively normal life."

Cormac winced a little.

"No, what she really wants?"

Eunan looked nonplussed.

"To be with child. She wants above all else to be with child."

Shock laid claim to Eunan's face and no amount of wishful thinking could evict it and put politeness back in its place.

"She wants a son to give to her father and her husband. A noble warrior, which would be her legacy in the world. I know I have expressed my disapproval to you in the past frequently, but she is determined. It is not for her father to take away her dream."

"But it is the last baby that deserted her and left her so unwell and you so opposed to her trying again."

"But now she is recovered and her father's money has bought her the finest physicians in all of Ireland to guide her through it. She is ready for you in both body and soul, if you get my meaning. You needn't worry when you go off to war. She'll be fine. Shall I also include in my letter to the Maguire that you'll be delayed by a few weeks but the men can go first as you have 'duties' to attend to here first?"

Eunan winced.

"Please don't put it like that."

"I will be very polite and say that you have to attend to important business for the O'Neill. We are all happy and your reputation is once more enhanced."

Eunan wished to test to see if there was any way out.

"Is this what Sorcha wants?"

"She is ready for you straight away. I can clear the corridor outside her room so you have no distractions."

Eunan stared at the ground, for he did not want Cormac to see his face.

"If it should please your daughter, it pleases me."

"Excellent! I shall have everything prepared."

Cormac leapt out of his seat and towards Sorcha's room. Eunan was left wondering if he should follow. He sat in the room for a few minutes and realised he was meant to follow. There was a flurry of activity outside Sorcha's room and Eunan leant on the wall opposite, unsure of what would happen next. A crowd of people were herded out of the room by Cormac. He dismissed them and told them he would summon them later if needed. He saw Eunan propped up against the wall. Cormac sat on the bench and pointed towards the door.

"She is waiting for you."

Eunan hesitated, hoping that Cormac would leave. But he didn't. He settled down on the bench.

"Go on then. What are you waiting for?" said Cormac.

Eunan pushed the door and sheepishly entered the room.

"There you are, my love. Come in."

Sorcha smiled meekly and lifted the side of her blanket to reveal her porcelain body and invite Eunan in. He reluctantly took off his clothes. Cormac now made himself comfortable on the bench. He quickly became bored and examined the wall for this mildew Eunan was talking about. He summoned his chief scribe and called for a ladder, a servant and his ledgers. He could supervise the siring of his grandson, maintain the castle and review the books of his lands all at the same time. For he had no time to waste.

# CHAPTER 43

# THE GATHERING STORM

E unan stayed in Augher Castle for the winter, spring, and early summer. He visited O'Cassidy House when he was able, where he left Faolán to both raise and train men, for he now had to replace those Galloglass that he lost. He had infrequent contact with Feargal and the MacCabes, which pleased Feargal greatly for the longer Eunan was away, the more he could turn Eunan's former men against him. The truce held until the late spring / early summer, until everyone seemed to realise that the steadily increasing raids no longer made up a breach of the peace but had become the simmering of war.

Sorcha gradually got better and by the deepest of winter could move freely around the castle and go outside in the brief periods the weather would allow a woman of her constitution. Eunan, however, was more restricted, for these dead children his wife miscarried were a burden on his soul. He could not shake off the thought that he was somehow cursed. However, once Sorcha was well enough, she nagged at Eunan.

"Is my beloved husband ready to sire a child once more?"

Eunan furrowed his brow. He could not sigh out loud for fear of offending his wife.

"Once more? Show me those children that make up once more?"

Once the words had left Eunan's mouth, he realised they were hurtful, and he was on the back foot immediately.

"I'm sorry, I didn't mean that. You want to try again after all that's happened? You are finally well. Why don't you concentrate on enjoying your health for a while before considering being with child once more?"

Sorcha rolled off the bed and pranced around the room to show off her health.

"I hear the war is going to start up again soon. Are you staying here to make the most of your health?"

"You know I can't do that. I have to go. It is my duty."

"What is my duty? To give birth to a son? How can I do that without the help of my husband? What if my father neglected to do his duty? Where would you be then?"

"Don't threaten me!" said Eunan.

"Then do your duty and everyone will be happy."

When the call came for Eunan to return to Enniskillen several months later, he did so with fifty O'Neill shot riding behind him and a child in his wife's belly.

The Maguire army was camped outside Fermanagh. The news from the south was that Marshal Bagenal had gathered a force of nearly two thousand men and was going to march to the Blackwater fort to resupply it. Rumours spread that the English were also going to land an army behind the O'Neills and the O'Donnells in Lough Foyle and both armies were going to unify in central Tyrone. However, the O'Neill had summoned all of his allies to come to his assistance. Hence, the Maguire summoned all his men. Eunan arrived and made camp beside the MacCabes. He sent Odhran to fetch Seamus and Faolán so he could unify those under his command. Once Feargal knew of Eunan's arrival, he summoned him to his tent.

Eunan walked through the camp of the MacCabes, saluting some but noticed the ranks had swelled with men he did not recognise and appeared hostile to him. Feargal, Cearbhall and Irial were waiting for him outside Feargal's tent.

"Good day, commander," Eunan said as he bowed. "I assume all is well with you before the resumption of another campaign?"

But the grim-faced Feargal was not for charming.

"Those men you have brought with you. They are not Maguires. They cannot be MacCabes."

"Well observed, lord. The Maguire gave me command of the shot and I have received fifty O'Neill shot to stiffen our ranks. I have also incorporated the South Fermanagh shot as they are the finest Maguire musket men bar none. It will be hard for any rebel unit to beat the quality of the MacCabe shot in the forthcoming campaign. That is the essence of the MacCabes, don't you think?"

"The essence of the MacCabes is the Maguires. We can recruit all the mercenaries we want but they are not MacCabes."

"Sometimes I think Irial and yourself are stuck in a ballad reliving a made-up past. The essence of the MacCabes is they were once Scottish mercenaries, a branch of whom came into the employment of the Maguire and who remained in his employment ever since. They may have replenished their ranks by recruiting Maguires but that was never their essence."

"You never understood the MacCabes and that is one of the reasons you were unfit to be their commander," snapped Irial.

"I am not here to argue with you, I am here to fight the English. If you think the essence of the MacCabes is Maguires, who are all the new recruits and faces I don't recognise?"

"They are all Maguires," said Irial.

"From where?"

"Connor Roe."

Eunan tensed his axe-throwing hand.

"You would endanger the Maguire by employing large numbers of his enemy's men in our ranks?"

"Go and ask your father-in-law who your enemy is for to the O'Neills Connor Roe is a friend. Now if you are not here to obey orders, relinquish your command. Unfortunately, I am needed in Enniskillen so I leave the command of the MacCabes to my worthy successor, Feargal."

"If you would like to make your way into the tent for the briefing," said Feargal.

Eunan nodded and bore the snipes and sneers in relative silence for the rest of the evening knowing that he would feel more at home once back with his own men.

The call for recruits went out all over the Pale and Taaffe was one of the first to heed it. He had used the money he obtained from his family wisely, firstly paying back the angriest and most violent of his creditors so he could enter and leave Dublin relatively freely, and spent the rest on recruiting men he could hire back to the Lord Deputy. He had also formed an understanding with Cormac O'Cassidy Maguire and borrowed freely from him as he knew the only way O'Cassidy could enforce his debts was through Captain Williamson and Shea Óg and without their support he was dead anyway. He had drilled his men so they looked as if they had presentable military discipline and they stood in a field waiting for Marshal Bagenal to inspect them.

In the intermittent truce in the winter of 1597/98 Thomas Butler, the Earl of Ormond, was left in charge of both political and military affairs in Ireland as the Crown decided who to send as a permanent replacement as Lord Deputy. Old and suffering from ill health, he gave the excuse that he was suppressing the rebellion in Leinster where his lands lay to avoid leading the expedition into Ulster. The Crown had sent over little in the way of reinforcements so Ormond had to rely on levies of soldiers from the loyal earls and the conscription and recruitment of native Irish.

Marshal Bagenal sauntered in front of the units of new Irish recruits with his right-hand man, Colonel Richard Billings, an Englishman with vast military experience, including several years in the Irish wars. The men in front of them were a ragbag of boys, casual farm labours and if they were lucky, men with previous military experience. They came to the front ranks of Taaffe's recruits all in their civilian rags, the same as they wore on the docks or in the field.

"This lot looks like they'd run at the first sound of musket fire," whispered Billings into Bagenal's ear.

"Unfortunately, these are the bricks we are given to build an army," said Bagenal. The Marshal walked up to the nearest man to him in the front ranks of Taaffe's unit.

"What clan are you from?" the Marshal asked. But Taaffe flew over before a word left the man's mouth.

"Oh, there's nothing like that around here. He loves the Queen he does, all he thinks about is her. His dream is to become a sir, like one of her knights. Isn't that right? You love the Queen."

The man took a step back, overwhelmed by all the attention.

"Go on, say it," said Taaffe. "Say you love the Queen."

"I love the Queen," repeated the man in the hope it would remove him from the spotlight.

"See? I wouldn't have any of those clansmen in my unit. Sure that'd be like robbing her own coin off poor Her Majesty. I wouldn't do that. My conscience would never have it."

The Colonel and the Marshal both looked at each other, eager to move on. Bagenal turned to his secretaries behind him.

"Sign up this unit under..." And he looked to Taaffe to confirm.

"William Taaffe."

"Under the name of William Taaffe. Note down how many men he brought and pay him for them."

The Colonel and the Marshal walked off leaving Taaffe delighted in the belief his luck had changed.

## CHAPTER 44

# BATTLE OF YELLOW FORD

E unan found himself near Armagh, digging a mile-long trench with his men. Their shovels easily cut through the moist soil, but there was some unhappiness in the ranks standing in the trench.

"For all the efforts I have put in for you," said Seamus, "why is it us that has dug this trench? Are you not supposed to be lording over some maps in a tent, sipping ale, while some farm boys dig this?"

Eunan forced his spade into the earth once more and tossed another lump of soil into the rampart they were constructing behind them.

"This is a punishment from Feargal upon me for the Maguire inflicting me upon him," said Eunan.

"That's nothing compared to what I've had to endure," said Seamus.

"Now is not the time for jokes."

"Who said I was joking?"

Eunan ignored him and changed the subject.

"It is Feargal and Cearbhall who have gone to meet the O'Neill and I will receive my instructions from them."

"Which no doubt will be 'attack the English single-handedly and try to die while you're at it'. I've had those instructions a few times myself," said Seamus.

"And you're not above giving them orders yourself," said Faolán as he rested on his shovel.

"Don't get cheeky, you, I'll leave you to dig this trench yourself," said Seamus.

"Maybe the trench is to defend us, we can stand behind it," said Faolán.

"More like somewhere to channel the enemy into," said Seamus. "He's a crafty 'oul fox, the O'Neill."

One of Eunan's men ran up to the trench and searched for his leader.

"Bagenal has left Newry and is on his way here. The Maguire has summoned all his commanders together. You must come now."

Eunan, Seamus, and Faolán needed little excuse to pick up their shovels and return to camp.

There was much excitement around the Maguire's tent. All his noblemen and officers gathered around a campfire to hear the Maguire speak before the impending battle. Songs and ale flowed, and the fires were topped with rabbit spits. They were elated to be part of the largest rebel army assembled to date. The Maguire got up from his revelries and called on everyone to be silent.

"Good evening, my friends and those I am less well acquainted with. On the eve of this great battle, we are all Maguires."

They met him with an enormous roar from Maguires from east and west and mercenaries and those invited to fight with them.

"We have assembled over four thousand warriors this evening, ready to fight for their homelands and their freedoms."

Another vast roar came in reply.

"Surely the enemy trembles in their camp tonight as they lie awake and dread what they will face in the morning. For they will face the wrath of the lords of the north!"

The men roared their appreciation.

"Now enjoy the revelries that have been laid on tonight, men, but do not be fearful, for the morn will bring the greatest victory the Maguires have ever known!"

The men were ecstatic and chanted "the Maguire, the Maguire!" They took the Maguire in their hands, held him aloft and threw him in the air.

Eunan, Seamus, and Faolán watched from the wings.

"They are pretty confident," said Seamus. "I hope they have a good plan."

Feargal, Cearbhall, and several of their bodyguards approached Eunan from behind and tapped him on the shoulder.

"Come on, it's time to discuss the plan for tomorrow," said Feargal.

"Don't forget us," said Seamus. "We're part of Eunan's command too."

Feargal thought about saying no but shrugged at Seamus's smirk.

He led them back to his tent where he unrolled a small map roughly drawn from the plans recited at the O'Neill's tent earlier that day.

"The enemy is powerful, but also arrogant. We expect them to march straight this way to the fort." Feargal's chapped finger drew an invisible line on the map. "The O'Neill is determined to stop them, so got men like you to dig this long trench. Once the enemy is confronted with the trench, then the O'Neill will spring his trap."

Eunan nodded along. So far, it was a typical O'Neill ambush strategy, with the trench being the stroke of genius, if it worked.

"Your job," continued Feargal, "is to harass the enemy with your shot, starting from here, where they enter this area of small hills until the trench. The O'Donnells will be with us and O'Neills will strike on the other side. Your difficulty is keeping your men supplied with ammunition. The primary force of MacCabe pike will sit below the trench and help spring the trap."

Feargal put his hand on Eunan's shoulder.

"We may have had our differences in the past, but you have a very important role today, which I know you can do."

"I know which direction to funnel the enemy, but as you said, ammunition is the issue."

"Now take your men and wait for the English to leave Armagh."

Feargal stuck out his hand to Eunan and Eunan took it.
"Good luck."

Dawn came, and there was a mixture of confidence and trepidation in both camps. Eunan had made his camp at the rear of a small hill between the trench and the English base outside Armagh. This was to be the initial point where the shot would harass the English column. Eunan had around two hundred men, a sizeable unit for the Maguires. He had fifty O'Neills, one hundred from south Fermanagh and fifty MacCabes. Morale was high, even though some men were a little nervous.

Seamus had taken care of the perceived supply issues. He had taken all the available shot and powder and split it in two. Eunan distributed as much shot and powder that each man could carry, along with words of encouragement for the day ahead. Seamus had taken the rest and placed it in several carts parallel to the route they thought the English would take. Several riders would ride between the carts and shot to ensure the men did not run out of ammunition. Nerves and anticipation condemned Eunan to a sleepless night.

The next morning, the English camp arose full of confidence for the day ahead. Blackwater fort was less than ten miles away and even though they expected to be attacked by the rebels, they had one of the largest armies the Crown had ever assembled in Ireland. They had around three thousand men and six hundred cavalry and drew up into six regiments of around six hundred men each. The core of the army comprised of English continental veterans, but they made up only a fraction of the force and the army had an unusually large reliance on Irish and raw recruits. They came out of camp and were divided into three units, each comprising two regiments. Bagenal led the vanguard himself with Colonel Percy, Colonel Cosby and Sir Thomas Wingfield leading the centre and the rear by Colonel Cunie and Colonel Billings. Sir Thomas Wingfield was the second in command. The army had two sleeves of shot out in front to stave off attack and in between the pairs of regiments were units of cavalry. They also had six cannons in the vanguard of the column and the baggage was at the rear.

They consigned Taaffe and his unit of raw recruits to the rear, as they were the more untrustworthy of the raw Irish units. Taaffe thought nothing of this, for even though he was a very experienced veteran of the Connacht wars, he had no particular desire to fight the rebels and was only there to further himself and see what opportunities may be thrown up by an invasion of Ulster.

They gave the command of the first regiment of English cavalry to Maelmora O'Reilly, the English-supported challenger for the title of O'Reilly who had been bitterly banished when the O'Neills and Maguires had previously supported and made Eamon O'Reilly the chieftain of the O'Reillys. Maelmora had gathered together the horsemen of the displaced Irish nobility and created a unit determined to crush the rebellion and stake their claim to rebel lands.

The army set off around eight a.m., confident it would reach the fort by the afternoon.

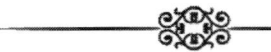

The army marched towards a terrain of small round hills, woods and bushes that lined the route they would take to the fort. The shot spread out to ward off any rebel attacks.

"Eunan, Eunan. The enemy is coming!" shouted the boys on lookout duty behind a bush at the top of the hill Eunan was camped behind. Eunan, Seamus, and Faolán immediately roused their men, and they split into their three prearranged groups.

Seamus and his men climbed the back of the hill they were camped behind while Seamus and his men hid in some nearby bushes and Faolán and his men went and climbed the hill behind them. Eunan and his men reached the top of their hill, lined up and started loading. They were immediately met by the sporadic shot from the English musket men below them.

"Quickly, hide behind the brow of the hill," cried Eunan, and his men retreated to cover.

"Load your guns, load your guns," shouted Eunan to his men so they would be prepared the next time they went over the brow of the hill. They waited until they heard the sound of gunfire from below the hills become more distant.

"Come on men, let's get them," Eunan cried.

They climbed to the top of the hill and let loose a volley into the massed ranks below. They saw some men fall, but Eunan was disappointed. They had met little resistance for the enemy shot was engaged further up the valley with few shot strung along the sides. Eunan thought they should have killed more with the free volley than they had done.

"Load and advance, men."

They advanced about ten yards and shot below them. This time, many more fell. The regiment had now passed them by and Maelmora ordered his cavalry up the hill to chase away the rebels.

"Retreat and regroup, men!"

They all ran up the hill and melted into the bushes as the cavalry came up the hill in pursuit of them.

It was now Seamus's turn for his men to jump from the bushes and exchange a volley with the English shot. About equal numbers fell on each side, and Seamus's men retreated to wait for easier pickings. When Faolán's men unleashed their first volley with the enemy shot, Seamus attacked the main column. There was quite a distance between the pairs of regiments which was supposed to be covered by Maelmora and his cavalry but he was so busy chasing away the different groups of rebel shot that seemed to randomly pop up on both sides of the column that a huge open space was created between the sections. Eunan contemplated attacking the rear of the vanguard regiments, but he did not have the manpower. He contented himself with signalling to Seamus's horsemen to come and replenish his supply of ammunition.

The next pair of regiments arrived, and they were less well protected by shot than the vanguard. Eunan's men stood their ground until the enemy shot retreated, and then Eunan's men could take pot shots at the column as it marched by. Eunan had broken the strength of the enemy shot, so by the time Seamus and Faolán and their respective men came to attack, they could discharge volley after volley into the enemy's flanks, almost without response. The cavalry between the regiments came and chased Eunan away and then carried on up the valley.

The last pair of regiments came within sight of Eunan, which were more robustly surrounded by shot. Eunan had to resort to hit-and-run attacks and suffered reasonable losses. But soon they were gone up the valley and he rallied his men together. He counted his losses.

"Eight men dead for at least thirty dead down below us. That's not too bad," said Eunan to Odhran, who had returned with Eunan's war dogs and ammunition for the men.

"We can still chase them up the valley and press them into the trench."

"Or follow them along the sides. Let us catch up with Seamus and Faolán."

Bagenal pressed his men further up the valley despite being harassed on both sides by enemy shot. Colonel Percy came back from riding ahead to scout out the way in front of them.

"We are taking casualties to both our left and right, sir. Our units are holding together, but it would be good to pin down an enemy we could get our pikes into. The bulk of the O'Neill forces is blocking our main path to the fort. What are your orders, sir?"

"We keep going until we reach the fort," said Bagenal. "The enemy dares not face us in an open battle, so it is up to us to force it upon him. We'll smash right through their ranks and straight into the fort."

"Very good, sir."

Taaffe felt relatively secure in his position in the rear of the army. He was relatively well protected by cavalry and shot and did not think the enemy would dare a full-on assault on an army of this size. He had been in these long-drawn-out battles that comprised constant skirmishing but rarely ended in a full-on assault and he could not think of one where the attackers had delivered a decisive blow. His men had kept their formation, and the fort was only three or four miles ahead. Tomorrow they could think of striking into Tyrone and ending this sorry war.

# CHAPTER 45

# THE FINAL CHARGE

C olonel Percy led his men forward with Bagenal's regiment just behind his. However, the land around the Yellow Ford was boggy and the cannons with Bagenal's regiment got stuck in the mud and the soldiers had to dig them out. All the while, the gap between the two regiments grew ever larger as Percy pressed forward. They were now getting bombarded by the front and both flanks and taking casualties. The shot which was supposed to protect the front of the column had by now thinned out. A sergeant came back to report to his commander.

"There's a trench across our route with no easy way to outflank it. It looks five feet wide and four feet deep, with a line of bushes on the other side of an earth rampart. The enemy shot is lined up behind that and God knows what else. What are your orders, sir?"

"The Marshal told us to march to the fort, so march to the fort we shall. Cross the trench, fill it and clear the way for the rest of the army."

"We are taking a lot of fire, sir."

"It takes courage to be in the vanguard, sergeant. Show some in front of your men."

The sergeant nodded and made his way around the formation of pike and began barking orders at the shot. The shot reorganised themselves at the head of the column and volleyed in front of them and over the trench. The rebel fire became more sporadic and Colonel Percy took this as a sign of their resistance waning in the face of a superior force that would not back down. The shot clambered across the trench with much difficulty but still sporadic fire from the sparse defenders, which did not reap many casualties but prevented the shot from neutering the worst effects of the trench. Next came the pike, which struggled to keep its formation. But it made it across relatively unmolested. The regiment climbed the hill beyond the trench and the men in the fort could now lay eyes on the relieving army and celebrated. Bagenal was desperate to close the gap between the two vanguard regiments. He charged towards the trench with his cavalry bodyguard.

Once the first regiment established itself on the other side of the trench, the O'Neill gave the order to execute his plan. With most of the English shot's ammunition spent, they retreated into the ranks of the pike for sanctuary. The O'Neill shot could now fire relatively unmolested at close range, into the English formations. Volley upon volley struck the pike and whatever remained of the protective shot. The pike ranks disintegrated as it took fire from three sides. The O'Neills, O'Donnells and Maguires charged into the front and sides of the regiment, slashing and stabbing in the gaps. The regiment broke and fled, but the retreating ranks got caught up in the trench and were slaughtered. Maelmora attempted to aid them with his cavalry but they could not surmount the obstacle of the trench. Bagenal could only watch in horror as the unit was destroyed in front of him. He rallied his men and attempted to charge over the trench to save the remains of Percy's regiment. He raised the visor on his helmet to survey the carnage. A bullet smashed through his forehead and took him from this earth.

All hell broke loose for the vanguard of the royal army. What men could escape climbed over the trench and streamed back in the direction they came from. They ran straight into the second regiment, which had done its utmost to make up the gap between it and the first regiment. The retreating men smashed into the formation, breaking it up. The rebel shot now concentrated its fire on the second regiment. The rebels who destroyed the first regiment now crossed over the trench. Maelmora O'Reilly and his loyal Irish horsemen came and tried to rally the fleeing troops, but all Maelmora got for his efforts was a fatal bullet.

The rebels now charged down the hills and attacked the second regiment in the flanks, and the destroyers of the first regiment assaulted it from the front. The second regiment disintegrated like the first.

The main body of the army made its way up the valley, unaware of the calamity that had overtaken the vanguard. It was being constantly peppered on both flanks by the Irish shot. With Maelmora charging ahead to support the first regiment, they had been stripped of cavalry support. The rearguard was a distance behind it. Suddenly, from in front of them, men from the vanguard ran past them. The beleaguered shot of the main army had been under pressure all morning and had run short of ammunition. A supply cart was brought up with powder and bullets. From nowhere came a stray spark and the whole cart exploded in a plume of black smoke, killing all that had previously surrounded it. The rebels took this as a sign to attack and came streaming down the hill. Colonel Cosby, the commander of the two central regiments, ordered a counterattack across the trench, which quickly ended with his getting captured. With this, the main army disintegrated as well.

Eunan and his men made their way up and down the series of small hills that were on the left flank of the marching English army. They first came across Seamus and quickly found Faolán and his men. The English army was below them, but all they could see was the rearguard slowly making its way up the valley. The rearguard was still well protected with shot on the flanks and cavalry chasing away any groups of shot that lingered after discharging their volleys. The rearguard left a trail of bodies as it advanced up the valley.

"How goes it, Faolán?" said Eunan when they caught up.

"It's just like shooting cornered rabbits, except more fun."

"Don't start congratulating yourselves just yet," said Seamus. "Just because they've given you a few free shots doesn't mean they're beaten. Have you heard what has happened at the trench?" he asked Faolán.

"I've heard no news, but the sound of gunfire is deafening from the hills beyond."

"We can't assume any more than they are giving free shots to everyone," said Seamus. "We must wait for the signal and make our assault with the others. I fear it may be bloody, for your friend Feargal may have given you the hardest cud to chew."

"Feargal is an honourable man," said Eunan.

"It is when you desecrate what gives an honourable man his values that you see what an honourable man he really is. I fear you may have to call on your Uncle Seamus to resolve your problems again."

"I am no longer a boy and do not need my Uncle Seamus to resolve anything for me, for anytime my Uncle Seamus intervenes, he causes more problems than he solves."

"Ha! Go back and tell that to your wife!"

"The enemy is down there, children, so save your anger for them," said Faolán when he noticed Eunan's burning eyes.

The horns of the O'Donnells sounded, and they heard drums from the other hill.

"The assault begins," shouted Eunan. "Make sure you have a sword, axe or another weapon, for the real fighting begins now."

Eunan strapped his battle axe to his back and felt for his throwing axes on his belt. They went to the top of Faolán's hill and saw the other rebels charging across the way. Eunan raised his axe.

"THE CRY OF THE MAGUIRE!" he roared at the top of his lungs.

"THE MAGUIRE!" came the response, and they charged down the hill at the enemy.

Eunan and his men swallowed up the yards. The O'Neills on the other side of the valley had a head start on them and slammed into the other flank. The prolonged skirmishing had used up most of the English musketeers' powder and bullets and it had been difficult for them to replenish themselves while they were under constant attack. Therefore, these two elements meant there was little resistance in the way of Eunan's assault. Eunan's men smashed into the flank of the last regiment, who did not have the time nor inclination to turn and face their pikemen in the direction of the charge.

Eunan charged down the hill, and swung his axe in an arc into the defenders who tried to step in his way. The blade sliced through air, skin, and bone with similar ease. To the right came a swinging musket. He parried it with the battle axe, ripped a throwing axe from his belt, and swung down as hard as possible over the musket. Only a second to remove the axe from the man's head. Someone charged from the left. He parried their weapon and head-butted him in the side of the head. Others came fast, and he swung his battle axe. Blood splashed all over his face and into his eyes. Thud! He was on the ground, tackled in the midriff. He saw the mangled face of a man possessed by the extremities of anger and fear summon the energy to deliver the death blow. There was another thud and an extended hand.

"Never say you don't need your Uncle Seamus," and he handed Eunan back his axe. He had a moment's respite to wipe the blood from his face. He was amongst a mass brawl of hand-to-hand combat, with the discipline of both sides now broken down.

"Come on. No time to dilly-dally," said Seamus.

They went towards the centre of the brawl. The English officers were now attempting to rally their men around the various unit standards. Seamus grabbed his men out of single combat scenarios by killing their opponent for them.

"Him." Seamus pointed a firm finger at a well-armoured man on horseback with the regimental standard. "Shoot him."

The men took careful aim with their muskets and, after several bullets bounced off his breastplate, his head exploded like a melon. Whatever men had gathered around his feet now took to their heels. The pike units had kept much of their structure but they made easy targets for the Irish shot and javelin-carrying Kern and cavalry and all the units did was absorb casualties.

Taaffe's men had been in the middle of the final regiment surrounding the baggage and but for the pikes they were carrying would have run long ago. They kept their formation and despite the heavy assaults, Colonel Billings was determined to achieve his objective and secure the Yellow Ford. They marched onwards because the English sergeants roared at them that they could not retreat. Eunan and his men concentrated on picking off those who were free and running around outside these formations. Colonel Billings marched until he reached the Yellow Ford. Sir Thomas Wingfield realised that all was lost and rallied men in the centre so they could turn around and retreat the way they came and rally outside Armagh. Colonel Billings' regiment was at the rear and had kept its shape so spearheaded the retreat down the valley.

Eunan rallied his men as Billings forced his way back down the valley and they assembled up on a hill. The men came back in dribs and drabs. Out of his original two hundred men, a respectable one hundred and fifty could still report fit for duty.

"The men are running low on ammunition and there is none left in the carts," said Odhran, who had been left in the hills to co-ordinate resupplying the men and to mind Eunan's dogs.

"There can't be too much of this battle to go," said Seamus as he took off his blood-soaked chain mail and threw it onto the ground. "Odhran should try to source some ammunition, and the rest of us can ready ourselves on the hillside and take pot shots at the retreating stragglers."

The rest of the men were lying prostrate on the ground, totally exhausted after an afternoon of hand-to-hand combat.

"I'll go to the top of the hill to see what's going on with the rest of the battle," said Eunan.

"I'll come with you," said Odhran.

"You can come some of the way," said Eunan, "but as soon as we see an opportunity to get ammunition, you must take it."

"I will also come with you." A young Galloglass stepped forward, one that Eunan did not recognise but he looked fit and healthy nonetheless. "It's too dangerous to go by yourself."

"Well, let us go. Seamus, please rally the men into some fit shape before I return, for I may have some work for them."

Seamus raised a hand to wave him goodbye.

They trudged up the next hill, which was slightly higher than the one they rested upon, for that should have given them a better view of the battlefield. When they were near the crest, Eunan saw some activity nearby on the rebel side that looked like men unloading carts.

"I think it's time for us to part, Odhran. Take Sionn and Olcan and see if they can spare any ammunition for us. If not, we'll have to pillage the battlefield for it."

Eunan bent down and patted his beloved dogs on their heads.

"Don't worry, my faithful friends, there is still plenty in this battle for you without placing you in too much danger."

"I will return quickly, successful or not," said Odhran.

Eunan continued to climb the hill with his bodyguard.

They reached the top of the hill, which had a commanding view of the battlefield and the valley below.

"Wow! Look at that carnage." Eunan could see the destruction of the English army in the trench and that they were rallying just below them.

"We must get back to the men and -." Eunan turned to see his bodyguard had pulled a blade on him.

"Why are you doing this on the cusp of our greatest victory? Are you a spy?"

"I am far from a spy. You bring disgrace to the Galloglass name."

The man thrust his knife forward and Eunan stepped back. A snarl came from the bushes and the muscular hulk of an Irish wolfhound took to the air. The knife was inches from Eunan's chest until the salivating jaws of the hound crunched down on the man's wrist and in amongst howls of agony chewed the man's hand right off. The man fell, holding his handless arm in the air as it spurted blood as if it were a fountain. Eunan had fallen over in his attempt to avoid the blade. When he got back up again, he was too late, for Sionn had already ripped the man's throat out.

Odhran burst through the bushes with Olcan on a leash in one hand and a broken rope in the other.

"Sionn has escaped! Oh my lord!" He saw Sionn standing over her kill. "I'm sorry, lord. It is my fault. I didn't check she was secure."

"It is no fault of yours. That dog of mine saved my life. She sensed I was in danger and came and saved me."

Eunan went over, knelt and hugged his dog, and did not regret for one second his shoulder got covered in blood and dribble.

"But alas, I have no time to stand here and be grateful for my dogs. The English return this way in strength and we must be prepared. I must rally the men."

They ran between the two hills while observing the fleeing royalist forces to their left.

They arrived at the hill and Seamus had gathered together the wounded so they could be tended to. But Eunan had no time for a task that could be done at the end of the battle.

"The English are below us at the bottom of the hill. We must strike now to ensure our victory."

"I am with you, but must warn you that the men are spent. They are low on ammunition and energy."

"All I ask for is one last push."

"And one last push you'll get." Seamus looked down and noticed that Sionn was covered in blood. "That was some rabbit she caught."

"Unfortunately, it was the man who came to assist me that was crushed in her jaws," Eunan whispered to Seamus. "He called me a traitor to the Galloglass after he pulled his blade."

"Leave me to my methods to rid us of Feargal and Irial."

"The only protest you'll get from me is if you don't include me in their deaths. My youthful naivety died with that man."

Seamus slapped him on the shoulder. "I knew I'd make you a Galloglass in the end."

"This Godforsaken war moulded me," said Eunan. "But one enemy at a time, and the nearest one is on the other side of this hill."

"One more charge and this battle is over," said Seamus, who extended his hand for Eunan to clasp.

They stood on top of the hill, ready to charge. They had their muskets and a handful of bullets at the most each and their swords, daggers or axes by their sides. The enemy was below and the vanguard, which was once the rearguard, still maintained good order. Eunan could see the massed ranks of the O'Neills on the other side. He looked at his men and the grim determination on their faces overcame any injuries, exhaustion, or nerves they had. Eunan raised his axe in unison with the O'Neills on the other side.

"FOR THE MAGUIRE!"

"KEEP IT STEADY, MEN!" Taaffe hollered from the top of his unit of pike. "THE ONLY WAY WE ARE GETTING OUT OF THIS IS BY STAND-ING TOGETHER. IF YOU DROP YOUR PIKE YOU'RE A DEAD MAN." Taaffe's constant messaging seemed to get through because his unit proved to be one of the best disciplined Irish units and therefore placed at the front of the column. The rebel shot slammed volley after volley into the flanks of the column until the gunfire suddenly stopped.

"THEY ARE OUT OF AMMO, MEN. THE ONLY WAY THEY CAN ATTACK US NOW IS THROUGH OUR PIKES. KEEP MARCHING."

Eunan and his men had by now charged down the hill, discharged their weapons and were picking off individuals as they tried to make their way to Armagh. Taaffe slipped between his pikemen for his own protection. He stood behind Shea Óg.

"You're my lucky charm. You always get out of these situations alive," Taaffe whispered in his ear.

"Look over there." Shea Óg pointed with his head to a melee just outside their pike formation. "It's Eunan Maguire."

"Give me your axe."

Shea Óg's neck stiffened.

"You're not going to go out there, are you? If you stay in formation, you get to live."

Taaffe cracked his knuckles.

"If it wasn't for Eunan Maguire, I'd be on my estate in Sligo, a rich lord. Instead, I'm here in the ignominy of defeat. If I can take one thing from today, it is Eunan Maguire's head. Give me your axe and lead the men out of here. If you see me get into trouble, come back for me."

Shea Óg sighed and handed him the axe.

"I know how these vendettas end up. Believe me."

But Taaffe grabbed the axe and forced his way out between the pikemen.

Eunan swung his axe, and the blood splashed on his face from another dead Irish conscript. He threw the body to the ground and shook out his limbs to rid them of the cramp and exhaustion. It did not work.

"MAGUIRE! MAGUIRE! COME AND FIGHT ME!"

Eunan turned to see the hulk of Taaffe behind him with an axe ready in his hands. He looked to see where Seamus was, but he was engaged in another melee with a group of retreating Crown Irish.

"COME ON, YOU COWARD! FIGHT ME FAIR WITH NONE OF YOUR TRICKS!"

Eunan was many things but not a coward. But he was without Seamus to talk some sense into him. He swung his tired limbs and charged towards Taaffe.

Seamus stood over a group of ragged, desperate Crown Irish conscripts armed with daggers, sticks and whatever else came to hand as they had long abandoned their pikes up the other end of the valley. Seamus's axe dripped, but even he was tired of bloodshed.

"I heard an accent in there. Are you men from Munster?"

"We are," said one man as he backed away and looked around to see if they were being lured into an ambush.

"Where from?"

"The old lands of the Earl of Desmond."

"Why are you fighting for these bastards? Against my better judgement and since I'm a MacSheehy Galloglass that served the last Earl, I'm going to give you a chance. Join me and we'll go back to Munster together and we'll take our lands back."

"How do we know we can trust you?"

"Well, it is either that or we fight it out now and I guarantee most of you will die. You won't be fighting for your lives, for I have already offered them back to you, along with your freedom. What is it to be?"

The men looked at each other, and most shrugged.

"We accept. Tell us what you want us to do?"

Seamus looked over at Eunan clashing axes with Taaffe.

"Prove yourselves. Kill that officer over there. He has robbed so many of our kinsfolk of their lands. You'd be doing it for revenge. If you turn coat again, my axe will make short work of you."

The man raised his knife.

"You heard him. Charge!"

Taaffe slammed the hilt of his axe into Eunan's, which was positioned to block a blow to his head.

"Long have I waited for this," Taaffe said. "You robbed me of the proceeds of all my work and reduced me to a beggar. But I can get a handsome price for your head."

Eunan threw off Taaffe and cast a blow towards Taaffe's side. It was easily parried away.

"You grow weak," Taaffe said. "It has been a long day of fighting for you, but all I have done is run. Throw down your axe and it will end all the quicker. I promise I will be merciful and sweep your head clean off. Cormac O'Cassidy will pay a handsome price for it."

"I have long heard tales of your cruelty and corruption. If it is to be, then it will be done the hard way," Eunan said.

Eunan summoned all his strength, but the fresher Taaffe easily absorbed his three consecutive blows.

"Then let us begin the downfall of Eunan Maguire," Taaffe said. "All I need is a recognisable face for Cormac O'Cassidy."

Three blows rained down from Taaffe, and Eunan could feel his knees buckle. Taaffe turned when he heard the cries of the Munster traitors turned rebels led by Seamus.

"Sorry I can't savour this." With the sheer force of strength, he knocked the axe from Eunan's hands. Eunan fell to the ground and raised his arm as his last line of defence. Taaffe raised his axe above his head to deliver the final blow. Eunan could not help it, but he closed his eyes. He thought of the lake and his village and running through the reeds with his wolfhound. He could feel no pain and wondered if Taaffe had struck yet. He heard the clash of steel and looked up to see Seamus above him. There was no sign of Taaffe. Seamus extended his hand downwards and dragged Eunan to his feet.

"Look," Seamus said.

Eunan saw in the distance the red face of Taaffe cursing himself and Shea Óg bundling his new master along.

"I KNOW WHERE YOU LIVE!" Taaffe said. "I KNOW WHERE YOU LIVE!"

"Look what I found."

Seamus held out a throwing axe with the Maguire emblem on it. "I found it in the mud and thought I would return it to you. I aimed for Taaffe's head but am not as well practised as you. It hit off the axe as he swung it to finish you and knocked it from his hand. Shea Óg came and yanked him away."

"Thank you, Seamus, for all you've done for me," Eunan said. "The spirit of Desmond looks out for me too, for he left the axe for you to find."

"Come on, let us rest," Seamus said. "The battle is done for today."

Eunan and Seamus retired to their hill to rally the men and count the survivors. Their men were strewn across the back of the hill from which they had initially charged. They had been joined by the Munster men that Seamus had turned mid-battle and who had proven themselves by attacking Taaffe's men. Eunan and Seamus went and spoke to each man individually, be they dying, wounded or well, collected their tales from the battlefield and thanked them for their day's service. They sent men out onto the battlefield to retrieve the dead and steal the weapons of the fallen enemy.

The clans lit fires in their original camps and Eunan and Seamus told the men to pack up their possessions and newly acquired weapons, for they were going to join the celebrations. But the noise of gunfire had not yet settled down, and Eunan and Seamus climbed to the top of the hill as the light faded. They sat down to rest their weary limbs. They surveyed the battlefield and then looked south.

"I wonder if Taaffe escaped?" said Eunan.

"That rat will have found himself a way to escape, there's no doubt about that," said Seamus. "But we'll get him the next time and finish off Shea Óg and Cormac O'Cassidy for good measure."

Eunan pointed towards Armagh, where the sound of gunfire was coming from.

"We could have had them good and proper if we hadn't run out of ammo," said Seamus.

"Yes, but with the Queen's army so badly beaten, the Pale, Dublin, even Munster lies open before us," said Eunan in the haze of a glorious victory.

"I've been here before," sighed Seamus. "I hope it turns out better than last time."

"So do I," Eunan said. His thoughts turned to his pregnant wife, and he imagined her ill and pregnant in bed. "So do I."

The End

# ALSO BY

If you enjoyed this book please would you leave a review on the retailer where you bought it.

To read more books in the *Exiles* series click on the QR codes below to be brought to your favourite online ebook store.

Bad Blood

★★★★ *"A new piece of Irish historical fiction that pulls you in through its protagonist, and is full of plenty of action," - Reedsy Discovery*

★★★★ *"To say this book is rich with action, adventure, and deep meaty history is putting it mildly," – The Historical Fiction Company*

★ ★ ★ ★ ★ *"a tale that is filled with twists, including stabbings-in-the-back, and one that puts readers on the edge of their seats," – The Book Commentary*

Uprising

★ ★ ★ ★ ★ *"Fully action-packed, this pulls you further into Eunan and Seamus' story; making you question who to support the whole way through," – Reedsy Discovery*

★★★★ *"Another action-packed adventure filled with rich historical information about Ireland in the 16th century embedded in the storyline,"*

*"for anyone who loves GOT stories, well this has it all – including a bloody battle at a wedding ceremony," – The Historical Fiction Company*

★ ★ ★ ★ ★ *"a real page-turner that leaves readers wanting more,"*

*"The conflict between the Crown and natives is brilliantly and elaborately written, the characters are rock-solid and relatable, and the plot is twisty as it can get," – The Book Commentary*

*It seems as if Eunan has succeeded beyond his wildest imagination. Once a lowly upstart, now part of the Maguire nobility and married to the woman of his dreams, the flames of the rebellion he continues to hold so dear also burn bright.*

*But enemies in the clan capture him and leave him to die in the Maguire's jail while they plot to sell the clan out to the English crown.*

*Will the bonds of family compel Seamus to save him or will he be dragged off to war to leave Eunan to be sacrificed in the cesspit of Irish politics?*

*Traitor Maguire is the third book in the epic Irish historical fiction Exiles series. It is set against the backdrop of the Elizabethan wars in Ireland in the 1590s. A world of Irish clans, their politics and the fight for supremacy, where spies and intrigue prosper, where the embers burn for a rebellion against the English crown. If you love fast-paced action and adventure orientated historical fiction then you will love this book.*

*Buy Traitor Maguire to discover this exciting new series today.*

FERMANAGH AND SURROUNDING DISTRICTS 1590s

Connacht 1590s map. Labels:

O'MALLEY BURKE · WALTER 'KITTAGH' BURKE · BELEEK CASTLE · O'CONNOR SLIGO · SLIGO · DROMAHAIR CASTLE · COLLOONEY CASTLE · BALLYMOTE CASTLE · BELCLARE CASTLE · GALLEN · LOUGH CONN · BURRISHOOLE CASTLE · CLARE ISLAND · CASTLEBAR CASTLE · MAC WILLIAM BURKE · CLAN MORRIS · CLAN COSTELLO · O'MALLEY · O'FLAHERTY · KILMAINE · LOUGH MASK · LOUGH CORRIB · EARL OF CLANRICARDE (BURKE) · GALWAY · ARAN ISLANDS · ATHENRY

CONNACHT
1590s

Legend:
- CASTLE
- TOWN
- LAKE
- FOREST
- MOUNTAIN
- LORDSHIP BOUNDARY
- INAUGURATION SITE

# CLANS AND MILITARY FORMATIONS

Clan structure

Irish clan structure came from ancient times. Clans were kinship groups that would have various septs beneath them. Therefore, there were usually various family branches, each with different strengths of claim to be the clan leader. The clan leader is usually referred to as being 'the' and then the clan name (e.g. 'the Maguire'). Within this system, you could have septs with a different surname that would still be part of the clan (e.g. Keenan Maguire).

They used a tanistry system to elect their leader, so to be elected leader, you had to galvanise support amongst the men eligible to vote. This inadvertently created several different power bases, and therefore rivals, within the clan. After being elected, and during the normal course of events, it was usual for the clan leader to demand the eldest male children of his rivals to be handed over for lengths of time as guarantees of loyalty.

These clans usually had subservient clans, outside their internal sept structure, that paid tribute to them. The example in the story is that the Maguires switch between paying tribute to whoever was the dominant O'Neill and paid tribute to the O'Donnells for a period.

Gallic military formations

At the time of the outbreak of the Nine Years War, except for the O'Neills, the fighting formations of the Irish were at best outdated, but in truth obsolete. The main European fighting formations were pikemen and shot. The main

Irish battle tactics were the ambush, to which their soldiers were suited. They were not capable of facing the English in a pitched battle. Hence the urgency of O'Neill and other leaders to train their men in the use of firearms, import weapons from the continent and Scotland, and get as many Spanish trainers as they could.

Below are the main troop types of the Irish clans at the time of the outbreak of the Nine Years War:

Galloglass – mercenary soldiers usually Scottish or from Scottish descent. These were heavily armed mercenaries who used long axes with curved blades. The main Irish houses usually had clans of Galloglass that worked for them permanently. A Galloglass leader was called a constable, a formation of Galloglass a battle and a Galloglass usually had the support of a horseboy or Kern and this was referred to as a spar. Galloglass got paid around three cattle per quarter.

'Cogin and livery' (referred to in the book as 'coin and keep' for simplicity sake) – the clan leader would hire Galloglass, and to share the burden of paying for them, he would assign them to different areas. The population assigned would be responsible for the payment and upkeep of the Galloglass for a time period at the discretion of the clan leader.

Redshanks are 'new Scots' or Scottish mercenaries hired directly from Scotland, usually on a seasonal basis. They were called Redshanks because they went barelegged. They were usually armed with swords and bows. They normally got paid the same as Galloglass, around three cows per quarter.

Kern – traditional Irish light infantry. They were usually not armoured and supplied their own weapons. The weapon of choice was the dart. They also used javelins, swords and bows. Their main uses were to support the heavier armed Galloglass, capture and herd cattle away from enemy territory, and against the English, they were used for lighting attacks and harassment. They usually got paid around one cow per quarter.

Horseboys – Galloglass usually had horse boys to support them. When they fought, they normally functioned as light infantry armed with javelins.

Horsemen – these were usually the nobility of the clan. They rode without stirrups, which potentially made them unstable when facing heavier English cavalry, and were usually armed with javelins.

Shot – these were armed with muskets. The Irish lords tried to retrain their Galloglass and other experienced soldiers to become either shot or pike as fast as circumstances would allow. The amount of shot the Irish armies could field would depend on the clan. The O'Neill formations were mainly armed with shot while the smaller clans were not.

Pike – there is little evidence that the pike was widely available to the Irish rebels. These formations also did not suit the Irish style of ambush warfare. Again, mainly the larger clans such as the O'Neills would have had the most pikemen.

The Irish formations were supported by experienced Irish mercenaries who had fought mainly with the Spanish army in the Dutch Revolt. These men would have been skilled in modern European warfare and made a vital backbone to the Irish military formations.

English military formations

The English forces in Ireland usually came from four sources: Irish conscripts (mainly from the Pale), Irish allies, raw recruits from England and veterans who had served in France, the Scottish borders or the Netherlands. There was much changing of sides between the Irish on both sides.

Shot – the English were mainly armed with calivers but also had a small number of muskets. The men armed with calivers, the lighter of the two guns, were mainly used for skirmishing. The muskets were used to support the pike as the muskets were heavier and less manoeuvrable.

Pike – Pikemen were the core of the army. They had a ten to fifteen-foot spear, a helmet and breastplate armour and were mainly used for defence. They could also make a very effective charge.

Horsemen – these were comprised mainly of Irish cavalry. They were more heavily armoured than the Irish cavalry and were armed with a lance, sword and occasionally a pistol. They were the most feared element of the English armies. They were mainly used for skirmishing.

English system of government in Ireland

Lord Deputy – the representative if the Queen and the head of the Irish executive under English rule

Irish Council – the executive branch of English rule in Ireland

Lord President (Governors) were the English military leaders for the various provinces of Ireland with wide-ranging powers.

London Privy Council – the body of advisors to the Queen

# ABOUT AUTHOR

C R Dempsey is the author of 'Traitor Maguire', 'Uprising' and 'Bad Blood', three historical fiction books set in Elizabethan Ireland. He has plans for many more, and he needs to find the time to write them. History has always been his fascination, and historical fiction was an obvious outlet for his accumulated knowledge. C R spends lots of time working on his books, mainly
in the twilight hours of the morning. C R wishes he spent more time writing and
less time jumping down the rabbit hole of excessive research.

C R Dempsey lives in London with his wife and cat. He was born in Dublin but has lived most of his adult life in London.

C R can be found at:

https://www.crdempseybooks.com/,

https://www.facebook.com/crdempsey,

https://www.instagram.com/crdempsey/,
Twitter: @dempsey_cr

# ACKNOWLEDGMENTS

Thank you to all my family and friends and all of those who helped to create this book.

Special thanks to Mena (endless patience and support), Eoin (advice and inspiration), Justin Moule (feedback and support).

Thank you also for the professional support of:

Book cover: Dominic Forbes

Editing: Robin Seavill

Both these individuals can be found on www.Reedsey.com

Printed in Great Britain
by Amazon

49791170R00205